I've counted nine different varieties of flooring,
every wall is made of a different material, no two windows
are alike, and I'm pretty sure I saw daylight coming through
the side of one of the closets. What we have here isn't a
fixer-upper so much as it is a tearer-downer. This house would
be a journey into the heart of darkness of home renovation.
We'd have to call it Apocalypse House.

continued . . .

"Laugh-out-loud. . . . Lancaster keeps the action fast and funny with a big, rollicking cast." —*Publishers Weekly*

"The situations and characters will keep readers in stitches and make this book a hard one to put down." —*Romantic Times*

PRAISE FOR
JEN LANCASTER'S MEMOIRS

MY FAIR LAZY
"Hilarious. . . . *My Fair Lazy* does not 'suck it.' It rocks it."
—Examiner.com

"Light and fun and full of pop culture musings." —*Chicago Sun-Times*

PRETTY IN PLAID
"Like that dreamy pair of heels that [is] somehow both comfy and chic . . . a hilarious tribute to her early fashion obsessions." —*People*

"Scathingly witty." —*The Boston Herald*

SUCH A PRETTY FAT
"She's like that friend who always says what you're thinking—just 1,000 times funnier." —*People*

BRIGHT LIGHTS, BIG ASS
"A bittersweet treat for anyone who's ever survived the big city."
—Jennifer Weiner

BITTER IS THE NEW BLACK
"She's absolutely hilarious." —*Chicago Sun-Times*

Nonfiction Titles by *New York Times* Bestselling Author Jen Lancaster

Jen Lancaster

If You Were Here

NEW AMERICAN LIBRARY

For Anne—

to, Jen Lancaster

NEW AMERICAN LIBRARY
Published by New American Library, a division of
Penguin Group (USA) Inc., 375 Hudson Street,
New York, New York 10014, USA
Penguin Group (Canada), 90 Eglinton Avenue East, Suite 700, Toronto,
Ontario M4P 2Y3, Canada (a division of Pearson Penguin Canada Inc.)
Penguin Books Ltd., 80 Strand, London WC2R 0RL, England
Penguin Ireland, 25 St. Stephen's Green, Dublin 2,
Ireland (a division of Penguin Books Ltd.)
Penguin Group (Australia), 250 Camberwell Road, Camberwell, Victoria 3124,
Australia (a division of Pearson Australia Group Pty. Ltd.)
Penguin Books India Pvt. Ltd., 11 Community Centre, Panchsheel Park,
New Delhi - 110 017, India
Penguin Group (NZ), 67 Apollo Drive, Rosedale, Auckland 0632,
New Zealand (a division of Pearson New Zealand Ltd.)
Penguin Books (South Africa) (Pty.) Ltd., 24 Sturdee Avenue,
Rosebank, Johannesburg 2196, South Africa

Penguin Books Ltd., Registered Offices:
80 Strand, London WC2R 0RL, England

Published by New American Library, a division of Penguin Group (USA) Inc. Previously published in
a New American Library hardcover edition.

First New American Library Trade Paperback Printing, March 2012
10 9 8 7 6 5 4 3 2 1

▉ REGISTERED TRADEMARK—MARCA REGISTRADA

New American Library Trade Paperback Edition ISBN: 978-0-451-23668-5

The Library of Congress has catalogued the hardcover edition of this title as follows:

Lancaster, Jen, 1967–
    If you were here/Jen Lancaster.
        p. cm.
    ISBN 978-0-451-23438-4
    1. Suburbs—Illinois—Chicago—Fiction. 2. Dwellings—Remodelling—Fiction.
3. Women authors—Fiction. 4. Marriage—Fiction. 5. Chicago (Ill.)—Fiction. I. Title.
    PS3612.A54748I37 2011
    813'.6—dc22   2011003171

Set in Bembo
Designed by Spring Hoteling

Printed in the United States of America

For the man who defined a generation.

Godspeed, Mr. Hughes.

Author's Note

Dear Reader,

This is not a true story, but was inspired by our adventures in suburban real estate. However, we quickly came to our senses and realized that buying a crumbling home by the lake was an incredibly stupid, potentially hazardous, ridiculously expensive, and almost-certain-to-end-our-marriage idea.

We did not purchase the house in this book.

We moved elsewhere.

This didn't occur.

(Yet.)

XO,

Jen

P.S. I feel it's important to note here that I love Stephenie Meyer. This might not make sense now, but it will later, I promise.

Prologue

I blame HGTV for what happens next.

Chapter One
THERE'S SOMETHING ABOUT ORNESTEGA

"No. *No.* Oh, *hell*, no."

I'm standing upstairs in my office when I spot someone in an oversize hoodie and low-slung pants paint ORNESTEGA in puffy silver letters on the flat red bricks of the building across the street.

Which is a *church*.

I imagine the Lord probably has His own way of dealing with little thugs who deface houses of worship, but I can't just stand here waiting for Him to scramble a swarm of locusts or turn rivers to blood. I imagine He's got a lot on his plate right now, what with war, poverty, the Sudanese situation, and all those reality-show contestants asking for His divine guidance as they navigate their way through the obstacle course and into the Jell-O pit.

The other thing is, if He does take notice and sends down hail mixed with fire, it's going to ruin my lawn. I think sometimes God expects us to act as His emissaries; ergo, *I* will fix this.

I press the "indoor talk" button on the intercom system. "Mac! Maaaaac! There's a tagger outside and . . ." Before I can even finish my sentence, my husband, Mac,[1] has exited his basement office/lair and flown across the street.

When it comes to wrongs that need righting, Mac fancies himself a modern-day Batman. I mean, if Batman were pushing forty, with a hint of spare tire around his waist, seven gray hairs, and a job in middle management for the phone company. The truth is he's more like Dilbert, only with a fully stocked arsenal.

Back in college, after we became friends, but before we started dating, Mac appointed himself my personal bouncer. Mac thought I was too hung up on being polite, so I'd always find myself cornered by some asshole I couldn't graciously escape whenever I'd go out. After Mac stepped in, woe be to any guy who hit on me or hassled me, because Mac was right there at my back. Eventually my friend Ann Marie pointed out that I could do—and had done—a lot worse than dating someone so anxious to keep me safe and happy, and we've been together ever since.

Anyway, despite the sixty tons of brick and cement block that comprise our house's exterior walls, and regardless of the soundproofed, supersealed, triple-hung windows, I can still hear every syllable of profanity Mac hurls at the aspiring gangbanger. I quickly search for some footwear, because I don't want to run barefoot into the snow to monitor the situation. My dog Duckie has the

---

1 Né John Brian MacNamara.

bizarre and annoying habit of taking one shoe and hiding it under the covers, so I have to tear through the unmade bed to find my flannel clog's mate. As soon as I can, I dash downstairs and outside just in time to witness . . . nothing.

Mac's cheeks are flushed and he can't suppress his smile. I've never met anyone who enjoys an altercation as much as this man.[2] "Mia, you should have seen that little bastard try to get away in those pants. He pretty much hobbled himself. Looked like he was running a potato-sack race. By the way, he disappeared into that building." He jerks his finger toward the dilapidated apartments a few doors down. I hate that complex; they cut their grass only twice last summer, both times at six a.m. on Sunday. "Apparently he's our neighbor."

"Who's stupid enough to tag a building in broad daylight? And then bravely run home across the street?" I wonder out loud. "Also, if that little shit wants to claim this block in the name of ORNESTEGA, then maybe *he* should be paying our rent."

"Not for long," Mac corrects. "Pretty soon he can pay our *property* taxes. Hey, ORNESTEGA," he shouts in the direction of the six-flat, "you owe us twelve thousand bucks!"

Mac and I are in the process of buying our house. Rather, we've started the process; we're currently waiting for the results of our appraisal so we can write a formal offer.

We moved into this neighborhood a year and a half ago. Originally our plan was to get out of the city of Chicago and into the

---

2   He's never anything but sweet to me, and I do my best to return the favor. He and I are like the Soviet Union and the United States during the Cold War: Whoever pushes the button pretty much sets our mutually assured destruction into motion. And like that nice pre–*Ferris Bueller* Matthew Broderick taught us in the movie *War Games*, the only way to win is not to play.

suburbs. Honestly, I've been dreaming of the bucolic towns ringing the north side of Chicago ever since I started watching John
Hughes movies on VHS with my older sister, Jessica.

I grew up in one of the bleak and depressing Indiana steel
towns that ring the wrong side of Lake Michigan. Jess and I would
snuggle into our rump-sprung plaid couch located in the drab
ranch house my family shared with my grandmother, located
down the street from the mill.

Jess and I were enamored not only by the characters in the
movies, but also the backdrop. We were astounded that people lived
so . . . nicely. I guess we assumed everyone had a yard full of rusty
patio furniture and broken swing sets, with neighbor kids running
around with dirty faces and stained pajamas well into the night.

We'd spend hours fantasizing about what it might be like to
live on a quiet, well-manicured street like Samantha Baker in *Sixteen Candles*, rather than being within earshot of the clamoring
from the blast furnace. While everyone else lusted after Cameron's
dad's car in *Ferris Bueller's Day Off*, we'd sigh over the darling
downtown shopping district filled with Tudor-style pizza joints
and charming shops and big, leafy trees. As far as we were concerned, Shermer, Illinois, was Shangri-la.[3]

Jess and I weren't unhappy, and our parents worked hard to
make sure we never went without, but aesthetics were never a
consideration for them. When we suggested they paint the walls
or buy some new couches, they'd tell us we could have a pretty
house or we could have a college education, our choice.

---

3 Much like Jay and Silent Bob in *Dogma*, I didn't learn that Shermer was a
fictional place until years after I first saw the movies. However, it's based on a real
town, so I wasn't too devastated.

I went from my parents' run-down ranch to an austere dorm room, to a claustrophobic five-person suite in my sorority house, then to a practically condemned apartment off campus.

After graduation, Mac and I moved to Chicago together. He had a well-paying job and upper-middle-class parents, so he was in a position to rent a swankier place in the Gold Coast or Lincoln Park, with amenities like doormen and fitness rooms and in-unit washing machines. However, I didn't have his kind of cash flow, so my options were more limited. Mac planned to cover my share on a nicer apartment, but I insisted I make it on my own. I didn't want to make a big thing about it, so I suggested he get his de-luxe apartment in the sky[4] and I'd rent something more modest. Yet he wanted to be with me, so he agreed to go halfsies on a terrible little studio apartment on a noisy street by Wrigley Field.

The first time we saw a rat in our grubby hallway, Mac went right out and adopted a cat. Savannah wasn't much of a mouser, but she did spark our love of pets, and she made us feel not just like boyfriend and girlfriend, but an actual family unit. We lost her to feline leukemia a few years back, but we've since acquired both dogs and an entire litter of kittens who've proved to be complete and utter badasses, hence their tough guy names like Agent Jack Bauer.

Mac claims that I'm the tenderhearted one, taking in all these pets, but you should have seen him bottle-feeding the kittens after their mother abandoned them.

Mac and I resided in a series of cheap, cramped urban dwellings long after we both started making money. I was so used to

---

4 Ten points if you caught the *Jeffersons* reference.

living beneath my means that it never occurred to me to upgrade as my means increased.

At some point, Mac started introducing a little bit of luxury into our lives, and we found it suited us. You know what? French-press coffee *is* better than Folgers. A down-filled leather couch feels a whole lot better than a lumpy old futon. And a new German sedan does indeed drive better than a fifteen-year-old Honda with a leaky sunroof.

Once I finally got comfortable with opening my wallet, we toyed around with the notion of buying a house. Soon enough, Mac and I were swooning at the thought of solid brick houses with big backyards for the dogs. Sure, our pit bull, Daisy, doesn't care for the outdoors, and Duckie[5] can't be away from her for a moment, but the *idea* of a yard was appealing.

We hadn't yet found the proper suburban outpost when record rainfall cracked our old rental home's foundation and caused our walls to fill with mold. Simply leasing a new apartment in the city seemed like the most expedient way to, you know, not die, so we began to scour options on Craigslist.

Our current place was one of the first listings we saw online, but we didn't even consider it a possibility; it was so nice we thought the rent had been posted wrong. I mean, there we were in a thousand square feet with walls full of deadly spores, but a couple miles west for a few bucks more, we could have three thousand square feet of new construction with a two-car garage *and* no specter of death hanging over our heads? *Really?* we asked each other. *And that's not a misprint?*

---

5 A Great North American Barkhound.

This house took our collective breath away the second we stepped inside. With eleven-foot ceilings, thick crown molding, and Brazilian cherry floors, we thought we'd died and gone to high-def HGTV heaven. We walked from room to room, admiring all the fine finishes. A butler's pantry? Yes, please! A second bathroom made entirely out of slabs of slate and tumbled river rocks? You know, I've been meaning to get me one of those! A Sub-Zero fridge and a six-burner Wolf range? Why, this gorgeous chef's kitchen may end my apathy toward fixing dinner once and for all!

We marveled at the idea of a city house containing four huge bedrooms. I mean, we wouldn't fill them up with kids,[6] but I was willing to wager we could put them all to good use. I could have a fitness room! And an office that wasn't really a hallway! And a guest room! We could have a guest room! Which meant we could finally have guests!

We couldn't figure out why such an amazing place was a) so cheap and b) unoccupied, but we didn't care. We wrote a deposit check as fast as our fingers would fly and we were settled in here within the week.

For the most part, we've been delighted with this place. I mean, everyone has a concept of what their dream house might be like, but all I have to do to picture mine is open my eyes.

And yet . . . I must admit a minor addiction to HGTV, no doubt stemming from my early John Hughes–based house lust. So, there's a part of me that mourns the loss of getting my hands dirty in creating a place in my own vision. I'd be lying if I said I didn't want to make my design divine with Candice Olson or see if

---

6 Seriously, no, thanks.

Carter really can. Mac and I both have a tiny, sexless crush on *Holmes on Homes*, and we'd adore having him get all self-righteous and blustery over shoddy masonry before he saved our bacon from the fire.[7]

The thing is, there's not a single thing this joint needs. What am I going to do? Tear up the gleaming hardwood to see if there's stained carpeting underneath? The bathrooms are already showplaces full of sunken tubs and six-headed steam showers. Should I replace the sinks with a cracked Formica vanity? The kitchen's gorgeous and functional, with forty-two-inch cherry cabinets, granite counters, and a French country chopping-block island in the middle of it. The only way to improve the kitchen would be to forbid Mac to cook in it.[8] Plus, I've got two decks and a patio and I've landscaped the hell out of all of them. Curb appeal? I've got it on speed dial, baby.

Okay, fine.

I'm sometimes discouraged when the rats eat from my artfully arranged, eclectically mixed herb and flower gardens. Also, the neighborhood's not the best. It's up-and-coming, or at least on the verge of it.

Or it was.

Our 'hood has gone a tiny bit downhill, with the way the economy's been going the past few years. And I might not love how the people across the street allow their unwashed kids to run around in their jammies well after an appropriate bedtime. But the

---

7 I don't actually know if this is a real expression, but it sounds vaguely Canadian, much like Holmes is vaguely Canadian.

8 And believe me, I've tried.

house is still perfect, and with the depressed market, we should be able to negotiate a better deal.

We're supposed to get our appraisal any minute now, and we're anxious to see the results. And even though we're already in the house we want to buy, we asked our Realtor friend Liz to help us navigate the process.

Liz insisted we get an appraisal to protect us from overpaying. Our landlord was shocked to hear that we'd brought a Realtor into the mix, but come on, that's how I roll! I mean, I have an accountant to handle my taxes, a financial counselor for the rest of my money, an attorney to keep my dumb ass from getting sued, a film agent for any television and movie stuff, a lecture agent for my speaking engagements, and a literary agent to hash out my print deals. (I write a young-adult series about teenage Amish zombies in love; it's surprisingly lucrative.) So why on earth would I enter into the biggest financial commitment of my life without a professional at my side? I might be a little loopy sometimes, but I'm not stupid.

We wait outside in the freezing cold for a few minutes to see if ORNESTEGA will make another appearance. He doesn't, so Mac shouts, "Buy a belt!" toward his apartment before we head inside to report the incident to the police. The beat cop who shows up advises us next time we see a tagger to call them and not to take the matter into our own hands. He said a lot of times tagging is step one of a gang initiation ritual and that we should be more cautious. I look over at Mac, who's nodding placidly at the officer, and laugh to myself. Yeah, like that's going to happen with Sergeant MacNamara on patrol.

Once the officer leaves, we walk up the wide steps to our

hand-carved front door. Right before we go inside, I ask Mac what's going to happen when the tagger inevitably spray-paints our garage.

"Don't you worry," he assures me. "I have a foolproof plan."

When I pull out of the garage today to meet my best friend, Tracey, for lunch, I find ORNESTEGA scrawled in eight-inch silver letters across our door. I hurriedly pound the keypad on my phone to dial Mac, who promises he's going to take care of it immediately.

Tracey and I live on opposite sides of the monument in the middle of the square. She's on the good side, with all the cute boutiques and darling cafés and trendy coffeehouses, whereas my side is Latin Kings–and-Cobras adjacent. I'd probably worry about living so close to two warring gangs but the thing is—and please don't judge—Mac and I are a tad conservative,[9] which means we may or may not have a small weapons stockpile. And unlike our Cobras and Kings neighbors, we actually know how to hit a target.[10]

Tracey and I have a fab lunch at Lulu's,[11] our favorite café, where we drink fair-trade tea and laugh at the twentysomethings clad in T-shirts boasting the names of my favorite shows as a kid. Listen, you with the fedora and hipster 'fro, five bucks says you've never even seen *Charles in Charge*.

I know, I know, that was bitchy and aggressive and unlike me.

---

9 Technically, we're Libertarians, but when's the last time they won an election?

10 Mac's expert marksman advice—turning the gun sideways to shoot works only in the movies. In real life it's an absolute guarantee you're going to a) miss and b) sprain your wrist.

11 Try the feta cheese plate. You'll thank me.

Seriously, I've kind of got a reputation for being a bit of a peacemaker, and I do my best to be polite. In fact, my sorority wanted me to join so badly they actually gave me a scholarship for all my dues. I guess when you stuff eighty girls who are all on their period at the same time into a single house, you're willing to pay a premium to have a calm, collected presence there to defuse situations.

So to be clear, I like everyone.

Except hipsters.

And hooligans.

And Stephenie Meyer. (Because everyone knows zombies are cooler than vampires.)

Anyway, I've all but forgotten about the tagging until I get home a few hours later. Upon my return, I see that Mac didn't opt to call 311 to request the city's Graffiti Blasters team, nor did he drag out soapy water and a Brillo pad to scrub off the offending moniker. He didn't buy a bucket of taupe paint and a brush, either.

No, my beloved opted for a less conventional solution. Now beneath the small, silver ORNESTEGA tag are much larger, thicker, blacker letters spelling out, IS GAY.

Yeah, this plan is *foolproof.*

Chapter Two
ONE SHEET TO THE WIND

We're in the wine department at Costco when we receive the news.

Normally I feel a little queasy in this section, because I always think of the time I paired a nice four-year-old bottle of Costco merlot with a bag of three-year-old microwave popcorn. Did you know microwave popcorn has an expiration date? Because it does. And you should never ignore it. I spent three days living in my bathroom after that and now microwave popcorn's on my permanent Do Not Fly list.

As Mac scrolls through the pages of our appraisal's supporting documentation, my stomach is in knots. I feel like I swallowed a fist or a hockey puck or a steak that Mac cooked. I'm dying to find out what our house is worth. When we moved in, the astronomical asking price was way outside of our budget, which was another reason we opted to rent.

But over the past two years, our income exponentially increased after my novel *It's Raining Mennonites* unexpectedly hit the *New York Times* bestseller list, which meant my next book, *Rumspringa-ding-ding*, recently sold for a tidy sum. Like I said, teenage zombies in love are fairly lucrative. I mean, they're not teenage-vampires-in-love lucrative,[12] but I'm satisfied. Between the two of our incomes, we can afford any asking price.

"Holy cats," Mac says succinctly. He holds out his iPhone for me to examine. I squint at the screen but can't make out what I'm supposed to be seeing, because I refuse to admit I need reading glasses.[13] "Here." Mac taps the number in the middle of the screen. "Look here."

I engage in more squinting and blinking and alternately bringing the phone closer and farther from my face. I finally see what he wants me to see and I'm confused. "But that number is way too low. Like, hundreds of thousands of dollars less than we expected."

His grin is best described as being of the shit-eating variety. "Uh-huh."

"What does that mean?"

Mac reaches across me to grab a couple of orange-labeled bottles from the Veuve Clicquot display. "*That* means we celebrate."

But I'm not ready to cheer yet, so I press for more answers. "Our house dropped about forty percent in value? In a year?

---

12 I bet there are no drive-by shootings *at all* in Stephenie Meyer's 'hood.

13 The way I see it, I can have a Barbie collection or magnifying readers; I can't have both. I choose Barbie.

Don't get me wrong; I'd love to snap it up at that price, but I can't see how that's possible. I mean, Vienna still owes more than that on her mortgage."

Vienna Hyatt owns our house, and she's the most unlikely landlord you've ever seen. She's a twenty-five-year-old trust-fund kid who pissed away the bulk of her inheritance on blow and Manolos.[14] Her real-estate-mogul parents decided to teach her a lesson,[15] so she's recently been forced into the family business, and now she's our problem.

Apparently part of their tough-love policy requires that she take a hands-on approach with her properties. When we blew a fuse on one of our dual-zoned air-conditioning units last summer, Vienna showed up in five-inch heels with a screwdriver tucked into her Louis Vuitton dog carrier, right next to Versace, her tea-cup terrier. She insisted she could fix the unit, but when Mac went out to check her progress, he found her disassembling our gas grill. I can't help but wonder if this is what her family had intended.

Mac narrows his eyes at me. "How would you know what Vienna owes on her mortgage?"

Okay, let me just say this and then we'll never speak of it again. Any mail that comes to my house is automatically considered mine. If you don't want me knowing how much you owe the bank, I urge you to fill out a change-of-address form.

"Um, it's just a wild guess." (Certain members of this household care not to be complicit in federal crimes.)

"The appraiser said that nothing on our side of the square has

---

14 This isn't gossip so much as it is fine, fine reporting from the folks at *Us* magazine.

15 As per the March 26, 2009, issue of *Star*.

sold in over three months, and he had a bitch of a time finding comps because everything's in foreclosure. Home prices around here dropped an average of thirty-four percent this year."

Mac has a spring in his step as we cruise the meat counters, but I'm a little more conflicted. On the one hand, I'm delighted that our house has become so much more affordable, but on the other, when I think of the hardworking people who poured all of their savings into losing investments, I feel like I ate that stupid popcorn all over again. Somehow this doesn't strike me as a victory.

When we get home from Costco, we find our garbage knocked over and trash strewn everywhere. Our cans are covered in ORNESTEGA tags.

Oh, kid . . . that was probably a mistake.

"So that's new," Tracey says, all deadpan, pointing to the top half of my house.

The sheet sign was not my idea. I hadn't even thought about them since college. In the nineties, sheet signs were a big deal in my campus Greek system. We used them to express all kinds of emotions, like how totally awesome our new pledge class was or the extent to which we were excited for team games played with various balls.[16] During homecoming weekends, rival fraternities would wage war against one another, dishing out zingers such as, THETA CHI, DON'T EVEN TRY, and PHI PSI—WHERE MEN ARE MEN AND SHEEP ARE SCARED, and, of course, the ubiquitous DELTS SUCK.

---

16 My sorority crafted a lot of signs of the WE'RE PI-FIRED UP variety.

Now I suppose college students simply design a logo on their MacBooks and FTP the file to FedEx Office[17] to be printed on a professional banner. They've probably never messed up their man-icures by dipping their fingers into cans of Kiwi shoe polish. Mock us if you will now, kids, but I guarantee that smelling like a pair of driving moccasins was an aphrodisiac in my day.

Anyway, Mac urged me to help him take this fight to the sheet-sign level. I resisted until I found a half-eaten lump of ham-burger studded with oblong pink pills in our backyard.

Fortunately, we're security-conscious enough to always keep the second gate between the alley and our garage locked, so the dogs never got near it. What's ironic is that the pink pills were antihistamines, and appeared to be the exact same brand and strength we give Daisy for her hay fever. (The unfortunate side note here is that the neighborhood rats are all emboldened and strong, since they're no longer troubled by seasonal allergies.)

Here's the thing—I can handle an aspiring gangbanger's half-assed attempts to mess with us. I wouldn't say I welcome it,[18] but I will say that I'm up for the challenge. I mean, I defy you to grow up in a steel town and not have it make you a little bit tough. Plus, those kickboxing classes I've taken have not been in vain.

Okay, fine.

All that time I've logged strolling along on the treadmill has not been in vain.

Okay, *okay*.

All the time I've spent watching Tae Bo infomercials has not

---

17 And when did it stop being Kinko's?

18 Even though Mac would.

been in vain. But, seriously, when someone threatens even one piece of fur on my precious doggies' backs, even if it's just with Benadryl, it is *on* like the fall of *Saigon*.[19]

"Oh," I quip to Tracey, "did we *not* have an enormous sheet sign proclaiming that ORNESTEGA wears ladies' underpants the last time you were here?"

Tracey shakes her head of chestnut curls. "I feel like I'd have noticed it."

I shrug. "We compromised. I told Mac he could hang it as long as he takes it down by tomorrow, when the Segunda Iglesia Hispanic Church has services. They don't need to worry about praying for ORNESTEGA's predilection for panties. By the way, that little asshole put squeeze cheese in our mailbox. Ruined a perfectly good Pottery Barn catalog."

"And you didn't shoot him in the thigh? I'm impressed." Tracey knows about the snub-nosed .38 Special revolver Mac insists I keep in my desk. Honestly, I dig having a weapon at hand when I write; it makes me feel like Ernest Hemingway. Although now that I think about it, Tracey's generally more concerned that I'll shoot *myself* in the thigh. Seriously, you mention having to move your gun one time because you accidentally filled it with pretzel crumbs, and suddenly everyone thinks *you're* the menace.

"Oh, come on, I have self-control."

---

19 Does this work as an expression? I had Ishmael say it to Mose in *Amish Is as Good as a Mile*. Later it occurred to me that pacifists might not study a lot of Vietnam War history, or engage in any sort of combat, even like punching a gangbanger in his smug face, for that matter. But come on, it's no less plausible than vampires who won't drink human blood.

Tracey says nothing, opting instead to raise a single eyebrow at me. Jealous . . . I can't do that myself anymore.[20]

"I *do* have self-control. I'm incredibly disciplined," I insist.

Tracey knows I'm a strict observer of what I like to call the Tao of Dalton. Remember in *Road House* when Patrick Swayze's character, Dalton, says that he's nice until it's time not to be nice? That's totally my philosophy.

Yet Tracey continues to smirk. "Fine, you win," I admit. "Truth is we heard from Persiflage Films and they may be interested in my writing a pilot for *Buggies Are the New Black*. I figured I couldn't have a laptop in jail, so for now, ORNESTEGA walks without a limp."

"Congratulations, Mia!" Because Tracey's an author, too, I don't have to explain to her how tenuous the whole film and TV business is. I can't tell you how many entertainment people I've talked to who say they love my writing and they're dying to work with me and then never call me again. Dealing with Hollywood folks is kind of like having a bunch of one-night stands, only I'm usually the only one who ends up with the clap.

Our kitten Agent Jack Bauer climbs into my lap and I scratch him behind the ears. "As far as I'm concerned, nothing's real until I see a check. Till then, they may as well be talking about Monopoly money."

"Speaking of real estate, what happened while I was on vacation?"

"Ugh, what an ordeal!" I settle deeper into the couch so I can share my tale of woe. Daisy flanks me, as I'm never allowed on a

---

20 Damn you, Botox, for making my forehead so smooth and expressionless but mostly smooth.

piece of furniture by myself. "I was worried that Vienna would be insulted if we went in with such a lowball offer, and if I've learned anything from *My First Place* and *Property Virgins*, it's that you don't want to offend the seller. Before we wrote up a formal offer, we had Liz call her to take her temperature on the whole deal. Not only did she laugh at the appraisal—"

"Did she know what an appraisal was?"

"Yes, *after* Liz explained it to her, whereupon she insisted on her original selling price."

"Any room to negotiate?"

"So far, no. What pisses me off is that I know how much she owes on this place, yet she wants tons more than that. Also, and maybe this is a stupid question, but she's a frigging millionaire: Why does she even *have* a mortgage?"

Tracey considers this for a moment. "Rich people don't stay rich by taking risks with their own money."

I nod. "You're probably right. Anyway, we came up with an 'everyone wins' kind of deal and made her an offer somewhere in the middle, but she was still having none of it. She claimed our appraisal was"—I pause to knead the thick fur on the back of Agent Bauer's neck while Daisy wedges herself in deeper between me and the couch—"in her words, 'not hot.'"

"Sounds like the path of least resistance would be to have a second appraisal," Tracey suggests.

I snort. "We're one step ahead of you. We had the bank's appraiser come in, and he estimated an even lower price because we live on a busy street. And you know what? Vienna still wouldn't budge. According to Liz, Vienna thinks the down market applies only to every other house in this neighborhood because *she* doesn't own them. After that conversation, she actually gave us a *higher* selling price. I suspect this has less to do with her real estate prowess and more to do with what I just read in *People*—apparently she needs the cash to live in Ibiza for the summer season. FYI, Southampton is 'so last year.' "

I begin to stroke Agent Bauer's back more aggressively and then have to raise my voice because he's purring so loudly. "What's so frustrating is that Vienna acts like this place didn't sit empty for two years because its price was too high before we moved in."

"Was that when she was in rehab?"

I concentrate for a moment. "Huh . . . you know what? You may be right. I think that's right after her sex tape broke on the Internet and she checked into Promises. Regardless, she told Liz, 'I could get a million for that place in a different location.' Well, yes. Duh. That's exactly how real estate works, honey. Unfortunately the house is in *this* location, where it's worth a fraction of that."

Mac pops up from the basement. "Hey, guys, what's with all the shouting?"

"We're talking about Vienna."

Mac rolls his eyes and heads to the kitchen for a soda. He's as fed up with the state of negotiations as I am. He suggested that if Vienna won't take the appraised price, then we go "fairy tale" all over her ass, speculating she might sell for a handful of magic beans, like in "Jack and the Beanstalk," as she seems that kind of gullible. I laughed when he first suggested this, but it may be our best option.

Tracey and I move on to happier topics and spend the afternoon laughing. At four p.m., she notices the time and announces she has to leave for her dinner date. Curvy and statuesque, Tracey's the Jewish hybrid of Marilyn Monroe and Mae West. Apparently this combination is like catnip to older generations, so her dates tend to be, let's say . . . more mature than her. Naturally, this is an endless source of amusement for me.

"Need to get ready?" I ask.

"Yep," she says, gathering up her coat and putting on her snow boots. "He's picking me up in a little while."

I cough into my hand. *"Earlybirdspecial."*

"What?"

I giggle. "Um, nothing." She frowns as she continues to bundle up. "So," I gamely continue, "a date tonight . . . How will you get sexy for that? Dab a little Mentholatum behind your ears? Fill your pockets with Werther's Originals? Surprise him with some fresh tennis balls for the tips of his walker?"

She sighs audibly. "He was born in October 1957. You realize that makes him six years younger than Sting. Would you date Sting?"

"Mac prefers I don't date, what with us being married and all."

Her cerulean blue eyes flash. "You know what I mean."

"Um, sure, I'd absolutely date Sting. But I don't picture your guy looking like Sting."

She glances up from her boot laces again. "How do you picture him?"

I close my eyes and try to envision her beau. I imagine a round face with soft jowls and a jawline that dips down into his collar. His hair is gray—or missing—and although his eyes show his age-borne experience, they've grown paler and a bit cloudy. He has crow's-feet and his lips have thinned. He's got laugh lines and forehead wrinkles and a host of other age-related maladies that I pay a lot of money to eliminate so my young-adult audience relates better to me at live events.[21]

"I guess in my head he looks like . . . Carroll O'Connor."

She snorts. "Archie Bunker? *That's* where your mind goes when you imagine an older guy?"

I nod.

"For your information, he does not look like Archie Bunker. He's been a weight lifter for thirty years and he's a vegetarian. He has a full head of hair that's got less gray in it than mine. I assure you he's in better health and shape than either of us."

I counter, "Yet I'm willing to bet his closet's filled with cardigans and Rockports and pastel Sansabelt pants."

Tracey's sheepish grin tells me everything I need to know.

"Maybe you should do your hair like Rita Hayworth tonight. All the GIs from the Greatest Generation loved her!" I call as she heads down our steps and out the heavy iron gate.

"Screw you and your sheet sign!" she cheerily calls back.

"Coffee at eleven tomorrow?"

"It's a date! See you at Lulu's!" She gets into her car and pulls away while I wave from the porch. The sheet sign whips in the breeze above my head while I quickly text her, *It's not a date; I'm too young for you.*

I go back inside and gather up all the detritus from our tea, depositing the dishes in the pristine farmhouse sink. After the kitchen's clean, I go upstairs to work on a new chapter featuring gratuitous barn building and brain sucking.

---

21 What, you thought I got all that crap done for vanity's sake? Come on!

The wind must have picked up, and I can hear the sign flapping against the wall outside. Time to take that thing down. I walk over to the intercom and call for Mac. "Hey, honey, church is in session tomorrow and the joke's getting old."

Also? I'm tired of people yelling, "Who's ORNESTEGA?" from their cars.

Mac comes up to my office, a parade of dogs and kittens in his wake. We go to either side of my bay window and release the zip ties securing the sheet. Once the sign's inside, we close the windows. I've just turned out the light and I'm about to shut the woven wooden blinds when I spot a shadowy figure moving quickly back and forth in the street in front of our house. What the . . . ?

"Mac, honey, get back here—what's going on out there?"

We see a hooded person on the street swivel his ski-mask-covered face around a couple of times and then pull what looks like a Powerade bottle out of his hoodie. The figure fumbles with something and then sticks a strip of fabric in the bottle. He whips out a lighter, ignites the bottom of the cloth, and hurls the bottle toward our house.

The first problem is that our fence is higher than the Masked Revenger anticipated, so when he throws his Molotov cocktail, it hits one of the finials on top of the gate and ricochets back toward him.

The second problem with Señor Ski Mask's plan is less about execution and more about design. Sports-drink bottles are efficient in their ergonomics because their wide openings allow for quicker refreshment deployment. When one's body is hot and thirsty for electrolytes, one wants to be able to gulp down that artificially flavored lemon-lime liquid as quickly as possible.

The thing is, there's a reason you never see James Bond blowing shit up by slinging a Gatorade container. Not only is a Château Lafite bottle a more elegant solution, but it melts at a higher temperature and its neck is much slimmer. Plus, being glass, it shatters on impact. However, the mouth on a sports-drink bottle is far too wide, and unless one stuffs in, say, an overnight maxipad, whatever fabric is placed inside is going to fall out once it's in motion and the bottle will melt once the fabric's ignited.[22]

Anyway, the person out front has found himself caught in a perfect storm of stupidity. One second he's standing there looking all smug and menacing in his ski mask, and the next, he's covered in turpentine and flaming harder than Boys Town on Pride weekend.

With the kind of deft swiftness one can employ only when one is, you know, *on fire*, our assailant whips off his mask, hoodie, and accompanying shirts and, in a single swift motion, hops out of his low-hanging pants. He then runs down the street screaming, clad in nothing but basketball shoes and a pair of colorful jockey shorts.

We're both quiet for a moment, taking in the gravity of what we just witnessed. I talk first. "I guess *that's* why ORNESTEGA doesn't wear a belt."

Mac nods. "But he has neatly answered the eternal boxers-or-briefs question; I give him that."

We silently watch the flames sizzle out when they reach a snowdrift, and finally Mac speaks again. "You realize this means we have to move to the suburbs."

---

22 Why, yes, Mac does make me watch a lot of Military Channel programming with him. How'd you know?

"Totally."

Mac is pensive for a moment before picking up the phone to call the police. "Of course, before we go, we'll have to change the sign to reflect recent events."

"Meaning?"

"Meaning now it's going to read, 'ORNESTEGA wears Spider-Man underpants.'"

Chapter Three
I'VE GOT YOUR GPS RIGHT HERE, PAL

"Turn left here. Left! Here! Turn left right now! The map says left! Left, left, left! Now, now, now!"

Mac glances at me in the rearview mirror, raising a single eyebrow. Okay, would everyone stop doing that? It makes me very self-conscious.

"Why are you not turning left? The blue line on this map is the most direct route to where we're going," I yelp. "Go! Left! Leeeeefffttt!"

Calmly, Mac replies, "Because I trust the GPS system more than I do your cartography prowess, and because the line you're looking at is a river."

Mac, Liz, and I are navigating our way up to see houses in the exclusive suburban town of Abington Cambs. We chose to concentrate our search in the Cambs[23] for a couple of reasons, but mostly because . . . this is *Shermer*! I'm so keyed up I can barely stay in my seat.

Abington Cambs was not only Hughes's inspiration for the fictional town of Shermer, but so many of his outdoor scenes were filmed here. We've already driven past the little stucco-and-beam shopping plaza from *Ferris Bueller*, and I'm pretty sure I just spotted the McCallister house from *Home Alone*. I mean, how perfect is that?

This is the most beautiful community I've ever seen; that's probably because it's also one of the wealthiest. *Forbes* magazine recently called Abington Cambs "the Hamptons of Middle America." Everything here is landscaped and manicured and tidy, exactly like I remember from the movies. I'm pretty sure if ORNE-STEGA wrote his name on anything, the zoning board would publicly execute him on the bucolic grounds of the market square.

Naturally this is where stupid, undeserving Vienna grew up, and, yes, that fact kills me a little inside.

Anyway, when I graduated from college and moved to Chicago, I was dying to see the Cambs firsthand. As it so happened, my first job was in sales, and I ended up servicing some hospital accounts close to here.

I'd often head to the Cambs after my meetings just to spot landmarks, and sometimes I'd stop to hit their McDonald's. The first time I went there, I almost missed it. Instead of sporting the familiar red-shingled roof and a big golden-arched sign, the Mc-Donald's in the Cambs is a pretty green wooden building with cream trim and shake shingles. Were it not for the tasteful little

---

23 Also known as the AC.

sign at the parking lot entrance, no one would know it wasn't a beautifully appointed—albeit oddly placed—barn.

From what I've read, the town is maniacal about more than just fast-food joints. Mr. T lived here in the eighties, and when he cut down his oak trees, the locals' outrage made the *New York Times*. Residents called it "The Abington Cambs Chain Saw Massacre."[24]

When the weather was nice, I'd opt to drive back to the city down the picturesque stretch of Meridian Road instead of the expressway. I'd go really slowly, making sure to take in all the mansions bordering Lake Michigan. Balustrades! Crushed-shell driveways extending half a mile! Sculpture gardens! Proud as I was of my first studio apartment by Wrigley Field, seeing those grand old homes on the water made me dream big. Matter of fact, I came up with the plot to *Valley of the Faceless Dolls* on that ride one warm spring night.

Between my blurting directions and Mac's ignoring them, we reach our first showing. We pull up to a diminutive taupe Cape Cod in a pretty subdivision far west of the lake. The trees in the neighborhood are bare save for a coating of snow, but I can already tell how pleasantly shaded this street will be when winter's finally over. Liz deftly works the lockbox, quickly extracting a key. She calls over her shoulder, "Let's have a peek."

The door opens into a sunny, inviting entry hall with plenty of room for coats and umbrellas and all the other detritus associated with living above the arctic circle.[25] I lean on Mac while I

---

24 I pity the fool . . . who disrespects dendrophiliacs.

25 Fine, the Cambs isn't technically located above the arctic circle, but it sure feels that way today.

kick off my snowy Merrell clogs and slide on a pair of blue flannel elastic booties. "You really don't need to wear those if you're in your socks," Liz tells me.

"Eh." I shrug. "I don't mind." The hardwood is made of thick planks of polished oak, stained to a lovely cherry color. There's a solidly protective level of varnish on top of it, so I already know the floor will stand up to years of muddy paws and throw-up kitties.

We first step into the small living room—or rather, I skid, as the combination of socks and booties turns the floor into a hot skillet and my feet into pats of butter—and we admire the picture window and the view. "There's not a crackhead to be seen out there," Mac remarks with more than a little awe.

We then wander into the dining room, which feels extra cozy with its raised hearth surrounded by built-in bead-board shelves. "Lovely," we all murmur. The walls are covered in wallpaper— normally my nemesis—but it's so rich and understated that at no point do I begin to look for loose corners to tug. We move on to the family room.

One of the rules I've learned from watching the home-buying shows is that you're not supposed to base your opinion on the homeowners' possessions; rather you're obligated to look beyond their stuff to see the real features, like double-paned windows, or the real problems, like a water-damaged ceiling. A professionally staged living room is great, but it doesn't matter if the furnace is on its last legs and the house is located in a floodplain.

Of course, the home-*selling* shows are all about staging, be-cause it's a fact that well-presented houses sell faster.[26] And even

---

26 I have a PhD in HGTV.

though my head understands that staging is nothing more than smoke and mirrors, my heart can't help but leap when I see their furniture. "Oh, my God," I exclaim. "They have the Lancaster sofa set from Restoration Hardware! That's what we have! We already know exactly what it would look like if we lived here!"

We pass through the breakfast area (sunny! airy!) and the well-appointed galley kitchen (a warming drawer! double ovens!) and into the narrow mudroom with the spanking new front-loading washer and dryer. Mac gets a faraway look on his face, lost in a daydream about all the towels and jeans we could wash in a single load.[27]

"Shall we check out the backyard?" Liz asks.

We put our shoes back on and step out onto a tidy stone patio that overlooks half an acre of young trees, all enclosed by a new fence. "The dogs would have so much fun out here," Mac remarks.

"Yeah, not really. Daisy would pee on the patio and then demand to be let back into the house, and Duckie would do nothing but stand in the farthest part of the yard and protect us from falling leaves and squirrels with his nonstop barking. Then I'd have to wade through snowbanks in my slippers to get him to stop, because he never comes when he's called," I reply. "No, thank you."

"We have plenty of room to put in a pool," Mac says.

"And now I'm back on board with the yard."

We return inside, stomping off snow and reapplying the sock-condoms. We check out the cute basement and find it more than suits our needs. The ceilings are high and the windows well positioned to eliminate glare when setting up the home theater.

---

27 Wait, this is a really sad fantasy, isn't it?

There's a wee office off the main part of the basement, and the second we step inside, Mac shouts, "Mine!"

Off the office, there's an additional storage area where we stumble upon a litter box. Okay, this? Is the biggest-selling feature of all. Even though our current house is huge, there aren't a lot of good places for the kittens' boxes. No matter where I place them or how often I change the clay, the open-concept layout means the stink wafts through the whole place to the point that when visitors come over, they don't notice the crown molding or cherry floors. Rather, the first thing out of everyone's mouth is, "How many cats do you have?" Shameful.

After a thorough basement inspection, we move up to the second floor. The first room we see must be the owners' little girl's room, because it looks like Easter has thrown up on a Disney film. Everything is either pale pink or mint green. Pink-and-green gingham ribbons suspend white wooden blocks spelling out SO-PHIA over the big window. The floor is covered in a floral pastel rug in shades of green and gold, and a white chair rail divides the walls in half. The bottom part of the wall is ballet-slipper pink, and the top part is covered in pink toile wallpaper. Only rather than the traditional eighteenth-century pastoral scene of oxen and farmers and straw-roofed huts, the lime green line drawings are of bunnies and frogs in repose.

"Obviously you'd want to change this," Liz notes.

Obviously.

I mean, I'd need to find blocks that spelled out MIA.

The other bedrooms are large and well laid out, and some come with attached baths where the fixtures are new and the water pressure impressive.

According to the MLS listing, the whole house has been recently renovated and everything's brand-new—the floors, the furnace, the water heater, etc. The house is compact, but it's move-in ready, and all we'd have to do would be to replace the owners' sturdy leather family room set with our own.

As we put our shoes on again and take one final glance behind us, Liz says, "The house shows really well and it's priced right. But what do you think?"

Mac and I glance at each other. In theory, this house is what we want. Granted, it's smaller than what we have now, but it's in a nice neighborhood, and it wouldn't require a single tweak before moving in. The best part is, we'd never have to deal with Vienna again.

And yet, now that we're standing here in the handsome foyer with the good closets and indestructible floor, something about the place doesn't feel right. There's no opportunity for us to make our mark on it, because everything's already been done just so. I mean, I don't want to do major construction, but updating things a bit would be a lot of fun.

Nothing particularly draws me to this house. At first, I thought because they had our sofa, that was a sign, but upon closer inspection, they've got the Maxwell model, not the Lancaster. The difference between rounded and squared-off arms is subtle, but crucial.

This house is like meeting a guy who's totally into marriage, comes from a fantastic family, has a well-paying job that makes him happy, and whose favorite hobbies include buying you designer handbags and watching reality television. I mean, where's the challenge? Where's the struggle? Where's the satisfaction that comes from finally breaking Mac—I mean *him*—of his bad habits?

"Liz, I have kind of a weird question. Is it possible that sometimes a house can be too perfect and it's kind of a turnoff?" I ask.

She smiles back at me. "I see that all the time. Remember, purchasing a house is more than just figuring out numbers. You buy with your gut, too. And if your gut says this isn't the one, then we have plenty more to see."

We walk out to the car and Liz asks me again if I wouldn't rather sit in the front seat.

"Nope," I reply. "If I do, Mac will try to make me use the navigation system."

"And what's wrong with that?" he calls over his shoulder.

"Listen, I did not spend all that time last night poring over my map just to have some officious German voice second-guess me. My map kicks ass. My map is *bank*."

Mac chuckles at me. "Still trying to make 'bank' happen?"[28]

"Of course." I have a running bet with my college roommate, Ann Marie. It started when I was convinced I'd come up with the expression "all that and a bag of chips." She didn't believe me, claiming I'd heard someone say it on *Oprah*.[29] I never forgave Ann Marie for crushing my dream, so ever since then we've had an ongoing challenge on who can make the Next Big Expression happen. She's been trying to get "sweet baby Ray!" into the collective unconscious, while I've been pushing "bank."

Despite being a blond-bobbed soccer mom from Connecticut, Ann Marie is vaguely terrifying. She once instigated a coup at a

---

28 And this is where the author breaks the fourth wall, noting that every book she writes has a nod to *Mean Girls* in it. What can Jen say? It was a really good movie.

29 This was back when her shows were still trashy.

Pampered Chef party . . . and it wasn't bloodless. Ann Marie works as a prosecuting attorney, and I sat in on one of her cases once. She showed up to court that day in a tangerine print shift, a padded headband, and a triple string of pearls. I had to laugh when the defense visibly relaxed upon spotting her. They had no idea they were about to be hit by a Lilly-clad guided missile. As the shell-shocked defendant was led out in cuffs, he kept repeating, "What just happened here?"

My point is that even with my international audience of socially networked teenagers reading my term, she's more likely to make her expression mainstream first. I'm pretty sure I heard a random person exclaim, "Sweet baby Ray!" at the grocery store last week, but I'm going to pretend they were looking at barbecue sauce.

Still, you have to admit that "bank" kicks ass as a turn of phrase. It's short for "Bank on it" or "You can take that to the bank," kind of like how Vince Vaughn[30] described everything as "money" before he got all famous and bloated.

I tell Mac, "I was thinking I'd work 'bank' into my next book, maybe have Ezekiel say it after a particularly successful barn raising or something."

"Do the Amish even use banks?" Mac wonders.

"No clue," I admit.

"Wait. You write about the Amish," Liz interjects. "Shouldn't you know? Wouldn't that have come up in your research?"

I shrug and smooth out my map. "Why would I research them? They don't read my work, so it's not like I have to worry

---

30 Also hails from the Cambs.

about my inaccuracies offending the Amish community. Or the zombie community, for that matter. What are they going to do, download my books on their Kindles? Read my Twitter feed? Does the milking shed have Wi-Fi? Seriously, you think Stephenie Meyer spends her time researching vampires' banking habits? Doubtful. She's probably too busy taking money baths."[31]

Liz wrinkles her brow.[32] "I'm curious, then: If you haven't done any research, then how do you know so much about the Amish?"

Mac speaks up before I get the chance. "She watched John Stossel do a report on them on *20/20*. Once."

"And yet my books about the Amish have done well enough to buy you this Benz," I calmly respond. I wonder what Mr. Stephenie Meyer drives. Probably a flying fucking car.

Mac's grinning when he glances at me in the rearview mirror. "Maybe if you knew a little more I could have upgraded to the big engine."

I know he's teasing me, but this still grates a little. I choose not to explain—again—how my books really aren't about being Amish or the undead eating flesh. Rather, they're about what it's like to be a teenager. I want kids to read my books and feel like I did when I watched *The Breakfast Club*; I want them to know that, like John Hughes, I'm quite aware of what they're going through.[33]

The Amish bit is really just a device for a couple of reasons. I like to write about stolen glances and clandestine feelings rather

---

31 Screw her and her eighty-five-million book sales right in the ear.

32 Knock it off!

33 Ten points if you caught the Bowie reference.

than big, blown-out, fully articulated sex scenes. The buildup to a first kiss can be every bit as riveting as a couple yanking each other's pants off, sometimes even more so.

I've gotten decidedly more modest as I've aged. At twenty-two, fresh out of college and four years of playing I Never at fraternity parties, I'd have had no problem going on and on about my character's o-r-g-a . . .[34] But I'm a proper[35] married lady now, and writing explicit scenes just doesn't sit right with me. I'm not judging anyone else who puts out racy novels—and I'll probably even read them—but writing them isn't for me. Plus, there's something very satisfying about keeping my characters innocent.

I've chosen to write about the Amish because their stories aren't going to get bogged down with technology, either. I don't want my writing to get all cloudy and convoluted because I didn't realize that Tumblr is the new Facebook which is the new Myspace.

Also, if I had to deal with characters that ran around spouting text message–speak like, "OMGWTFBBQ!" I'd probably want to kick a lung out of myself. Sure, the technology, lingo, and costumes change from generation to generation, but the pressure of being trapped somewhere between childhood and adulthood is universal.

In other words, the point isn't about getting sparkly in the sun, *Stephenie*.

While I pout in the backseat, we get to the next house. We're a little farther east in the Cambs, and the trees in this neighborhood are more mature, forming what's got to be a spectacular

---

34 You know what? I'm too embarrassed to even finish that sentence.

35 Read: boring.

canopy over the street when the leaves fill in. That's the one down-side of new construction in a subdivision. Sure, you might get a fancy community clubhouse and wide, smooth streets covered in fresh blacktop, and a brand-new roof, but unless the builder spends a mint on landscaping, the tiny little trees are dwarfed by whatever house they're placed next to, no matter how modest. Given the choice, I'd prefer a house that's older, maybe in a more established neighborhood.

The driveway is way longer than the last one, and under the snow I detect the sound of crushed shells. The house is solid brick, not just a brick facade, like where we live now, and the yard is substantially larger than the last. Homes in this neighborhood are set farther apart, and if you squint just right, it almost looks like an estate. This is a promising start.

Our promising start comes to a screeching halt the second we step inside.

"What's that smell?" I ask, pulling my woolly scarf over my nose and mouth. I'm assaulted by an aroma that stings my eyes and burns my throat. My lungs instantly feel like there's a steel vise around them.

Liz breathes into her gloved hand while consulting her MLS listing. "It says here they had a tiny problem with mold."

Mac points to an enormous black bloom on the far wall in the kitchen. "*Had* mold? Ladies, that ain't modern art. More like *has mold.*"

"Do we even need to look at this one?" I ask.

"Been there, done that, burned the T-shirt," Mac replies.

We dash back outdoors and gasp for fresh air. "No wonder it was in our price range."

To start this process, we ran our financials past our banker again. We'd been approved for a generous amount before, but with my recent book sales, we wondered if that would alter our budget. Turns out our bank is very enthusiastic about teenage Amish zombies in love and they increased our preapproval amount substantially.[36] We're not ready to spend our self-imposed limit, but we did allocate more funds to the search.

With this sum, we could get a spectacular home anywhere in the whole Chicagoland area . . . except here. Since this is such an elite enclave, prices are ridiculously inflated compared to other suburbs. A sane person would simply go where he got the most bang for his buck, but come on, this is Shermer! I've waited my whole life to live here!

We load back up into the car and drive another mile due east. Yay, east! From what I've read, the farther east you live in the Cambs, the better. Apparently there's a whole east side/west side rivalry raging up here. The west side is where *Pretty in Pink*'s Andie lived, and the east side is where the sad-little-rich-boy-Blane-who-was-conflicted-about-liking-her (and-who-was-not-in-fact-a-major-appliance) was from. What John Hughes couldn't have predicted back then is that twenty years later, even Andie's teardown would be worth half a mil.

We pull into the circular drive of the third house. "Circular drive!" I exclaim. "All the best homes on the lake have circular drives! I feel good about this place!"

The house has an interesting footprint—from the front, it looks like a modest ranch, but in the back it balloons up to two

---

36 And they don't ask any pesky questions about my research methods.

and a half stories. The entire south wall is made of glass and it looks out onto acres and acres of forest preserve. I'm already mentally leashing up the dogs and taking them on long, luxurious, woodsy walks where I don't have to worry about them stepping on glass or trying to eat a syringe or a cigarette. Once while we were out walking, I had to wrestle a chicken wing out of Daisy's mouth. Seriously.

Liz punches in the code to get the key and we step out of our shoes and into the flannel booties. We're prepared to be wowed. The ceilings inside are low and sloped, and there's nothing but pale wood planks everywhere we look. There's wood on the walls, wood on the countertops, a wood-covered refrigerator, wood paneling over the dishwasher, and wood on the slanted ceilings. The only place in our line of sight that's not decked out in wood is the sunken living room. It appears to be about a foot lower than the rest of the house, but the carpet is so shaggy it's more like six inches. I sort of want to do the Nestea plunge onto it.

"What do you call this architecture style?" Mac asks.

Liz scans her sheet. "The listing says it's 'Colorado contemporary.'"

"The listing should say, 'Mork and Mindy's house,'" I correct.

The decor doesn't get any more contemporary[37] as we move past the entry. We notice the living room contains nothing but one of those big egg-shaped chairs and a curved chrome lamp.

"Suddenly I have the urge to sit in here wearing my hiking boots, listening to Dan Fogelberg on my eight-track while I read *Jonathan Livingston Seagull*," Mac says.

---

37 Or Colorado.

"While feathering your hair with your enormous plastic pocket comb," Liz adds.

I chime in, "In rainbow suspenders. While smoking an enormous doob."

There are three different spiral staircases leading to oddly angled nooks upstairs, and every bedroom has either a water bed or access to a hot tub or both. And wood. So very, very much wood.

"Anyone else get the feeling this place was a porn set?" Mac asks.

I nod gravely. "So very, very much porn."

We continue the tour, mostly because it's funny.

"Who would buy this place?" I ask.

Liz consults a column of dates on the second page of the listing. "It's been on the market for a year. You know, the construction is solid and someone obviously spent a lot of money on the paneling, but design like this can't be fixed without a bulldozer. Unless they drop their asking price several hundred thousand dollars—"

"Or find Pam Dawber," I interject.

"Or find Pam Dawber, no one will buy this place."

We bid good-bye to Porn House and move on to the next listing. We're there before I can even locate the place on the map. We park in front of a sagging colonial bordered by a couple of scruffy trees. "Okay, here we go," Liz says. "This is it, 613 Maple Knoll Road."

Hmm. Why does this address sound familiar? Have I been here before? No, today's pretty much my first foray into anything other than the Cambs' McDonald's. And yet this address rings a bell. Why?

"Have you mentioned this place to us before?" I ask Liz.

"Not that I know of," she replies.

"Mac, does this seem at all familiar to you?"

Whenever Mac really needs to concentrate, he squints and puts his hand to his mouth. He finally opens his eyes and says, "The place looks a little like a down-market version of my grand-parents' house, I guess?"

"No, no, that's not it. But the address, it's right on the edge of my subconscious. What is it? What could it be?" I stomp around the porch, shaking snow off my clogs. I notice a lady walk by with a dog and I smile and wave. In return, she scowls. Okay, what was that about?

The lock is sticking, so we have a couple more moments to cool our heels before we enter. I continue to try to jog my memory. "Maple Knoll, Maple Knoll, Maple Knoll . . ." And then I notice the street address in big brass numbers on the mailbox and it comes to me. "I've got it! I know how I know this house!"

"Yeah? How's that?" Liz asks. "Have you been here before? I just showed a place to a couple, and in the middle of the tour, the wife exclaimed, 'I threw up in these bushes!' I guess she'd been to a party there once in high school."

"That's hilarious, but we didn't grow up in Illinois—we're from Indiana. We only moved up here after college. But I remember why I know this address! A child molester lived here!"

At the same time, Mac and Liz exclaim, "*What?*"

"I cross-referenced the MLS with the Illinois Sex Offender Database." Both Liz and Mac stare at me incredulously.[38]

Liz looks worried as she works the locks. "Was it one of those

---

38 What, they didn't?

situations where the guy was nineteen and the girl was seventeen and it was more of a parent thing and less of a sex crime?"

"Oh, no," I exclaim. "This guy was a full-on perv. Child pornography. Videotaping and shit. Don't even worry about the lock, because we can't live here. Too much terrible karma."

Mac quickly agrees. "You're right. The neighbors might not know we were the new people and we'd be ostracized."

I nod. "I guess that explains why the woman who just walked by here was staring daggers at us. Also? I'd hate to get a pedophile's mail."

We quickly leave and spend the rest of the afternoon trolling around the west side of Abington Cambs. What's really unfortunate is that the Porn House and the Perv House are the highlights of the day. Everything we see next is small or chopped up or completely overpriced or full of questionable wiring and a hundred layers of hideous wallpaper and totally not worth removing our shoes. Mac and I are both really frustrated that we may not be able to find a decent place up here.

"Hey, is anyone thirsty?" Mac asks. "We should find a 7-Eleven or a Starbucks or something."

I'm quick to help. "Let me see what I can locate on my trusty map."

Exasperated by our lack of success, he runs his hand through his hair. "Okay, seriously, enough with the frigging map. You're using what's essentially a child's place mat from a seafood restaurant, and you keep telling us to turn left into bodies of water so we can avoid pirates while we search for the goddamn buried treasure! This is like driving around with Homer Simpson. I guarantee you there's no place to get a hot beverage on that thing, so please stop barking commands and let me see what I can find."

I cross my arms and lean back into my seat. If my navigational skills aren't wanted, then I'll keep them to myself.

We cruise up and down Whitefish Bay Road for fifteen minutes, passing the oddly placed green barn no less than five times.

At no point do I mention that that's the McDonald's . . . which is clearly marked on my map.

Chapter Four
THE REAL HOUSEWIVES OF LAKE COUNTY

"No luck yet?"

I'm sitting at a window table at Lulu's with Tracey and our mutual bestie, Kara. Our schedules have been so hectic that this is the first time we've had a chance to get together in almost a month. "Oh, no," I say, stabbing a hunk of feta cheese, "we've found a place. In fact, we've found a bunch of places. We just can't buy any of them."

Tracey smirks. "I'm so sorry to hear that." Tracey hasn't quite been behind our move to the suburbs. She thinks we should simply find a house here in the city, but unless we colonize Grant Park, we're not going to get all the land, lake, and privacy that we want. Every time I recount an unsuccessful real estate outing, Tracey cheers, "Team City!"

Kara's from the Cambs and her mom's still a practicing ob-gyn up there, so she's been far more supportive of Team Suburbs. Plus, if she comes to see us, she has the option to tack on a visit to the 'rents, too. "What's going on?" Kara asks sympathetically, pushing a big hank of black hair back from her face. Her stacked, intricately carved gold bracelets clink merrily with the movement. Her jewelry's the one nod to her Indian culture. "My parents said there are ten houses for sale in their subdivision."

"Hey, I love their house! All those pretty trees and winding drives! You know, I should look at places in your parents' neighborhood," I say.

Kara shudders. "Please don't. I'll never be allowed to see you if I don't swing by their place, too, and I already see them plenty. *Plenty*. I'm begging you as a friend to buy on the east, north, or south side."

I've met Kara's parents many times and they're sweet and kind and adorable . . . and absolutely merciless when it comes to their opinions on Kara's life. As I'm sort of charmed by my overbearing family, sometimes I don't realize that others frown on being told what to do quite so much.

"Oh, honey, I'm sorry; I forgot."

The last time we got together, Kara shared her latest story about a mandatory parental fix-up. Not only was her date forty and still living at home, but he spent the whole evening lecturing Kara on the evils of high-fructose corn syrup and liquor after she ordered a rum and Coke. As she saw it, her only course of action was to drink more. So she did. But then she had to endure a hangover-tinged lecture the next morning from her mom after getting a "bad report"[39] from her date.

---

39 Mrs. Patel's words, not mine.

"She's right; it's a bloodbath up there," I agree. "Just about everything in our price range is either a short sale or in foreclosure."

"Short sales are tricky," Tracey adds. "Lenders are really hesitant to allow owners to sell properties at a loss, especially now."

I add, "We're finding that the problem with buying a short sale is that the seller's bank has to approve our offer, and in a lot of cases we're dealing with a third-party negotiator who won't give us any idea of what we're bidding against so we know what to offer. On the one hand, we don't want to strong-arm anyone out of their family home with a superaggressive bid, but on the other, we question the wisdom of paying full price in this market. Every time we've guessed at an equitable price, we've been shut out."

I take a bite from my feta plate before I continue. "We fell in love with one house with a big pool and an enormous wooded lot with hiking trails—"

"You don't hike," Tracey interjects.

"I might if I had my own trail," I argue. "Plus there was a four-car garage—"

Tracey interrupts, "You have two cars."

"I'm aware of that. But the storage would be nice, and Mac could have used part of the garage as a workshop. And there was a fab sunroom and a sweet media room, but it doesn't matter, because there's a third party involved and our bank won't work with them and we lost out. Then we saw a house that we completely loved, but the taxes alone would add almost three thousand dollars to our monthly mortgage payment and we just *couldn't*."[40]

---

40 Okay, technically, we *could*, as my sales in Germany are currently through the roof. Seriously, I'm like the second coming of Hasselhoff over there.

Tracey stirs raw sugar into her iced tea and remarks, "You're paying for their amazing school system, which . . . Oh, I'm sorry. Remind me again which of your offspring will be attending Abington Cambs Country Day. Daisy? Agent Jack Bauer?"

I purse my lips at her[41] and continue. "Then on Sunday, we found the frigging promised land. Our banker called us and told us about a foreclosure. It was light-years beyond the top of our comfort level in terms of price, but he said the word on the street was that their bank would take any offer."

Mac and I were dying when we pulled down the private lane and saw the house. We were looking at an estate with towers and everything, and there was no squinting involved.[42] We could not believe our luck as we passed under the wisteria-vined arbor and down the winding bluestone path. "No way!" we kept exclaiming to each other. "No way!" Right as we got to the door, a family of deer dashed across the lawn. What timing! It was as though a film crew were right offstage shouting, "Cue the deer! Cue the deer!"

Liz was doing an open house that day, so she couldn't come with us. Instead, she arranged for us to meet with the Realtor who was working with the bank.

Mac and I walked around with our jaws slack. Not only was it eleventy thousand square feet,[43] but the original owner was a builder and this place was his baby. Every detail was pitch-perfect, from the custom millwork to the library with the mahogany built-ins to the eight-jetted steam shower. And the home gym with the

---

41 Can't actually frown.

42 Picture the Playboy Mansion, only with more ivy and less booty.

43 Give or take a few kajillion hundred.

rubber matting and the ballet bar and mirrored walls? My God, I've belonged to health clubs that weren't as nice. Or big.

This was our better-than-our-wildest-dreams house! And according to our inside source, it was in our budget! We were ready to write a check on the spot until we climbed up into the south tower.

"The place was insane," I tell them. "But then we ran into the owner's teenage daughter up in the third-floor library loft, working on her computer. The Realtor congratulated her on the nice job she'd been doing, which Mac and I didn't understand.

"As soon as we got down to the second level, the Realtor leaned in to us all conspiratorially and mentioned that the daughter had been industriously listing the family's possessions on Craigslist and eBay. Turns out the bank was allowing the foreclosed family to live in the house until they found a buyer, and the kid was trying to raise cash to help with moving expenses."

Kara inadvertently clutches her chest. "Oh, *God*."

"Yeah," I continue. "What was I supposed to say? 'Yo, kid, sorry your dad lost his empire. Pack up all your gymnastic medals and shit, because I'ma keep my Barbie collection in *your* room!' I mean, maybe we're fools for not jumping on the opportunity, but we couldn't do it."

"Of course you couldn't," Kara confirms.

"Chef's kitchen?" Tracey asks.

"The kitchen alone was a thousand square feet, with furniture-grade cabinets, and they weren't messing around with some rinky-dink Wolf stove. Oh, no, they had a freaking AGA cooker. And there was a TV in the fridge door."

"How many bathrooms?" Tracey prompts.

"Five full, three half. And one of them had an onyx counter-top. Ridiculous."

Tracey toys with her spoon before placing it by the side of her plate. "Did it have a wet bar?"

"One on the main level, a full bar in the walkout basement, and a bar area with the outdoor kitchen by the pool's waterfall."

"Oh, yeah." Tracey smirks. "You made the right choice." She doesn't gloat and exclaim, "Team City!" like she normally does. She doesn't have to.

"My point is, we need to find something soon before I shoot Vienna in her hair extensions," I say.

"Accidentally, of course," Kara adds.

"Yeah." I snort. "*Accidentally*. Get this—she's aware of the problems we have with gangs in the neighborhood. And she real-izes we trend a tiny bit militia and we're always on high alert, right?"

"Is it just exhausting to be you sometimes?" Tracey asks.

I glance over at Tracey and answer her honestly. "Sometimes. Anyway, Mac's fairly serious about hitting the gym before work ever since he saw himself in that three-way mirror at Blooming-dale's. So last week, it's about four thirty a.m., and he's just about to go out the back door when he hears noises up front. Right as he gets to the front door, it swings open and Vienna staggers in wearing this ridiculous pink chinchilla bolero. Mac is all, 'Can I help you?' And she slurs, 'I'm here to show the house,' and then he notices a drunken guy in tow. I guess she met him at a club and he wanted to see the house she had for sale. When Mac yelled at her—and believe me, there was yelling—she was all, 'It's my house and I'm allowed to be here!' The whole situation kind of devolved from there, and when Vienna finally left, Mac honestly couldn't figure out whether she was that stupid or that arrogant."

Tracey quips, "Can't it be both?"

"Ooh," Kara squeals. "I saw her in that exact coat in *OK!* when I was at the nail salon last month. Wow, times must be tough for her if she's recycling her outfits."

"Really?" I ask. "*That's* your takeaway from this situation?"

Kara's suddenly sheepish. "Oops, sorry. What are you gonna do?"

I shrug. "We keep searching. I don't care if we have to look at every house in the AC; we *are* moving there."

"Thanks for coming with us. These places are starting to blur together and we're at the point where we're having trouble keeping them straight," Mac says. Tracey's accompanying us to a house we saw earlier this week. We feel like it has potential because of a couple of key features, but want a second opinion from a trusted adviser. She's up front with him, as we both hope to gauge her first reaction of the house when we drive up.

"Here's the thing, Trace," I begin. "When Liz showed us this place, she said, 'A house like this takes a specific buyer.'"

Tracey's mom is a Realtor, so she knows all the code words, like how "cozy" means "microscopic" and "conveniently located" means "freeway-adjacent." "So you want me there to help you determine whether the home's tackiness is superficial or goes all the way down to the bone."

"Bingo. I guess because my taste trends a bit juvenile when it comes to decorating I can't get a bead on this place. I'm not sure if the house is over-the-top or really elegant," I reply. Tracey has exquisite taste in antiques,[44] so I will absolutely do as she advises.

Because I grew up in a house that was so austere, I have trouble determining what's stylish in terms of interiors. I've seen tons of television shows where designers demonstrate how to replicate a high-end piece with a low-cost improvisation, and I almost always prefer the inexpensive knockoff. So I figure if we're going to make the biggest investment of our lives, I don't want to discount a place for being gaudy when it's actually gilded.

After we get off the highway, we wind down a couple of wooded lanes on the way to our potential street.

"Great neighborhood so far," Tracey tells us as we pass a couple of lovely Arts and Crafts–style homes with stunning river-rock stone supports, exposed roof rafters, and wide triangular eaves. One of them has the most gorgeous stained-glass windows I've ever seen, all done up in brown and gold florals. Tracey amends her approval with, "I mean, *if* you have to move to the suburbs."

We pass a number of houses running the gamut from cute to spectacular. "I like that one a lot," I say, pointing out the Prairie-style place with tons of symmetrical clerestory windows as we round the corner to the listing. "It's so, like, Frank Lloyd Wright."

"You ought to research that address—Wright built many homes up here. That may be one of his actual designs," Tracey tells me.

Mac replies, "Cool," and slows as we approach the circular stone driveway. Tracey's not looking at what might be our house, because her attention has been drawn to the massive Shingle-style home across the street.

---

44 Furniture and men.

"How fabulous is that?" Tracey crows about the home's elegant, understated simplicity. "It's like a perfect beach house all tucked away here back in the woods. This is my favorite kind of home. Did you know Shingle style was the backlash to all those fussy Victorian-style places at the turn of the century? I bet those shingles are made of white cedar, because—" And that's when Tracey realizes we've parked.

"We're here," Mac tells her. He and I both hold our breath while we anticipate her initial reaction.

Tracey leans forward to peer through the windshield.

"Oh, sweet mother of Jesus."

Mac and I exchange glances in the rearview mirror. I was bracing myself for that reaction, as this house definitely doesn't look like anything else in the neighborhood, with its modern twist on French Provincial architecture. The house is massive gray stucco with a high hip roof, lots of balustrades, and matching twin chimneys. The windows are tall and paned, cutting into the cornices, and their shape is outlined by continual lines of raised molding. The whole house is balanced and symmetrical and . . . a tad dramatic.[45]

"Is the entry over-the-top?" I ask. Part of me already knows it is, and yet the part of me from a crappy Indiana ranch house can't help but being impressed.

"Just a little," Tracey agrees; then she points to the oversize cement urns flanking either side of the door. "Also, the owners need to get Sabrina Soto on the phone stat to talk about staging. Because nothing says 'million-dollar home' more than four dollars' worth of plastic plants spray-painted green."

---

45 Kind of like RuPaul is a tad dramatic.

We knock and then let ourselves in, where Liz awaits.

Last time we were here it was overcast and gray and we didn't get a great look at some of the rooms because it was so dark. We struggled unsuccessfully with the lights in the foyer, so we didn't experience the fully lit impact of it until now.

"Hey, you figured out the switches," Mac comments.

"Okay, Tracey, here's where I need your expertise. All of this crown molding—is it rich and expensive or is it too much?" The painted woodwork crisscrosses all over the foyer, running up and down the walls and across the ceilings, following the flow of a staircase that first curves in one direction and then the other. The banister's wound with an ivy swag that trails up the stairs and across the Juliet balcony. An ornate chandelier hangs low over the entryway, draped in string after string of beads and crystals, branching off into hundreds of little light-topped arms, which make the foyer as bright as an operating room.

Sure, my eyes are distracted by all that's going on in the vicinity of the walls, but then again, I can't help but notice how open and airy everything is. Plus the scope of the staircase is nothing short of grand. That's worth noting, right?

Tracey takes in the whole room before answering, "It depends."

"On?" Mac prompts.

"On whether or not you're a Real Housewife of New Jersey."

Ouch.

We pass from the flamboyant hallway into an equally ornate and scroll-y dining room. "I figured out the lights in here, too," Liz informs us. "Look up." The last time we were here in the relative darkness, we thought the tray ceiling had been painted with some light gray paint for a little architectural contrast. Yet when Liz hits the switch, the whole thing begins to glow from the silver-leaf treatment and tiny LED lights sprinkled randomly throughout twinkle like miniature stars.

"Did not see that coming," Mac notes.

Tracey says nothing, instead simply choosing to nod. Yet I have to wonder how twinkly and festive the ceiling might feel around a properly set table full of family and friends. I bet it's not awful.

We circle around the foyer to the powder room. I actually thought this room was pretty cool the last time we were here, but in watching Tracey's reaction to the enormous tufted button holding up swags and swags of alternating cranberry and forest layers of silk on the ceiling, I rethink my position.[46]

"It's like being at the circus!"

"But the ceiling's made of silk," I protest. "Silk is a nice fabric, right?"

"Oh, honey, yes, but not on a bathroom ceiling. The material's not the problem—it's the context." She continues to peer at the fixtures. "Wait. There's a hookah in here—no, this isn't a circus. Rather, it's more like *The Thousand and One Nights*. I shall call this room 'Scheherazade Takes a Shit,'" Tracey says, attempting—and failing—to not bray with laughter.

We pass into an electric green reading room filled with fake potted palms. Dusty plastic leaves form an awning over our heads. Tracey strolls the perimeter of the room, first taking in the paint choices and then inspecting the zebra-skin couch topped with

---

46   Note to self: Subscribe to *Elle Decor*, like, yesterday.

round fuchsia, yellow, and royal blue throw pillows. "This room looks like Tommy Bahama banged a bag of Skittles."

There's an enormous lion-headed water feature in the corner, and the window looks out over the statue of a bear on the patio. "So, what do you think, kids," Tracey asks, "Russian Mafia or Italian Mafia?"

"But," I protest, "paint can be changed. Candice Olson says so all the time. And check out the window treatments!" Last time we were here, I fell in love with the thick white wooden-slat blinds. "Those are custom-made plantation shades!"

Tracey's not having it. "Yeah, and you certainly could never replicate those, right?"

Ooh, good point.

"To be fair, Tracey, you've told me how much you love French Provincial houses."

"Yes," she agrees. "In Provence."

I feel like I have to defend our bringing her here, so I say, "I swear this place didn't seem nearly so over-the-top with the lights off."

Before she can get in another snarky remark, I add, "Plus, this room isn't what sold us. You haven't yet seen the adorable guesthouse off the back patio. A guesthouse! As in a separate house for guests! You know what people in Indiana don't have? A spare house for visitors. How exciting is that? Guests could have all the peace and privacy they wanted. Genius! And more important, there's a pool and a pond. Do you realize if we buy this house we could be all, 'We've got a pool and a pond. Pond would be good for you,' every time someone came to visit. How hilarious would that be?"

"Mia, you can't drop that kind of cash on a house just because you want to quote *Caddyshack*."

I guess we'll see about that.

"Let's just finish the tour before we completely rule it out," I reason.

We move on to the ultra-high-end kitchen, with its custom cabinetry and PRO series Sub-Zero fridge and wine cooler and double dishwasher and . . . ropes and ropes of fake ivy and pretend grapes. They seem to have snaked their way from the entry hall, over the balcony, and back down the wall in here. The plastic vines are strewn everywhere—on top of cabinets, over the fridge, looped from the ceiling, and woven into the window treatments. Tracey grows increasingly appalled. "No, seriously, the owners have to fire this home stager. Hell, I might just e-mail some photos to *Get It Sold*, because *clearly* they could use the help."

Then we get to the big dance—the two-story family room with its trompe l'oeil tray ceiling with its columns and cherubs. Tracey doesn't notice it until I point up, and when she does, she jumps a little. "It just gets better and better."

"To be fair, that wasn't done cheaply," I say, attempting to be the devil's advocate for the house. I'm coming around to agreeing that it might be a tad much, but someone dropped a ton of cash upgrading this place, and I really do like the pool and the pond.

Okay, I can't not say it again.

Pond would be good for you.

See? Hilarious! Every time!

"Oh, no," Tracey agrees. "You're right on target there. Someone paid big money on these hideous treatments, thus proving the axiom 'You can't buy taste.'"

Mac's been looking in the pantry (which, of course, boasts another ginormous chandelier) (and, of course, impressed me on our last visit) and comes out to rejoin the conversation. "Obviously the place isn't our taste—"

"This is no one's taste," Tracey insists.

Mac is undeterred. "But the reason we brought you here is to get your opinion on the bones of the place. Is what's underneath all the grapes and sparkles worth salvaging?"

Tracey pulls out a chair and has a seat at the rococo-legged kitchen table with the five-inch-thick marble top. "Here's my issue with that—you said the house was priced reasonably but not great."

Liz sits across from us and she nods, toying with the enormous bowl of fake plastic grapes in the center. "I feel like they'd really need to come down on the asking price to make this place a good deal, and from what the listing agent says, they're not terribly negotiable. It's not a short-sale situation, at least not yet."

Tracey processes this information. "To me, it doesn't make financial sense to pay a premium for expensive fixtures and then get rid of them. You're going to have to fork over multiple thousands to chase the ghost of Carmella Soprano out of here. You want to rip stuff out? Then I suggest you find a house that's priced accordingly or needs rehabbing."

Mac nods. "That's what I've been telling Mia. I say if we want the most house for our money, we buy a fixer-upper, but she's totally against it."

"That's not a bad idea, Mia. Why so opposed?" Tracey asks.

"Redecorate? Yes. Rehab? No. I mean, remember when we had the leaky shower pan in the rental house on Old Gold Ave., and the one-week repair job turned into a two-month bath-gutting odyssey? No, thanks. I'd rather keep looking," I reply.

Mac turns to me, "So this place? It's out of the running?"

"Tracey makes a lot of sense about not tearing down expensive finishes," I have to admit. "Should we go?" I rise from the table.

"Oh, no, no—I've got to see what treasures await upstairs," Tracey says.

I'm not sure what particular feature finally pushes Tracey over the edge—whether it's the Wild West saloon doors separating the hot-pink master toilet from the hot-pink sunken tub[47] or the massive elk-antler chandelier in the upstairs den or the wire-enclosed children's bed that's supposed to look like a princess coach but instead resembles a coast guard marine-rescue cage. She spends most of the ride to the city cackling and wiping her eyes.

On the plus side, I'm so glad we brought Tracey, because now we're not buying a house that can't be made tasteful.

The downside is, we won't have a pool or a pond, and either one would have been good for me.

"Anything worth noting today?"

I say nothing, choosing only to grit my teeth in response.

"That bad?" Mac asks gently. I've just come in the back door from an entire day spent up in the Cambs.

While Mac's at work, I've been tasked with running real estate recon missions. During the week it's my job to weed out the stinkers so he doesn't have to spend his weekends grimacing at faux-

47 Now with twenty percent more plastic grapes!

wood paneling and unfinished basements. I'm fine with the arrangement, because I have a looming deadline, which means I want to do anything except what I'm *supposed* to be doing.

The truth is that the places I saw weren't *so* awful today—at least comparatively—provided one has a deep and abiding love for mauve paint, gold faucets, and flood damage. At the moment, my glowering is due less to the fruitless search and more because of what I catch him doing. He's standing over the stove massacring thirty dollars' worth of fresh ingredients from Whole Foods in an attempt to make dinner.

A few weeks ago, while we were at the market, I spotted a jar of herbs and sauce called Bush's Chili Magic Chili Starter. I launched my body in front of it, hoping Mac wouldn't notice, but I was too slow. He grabbed it, announcing, "Let's make 2010 the year I learn to master chili!" just as I was thinking, *Let's make 2010 the year you stop trying to master chili.* I realize some wives would love it if their husbands took the initiative to cook dinner, but perhaps they don't realize they'd have to *eat* whatever their husbands make.[48] Because I hate the idea of wasting food—or hurting his feelings—I always choke down whatever he serves.

I take off my coat and come over to kiss him. Then I sneak a glance into the saucepan. I'm no chili aficionado, but I'm pretty sure it's never supposed to be that color.

"See anything worth noting today?" he inquires.

"Sort of," I say, grabbing a glass of wine from the fridge. I'm having chardonnay, not so much because I need a drink, but more because I'm hoping the oak resin will set up a *Flavor Protection*

---

48 Also, I'm getting tired of throwing out all my good pans.

Perimeter between my tongue and his chili. (I also keep a secret stash of peanut-butter–filled pretzels in my desk for nights Mac cooks dinner.)

I take a deep, protective swig before continuing. "The place on Goldenmill had a Liberace bathroom."

Before I continue, here's where I need to apologize to everyone who's ever prompted me to roll my eyes on HGTV. I always get so mad at the people who can't see past the aesthetics of a place, but it turns out that's easier said than done. Sometimes when I spot something so blatantly hideous, like fake bamboo wallpaper or one of those knit toilet-paper holders topped with a doll's torso, I question all the homeowners' decisions, starting with the one to buy this particular house. I mean, a tufted silk ceiling is one thing, but a sad clown painted on velvet? No.

He glances up from his simmering pot of unpleasantness. "Meaning?"

"Meaning the bathroom was mirrored everywhere, and I'm not kidding. I'm talking on the ceiling, on the back of the door, on the vanity, and on the floor. Plus there was a rounded wall, and in the curve there were about twenty long, narrow strips of mirror. Topping it all was a gigantic mirrored chandelier."

At that point in the day, I'd had about six lattes, so I ended up needing to use that bathroom. I now know what I look like while taking a leak from fourteen different angles. I kept swinging my head around so I wouldn't make eye contact with myself, but no luck; I was everywhere. FYI? There's some stuff you just can't unsee.

"Nice." He stirs his pot, and then licks the spoon when he's done. Did he just wince? Yeah. That bodes well. "What about the

Cape Cod on Foxfield? I took the virtual tour and it seemed right up our alley."

"They must have shot the MLS listing photos while lying on the ground or something. The bedroom ceilings were so slanted I couldn't stand upright. A place like that would require major reconstruction." I rub the sore spot on my forehead. I hope the sellers aren't too mad I dented their wall with my face.

"Then maybe renovations should be an option," he says, dumping a handful of salt into his bubbling potion. I shudder inadvertently. "If it means we get a bigger house or a better neighborhood, we should consider expanding our search to rehab properties."

Ack, the rehab-versus-redecorate discussion. This has been our perpetual "tastes great"–versus–"less filling" argument, and it's the biggest reason we're still in a rental house. He's dying to take something down to the studs, while I'm really confident in our ability only to switch outlet covers and paint trim.

Seriously, every time he says the R-word I can't help but recall the time we bought our new chandelier for the dining room. Mac was convinced he could install it himself despite having never done so before, and even though the instruction sheet from Pottery Barn clearly stated, *You should really call a professional for this; no, really, we mean it.*

To his credit, he was able to manage the assembly and the mounting of the fixture. After it went up and he went to the basement to flip the breaker, I was awed by how merrily the chandelier twinkled for six whole seconds before the switch plate sparked and we lost power in half the house.

The best part was when Mac tried to get the electrician to

convince me of what a good job he'd done up until the part where he almost started an electrical fire. The electrician agreed, saying that if indeed Mac had realized we had a triple rather than a double switch, he'd have done everything right. And yet as I wrote out the two-hundred-and-fifty-dollar time-and-a-half check for the repair, I failed to recognize this victory.

As Chandeliergate 2008 is still a sore point around here, I don't bring it up. Instead I say, "I thought we agreed renovations would be too troublesome. I mean, I want to put my mark on a place, but I had new paint and carpet in mind, maybe a little crown molding. Possibly some light cabinet hardware shopping."

An oddly determined look crosses his face. "Listen, we've spent every Saturday for the last year watching HGTV. What they do only looks difficult. Do you know how easy it is to rehab a bathroom if you're just swapping vanities and exchanging fixtures? Most of the work comes from the teardown, and I can swing a sledgehammer and rewire an electrical panel. The only hard part's moving pipes, and we can outsource that to a professional."

"You spend one high school summer working in a lumber-yard and all of a sudden you're Bob Vila?"

He wipes his hands on a dish towel and begins to ladle out our dinner. "No, I'm saying we're capable of doing more than you'd guess."

I mull this over while collecting napkins, spoons, and enough bread and butter to absorb the taste of our dinner. When he's finished preparing our bowls, he sits down across from me and places his hand over my left hand. "Promise me you'll at least consider our buying a rehab."

I glance down at the gelatinous blob in my bowl and I cross

the fingers on my right hand under the table. "If we can't find a house that's move-in ready, then yes, I promise."

And I mean it. Mostly.

Yet there's a part of me that also recalls spending a year of Sundays watching the Food Network. For all our copious research, I'm still about to eat a bowl of blue stew.

We've officially looked at every move-in-ready house in Abington Cambs.

Now what?

I've spent the past few days furiously trying to complete an overdue chapter, and the eyestrain from staring at the computer is killing me. Between the pressure of the deadline and the anxiety of not finding a house, I'm completely wound up and stressed-out. I decide the best way to reward and revive myself is a long soak in the tub with a couple of chamomile tea bags over my eyes.

I've been in the tub for about twenty minutes when I hear an odd noise. It's almost like . . . whispering? I sit up for a second, removing the washcloth that's keeping my tea bags in place. I pause to really listen, but then I don't hear anything. I'm not terribly concerned, because the alarm system is set. I have it armed at all times now, ever since ORNESTEGA's little pals flashed their gang signs at me.[49]

I reapply my tea bags, reposition the washcloth, and, using my foot, nudge the faucet to run enough hot water to revive my bubbles. Ah, that's the stuff.

---

49 FYI, kids, flashing gang signs is a lot less scary when you're wearing mittens. I suggest you either buy gloves or wait until it's warmer to represent.

A few minutes later, I hear the weird sound again, but I ignore it. It's probably just the TV downstairs. I've taken to leaving HGTV on twenty-four/seven. Every time Sandra Rinomato helps her Property Virgins find their first place, my hope is renewed. I mean, if people who have almost no budget can find their dream home, we're destined to find something great, right?

Anyway, sometimes the volume goes up during commercials, especially when the ShamWow guy's ads run. No big deal.

I hear the odd noise a third time and that's when I smell something akin to cologne and cigarette smoke. I pull off my jury-rigged chamomile mask, and when I do, I am faced with what appear to be two Japanese businessmen inspecting my steam shower.

I scream and then they scream and we all scream, yet with all the screaming going on in my bathroom, no one gives us any ice cream.

The screams do bring Vienna running, though. So that's a plus.

"Ohmigod, break my eardrums, why don't you?" She stands in my doorway, hip-slung and aggravated, clad in a sundress constructed of what appears to be a fitted yellow shower curtain, paired with four-and-a-half-inch gladiator sandals.[50] She points at the two men peering down curiously at me before returning to texting while talking. "This is Mr. Oshiro and Mr. Takamoto. I don't know who's who, but whatever. They're real estate investors from Japan. They might want to buy a piece of my company." And on cue, both gentlemen bow.

This is surreal.

---

50 Apparently in her world, it's not fourteen degrees outside.

"Hi, nice to meet you and welcome to my home," I say with a nod to the men. They bow again. "Oh, Vienna? In case you failed to notice, I'm taking a bath here!"

"Yeah, I noticed." She snickers. "I noticed your shoulders are totally fat." Then she briefly removes her fingers from her crystal-studded cell phone and puffs her cheeks and presses her finger to her lips. This causes the Japanese men to nod appreciatively at her gesture before bowing again.

What does . . . ? How could . . . ? I'm so torn between complete rage and abject mortification I can hardly form a complete thought. I finally sputter, "I'm sorry, but are you *insane*? Why are you here? You're obligated to give me two days' notice before you let yourself in, and you know that. You're trespassing, and technically I could have you arrested right now."

"Doubtful," she replies with a toss of her clip-on hair. What sucks is, she's right. If the Chicago PD didn't haul her in the night she drove her Bentley into all those "boring people"[51] at Enclave, I imagine this is small potatoes.

I curl into myself and sink as low as I can under the bubbles. "How did you get past the alarm?" I hiss.

She begins to twirl one long, white-blond polystyrene extension. "Ugh, your stupid alarm. Pain in my ass. I had the guy cut the wires a few weeks ago because it kept going off, like, every time I came in."

I can feel my blood boiling, and if it weren't for my overwhelming fear of public nakedness, I'd have leaped out of the tub and throttled the bitch by now. With gritted teeth I ask, "Where

---

51 Her words, not mine.

are my dogs?" I suddenly have a vision of her simply opening my gate and letting my pups run free. And if that's the case, I cannot be held responsible for my actions. I'm about to go full-on Swayze up in here.

She shrugs and bats her overly mascaraed eyes. I take great pleasure in noticing that the left one is a tiny bit wonky. "Last I saw, they were on the couch. They totally love me; all dogs do. It's one of my, like, many gifts."

"That's just great. Oh, FYI? You can leave anytime now," I suggest. "Or not, of course. Because there's nothing at all embarrassing or inappropriate about my being nude while you conduct business with a couple of Japanese dudes. I'm sure they're used to it, what with bathhouses being a big part of their culture." When I thrust a soapy finger in the men's direction, they both bow. Argh.

She doesn't budge from her spot. "Whatevs. Listen, can you get up? The guys wanna see if the tub's jetted."

And now it's time to not be nice.

I hurl my bubble bath at her. *"Get out, get out, get out!"* She scurries out of the line of fire as the bottle splats against the glass door, oozing big emerald green streaks. Misters Oshiro and Takamoto follow her, but not without giving me a cursory bow first.

You know what?

Maybe I *could* live with a little construction dust.

When I get home from today's search, I don't even flinch when I see Mac slaughtering twenty-two dollars' worth of grass-fed, antibiotic-free, organic beef.

I don't worry when he tells me about the mysterious bandaged person lurking in the alley; nor do I frown[52] when he informs me of Vienna's latest antics involving a backhoe and my row of lovingly tended, winterized peony bushes.

You see, I found our house today.

---

52 You know what I mean.

Chapter Five
SOME KIND OF WONDERFUL (HOUSE)

"Oh, my God, you guys, are you sitting down?"

As I dash toward their lunch table, Tracey and Kara shoot each other puzzled looks before looking back to me. "Um, Mia?" Tracey asks, drawing out her vowels as though she's speaking to a dog or a particularly dim child. "Do you need us to get off our chairs and move to the floor, or are you preparing us for some piece of potentially advantageous news?"

"News! News! News!" I yip, waving my hands in front of my face like I'm trying to cool myself down as I fall into my chair. I'm so excited I can barely form multisyllabic words.

Kara immediately mirrors my excitement and begins to bounce in her seat. "What? Movie deal? The Persiflage Films thing? What's happening?"

"Better! My house! I found my house! I got a house!"

Tracey rests her hand on my forearm in an attempt to calm me. "Whoa, slow down there, Speed Racer. I saw you yesterday and you hadn't even mentioned anything worth a second look. Now you're what? Making an offer? Already under contract? How can that be? You are not Little Miss Snap Decision. I mean, last week you spent twenty minutes at the Whole Foods meat counter debating between the prime rib eyes and the grass-fed filets. But you could pick a house—the biggest investment of your life—in an afternoon? Tell me how this works."

My words come rushing out. "Okay, number one, protein is a priority in my life, and number two, because the universe essentially rented a billboard and said, 'Hey, Mia, this is the place.' It's fate. I am destined to live in this house."

Kara grabs me for a quick hug. "Yay! I'm so happy for you! Tell me everything . . . starting with how you're not buying in my parents' neighborhood!"

I take a big breath and try to steady myself. "No worries. We're going to be east-siders, so you're totally safe. Anyway, we're up in the Cambs yesterday and Liz's looking at her MLS printouts. She'd pulled a listing that was outside of our set budget, but she said there was something about it that made her want to take me there."

"Pumpkin, that 'something' is called 'commission.'"

I cut Tracey a sideways glance before continuing. "So, like, Liz is all, 'There's an interesting notation in the remarks section,' and I'm, like, 'What?' and she's, like, 'Lemme read the whole thing,' and I'm, like—"

"And you say you have trouble mastering the modern teenage dialect." Tracey smirks.

"Ignoring you. Anyway, she goes, 'I guess this house has a claim to fame. Someone used it in a movie a while back.' Which, hey, that's kind of cool, right? Then we look at a bunch of lame and boring houses and I forget she mentioned it. Then we eventually pull up and I see what she's talking about, and right then and there in the passenger seat of Liz's Volvo, I shat myself."

"Oh, sweetie!" Kara gasps. "Are you okay?"

"Figurative shat,[53] I'm fine." I take another huge breath and I inadvertently start grinning, remembering yesterday. "I'm actually pretty goddamned great, to tell you the truth. Listen, do me a proper. Close your eyes and picture this. Imagine yourself going down a long, circular driveway to a big brown-and-white Tudor tucked back in the woods. And in the distance? You can hear the lake." I clear my throat and try to stop beaming.[54] "*Ahem*, big lake."

"Mia, that sounds awesome!" Kara gushes. "Particularly since I can just sneak up Whitefish Bay Road to get there and I won't be spotted."

"You really think your parents or their friends are going to have a watch out on the roads you might drive, all in an effort to bust you if you don't stop by home?" Tracey demands.

Kara begins to gaze off into the distance with a melancholy expression all over her face. "Without a shadow of a doubt."

"Um, hello? Not done! So, you're imagining this house, yes?" Then I realize I don't actually have to have *my* eyes shut during this exercise and I open them. "Now visualize a big picture window. Do you see it?"

---

53 Figurative Shat—would that not be an excellent postpunk band name?

54 Which is impossible.

Tracey's and Kara's lids are firmly closed, but one of Tracey's eyebrows is getting dangerously close to raising itself in exasperation.

"Envision this big window and on the other side is a shiny glass dining table and it's, um . . . all *aglow*, as if being lit by candles on a birthday cake. And two people are kind of hunkered over it. Now as you're taking in this scene you start to hear the opening notes of a really amazing song, like . . . 'If You Were Here' by the Thompson Twins."

Tracey's eyes snap open. "You've just completely ripped off the final scene of *Sixteen Candles*."

Kara does the math a couple of beats quicker than Tracey. "No . . . no! No way!"

I say nothing and just nod.

Kara begins to shriek, "*Holy shit, you're buying Jake Ryan's house!*" causing all the hipsters at Lulu's to look up from their graphic novels and Vonnegut books. Listen, kids, when you stop trimming your beards like bonsai trees you can judge. Until then, *I'll* be the one doling out snide looks, thanks.

"How is that even possible?" Tracey wonders.

I reply, "The Jake Ryan character lived in Abington Cambs, so it makes sense that's where his house would be. John Hughes filmed a ton of stuff up there, so it figures he shot a real place. Plus, all homes go up for sale eventually, right? Why not that house and why not now? My point is that this is the universe's way of telling me I'm meant to buy Jake Ryan's house."

Tracey persists: "Wasn't that place kind of a mansion? And it's close to the water? I'm not sure how to say this, so I'll just say it—I realize you're doing well, but I didn't realize you were doing mansion-on-the-lake well."

"Weeeeell," I drawl. "Remember how the house was so quin-tessentially eighties?"

"Oh, yeah," Kara agrees. "All the chintz and the glass tables and brass accents. That movie's like a living time capsule."

I nod. "Right. The good news is that, um, the eighties never quite ended there. I guess the couple who owned it during filming sold it, and *they* sold it to someone else, who died shortly after-ward, so nothing's been touched in at least twenty years. A trust owns the place now, and they've priced it to sell to anyone who wants to take on the renovations. Mac hasn't even seen it yet, but when I told him he could tear out drywall, he was totally behind me."

"Mmm-hmm, mmm-hmm, right. But it's still a mansion on the lake, and those aren't cheap," Tracey persists.

I begin to squirm a bit in my seat. Sometimes I wish Tracey would stop writing terse police dramas and go back to chick lit. She was a lot less intense back then. "You'd make one hell of an interrogator," I observe.

"Uh-huh," she agrees, not breaking her gaze.

"Fine, it'll be a bit of a stretch financially, but we can do it, especially if we tackle some of the rehabbing ourselves. Plus, I'll get a big check once I finish my work in progress, which, ugh, don't remind me about right now. Anyway, if I get in a financial pinch, I can create a new book series, maybe for adults this time. Come on! It's *Jake Ryan's house*! You can't put a price on that!" I exclaim.

"Except you can, because that's the nature of real estate," Tracey says.

"No, Mia's right," Kara agrees. "Ask any woman between age

thirty to fifty and she'll tell you that Jake Ryan was her ideal man. I mean, who wouldn't fall in love with the hot guy who actually gave a shit about inner beauty? And when he showed up at Samantha Baker's sister's wedding in the Porsche? That's every modern girl's dream of the knight on the white horse. Did you know the *Washington Post* did a big article about his enduring legacy a while back? Twenty-five years later, women still want Jake Ryan to do filthy things to them. Fiiiillll-theee. I know; I read their e-mails."[55]

Tracey rakes her hand through her curls. "Honestly, I never saw the appeal. Too pale, too brooding. Not for me. Also, it bears repeating that a) Jake Ryan is fictional; ergo b) he never lived in that house, and c) you absolutely *can* put a price on that. In fact, I'll wager that price was clearly marked on the MLS sheet."

"Listen," I say. "The bottom line is this: I have faith in fate and I take stock in signs."

This is no exaggeration; I'm a firm believer in destiny. Maybe this is because I grew up listening to my right-off-the-boat Polish grandmother's stories. The only time her fairy tales ended badly was when those involved ignored the signs. To this day, Babcia[56] Josefa swears that fate has already determined every nuance of our lives, and all we have to do is look for the hand of divine guidance.

Irina, my mother, grew up under this same philosophy, which she then manipulated to convince Babcia that it was the universe telling her to marry that Italian steelworker.

---

55 Kara's a nationally syndicated sex and dating advice columnist and not just a conduit for dirty correspondence. When she was pitching her work, I begged her to call the column "The Kara Sutra," but apparently that's already a porn site. Damn.

56 Polish for "grandmother."

By "universe" what she really meant was "pregnancy test."

They got married anyway, despite conflicting signs.

They're divorced now.

Universe—1, Mom—0.

I continue. "Here's the thing, Trace. I've spent the last twenty-five years obsessed with all things John Hughes. I mean, I want to live in the AC just to be in the environment that used to inspire him. So when Jake Ryan's house practically falls into my lap—much like Samantha Baker's ill-fated sex quiz fell in front of Jake in study hall—divine will is sending me a message and I can't ignore it."

"I'm curious. Is the universe telling you to take out million-dollar mortgages? Is the universe suggesting that you burn things? Does the universe send you secret messages about your neighbor through your dogs?" Tracey queries.

Kara and I both fold our arms in soundless solidarity.

"I'm simply saying that sometimes the universe is an asshole." We continue to scowl. Or Kara does, anyway. Then Tracey shrugs her shoulders and picks up her menu with great resignation. "Fine. I'm not going to be able to convince you otherwise. So, I guess . . . mazel tov and let me know how I can help."

"Thank you," I say, squeezing her hand. I go through the motions of reading the menu, but I'm pretty much having the exact same feta cheese plate with a side of chicken I've been ordering for the past four years.[57] But something still bothers me.

"Tracey, do you mean to tell me you really weren't into Jake Ryan?"

---

57 Like I said, protein is a priority.

She arranges her face in a moue of distaste. "Not so much."

I think about that long and hard.

"Is it because he didn't have an AARP card?"

"Do you love it? You love it, right? I already love it but *you* need to love it."

Mac leisurely and deliberately takes in the view. "I've been here for fifteen seconds and I've only seen this one spot. We probably need to have dinner and go to a couple of movies before we decide if we want to take this relationship to the next level."

We're with Liz, standing in the gracious entry hall of Jake Ryan's house.

Okay, maybe it's not so gracious anymore.

Maybe it looks a bit like the lobby of a transient hotel, with all the weird black and white octagonal inlaid tiles and grimy windows. The only thing that's missing is a Plexiglas cashier's booth and a sign detailing hourly rates.

Every other time we've viewed a home, we've had to slip on the blue booties before embarking on the tour, but the pile of shoe covers has long been abandoned on the other side of the hall. I guess people walked in, saw the state of the floor, and decided that a little mud could only improve the situation.

"You have to use your imagination," I assure him. "Don't be like all those assholes on HGTV who won't buy a house because of the wallpaper. It's not load-bearing wallpaper, people! All you need is a steamer and some elbow grease! Please, Mac, just clean it all up in your head. Do a little mental mopping. I bet that's why no one's snapped this place up yet. They don't have our kind of vision. You can't let an ugly floor distract you from the vaulted ceiling. Picture a beautiful crimson Persian rug in the middle of this room and a nice round table that would be handy for mail and keys and stuff. We could do this up like a Four Seasons lobby, with giant sprays of fresh flowers. Gorgeous!"

"When you showed me the listing online, I couldn't comprehend how this place could possibly be in our price range," Mac muses. He touches a closet door and it immediately falls off its hinges. We all jump. "I have a better understanding now."

We proceed to the left and enter a two-story ballroom. "A ballroom, for crying out loud! We could have balls!" I exclaim. Okay, fine, I may be giving him a bit of the hard sell. I can't even envision what a ball might look like, but I maintain it would be nice to have the option. Most likely the only balls this room would see would be of the tennis variety, with Daisy and Duckie chasing after them.

Mac laughs. "Number one, that's what she said, and number two, come see these picture windows in the dining room."

"I do see them—and the view in front of them!" Majestic fir trees form a semicircle around the bay window. Beyond that, there's a thicket so dense I can't quite determine how deep the ravine is that runs behind the house. The seller's Realtor says that after the ground dips down, it goes back up and the lake is just beyond it. Right now the whole area's too snow covered (and lovely) to inspect firsthand.

"No, I want you to take a look right here." I can't help but turn around first to see where the glass table would have been in this room. Suddenly I have a craving for birthday cake and Thompson Twins music. Snapping me out of my reverie, Mac begins to point at various parts of the main window. "The seal's broken on all of them. You can tell because of the condensation between the two panes. These are huge and custom and they'll need to be replaced. That's hundreds, if not thousands, right off the bat, and we're only five feet into the house. Plus, these parquet floors? Their best days are behind them. Do you notice how worn and thin they are? They may be so far gone they can't even be refinished."

I'm not sure how to argue this, and then it comes to me. "We'll ask for a buyer's credit!"

"Ooh, no, sorry. Can't do that," Liz says, waving her MLS listing. "The trust that owns the house is selling it 'as is.' However, if you go under contract and the place inspects badly, you'd have the option of walking away without losing your earnest money."[58]

"I can't imagine this place would inspect badly," Mac notes, tapping the wall, which results in a small rain shower of plaster dust.

I decide my best bet is to distract Mac from the grotty floors and imperfect windows. I brush the powder off his shoulders and hustle him into the next room. "Check this out—a formal library!" We move into a room that's covered in a rich mahogany paneling and lined with what seems like a hundred shelves. "I mean, think of what my book collection will look like in here!"

"Probably a lot like *Masterpiece Theatre* meets *Bridget Jones's Diary*."

---

58 Earnest money is what you put down in a real estate transaction to secure a buying contract. Typically it's about five percent of the purchase price, and the point is to show the seller the buyer has skin in the game. Once the house is under contract, the earnest money doesn't get returned if the buyer flakes out for any reason other than a bad inspection. This public service message has been brought to you by HGTV.

"What does that mean?"

"You own ten thousand books and they're all pink, paperback, and have shoes on the cover."

"You say that like it's a bad thing."

"No, I say that like they don't require being displayed in a room where smoking jackets are appropriate. It would be like cutting butter with a chain saw, or hiring a chauffeur to drive the dogs to the beach. Yeah, you *could* do it, but what an enormous waste of resources."

"I disagree. An enormous paneled library is just what my books need to give them a bit of gravitas. And Daisy would love to go for a ride."[59] Granted, my hilarious *Save a Buggy, Ride the Amish* framed print wouldn't fit in so great here, but otherwise? Perfect!

As we pass from room to room, Mac remarks, "I don't remember most of this in *Sixteen Candles*."

Naturally Mac's familiar with Hughes's entire oeuvre, having taken a couple of film classes in college. The first time Mac referred to Hughes as "a brilliant filmmaker" during a group discussion, my ears perked up. As he rattled on about Hughes's prowess in developing minor characters and punctuating poignant moments with the perfect song, I found myself wondering why I'd kept Mac in the Friend Zone for so long.

"Wouldn't they have filmed the inside scenes on a set?" Liz asks.

"Actually, I believe the bulk of the interiors were filmed onsite. The producers rented out the house for the duration of filming. Most likely what we're seeing is different because of

---

59 Also, *Bridget Jones's Diary is* classic literature. Ask anyone.

renovations made postshooting." Hey! Look at me and my fancy film knowledge! I've thus appointed myself the expert of All Things Hollywood as a result of my sporadic meetings with a handful of entry-level entertainment folks over the past few years. Once I had a sit-down with a film studio flunky who spent the whole time talking about his Facebook page. Sure am glad I paid for a full-fare ticket to LA to take *that* meeting.

I continue to dazzle the crowd with my insider information. "Remember the part in the movie where Dong and his date crash through the floor on the exercise bike? The owners actually had a huge hole in the ceiling because of a leak. John Hughes thought it was so funny that he wrote it into the script."

Mac nods along with my monologue. "What you're saying is that this house has a history of water damage."

Oh! Hoisted with my own petard!

When we get to the kitchen, Mac marvels at the antiquated appliances. The bizarre—possibly sparking—track lighting in the bedroom causes him to scratch his head in disbelief, and the state of the laundry room makes him shudder. I didn't realize you could stick linoleum floor tiles to the ceiling, either, but maybe that was the style back then?

"What do you think so far?" Liz probes.

"You already know my vote," I say.

Mac's a lot more skeptical, especially when the floorboard beneath him cracks. I try to cough really loudly to cover up the noise, garnering a knowing look from Mac. Busted. "Mia, I've counted nine different varieties of flooring and we haven't even been to the basement yet. Every wall is made of a different material, no two windows are alike, and I'm pretty sure I saw daylight coming through the side of one of the closets. It's like this place was an elaborate game of handyman Truth or Dare."

"There's so much space!" I insist. "And so many rooms!"

"We've passed six bathrooms so far," he observes. "Each one of them has had a different color and style of toilet. I've seen black, white, mint green, powder blue, baby pink, and light purple—"

"Lilac. Technically that shade is lilac," I inform him. What can I say? I watch a lot of *Color Splash* with David Bromstad.

"Who installs a *lilac toilet*? Prince? On top of that, functionally, not a single bathroom countertop hits higher than my inseam. Great if I'd like to wash my crotch, but I'd have to bend at a ninety-degree angle to brush my teeth. Who lived here? Circus folk? Carnies? Plus, we are only two people. We don't need six toilets. Let's face facts, Mia—this house is a disaster. We'd have to call it Apocalypse House."

"You wanted a fixer-upper," I protest.

Mac tries to break the news as gently as he can. "This house would be a journey into the heart of darkness of home renovation. What we have here isn't a fixer-upper so much as it is a tearer-downer."

"Please do me a favor and don't rule it out until you've seen the whole thing," I beg.

"You're the boss," he says with more than a little resignation, following me down the too-steep stairs.

Liz is fully versed in all the reasons I want this house, a few flaws notwithstanding, but I need her to help me sell Mac. After we tour the bedrooms, she pulls out the big guns. "Mac, perhaps you'll be interested in the full English basement. Plenty of space for a pool table!"

"Honey, see? There's a bar down here!"

When I say a bar, I don't mean a small slab of countertop and room for a few stools. I mean a full, operational, ready-to-open-for-business bar with a keg cooler, an industrial-strength ice maker, and seating for fifteen, all covered in a really retro knotty pine paneling. Plus, you have to go through a separate door to be able to stand behind the bar, so it's particularly authentic.

"Huh," he says, running his hand over the place where I'll wager he's already mentally stocking cut lemons, limes, and other assorted cocktail garnishes. I saved the basement for the end of the tour because I'm counting on Mac's unresolved bartending issues. He was hired as a bartender during college but he kept yelling at people when they'd order blender drinks and was eventually demoted to bouncer. Actually, that's how we met—he stormed into the dining area one night because he wanted to see what kind of person[60] ordered a banana daiquiri in an Irish pub. Oh, and FYI? This is the perfect example of the hand of fate at work. If I didn't have a lifelong love of Cool Whip–topped cocktails and he weren't so fussy about what he mixed, we'd have never met.

"Nice, right?" I prompt.

"Hmph," is all he says in response.

After we're finished (grudgingly) admiring the bar, we head into the adjacent area. There's a big spot in the middle of the carpet where someone's laid down more parquet to form a functional dance floor. I point down at it, saying, "How many homes have you seen that come with their own disco?"

"Other than in *The Jerk*? None," he replies before something

---

60 The exact word he used was "moron."

in the corner grabs his attention. "Hey, what is that over there?" He points to a platform that's surrounded by paneling, covered in carpet, and buffered by stairs.

"Not sure," Liz admits. "We couldn't figure it out last time." She and I kind of thought it was a stage for midgets, but don't want to say this, because Mac's already convinced this house was built for little people.

Mac takes a small jackknife out of his pocket. He very gingerly peels back a section of the carpeting and lifts a small portion of plywood. Then he whips out a mini Maglite and shines it in the crevice, leaning in close to get a better view. "There's a . . . Jacuzzi under here."

Liz and I are both completely perplexed, although this does make slightly more sense than a little-person karaoke stage. "Does it have water in it?"

"No, no, it's empty. I guess that explains why there's a huge exhaust fan over there." He gestures to a massive grated system behind the hot tub.

"That's just badass," I exclaim. "How often do you pull up the carpet and discover *a hot tub*? How much fun would that be? You could stand behind your bar and I could sit in here and have fruity blender drinks. If that's not the key to happiness, what is?"

"Let's be realistic, Mia. The hot tub is obviously broken if it's covered up with panel and carpet. Plus it's so big they probably built the basement around it. I doubt we could get it out," Mac cautions.

"Details! Silly, torturous details! We can get it fixed," I promise.

We move on to the main part of the basement and Mac grows really quiet. We've just entered the area that meets his exact specifications for his dream home-theater system. Not only is this room the right shape and height and width for ideal sound quality, but the windows are positioned in such a way that they wouldn't cast a glare on the plasma screen. He won't look me in the eye and all he manages to mumble is, "I might be able to work with this."

Yes!!

We move on to the basement kitchen. "What is this?" Liz wonders, poking at the black screen and weird knobs. "Like an old TV or something?"

"Ha!" Mac barks. "That, ladies, is a microwave. In fact, I'm pretty sure it's the first microwave. Ever."

I feel like all my good work with the bar and media area might be for naught, and I can sense I'm losing him again. "Mock it if you want, but a microwave is what, a hundred dollars to replace? What you're failing to see is that there's a whole extra kitchen down here with a fridge and a stove and a dishwasher. Yes, it's all a bit *Brady Bunch*, but I bet it's functional. Which means you'd still be able to prepare your gourmet meals[61] while the upstairs is under renovation. So this is actually a really good thing."

Actually, if any of these appliances are functional, I'll be shocked, but I feel it wise not to mention this.

After Mac mocks the kitchen a bit more[62] he moves on to the basement bathroom, and we add one more color (beige) to the toilet collection. He's appalled by the state of the water heaters, and I'm not sure what he might have thought about the furnace, because he is bent over, clutching his sides and laughing.

---

61 Theoretical, of course.

62 Apparently harvest gold and avocado appliances are not the new black.

When Mac finally composes himself, he takes my right hand. "Mia, this isn't going to happen. We cannot in good conscience buy this house."

I begin to panic and speak almost exclusively in exclamation points. "But it's huge, it's close to the water, and you'd get to renovate! This house has great bones! Think of all the new tools you can buy! And the location! Come on, this is east Abington Cambs! You can't get a better address than this! Yeah, there are a few cosmetic issues, but those will be fun to fix! If this house were fully operational and perfect, we'd never be able to afford it!"

He appears wholly unmoved by my monologue.

Then I do something I'm ashamed to admit. I try to get my eyes to water, knowing full well that crying is his Kryptonite. I generally follow Spider-Man's aunt's dictate of great power coming with great responsibility, so I rarely trot out the tears without due cause. Yet my eyes stay dry for some reason, so I surreptitiously snake my left hand up to the thin, sensitive skin beneath my armpit and I give it a solid pinch to see if that prompts the waterworks.

It doesn't.

Damn it.

"Mia, stop that. You're going to leave a mark." He pulls my left hand out of my cardigan. "We'll find our house. But this isn't it. There's too much to do. I mean, maybe renovating this place wouldn't be impossible, but it seems like an awful lot for a couple of first-time home buyers to take on. I don't want to put that kind of financial or emotional stress on us. I mean, *we* are too important, and I worry that the strain might mess up what we have. Does that make sense?"

Numbly, I nod. He presents a cogent case for his findings. I can't argue with his logic . . . and yet I don't understand how this can be. I'm *supposed* to live here. I feel like this place is my destiny, the manifestation of all my childhood dreams. When my sister and I were home at night while Mom worked her second job to give us a better life, *this* is where I'd imagine I'd be once it got better. The universe told me so; all the signs pointed to it. Then to be so close and have it not work out? I don't get it. What are the odds *another* John Hughes movie house is going to open up in our budget (stretched though it may be) in the next couple of weeks? Walking away from this place feels wrong all the way down to my soul.

Liz concludes our tour, saying, "I guess that's everything. Why don't we head up the back stairs, since we forgot to look at them last time?"

Just as we're about to ascend, we pass one more door. "What's in here?" Mac asks.

Bitterly, I respond, "Probably just another utility room full of 'fire hazards' and 'red flags' and all the other scary words that mean we don't get to buy Jake Ryan's house."

He pushes open a heavy steel door to reveal . . . nothing. We're enveloped in darkness. "Let me see if I can find a light." Mac feels the walls until he finds a switch, flips it, and illuminates a vast expanse of cement walls and wire shelves. There's an exhaust system similar to the one over by the defunct hot tub, and in the far corner, there's a low door with a dial on it. On the opposite side, I spy another junction box with a bunch of thick blue wiring coming out of it.

"What a perfect area for dry storage," Liz remarks.

I'm not so sure about that. "Maybe. But I don't like how there aren't any windows. I feel kind of claustrophobic in here. Plus the door's so heavy that I'd worry about getting trapped."

Confession time? Being trapped is a real concern, because I kind of get stuck a lot. It's not because I'm fat—regardless of what that jerk Vienna says. I'm actually in fine shape, especially when you consider my deep and abiding love of butter. But I'm a bit of a disaster magnet. Things just seem to happen to me, like once when I was vacuuming in front of this huge antique mirror in the bedroom. Somehow the cord must have caught and the whole thing came crashing down on me. Luckily it didn't shatter, but I spent half an hour screaming for Mac to get it off me, and he couldn't hear me over the roar of my Dyson.[63]

If a locked door's going to break, I guarantee you I'm on the inside of it. One time Ann Marie and I were staying in her brother's loft in New York and the bathroom doorknob fell off while I was in the shower. Fortunately Ann Marie is the unholy love child of MacGyver and Martha Stewart, so she not only had me out in ten seconds flat using nothing but items from the fridge and spice rack, but she also whipped up a miracle hair serum that kept me from getting the frizzies the whole time we were in town.

"Anyway, are we ready to go?" I don't want to leave, but I don't really have a choice.

I guess this isn't, in fact, going to be my house. Mac and I are a solid partnership precisely because we listen to each other, so I'm not going to insist we buy this house just because I have some weird tie to a couple of movies made a quarter of a century ago. We function well as a couple because we make our decisions to-

---

63 Yes, I gave in and hired a maid service after this. When the universe drops heavy shit on you, you tend to listen.

gether. We're a team. I mean, separately we're both one hundred percent, but when we band together, we're one thousand percent. That's why we've come so far from our humble postgrad beginnings. If one of us makes our mind up based on rational thought and solid arguments, the other has to respect that.

Liz and I turn to leave but Mac just stands there. "Mac? Mac? Honey? Are you coming?"

"This room . . ." he says in a voice full of awe and wonder. "Do you know what this room is? This is a *panic room*."

"A what?" Liz asks.

"Like that Jodie Foster movie?" I add.

"Right, exactly." He begins rubbing his hands together, almost as though in anticipation. "You see, over there, someone installed a ventilation system and a pumping system, and that over there is enough CAT5 fiber to support a government-grade surveillance system. There's a ton of room to lay in supplies, and with a foundation like this, someone could easily survive any disaster, up to and including nuclear war. And over there? That's a gun safe big enough to house an actual arsenal. You know what? I'd like to see ORNESTEGA try to breach this perimeter! Ha! This is . . ." He trails off again as he takes in every bit of the room.

He touches the walls with quiet reverence, and it's the first item he's come into contact with in this place that hasn't cracked, splintered, or crumbled. "This is . . ."

"This is what, honey?" I prompt.

"This is . . . our new home."

Chapter Six
WE DON'T NEED NO STINKING SECOND OPINIONS

"Tell me again why we're doing this ourselves."

I can't see Mac while he says this, save for the very top of his head, as he's hidden behind a mountain of moving boxes and flanked by huge rolls of Bubble Wrap and both dogs. "Do you know how much it costs to hire someone to pack for us?" I ask rhetorically. "We're totally capable of doing it ourselves. Plus I'm not forking out all that money for some company to come in here and parcel up all my free-range drawer pretzels."

What I don't mention is that every minute I spend packing is a minute I don't have to be working on my new book. Let's just say the writing isn't going so well. For some reason, the only scenes I can imagine go like this:

Mose: What are your plans after the harvest?

Amos: First, of course, I'll thank the Lord for being with us during the long, hard autumn days. I'll praise Him for keeping our backs strong and our hearts full. I'll extol the glories of His bounty and the virtue of His grace and mercy. I'll pray that our work proves fruitful and that the grain elevator will give us a fair price for all our toiling so that our families may enjoy a warm hearth and a full belly all winter long.

Mose: Aye, the Lord is good indeed. But what of after we give thanks?

Amos: My beloved Miriam has her sights set on a trip to the wicked city. She showed me some glossy photographs of what she calls her "heart's desire."

Mose: Surely she doesn't yearn to give in to carnal pleasures? Let her not be Eve to your Adam and lead you down the sinful path!

Amos: Oh, but no. I wish that it were me who captured her attention so. She seeks not the glory of God, but the opportunity to visit a special barn for pottery. My forbidden love cannot stop speaking of her lofty desire for oil-rubbed bronze fixtures and granite-topped vanities for her en suite bathroom and . . .

And it kind of rambles on like that for a while.

The thing is, I'm not even sure the Amish *go* indoors.

I should probably Google that sometime.

Anyway, Mac and I hired packing help for a previous move and . . . pack they did. Did they perform beautifully in protecting our delicate furniture and fragile mirrors and flat-screen televisions during the rigors of a crosstown trek? Yes. Did we lose a single lightbulb or a one-dollar wineglass over the course of the move? No. The problem was that their precision extended to each item they touched. The packing ladies gathered every single spilled Spree and Jolly Rancher still floating around my desk drawers from my '07 Christmas stocking, each dried out rollerball pen, and nine thousand loose paper clips, grouping like items in tight brown paper packages surrounded by cushioning layers of Bubble Wrap. They devoted entire moving boxes to garbage cans stuffed with empty macadamia nut jars, junk mail, and dirty Kleenex. We opened packet after packet of chewed dog bones and rusty bobby pins and wine corks cats had batted under beds.

To be fair, I wouldn't have expected the team to take stuff out to the Dumpster, but I didn't anticipate bringing the individually wrapped contents of my recycling bin to my new place, either. Every time we opened one of their boxes, it was like the worst Easter basket ever.

On top of all of that, we had to give the packers an extra-huge tip, because one of the ladies ran across Mac's box of army flash grenade simulators[64] and almost had a heart attack.

"We can weed out stuff this way," I add. Although I'm not actually very good at purging, seeing how I just boxed up every single business card I received back in the nineties, when I sold

---

64   According to Mac, you never know when you might need to disperse a riot in front of your house.

medical supplies for a living. But hey, maybe Dr. Aparajita Gupta and Dr. Trip Wadsworth *enjoy* books about teenage Amish zombies in love and they're waiting for my calls, which I can't place without having their numbers, right?

Obviously, we're packing because . . . ta-da! We got the house! After an annoyingly expensive bidding war with another Hughes fan, we were victorious! Hooray, us! Hooray, universe!

The shocking news was how well the place inspected. We anticipated being crushed by repair costs, but the patriarch of Angie's List–recommended Sandhurst and Sons Home Services assured us the house's problems were minor and primarily cosmetic. Mr. Sandhurst was so cute in his Mr. Magoo glasses and nubby cardigan, too. He kept calling us Mackey and Minnie and pretending we were his grandchildren—he was hilarious! I was surprised he filled out his report by hand, but I figured he's been doing business this way for fifty years, so why fix what's not broken?

"Oh, I keep forgetting," Mac says, grimacing at our collection of every cell phone we've owned since we met in 1994, "your grandmother called again. That's what, three times? Why aren't you calling her back?"

"Because I'm avoiding her. Duh. All she wants to do is give me decorating advice."

After my folks divorced, my mother, sister, and grandmother migrated south. They live in Miami Beach now, and together they own Two Polish Ladies Maid Service, the East Coast's largest residential and commercial cleaning operation.

I know, right?

I couldn't be prouder of how they built their business from the ground up. Jess and I weren't the only ones inspired by

Hughes's films. One night Babcia watched *Home Alone* with me and spent the whole time bitching about the state of the McCallisters' house.

"They rich—so why house not sparkle?" Babcia groused. She'd parked herself next to me on the old plaid couch with a mason jar of her homemade grain alcohol. Smelling strongly of gasoline and horseradish, Babcia's mash was so potent I'd get a contact high just being around it. This stuff sparked my lifelong aversion to any liquor not best served with a tiny drink umbrella.

"Babcia," I explained, "Kevin McCallister is eight years old, and more important, he's *home alone.* Things are bound to get messy."

"No! Is filthy before. Look hardwood! No shine! Look window! Is need clean with newspaper! Look rug! Is terrible crunchy. I make potion, clean whole house. Get lots rich people money."

"Babcia, you can't 'make potion' and clean this particular house, because it's a movie," I argued fecklessly, fully aware that rational thought held no weight. I'd recently made the mistake of watching *Field of Dreams* and *Teenage Mutant Ninja Turtles* with her, and for weeks all I heard was, "Why dead men play baseball? Why turtles eat pizza? You find and tell stop."

Point? Babcia's threat about cleaning rich people's houses turned into an obsession, which turned into a business, which eventually turned into an empire.[65]

Since becoming entrepreneurs, Babcia and my mother lost their aversion to aesthetics, and they wouldn't admit to having owned that shoddy old plaid couch on a bet. Between the two of

---

65 My dad now owns an auto body shop in Ohio. Was he inspired by Keith in *Some Kind of Wonderful?* Who can say for sure?

them, they've filled their Ocean Drive penthouse with acres of claw-footed chairs, chandeliers the size of water buffalo, rich tapestries, and gilt-framed paintings. Even with twenty-foot-high south-facing windows, they've managed to make their place as dark, foreboding, and gothic as a medieval castle. Jess and I call their style "Eastern Bloc chic," but Mac says it's more like "Donald Trump Meets Count Dracula."

"You have to call her back. I can't put her off again. Now. You should call her now," Mac insists, a rising edge of panic in his voice. Mac fought in Desert Storm before he went to college—he saw real combat and experienced all the horrors of war, but the only thing in the world that scares him is my Babcia. He swears the mole above her left eye stares into his soul.

Pfft. He should have seen it before she had the laser hair removal.

Over the years Babcia's upgraded her Stalin-era babushkas for Hermès scarves and stopped turning her tresses pink with at-home colorings, but she's still got enough Old World in her that I get why she'd be terrifying to an outsider.

I set down what I'm about to pack—a bunch of empty CD jewel cases—and reluctantly pick up the phone.

"Hello, talk." There's something wonderfully imperious about how my grandmother answers the phone.

"Babcia! Hi, it's Mia."

"Ah, *moja zabko!*"[66] Her pleasantries don't even last a second before she launches into me. "Why I call eleventen times? *Why?* I tell call Babcia, you call Babcia now! I see, I spank! Bad girl!"

---

66 Literal translation is "my little froggy." This term of endearment never quite caught on in English.

Interesting side note—the family business didn't really catch on until Jess took over all the customer interaction. Turns out most people don't enjoy being yelled at—or threatened with a spanking—particularly when paying ninety dollars an hour. Now Mom does the accounting and deals with vendors, Jess is the face of the business, and Babcia commands her army of maids with an iron (curtain) fist.

The only way to beat Babcia is to blithely ignore her threats. "So how's Miami?"

"Yellow," which I take to mean "sunny." At this point, I'm pretty sure her dialect is a ruse employed solely to lend authenticity to her business. I mean, she's been living in the States for almost sixty years; it's time to make indefinite articles happen. "Listen, I buy something. You put in house."

Oh, this can't be good.

I try to sound gracious. "Thank you, Babcia. May I ask what it is?"

"Is cross. Very big. Tall like man. Much gold."

"Wow, Babcia, that sounds awesome; I can't wait to see it!" My tall-like-man gold cross will hold a special place of honor.

In my new garage.

"When move?"

"We close on the house Monday and we head out the day after that. My friend Ann Marie's coming into town tomorrow so she can see it before we go. Perhaps she can give me some ideas about where to put your beautiful gift."

Ann Marie and my grandmother have always been kindred spirits, but ever since Ann Marie downed a shot of Babcia's jet fuel, they've had a particular affinity for each other.

"She good girl, not like you. You tell her come work here."

"I will. I'm sure she'd be delighted to quit practicing law and move her whole family down to Florida to be a maid."

"YOU DON'T MOUTH-SMART."

"I'm teasing you, Babcia. Anyway, how's it all going? What's Mom up to? And Jess—is she going to start that grad school program?"

"No more talk bye." Babcia puts the phone down with a bang. She's not rude so much as deeply efficient. After she delivers her message, she sees no point in hanging around for chitchat. Our phone conversations are like tearing off a bandage—painful and vaguely annoying, but ultimately over quickly.

I return to Mac and his box stack. "Babcia needs to talk with you." Mac instantly blanches. "Honey, I'm *kidding*. Why are you so afraid of her? She's, like, eighty pounds!"[67]

He stares into the distance while he appears to be shaking off a chill. "Evil takes many shapes and sizes."

I mentally snap my fingers. "Speaking of evil, we're doing a walk-through with Vienna on Friday to assess damages for our security deposit."

"During the day, or is she going to pay us another middle-of-the-night visit?"

"She said three o'clock, but a.m. or p.m. is anyone's guess. Ann Marie may still be here, so I'm rooting for a.m."

"Have they ever met?" Mac wraps a portion of tape around a box containing manuals for appliances we had four apartments ago.

---

67 Without the mole. Maybe eighty-one with it.

"Nope. But I imagine if they do finally encounter each other, we'll see it on the news."

"Mmm-hmm, that is indeed Jake Ryan's house."

I cast a sidelong glance at Ann Marie, nodding to herself in the passenger seat. "You say it like there was a semblance of doubt."

"I didn't doubt you; I simply need to see things for myself."

We exit the car and make our way to the front door. The weather has warmed to the point where coats aren't necessary, so I'm clad in a fleece pullover and yoga pants. Ann Marie's done up in her usual early-spring uniform of slim-fit oxford, rose pink corduroy Laura Petrie pants, and a cashmere wrap looped artfully around her shoulders. For an extra splash of color, she's held her honey blond bangs back with a floral silk scarf. I've long since stopped making *Stepford Wives* jokes around her; she takes them as a compliment.

"Let's go in." The seller's agent couldn't be here, so she gave us the lockbox code. I clumsily release the key and open the door. "The place is a little rough around the edges, but the inspection wasn't bad. Most of what we'll concentrate on is painting, papering, and swapping fixtures. We'll need to do some minor bath upgrades, too, but that's not a huge deal."

"Noted."

Ann Marie is completely silent while I lead her on the tour. She's always quiet when she's concentrating. And as most defense attorneys learn the hard way, she's almost impossible to read. Of course, I could have told you that fifteen years ago, when we played strip poker at the Phi Delt house. All of us were down to our underpants while she hadn't even removed her signet ring.

I talk through how the real layout compares to that of the

movie. "The dining room was over there in the film, and the kitchen was way smaller, so this huge room is kind of a bonus."

I show her all our favorite parts and elaborate on our plans to fix those that aren't. I point out where I'll put my writing room. "See?" I say. "I'll have the perfect view of the apple tree when it blooms next month!"

We go all the way from the third-floor loft to the basement bar and then back out into the treelined yard. Rain's left the soil too damp to make our way down to the lake, but it's so windy we can hear the water slapping against the bluffs.

"So," I say when our tour concludes, "what do you think?"

Ann Marie lifts the bottom of her scarf and inspects its edge. She's stalling; that's her one tell. Finally, she replies, "Purchasing this home is fucking insane."

I let out a short barking laugh. "Tell me how you *really* feel. Seriously, what do you think?"

Ann Marie's eyes are as steely gray as I've ever seen them. "What I really think is you should run away from this house. Very fast. The level of disrepair is profound and it's going to cost hundreds of thousands more than you anticipate."

Argh. Tell Ann Marie about the potential for rain and she'll prepare for a hurricane. Show her your tan line and she'll force you to get a cancer screening. I'm not saying she's one to overreact, but . . . Oh, wait. Yes, I am.

"Honey, I respect your opinion—you know I do—but I've got to politely disagree. Our inspector gave it two thumbs up."

"Then he's either mentally ill or incompetent."

Before I can argue, she plows on. "I can see a dozen very expensive things wrong with this place from here. For example, there—the lintels over the window aren't painted. They show signs of rust. Seems innocuous, yes? But eventually they'll lose strength and won't support the weight of the masonry. Was that noted in your report?"

"Um . . ." I don't even know what a lintel is.[68]

"Right. Over there now, where the ivy grows?"

"I love the idea of ivy!" I exclaim.

"Yes? Then you must also love the growth of mold and mildew? Do you want to promote rot or allow access to small animals and bugs? Hmm? No? Then lose the ivy."

"Fine. *That's* a landscaping issue and not terribly expensive." I feel a tad smug because I can almost never get anything over on Ann Marie, and when I do, I suspect it's because she lets me.

"Your chimney cap is cracked and the exterior lights are loose, both of which sound small but can lead to a whole host of problems. Your gutters are deteriorated to the point that they're leaching water into the soil around your house, which can impact the foundation. Want me to continue? All right, I shall. How about your roof? Mia, if you don't want it to rain inside the house, I suggest you install a new one straightaway."

"Listen, Chicken Little, the inspector—"

"Crazy, stupid, or senile."

While I attempt to spot these so-called deficiencies, Ann Marie removes a linen handkerchief from her Kelly bag and dusts off her Tory Burch shoes. "Judging from the fine texture of this sawdust, I'd imagine you have termites. My guess is drywood, but

---

68 A bean of some sort?

I'd hesitate to rule out Formosan subterranean. And that beam over there, under your writing window . . ."

At this point, I'm having trouble mounting a defense. I wonder, *was* Mr. Sandhurst a little lax in his estimation? He did wear those huge glasses and he was kind of elderly and . . .

Sensing my hesitancy, Ann Marie goes in for the kill. Suddenly I feel a tiny pang of empathy for any criminal who ever had the misfortune of facing off against her. "Pay attention to the long line of holes," she explains, raising a neatly buffed pointer finger in the direction of the front right corner. "Caveat emptor, my dear. Woodpeckers caused those, validating my theory that most of the wood in this house is infested. Think about it. Woodpeckers don't eat wood; they eat bugs. Ergo, if you have a woodpecker, you have bugs. How are you going to finish your book with the constant metronome of a woodpecker outside your window, hmm?"

Flabbergasted. That's what I am. Flabbergasted.

"I . . . I don't know what to say, except that our inspection didn't show any of this. I mean, are you trying to scare me out of living here? If so, you're doing a swell job."

"Yes! Absolutely I am! Run! I beg you to run away from this deal."

This simply cannot be, so I persist. "What you're telling me— it's all fixable. A roof can be replaced. Termites can be killed. Ivy can be trimmed."

"Mia, the heart of the matter is, you don't understand what you're undertaking," Ann Marie says in an uncharacteristically gentle voice. "Yes, you can almost always predict which option the homeowner will choose on *House Hunters*, and I believe with your taste you'd shine on *Design Star*." She quickly amends her statement. "If you were putting together a room for little girls or gay men. What I'm trying to impress upon you is that renovations are long and ugly and demanding. You won't grasp how invasive it is until you live it. Our powder room remodel took a month. No matter how much we tidied up, it was like every day the contractors came in and shook a five-pound bag of flour all over the house. I worry that this will put undue pressure on your and Mac's shoulders. I just worry. That's all."

I have complete confidence Ann Marie has my best interests at heart and I believe her. . . . I do. She's rarely wrong in spirit, but she frequently overestimates the scope of a problem.

Plus, I might just believe in fate a little bit more.

Destiny wouldn't have led me to Jake Ryan's house if it weren't the one for us.

Right?

But just to be safe, I'm going to move my writing room to the library.

Chapter Seven
I'VE GOT TWO CONCUSSIONS AND A MICROPHONE

Chaos. That's how I'd describe the situation here. Chaos.

Our closing yesterday was smooth sailing over calm seas. *Then* I was expecting chaos. I'd heard so many closing horror stories prior to the event, like problems with financing, parties not showing up, or worse—sellers dropping dead and the property going into probate, fights breaking out over Realtor percentages, paperwork snafus that took weeks and thousands to fix, but our closing entailed us signing our full names a bunch of times in blue ink and then receiving a set of keys. Easy peasy.

Start to finish, the whole thing took half an hour. We would have been through sooner if the seller's attorney and I didn't spend a few minutes bonding over our mutual distaste for cheesy vampire romances.[69]

But after that? Nope, didn't expect what happened after that.

Our last few minutes of Zen came after we walked out of the real estate office and stepped into the car. "This Is the Day" by The The was playing. With lyrics like, "This is the day / when things fall into place," Mac and I grinned at each other like a couple of lunatics. Truly, yesterday *was* the day our lives changed, you know? I'm not sure either of us could have contained ourselves if "If You Were Here" had come on. Hearing that song reinforced my belief that there are always signs when something's right, which is why I didn't even bother to tell Mac about Ann Marie's advice. The universe knows what it's doing.

We stopped by the new house briefly to make sure the keys worked, then hightailed it back to the city, because we hadn't come close to boxing up all our belongings for this afternoon's move.[70]

I was unloading the hutch in the living room when I noticed this spinning-rimmed low-rider making loops past our house. At first I was annoyed by the thumping bass but shrugged it off, knowing I was spending my last night in the 'hood. If the hipsters and hoodlums wanted to take ownership of this block, fine by me.

But as they continued to cruise around the house, I paid more attention. A pattern soon emerged—whenever the car full of shaved-head thugs passed our yard, they'd drive extra slow and lean out as though they were trying to get a peek at us.

---

69 Yeah. I went there.

70 Apparently I enjoy "not packing" almost as much as I enjoy "not writing."

"Mac!" I called into the intercom. "Mac! ORNESTEGA and his idiot friends keep circling the house. I'm worried they're going to attempt a drive-by." *Seriously*, I thought, *if these little punks shoot me on the day I bought Jake Ryan's house, then . . . I guess that really would be the day that my life changed.*

"Oh, for God's sake," Mac groused, stomping up the stairs. "These morons have no concept of physics, do they? If they were smart, they'd set up a sniper nest on the roof across the street. They can't shoot us from a car, you know. Unless you're a Ranger or a trained assassin or Agent Jack Bauer,[71] it's almost impossible to *hit* a moving target *from* a moving target. That's why you always hear about innocent bystanders getting caught in the cross fire. If these derelicts had any concept of how to work a weapon, they'd all peg one another and social Darwinism would go a long way toward resolving the Cobra/Latin Kings territory dispute."

"Uh-huh, great. I'll just go ahead and call the police then." I herded the pets in front of me so we could all scurry down to the basement. Then I noticed the determined set of his shoulders. "Please don't do anything stupid."

"No worries!" he assured me as he dashed up the stairs to the second floor. "My plan is foolproof!"

Well, shit.

I hid in the basement, waiting for the police to arrive and trying desperately to avoid getting a face full of hot lead.

In the interim, Mac went to work. Using a broom handle, a long down coat, and my Fashion Fever Barbie Styling Head,[72] Mac

---

71 The one on *24*, not our kitten.

72 What, you *don't* have one?

made it look like a person was moving around behind our window sheer. I'd have congratulated him for his ingenuity, but considering he got the idea from *Home Alone*, I gave him only partial credit. And unlike Kevin McCallister, he was trying to lure OR-NESTEGA and Co. in, rather than scare them away.

When I heard the hail of gunshots and the subsequent shattering glass, I sprinted upstairs to find Mac standing next to our broken window, *tsk-tsk*ing and wearing an oddly amused expression.

The forensics experts told us that out of the shots fired, seven bullets went straight into the ground, one hit our neighbor's satellite dish, two lodged in the mailbox on the corner, four ricocheted back into the trunk of the car, and one grazed the driver's right thigh.

No one was seriously harmed in the firefight,[73] but ORNES-TEGA suffered a broken leg and concussion when the injured driver floored the getaway car and bashed into the church across the street.

If that's not God's payback for the graffiti, I don't know what is.

Well played, Lord. Well played.

By the way, the bullets didn't shatter our window. None even landed on our property. The window broke when one of the spinners flew off the car and bounced into our house after the crash.

Between giving statements and tracking down a window-boarding service, we didn't have a lot of time to shove stuff in boxes last night. Tracey and Kara brought us dinner and lent a hand, but at that point the evening was shot.[74]

First thing this morning we called (begged) for some boxing

---

73 Mac says you may as well be firing a staple gun if you're going to use a .22-caliber weapon.

74 Pun intended.

assistance, and now there's a team of six ladies making time and a half to Bubble Wrap our unmentionables while ten movers load out what's already in cartons.

Mac isn't even here to help supervise this three-ring circus. I figured the most appropriate punishment for, you know, *drawing gunfire* was to transport two hyperactive dogs and four angry kittens to the new house in his prize Mercedes. He called earlier to tell me that with all the yowling and barking, it was like driving up the expressway with six air-raid sirens.

I told him as soon as I stopped smelling lead dust, I'd be more sympathetic.

As it turns out, the sixteen strangers currently scurrying in and out of my house are not the source of the chaos.

Oh, no.

That honor belongs to Vienna, who's presently standing in my front door.

She didn't show up for our final walk-through on Friday. Per her Twitter feed, she had a "really important colonic" that took precedence. Now she's here, unannounced, unscheduled.

And she's brought a camera crew.

Vienna thrusts a piece of paper at me. "Sign."

I take the document from her, more out of curiosity than courtesy. "What is it?" I squint but can't make out the fine print.

Vienna blows an enormous bubble in my face, sucks it back in, and gives her gum a couple of aggressive chews before answering. "We're, like, capturing how I'm a savvy business working executive woman. People want to see me perform jobs.[75] I'm, like, a

---

75 It would be indelicate for me to mention that anyone with $9.99 and a broadband Internet connection could watch Vienna "perform jobs."

one-two-pre-noor and everything, which is the oldest profession. My show's gonna be all uplifting and shit. For poor people. Now let's do this thing already!"

A guy in cargo shorts carrying a boom mike explains rather sheepishly, "That's a consent and release form, pretty standard language. Can you please sign it? Please? We're shooting Vienna's new reality show, *One Night in Vienna*." For a brief moment, I see something almost haunted in his eyes, but before I can ponder it, I mentally rewind what he just said and . . . Hold up a minute.

What?

Then my memory clicks. I read something about this recently on PopSugar.com. I guess Vienna wants to one-up her frenemy Paris and do a business-oriented version of *The Simple Life* to prove that she's no longer the coke-snorting, paparazzi-shoving, assistant-abusing diva the media's made her out to be. I imagine that's why she's clad in a business suit.

Of course, most executives I know tend to wear a shirt/bra/camisole/*something* under their single-button blazer, but it's possible I just don't understand every nuance of haute couture. The September issue of *Vogue* can teach one only so much.

To confirm, I ask, "You want to film our walk-through?" The producer accompanying the sound guy nods.

"We need to show Vienna taking command in a professional environment," the producer confirms. "When she speaks to you, try to defer to what she says. We want to put a positive spin on this. We're out to show a whole new side of Vienna."

According to Dlisted.com, her last few ventures ended badly. Turns out even the most avant-garde fashionista draws the line at carrying a cat-skin handbag. Rumor has it that Anna Wintour decreed Vienna's signature perfume smelled like "hepatitis B and poor decisions."

I'm still holding my consent form and processing what's happening around me. If I sign this, does that mean they'll use *my* image on-screen? I'm a bit ambivalent about this. On the one hand, no publicity is bad publicity; on the other, I'm not sure that particular axiom applies to publicity in conjunction with Vienna.

Vienna's entourage includes a cameraman, a couple of guys carrying heavy lights, a makeup artist, two hairstylists, and a personal assistant, in addition to the aforementioned sheepish sound engineer and producer.

"What are you, like, waiting for?" Vienna snaps. Then she grabs her assistant, bends her over to create an ad hoc writing surface, and slaps my consent agreement on the center of the assistant's back before thrusting a pen in my face. "Sign it."

In the background, ten movers and six packers have gathered to watch the action unfold. A few are taking cell phone pictures, and who could blame them?

I hastily autograph the sheet while the first hairdresser tries to fluff Vienna's coif. Vienna's seemingly already satisfied with her do—a prim French roll adorned with feathers, sequins, and dangling crystals—and shoves her out of the way with the heel of her palm. Luckily, the stylist's fall is cushioned by a battery of empty boxes no doubt destined to hold the contents of my wastepaper baskets.

Vienna waves her arm in the air as though roping some imaginary cattle and begins barking orders to various crew members. "Hey, fatty! Yo, retard! Smelly guy! You, dead tooth, come here and get me in profile. I'm ready for my close-up! And . . . action!"

I guess that neatly explains the crew's pained looks.

While Vienna and her posse move to the center of the living room, a packer notices the few remaining glass shards from last night's altercation and attempts to retrieve them. "No, no, please!" I blurt. "We're not taking that with us! Those are pieces of broken window."

Vienna's interest is suddenly piqued. "Wait, my window? You broke *my* window?"

"Um, didn't you notice the enormous board where the center casement window used to be? We had a drive-by shooting here last night. Pretty scary, but don't worry: We're fine and insurance will cover the replacement costs, so, really—"

Vienna snaps her fingers behind her back and mouths, *Make sure you're getting this*, to the camera operator. She lunges toward me and stands an inch from my face in classic reality-show confrontation mode. "*You* broke *my* window? You bitch! You fucking fake-ass phony bitch! I'm going to sue you! I'm going to sue your fat ass off! *You* don't get to break *my* window. You're not seeing a dime of your security deposit. I mean, I could, like, buy and sell you! Yes! I'll do that. I will do *that*! Buy you! Sell you! Because you suck! You're, like, a big ugly bag of Polish sausage stone-face slut!"

I'm a *what*?

I mean, I understand the words she's saying individually, but all together like that? Not so much.

Vienna continues her tirade, now with twenty percent more spittle and some intense neck rolling. Is she going to bust out the you-go-girl finger wag? And . . . there it is! "I hate you, I hate this house, I hate work, I kind of love Britney, but you? You I hate and I hate your asshat-face."

I look around at a roomful of stunned personnel. "I'm sorry.

Is anyone else following this?" Vienna's personal assistant points behind Vienna's back and pantomimes inhaling an enormous rail of coke off the staircase. Her makeup artist sighs and quickly repacks all the lotions and potions she's just unloaded, while the lighting gentleman snaps off the big box lights. Her producer has assumed a position best described as "face-palm." I'll bet when he envisioned Vienna "taking command in a professional environment," it didn't shake out like this.

Vienna's not finished with her diatribe. She starts in on what I assume is her thesis statement.

"So fuck you, fuck your bathtub, fuck the Japs, fuck your grill, fuck your mother, and fuck your fucking fuckity fuck. Your dogs are cool. But fuck your cats *and* your fucky face."

I wonder, am I supposed to be intimidated by her yelling? Cowed? If so, I'm going to make for terrible television. I mean, I've heard worse stuff coming out of Babcia's mouth while wishing me a happy birthday. And really, I'm too busy for this nonsense, especially when Jake Ryan's house is waiting for me. I've got to put a stop to this.

"Um, hi, listen, sorry to interrupt while you're rolling," I say, offering the producer an apologetic look. "Quick favor? Those guys over there?" I gesture toward the movers. "I'm paying them by the hour. So if it's not too much trouble, could we either start the walk-through or finish up with the fucking fuckity fuck?"

A giggle escapes from the previously unscathed second hairstylist. And that's all it takes.

In one deft motion, Vienna whips off her impossibly high sandal and hurls it in the direction of the laughter. Thanks to Sir Isaac Newton's first law of motion, a triple-strapped Alexandre

Birman python wedge produces more drag than, say, a baseball, so despite what I'm sure is Vienna's extensive knowledge of all things aerodynamic, she ends up picking off Manny, the foreman of the moving crew. She clocks him right in the head, and Manny crumples and hits the ground with a thud.

At this point, the producer grabs Vienna around the waist and begins to drag her out the door. "I think we're finished here. Thank you," he calls as he wrestles her down the steps and to the gate, the rest of the crew scuttling out behind them.

I rush over to Manny to see how he's doing while his co-workers offer up yet-to-be-packed bags of frozen peas and cold drinks. We get him up and try to assess his level of consciousness. Manny insists he's fine, but I'm not so sure. That shoe must have weighed six pounds, and she pitches like a Cy Young Award winner. I set him up on the couch and beg him to rest as long as he needs.

As I try to calm everyone and reorganize the boxes, I have to wonder—how does that girl go through life generating so much bad karma with so few repercussions? Every time I think, *Oh, the universe will eventually right itself*, in regard to Vienna, she ends up making out with Robert Pattinson[76] or appearing on the VMAs. Sure, she had a few bumps in the road—like her family attempting to make her work[77] for a living—but for the most part, she's bulletproof.

That's when I notice something important I've left unfinished, and I can't help myself. "Wait, wait!" I call, running after Vienna

---

76 I don't hold *Twilight* against him.

77 With her pants on. (Blouse optional.)

and her crew. I reach them just as they're done putting all their gear back in the van and are about to take off.

"Do you guys still need my consent form?"

Mac and I are tucked into bed after what's proved to be an arduous thirty-six hours.

Unfortunately, we're not tucked into bed in our new house. Due to Vienna's antics and Manny's head injury, the movers didn't have enough time to unload the truck in Abington Cambs after filling it up. So we agreed that they'd simply store everything overnight and we'd see them in the morning.

Kara's parents insisted we stay with them, and you don't say no to the Patels,[78] so we're upstairs in their guest room watching television before we go to sleep. My sweet little Daisy and Duckie are so exhausted from running around their new backyard that they're too tired to climb up on the bed with us. This may be the first time we've slept alone since we adopted the dogs.

"I can't keep my eyes open." Mac yawns. "Where's the remote?"

I reply, "I don't know, and I think I'm too tired to get up and find it."

"Maybe we'll just close our eyes for a minute and . . . mmph." And like that, he's out.

I'm about to drift off too, when I hear the opening credits of *TMZ*, followed by a familiar voice and a bunch of bleeps. I sit up and grope for my glasses.

"So *bleep* you, *bleep* your bathtub, *bleep* the Japs, *bleep* your grill,

---

78 Kara and I have had many a liquid lunch discussing this fact.

bleep your mother, and *bleep* your *bleep*ing *bleep*ity *bleep*. Your dogs are cool. But *bleep* your cats *and* your *bleep* face."

What the *bleep*?

Glasses finally on, I see shaky cell phone footage taken *from my house*, replaying everything that went down today. Then Harvey Levin comes on-screen, reporting, "Producers have pulled the plug on Vienna Hyatt's new reality show after today's violent outburst."

The cute surfer-boy reporter with the wild mane of blond hair adds, "Yep, it's over before it even began. I guess anyone wanting to spend *One Night in Vienna* will have to do it the old-fashioned way!"

Harvey continues. "Ha! You know that's true. I'd hate to be in her shoes. No, wait. I'd hate to be *hit* by one of her shoes!" Cameras pan to the whole team at *TMZ* laughing before the scene cuts to a shot of Manny trying to shake away all the cartoon birds flying around his head. "Will our favorite bad girl seek revenge for her axed show? Wait. What am I talking about? This is Vienna Hyatt! Of course she will!"

Then *TMZ* launches into a long retrospective of all her old feuds. My God, that woman's fought with everyone. And I'm not just talking about the usual Paris-Lindsay-Kardashian-du-jour-Britney conflagrations, although by Vienna's own admission, Ms. Spears currently holds a spot on the buddy list. Her extended enemy list includes the regular suspects, such as all the kids from *Laguna Beach*, *The Hills*,[79] *The City*, and even *Jersey Shore*. But it doesn't end there, oh, no. Vienna's had words with everyone from

---

79 Particularly Speidi, although who doesn't hate them just a little?

Arnold Palmer to Ahmet Zappa. According to *TMZ*, she even pissed off the Dalai Lama by shoving him when he accidentally walked in front of her at the step-and-repeat banner wall at a Free Tibet event.

Harvey returns to the screen. "And when Vienna gets revenge, you'll hear it here first!"

After the segment ends, I hop out of bed to find the remote, which is located directly beneath Daisy's ample rump. I give her a quick smooch on the snout, switch off the television, and climb under the covers.

Before I fall asleep, I snuggle closer to Mac; then I say a little prayer of thanks that we're up here in Abington Cambs now and will never have to deal with Vienna again.

Chapter Eight
FOR WHOM THE BELL TOLLS

"Doorbell! Mac, the doorbell! Come on, let's get the door!"

We've been waiting for our first official doorbell ring for what feels like forever. The movers mentioned that coming up to Abington Cambs is a huge pain for them, because the neighbors are always getting in the way with all their welcome baskets and impromptu wine-based meet-and-greets.

At the moment, I'm not concerned whether the new neighbors might cause the movers "a pain," since we've waited over a week for our stuff to arrive. Thirty miles away! Eight days of waiting! Turns out after foreman Manny was hit in the head, he had a little trouble reading the bill of lading back at the warehouse and our things were shipped via rail to Atlantic City, not Abington Cambs. Straightening this all out took forever—and more than a little yelling on Mac's part. Every day the moving company would promise "tomorrow," but after a few days, we wondered if tomorrow would ever actually come. (Please don't tell Mac, but part of me wonders whether, if he'd been a little less shouty on the phone, things might have been resolved faster.)

Anyway, after we left the city, we slept at the Patels' house for three nights while we waited for our beds and stuff to arrive. Kara's parents assured us we could stay as long as we wanted, but that seemed like such an imposition. Also, after a couple of days, Kara freaked out over being obligated to visit, and Mac became really interested in learning to cook Indian food, which . . . no. So we bought an air mattress and a couple of beanbags and officially moved in here. Those three items plus what we packed in overnight bags comprise all of our accessible belongings, as I refuse to replace what I already own.

Mac and I have been "urban camping" for five days, and all I want to do is sit on a chair with a back. I've been trying to write my novel since we got here, but I keep going off on tangents about sturdy, comfortable Amish furniture. I've waxed on and on about stately farmhouse tables and wide-slatted rockers, varnished and lovely and solid. I devoted eight pages to the matching bedroom set Amos handcrafted for his zombie crush, Miriam, but instead of reiterating how conflicted he was about his unrequited, undead lust, I . . . Well, why not just read it for yourself?

Amos: Miriam, my sparrow, please direct your loving gaze to the dovetail joints on this fine sleigh bed that are as firm and strong as my bond to you. Pay special heed to the curved footboards I crafted with my own hands.

Miriam: Why, Amos, are you making your wanton inten-
tions clear, that this shall be our marriage bed?

Amos: Uh, sure, yeah. But please note the ergonomics that
went into the curved shape of the headboard that
would make it ideal for late-night reading or snack-
ing or perhaps watching television. I mean, if we
watched TV. I didn't make the headboard out of any
kind of stupid fabric, so it's not going to hold stains
or any odors. And I hand-tooled and lacquered the
wood in a cherry stain because I know it's your favorite finish, because it's not too light like honey
oak and not too dark like mahogany, and really, this
particular color would go so great with, say, a really
awesome antique Persian rug, you know?

I ran some of the new pages past my niece Claire, and she said
they "sound like an IKEA catalog, only boring-er."

Another downside of not having our things—and trust me,
there are plenty—is that we haven't been able to prepare meals,
since our pots and pans have been wending their way back from
the boardwalk. For the first few days we lived on takeout, and that
got so old that I found myself missing Mac's culinary abomina-
tions.[80] All I wanted was something from my own kitchen, so we
resorted to microwave cookery. As luck would have it, the nice
microwave in the big kitchen died the second I tried it, so we've
been using the antique one in the basement. Said microwave is
perfectly functional, but I'm afraid it's going to go all *Hot Tub Time*

---

80 Almost.

Machine on me and send me back a few generations every time I nuke a hot dog.

But now the moving truck is here at long last, which means the neighbors have been alerted to our presence. Somebody's at the door, and I may be even more excited than the dogs, who are leaping and howling at the possibility of visitors. I can't believe I'm *finally* living in a place where I'll know my neighbors. I'm not the kind of gal who'd run next door to borrow a cup of sugar, but after so many years of being anonymous in the city, I've taken a shine to the prospect of brief, friendly chats with other homeowners when we're getting our newspapers in the morning.[81] I'm cool with the idea that someone might keep an eye on our place when we go on vacation, not because they have to, but because they want to. I'm a little bit enamored by the idea of trick-or-treaters, and I'm thrilled with the notion that someone might sell me Girl Scout Cookies.[82]

When I was growing up, the street where we lived looked run-down and depressing, yet a closer-knit community could not be found. Sure, a few families allowed their dirty children to play outside at night in their pajamas, but even so, every single adult in the neighborhood watched out for those ragamuffins. We banded together to shovel Mrs. Kingery's driveway, and we picked up Mr. Signorelli's arthritis medicine once he got too old to drive, and brought casseroles every time the Kubiaks had a new baby.[83] If indeed it takes a village, Spring Street was that village.

---

81 Note to self—stop reading the paper online.

82 I'll take three boxes of Samoas and two Thin Mints, please.

83 Bred like rabbits, those people.

As we make our way to the door behind two elated, scrambling dogs, I quiz Mac. "What do you think we're getting, a fruit basket? Maybe a pie? Ooh, I hope it's wine!"

"I'm dying for a nice, heavy casserole, with ground beef and macaroni and cream of mushroom soup." Mac rubs his stomach. "I can't eat another hot dog. I can't."

I settle the dogs and smooth my ponytail, running my tongue over my front teeth to make sure there's no stray lipstick before I make my first impression on our new neighbors . . . and possibly our new friends.

I grab the door handle—hmm, that feels a bit loose—and I swing open the door. Not too enthusiastically, mind you. Don't want to appear desperate, just welcoming. "Hello! I'm Mia! And this is Mac and Duckie and Daisy," I say, pointing to each of them.

A small, fastidious middle-aged man stands in front of me. He's wearing undersize round tortoiseshell glasses, and one of those tweedy blazers with the sewn-on leather arm patches, and . . . Oh, Jesus Christ, is that an *ascot*?

No, wait. It's just a scarf.

But still, it *could* have been an ascot. How badass is that?

Seeing my neighbor here dressed like it's casual Friday at Harvard Law School makes me laugh about how far I've come from Spring Street. The only jackets neighborhood men wore were of the Carhartt variety, except for state occasions such as christenings and weddings, which called for synthetic sport coats festooned in plaids best described as "tasty."

Mac and I stand next to each other in the doorway, two dogs sitting nicely behind us, all waiting for our new elbow-patchy neighbor to say something. I can't help but notice his well-manicured hands are empty, but maybe his wife's on her way with something potable or macaroni-based and delicious? Mac and I grin briefly at each other and then back at our neighbor.

"Would you like to come in?" I offer.

"Are you the new owners?"

I'm a bit taken aback by this stranger's brusqueness. But maybe he's cranky because he couldn't find his ascot? Self-consciously, I try to knock the excess dust off of me. I bet my stupid yoga pants and dirty hoodie are throwing him off. We've been busy cleaning and I must look a mess.

Mac's detected something off about the man's voice, too, and I notice he pulls himself to his full height. Duckie stops wagging his tail, and Daisy slinks down to the floor. "We are. Can I help you?"

"Yes, you can help me. You can help me by taking care of your diseased tree, southeast corner, three paces in." The man whips out a digital camera and begins to scroll through the photographs of limbs and sticks. "Here, you see the flagging on these branches? And the brown streaking in the sapwood here? And this bark beetle gallery! Ugh! Listen to me: I *will not* lose my elm tree because you people refuse to service your property, and I've already reported this to the city."

"Whoa, hold on," Mac says, and gestures at the team carrying in our couch.[84] "We're just now moving in." At this point Daisy slinks away and Duckie's hackles raise.

"It's my understanding that you've been here for a week. My expectation is that you would have taken care of this the first day.

---

84 I see a long, soft sit in my future.

We have standards around here, and you're already in violation." With this, Mr. Elbow Patch removes his glasses and gives them a quick polish with his handkerchief.

As Mac's drawing his breath to set him straight,[85] I surreptitiously pull him back a step and attempt to defuse the situation. I don't want to be disinvited from the block parties for the next twenty years because we're tired, dirty, hungry, and sore from sitting on bean-based furniture for most of the week. "Yes, of course, I'm really sorry. We'll take care of this immediately. Is there a landscaping service you can recommend?"

Elbow Patch's disgust is almost palpable. "Hiring a service? We keep our gardeners *on staff* around here." And with that, he spins on his heel and marches up our driveway.

Mac makes a stern face at me and repeats, " 'We keep our gardeners *on staff* around here,' " and we both crack up, causing the dogs' moods to lighten as well.

"Who says stuff like that?" I wonder, wiping my eyes.

"People who wear elbow patches," Mac replies.

I glance down, noticing a small splotch of mustard on my jacket, and I absently scratch at it with my thumbnail. "I guess there's one grumpy person in every neighborhood. Although I can't remember who the meanie was on Spring Street."

"Didn't you tell me that Babcia used to confiscate all the balls that landed in your yard and would then sell them back to kids at garage sales?"

"Ha! Yeah, I forgot about that. I guess she always had entrepreneurial tendencies." Nothing used to make Babcia's blood flow

---

85 Read: shout him stupid.

quicker than a stray baseball or Frisbee in our grass. She'd practically vault over the ottoman to get around to the door in order to snatch the wayward toy before its rightful owner could get to it. Babcia fetched balls faster and with more vigor than a purebred Labrador retriever. "I wonder if people thought she was the neighborhood crank?"

Before Mac can answer, the bell rings again.

"Showtime!" I exclaim. We move toward the door, and I'm a tad more reserved when I open it this time. This time, the dogs don't follow because we've put them out. A woman about my age stands in front of us. She sports the kind of sassy haircut made up of points and flips that no one over a hundred pounds can get away with. She's all done up in Lululemon togs. Aha! I knew people had to wear athletic gear up here at some point.

I suspect the weird looks I've been getting at the coffee shop all week have had to do with how I've been dressed. Whereas I've been tooling around in the same workout clothes and ratty old Nikes, everyone else appears to be ready for lunch with an ambassador. Seriously, it's like every woman in the AC is channeling Grace Kelly, with superstarched Peter Pan–collared blouses or twinsets, pencil skirts, or tailored pants, finished off with kitten heels or ballet flats. And the jewelry? Don't even get me started on the jewelry. Charm bracelets and pearls and, oh, my God, the diamonds! I'm talking studs the size of horseflies and solitaires big enough to skate across.

A woman last week must have been sporting twenty-five carats between her neck and wrist alone. So I said to the guy in line behind me, "I bet she's having a bling-uccino." Then he looked at me all blankly, so I pretended I was talking into my Bluetooth instead.

My point is, I don't understand how these gals manage to be so pulled together at ten o'clock in the morning, at Starbucks of all places. I can barely remember to put on pants before I have my coffee.

Anyway, I notice our new, sporty neighbor doesn't have any kind of obvious welcome gift with her either, unless the enormous SUV stroller containing two apple-cheeked toddlers is meant for us, in which case . . . thank you?

I handle the introductions. "Hi, I'm Mia, and this is my husband, John MacNamara. But most people call him Mac."

"Do you have dogs?"

Wow, Abington Cambians don't waste a lot of time with conversational foreplay, do they?

"Um . . . yes, we do," I tell her. "They're on the back porch right now. Their names are Duckie and Daisy. Did you . . . want to meet them?" I can't imagine where she's going with this until I glance down at her sleeping children. *Oh.* I bet she's concerned about the pit bull, so I need to put her at ease. "Please don't worry; they're totally sweet and docile unless you're, like, a pork chop or a squirrel."

Lululemon's expression darkens. "Do you, by chance, have a doggy door?"

"We do." Pride practically radiates off Mac as he replies. With a little elbow grease—and a lot of swearing, so very much swearing—Mac successfully completed his first DIY project here yesterday.[86] The door works like a charm, and the dogs are delighted to have a say in whether or not they go outdoors.

---

86   Estimated installation time on the package? Two hours. Actual installation time? Six days.

"I see. Then please take this." Lululemon roots around in the storage area on the back of her Bugaboo.

Ding, ding, ding, jackpot! The new neighbor *does* have a welcome present for us! So maybe this lady isn't that great at conversation, and perhaps it would have been nice if she'd told us her name, but I don't care, because we're getting a present! Hooray!

Lululemon hands Mac a small blue-and-yellow bottle. Ooh, what is it? Some kind of small-batch Scotch? A wee container of yummy dessert wine? Possibly an exotic bath soak?

Mac turns the container over and up and down. "WD-40?"

"Yes. Your door is banging open and closed and it's clearly in need of a lubricant.[87] I'll thank you to fix it at once, because your dogs are disturbing Calliope and Gregor's afternoon nap."

As we stand there, astounded, Lululemon executes a perfect three-point turn and trots up the drive and onto the street.

"Calliope and Gregor?" Mac's expression vacillates between shock and awe.

I reply, "Don't look at me, dude."

We try to shake off the incident, chalking up Lululemon's attitude to toddler-based exhaustion and a desperate need for carbohydrates. Then we spend a few minutes discussing furniture placement with the movers before the bell rings again.

"I'm almost afraid to answer it," I tell Mac.

This time there's an old man—ancient, really—standing in the center of our porch, and he doesn't look happy.

Of course he doesn't.

Even his wrinkles are frowning. We joked about buying a

---

87 That's what she said. (Sorry. Couldn't resist.)

welcome mat that said, GO AWAY, but now that seems like it might have been a wise investment.

Before we can say anything, the old guy begins to wave an eagle-headed cane at us. "Tell your kids not to park in my driveway," he hisses.

"Is someone parked in your driveway?" I query. I thought everyone here arrived via the moving van, but I double-check. "Hey, guys? Anyone parked anywhere other than this driveway?" I confirm they haven't and turn back to the visitor. "If someone's there, it's not us."

He scowls so hard his jowls tremble. "I didn't say there was someone there now, missy. I *said* I don't want your kids parking in my driveway."

Mac is utterly confused, so I field this one. "I promise that won't be an issue, sir, as we don't even have kids." Because I'm polite, I don't add that if we were to reproduce, by the time our children were old enough to get a license, he'd be dead.

His beady little eyes dart back and forth beneath fleshy lids. "Well, keep it that way." Then he totters off our porch and proceeds to slowly traverse the cobblestone path. When he gets to the street, he kicks our mailbox.

"Did you sign us up for a reality show and not tell me?" Mac demands.

"I tried to get us on *Property Virgins*, *House Hunters*, and *My First Place*, but no luck," I admit. Apparently the producers at HGTV aren't doing a lot of episodes where first-time buyers purchase starter mansions.

When the bell rings for a fourth time, I send Mac out to oil the doggy door. I'm a lot better in confrontational situations, since I'm not so quick to escalate.

Although, really, odds are good that someone's going to bring us a damn casserole soon and that we're finished with all the Negative Nellies. We've already been yelled at by neighbors on either side and across the street. Surely there can't be anyone left in our immediate proximity who has reason to dislike us without even having met us.

You know what?

There are a lot of angry people in this neighborhood.

My shoulders are killing me. Between yanking open the heavy front door and tensing up when strangers yell at me, I'm in desperate need of a massage.

By the time the bell rings for the fourteenth casserole-free time, I'm spoiling for a fight. I'm tired of being told that my driveway needs to be power-washed, that I'm remiss in planting my purple ornamental cabbage to show support for the high school's baseball team, that I put my recycling in the wrong kind of bin, and that the moving van needs to be repositioned because it's causing "an uncomfortable glare while I'm trying to watch *Wheel of Fortune*."

How is everyone around here so mean? These people live in amazing houses on the most beautiful street in the coolest town and yet no one's happy? How does that work? At this point I don't blame this home's caretakers for not keeping it in better shape; there's no pleasing anyone around here, so why bother?

Despite the pain radiating up my shoulder, I whip open the door with all my might. "What now?" I bark into the shocked face of Liz, our Realtor.

"Is this a bad time?" she asks, then tentatively offers me an enormous basket filled with lots of wine and cheese and serving accessories.

I apologize profusely, call Mac, and crack open one of the bottles of pinot.[88] We move to the couch, where we give her a rundown of our afternoon.

"I don't get it," I cry. "Everyone seemed really nice up here when we were looking at houses. What went wrong?"

"Why don't we have any casseroles?" Mac adds.

"I don't really know what that means, Mac," she replies. "But I'm afraid what you're saying makes sense. After the closing I ran into the trust's attorney at Starbucks. I found out that if the trust wasn't able to sell this place by April first, there was a plan to turn the property over to the community."

"Turn over? I'm sorry. I'm lost," I tell her.

Liz sighs and takes a small sip of her wine. "Meaning that this property was going to be torn down and made into open lands. Basically, your house was earmarked for a nature preserve that the neighbors would be able to access, and now that you're here, they won't get it."

Mac leans forward and sets his glass on the coffee table. I'm so relieved about finally having furniture that I don't even dive for a coaster. "We were in a bidding war! If we didn't buy this place,

---

88 Not necessarily in that order.

someone else was going to. The neighbors wouldn't have gotten their park regardless."

A pained expression flashes across Liz's face. When we asked Liz to represent us, she balked, insisting she wasn't that familiar with the Abington Cambs market and that having the inside scoop could be crucial. But we insisted harder, and now . . . here we are.

"So what you're saying," Mac continues, "is that we're already in the proverbial doghouse with these neighbors. They're predisposed to dislike us." Then he slumps back onto the couch, mourning the loss of casseroles in perpetuity.

"Unfortunately, that's about the size of it. I can't tell you how sorry I am. I should have turned you over to a local Realtor and—"

I'm not accepting this brand of defeatism. "Stop right there. You did a great job, because we're here, aren't we? Maybe we'll have to try a little harder to win over the neighbors, but I'm sure we can, because, need I remind you, *we were destined to live here.* I mean, if the Jablonskis could get over Babcia rewashing everything on their clothesline[89] and the Pasquesis forgave her for annexing their yard for her vegetable garden,[90] then we can rally. All we did was buy our dream house, and all they need to do is get to know us."

Liz smiles at me. "I admire your determination."

"Or your delusion," Mac adds.

"Everything's going to be fine. We just need to give it a little time. Trust me."

---

89   She found their whites to be too "dirt filthy."

90   Babcia claimed, "God tell give Babcia. You no like? You tell God; I send you see Him."

After we finish our visit, I walk Liz to her car, hugging her briefly before she leaves. "Thank you for everything, and we'll see you soon."

When I close the front door, a blinding flash of pain travels up to my neck and the knob comes off in my hand.

This had better not be a sign.

Chapter Nine
FALLING THROUGH THE EARTH (OF SORTS)

"Love what you've done with the place."

Tracey and I are standing in my front hallway. The area that had once been dated and dingy is now—hmm, what is the proper designer term for it?—ah, yes, a frigging war zone.

The Dumpster we requested a week ago hasn't yet arrived, so Mac thoughtfully placed every piece of broken vanity top, each shattered tile, and four metric tons of drywall in the foyer beside the front door. He argued that the neighbors would have our heads if we placed the refuse outside without a bin, and I'm inclined to agree with him. We've already been on the receiving end of three different neighborhood petitions regarding our trees, our dogs, and our ability to accessorize.[91]

---

91 I might be phrasing this wrong, but my point is, should neighbors really have a say over what kind of mailbox I choose?

"You like it?" I ask.

"Oh, yes," Tracey dryly asserts. "Very fetching and postmodern. Reminiscent of Bosnia. Or Herzegovina. The broken tile has the insouciance of a land mine, while the plaster hunks scream 'ethnic cleansing.' I believe you'd describe this whole look as 'bank.'"

All I can do is nod.

"Really, Mia—might I ask what you were possibly thinking?"

I explain, "Mac has a ton of vacation time. He's been with his company since graduation, so the amount of time off he gets is ridiculous. He's taken the whole month of May off, and he has tons more days accrued after that, too. Anyway, he decided that since we're not going to be traveling—"

"As you've invested all your money in this house," Tracey offers.

"That, and because I have a book due, we're not going on vacation, so Mac was trying to figure out what to do with his time. Point? After spending a weekend watching Genevieve Gorder make over outdated baths, he decided he was ready to start renovating, and he's been ripping out fixtures ever since."

"Clearly this"—Tracey makes a broad sweeping motion over the shoulder-high piles—"came from more than one place. What happened to your plan to take your time and finish one room before moving on to the next?"

I exhale deeply, and my breath sends little plumes of construction powder into the air. Somehow when Mac explained things, ripping out all the upstairs bathrooms made sense, but now I'm not so sure. "I suspect he may have gotten carried away." While we're standing there, the core of Mount Drywall destabilizes, followed by a minor avalanche that spills across Tracey's Pumas.

She shakes her foot, creating swirling eddies of dust motes. "You think?"

Before I can come up with a snappy retort, there's another knock at the door. I wipe away the grime coating the side window and see a familiar dark head. "Hey, Kara! Welcome! How was your visit with your folks?"

Kara plows into the house so quickly that she churns up all the dust and she's suddenly nothing but a blur of bangle bracelets and bouncy hair. "You mean other than the four hundred and twenty-seven conversations we had about my being in my thirties and not yet married? Great! Just great," Kara responds through gritted teeth.

"Did you finally come clean?" Tracey inquires. Kara's folks are so old-school that she's terrified to admit to them that she's the Kara behind the wildly successful relationship column. Of course, they don't call her Kara. They refuse to acknowledge anything but her given name—Karunamayee, which means "full of pity for others."

Seriously, how perfect is that?

It's like she was *predestined* to give advice for a living.

Kara shakes bits of drywall out of her hair and her bracelets jangle with all the movement. "Not even a little bit. Ironically, my column ran today, and it was racier than usual because I answered a question on threesome etiquette."

"There's *etiquette* involved?" Wow, sometimes I wonder if I really am Amish.

Kara regards me quizzically. "Of course—there's etiquette involved in any social situation, and what's more social than a three-way?" Kara then notices I'm blushing all the way to the tips of my ears, so she doesn't really elaborate. "The long and short of it is, share and share alike. Anyway, while we're sitting there having tea after breakfast, both my parents went on and on about the shame that *other* Kara must heap on her family, and I wanted to fall through the floor and die."

"Sounds like you need a drink," I declare.

Kara blithely steps over the piles of rubble, and both girls follow me to the kitchen. "Have you got anything that isn't pink or sugary?"

I ponder the contents of our fridge for a second. "Of course. Wine okay?"

Tracey chimes in, "Is it sugary pink wine?"

"No."[92]

"Something stronger?" Kara pleads. "I may have trouble washing away the thirty-four years of shame and disappointment I've heaped on the Patel name with sauvignon blanc."

"Oh, honey, I'm so sorry." I give her a reassuring hug before I root through the liquor cabinet. "Most everything's downstairs in the bar, but Mac may have some sipping whiskey up here." I locate a bottle of Elmer T. Lee bourbon and set it on the grit-covered countertop,[93] and before I can even reach for a glass, Kara downs a shot straight from the bottle.

"You poor kid," Tracey sympathizes. "That is so not *bank*."

You know what? I'm willing to admit "bank" doesn't work as an expression.[94]

---

92 *Yes.* And what's wrong with rosé? It's delicious!

93 Yes, Ann Marie was right about the "five-pound bag of flour" business, damn it.

94 Oh, *Mean Girls* Gretchen, I feel your pain.

Drinks prepared, we make our way to my library/office, part-ing the thick sheets of dust-repelling plastic as we enter. This is the one clean, organized room in the whole house. Because of the majestic paneling, we didn't need to cover up any horrible eight-ies peach paint or vertigo-inducing wallpaper.

A word about the wallpaper, if I may?

I realize I've previously ranted about how home buyers on HGTV always seem daunted by the littlest bits of wallpaper. In the scheme of things, wallpaper simply isn't that big a deal. I mean, it's paper. Anything made out of paper can't be inherently so chal-lenging, right? And yet now I'm forced to admit that wallpaper can be so aggressively awful as to cause actual distress.

Take my living room, for example. My walls are covered with yards and yards of paper you wouldn't believe if you saw. Picture a whole bunch of monkeys sitting around on large swirls of paisley perpetrating hate crimes against a group of Asian men who are just hanging out, minding their own business by playing their lutes and dancing their jigs. In alternating scenes, lions climb bamboo trees, tigers run away from monkey-tossed spears, and jaguars poise, ready to launch an attack on the pesky monkeys who started everything. The whole scene is about five seconds away from im-minent bloodshed.

The kitchen walls are plastered with paper featuring dogs dancing with clowns in what appears to be a Venetian circus. The dining room boasts large multicolored pheasants on a mustard yel-low background sunning themselves in what must be a nuclear-waste-rife raspberry patch, as each of the berries is three times the size of the birds' heads.

One of the powder rooms has walls covered in pink and fuchsia checks bordered with repeating scenes of Chinese men who are either working in a rice paddy or washing their socks.[95]

Or how about the loft on the third floor? The room spans the length of the house, although the ceiling follows the roofline, so it begins to angle at shoulder height. What would make this room less oppressive? I know! Eight thousand square yards of pastel blue and white Boats of Many Sizes alternating up and down the walls in the maritime version of my nightmares. Or what about the bedroom made up primarily of Chinese men whipping yaks and feeding chickens?

Funnily enough, the horrible wallpaper was the only stuff Ann Marie did like about this house. She says this style is called "chinoiserie" and that it's very happening with the senior set in Florida. Yeah, well, so is Super Poligrip, but I'm not about to smear denture cream on my walls, either.

Anyway, I love coming into the library because I can avoid the "noise" of the many, many wallpapered rooms. I spent an entire day lemon-oiling the wood walls and ceiling and now they're as glossy and shiny as the steering wheel in Mac's car. Beautiful!

After I accomplished that project, I felt divinely inspired, and I tore through my latest chapter. This room is kind of my sanctuary, as no matter what Mac's ripping down in the house, I can come in here and work in peace. And that's a real relief, considering how behind I am on this manuscript.

We bring our cocktails to the sitting area over in the corner. As Duckie and Daisy love Kara more than almost anyone, they immediately dog-pile on her. Due to their size, breeds, and thor-

---

95 I can't quite tell.

ough distaste for being groomed, she's one of their few fans. Kara welcomes their sloppy kisses and has to peek around wagging tails and nuzzling snouts to continue her story. "I wouldn't have even gone to their house, but I had to borrow a car while mine's in the shop. I swear, if that thing gets any older or more decrepit—"

"Then I'd date it!" Tracey insists as Kara and I both blink in amazement. "What, I can't acknowledge I like old men, too?"

"It's decidedly less funny if you own it," I admit.

"She's right," Kara agrees. "Sorry, Trace. Anyway, I need to get a new car, because asking them for help only serves to highlight how I *can't possibly function* without a husband." Before Tracey and I can jump in to protest, she continues, "No, no, I'm aware I function just fine on my own. Great, actually. I couldn't be happier most of the time. But convincing Dr. and Dr. Patel I'm capable is an entirely different story."

"Would they have given you this much shit if you'd gone to med school instead of J school?" Tracey and Kara met as grad students in the Medill School of Journalism at Northwestern in the nineties.

Kara mulls over my question before answering. "Probably."

Before we can pursue this line of conversation, we hear a loud banging upstairs, followed by what sounds like two bears wrestling, capped off with an enormous thump.

"Do I want to ask?" Tracey points to where my fantastic flea-market-find crystal chandelier sways dangerously above us.

"Mac has proclaimed today New Toilet Day! Which will be nice, because I'm tired of coming downstairs every time I have to take a leak. Do you realize that out of seven bathrooms, we're presently down to three?" I grouse. And then I feel a weird stab of guilt at bitching about being down to three bathrooms when I grew up in a house with five people and one full bath.

"Everything will be totally worth it when you're done." Funny, but the second Kara stops dwelling on her parents, she returns to her usual upbeat self. "That reminds me: I've got some recipes for Mac. He mentioned on Facebook that he wanted to learn to make palak paneer and lamb curry." She pulls a couple of cards out of her bag and I dive on them like I'm protecting the room from a live grenade.

"Jesus, God, no!" I exclaim. "No, no, no! Before that man even thinks about making Indian food, we need all seven toilets operational. All of them. Trust me on this. I'll just hang on to these," I say, stuffing the cards into my well-worn copy of *Shopaholic Takes Manhattan*. "He'll never look in here."

We hear more crunching and cracking above us. "Everything okay up there? Do you need me to call the plumber yet?" I worry that plumbing isn't a place to economize in our renovation process, but Mac swears he has the situation under control.

"Negative!" he calls back.

Okay, then.

"You hear any more from Vienna?" Kara asks. "Last I saw on Perez Hilton's site, she was swearing revenge."

I brush off the notion of impending doom. "Revenge for what? For dropping a thousand f-bombs at me on camera? For throwing a shoe at my mover? What did I do except pay my rent on time and put up with a lot of foolishness?"

I don't mention that all the contrarian teenagers who hate Vienna and her impact on pop culture now look at me as kind of a folk hero. They've been snapping up my entire backlist, so how is that not win-win?

Kara leans forward in her seat. "Mia, she's not rational. Never has been. You don't understand—I grew up around here, and that girl has a long reputation of being vicious. In high school, my younger sister Alex[96] made the mistake of saying hi to Vienna's boyfriend, and the next day she was kicked off poms because of some risqué Myspace photos. The pictures were obviously Photoshopped, but my parents were so mortified by the whiff of scandal that they refused to fight for my sister's spot on the squad."

"You sure that was Vienna's doing?" I ask.

"Yep. The work was quality, meaning Vienna paid someone to do it, but the body was Angelina Jolie's in *Tomb Raider*, meaning absolutely no thought went into it. Also? Vienna bragged about it."

I shrug. "Yeah, that sucks for Alex, but you're not convincing me. What's Vienna going to do, withhold my security deposit? Too late! I already got a check! Although I suspect someone who works for her sent it, as the 'i' in her signature was missing its trademark heart."

"You need to check the gossip sites more often, Kara," Tracey admonishes. "Vienna took off for the ashram in *Eat, Pray, Love* a week ago. She was quoted as saying she 'wants to be more spiritual and shit.' Deep thinker, that one. I read that she and fifteen of her closest friends flew there on her dad's custom-built Global Express XRS."

"Because nothing gets you down the path to enlightenment faster than a forty-million-dollar private jet." Kara giggles.

---

96 Alaknanda, which means "flawless."

Somewhere above us we hear an enormous crash, followed by a *TMZ*-worthy string of profanity, followed by . . . silence. "No, really!" I shout at the ceiling. "I can call a plumber anytime you'd like."

Mac's response is muffled but audible. "Still fine. Not to worry."

Ten minutes later, we're onto the topic of Tracey's recent breakup. She says they had "irreconcilable differences," which we've interpreted as "an expired Viagra prescription." We're teasing Tracey about cruising senior centers for dates when we hear the first groan.

"Was that Daisy?" Tracey asks. Fair question. Were farting an Olympic sport, Daisy would easily medal.

"Ha," I snicker. "If Daisy tooted, there'd be no confusion about it. You'd know." Because pit bulls have shorter, wider snouts, they take in more air when they eat. And because Daisy's plump as a pork roast, she eats an awful lot. You see where I'm going with this? Mac always says the Department of Defense could weaponize what comes out of her.

We resume our conversation, and thirty seconds later, we hear another groan, this time longer in duration and a bit more urgent. "What *is* that?" Kara asks.

"Eh, it's an old house. Old houses make noise," I reply. The main part of our home was built in 1891. I love living somewhere with a real history about it.

"So, anyway, Tracey, I'm writing about May–December affairs, and my readers want to know"—*groan*—"if there's snow on the roof"—*GROOOOAN*—"does that mean there's frost on the—" But before Kara can complete her thought, the groaning noise grows exponentially louder and is immediately followed by the sound of a thousand wood fibers snapping.

After that, and almost as if in slow motion, we witness my prized polished paneling begin to bow before completely giving way.

The chandelier is the first casualty. It comes down slowly, serenely, almost lyrically, with each individual crystal creating its own bit of music before swinging toward the bay window and smashing into a veritable Kristallnacht in the side yard.

Fortunately, we're all sitting opposite from the fulcrum of broken paneling, and other than the window, there are no additional victims.

According to the entry about gravity on Wikipedia: *Under an assumption of constant gravity, Newton's law of universal gravitation simplifies to $F = mg$, where m is the mass of the body and g is a constant vector with an average magnitude of 9.81 m/s^2. The acceleration due to gravity is equal to this g. An initially stationary object which is allowed to fall freely under gravity drops a distance which is proportional to the square of the elapsed time,* which is really just a fancy way of saying that pastel pink toilets fall from a hole in the ceiling pretty fucking hard.

"You guys?" I shriek. "Kara, Tracey, talk to me." There's so much dust I can barely see either of them. They both answer affirmatively, and a massive feeling of relief rushes through me.

Fortunately, the dogs are also fine, because they both raced out of the room after the first few groans. Funny, but animals can always sense impending danger.

Or in this case, impending stupidity.

In unison, we look up at the massive hole in the ceiling about the same time Mac peers down. "You okay down there? Oh, hey,

Tracey, Kara, didn't know you were here." We're all speechless, gawping back at him in stunned silence. "I think I dropped the toilet," Mac adds helpfully.

"No shit," I reply.[97] I survey the wreckage in my office. Aside from the gaping hole in the ceiling and the bashed window, the toilet has taken out my desk, my computer, my monitor, my chair, and has smashed into enough pieces to make Humpty Dumpty, all the king's horses, and all the king's men look like a bunch of rank amateurs.

"I guess I needed a plumber after all. Possibly a carpenter, too," Mac admits sheepishly, causing a whole bunch of blood vessels in my brain to spontaneously burst.

"Hey, Mia?" Kara prods me gently. "Looks like the bourbon survived."

And then we drink.

And then we barf in the three remaining toilets.

"It could have happened to anyone," Mac reasons.

"Is that right?" I snap. "Because I watch even more HGTV fix-up shows than you, and some of those homeowners are beyond dumb, like they don't understand the concept of not touching live wires or wet paint. Yet I've never once seen a single toilet fall through their ceilings, let alone *two*."

After Toiletgate, the girls and I spent the whole night cleaning up the library . . . and swilling bourbon.[98] Shards of potty flew into

---

97 Pun not intended this time.

98 With enough maraschino cherries in it, it's not bad.

every corner of the room—under couches, behind books on the shelves, in the fireplace, etc. After we'd finally retrieved all the pieces that could pierce tender paw pads and bare feet, we hauled my trashed desk and computer equipment into the hallway, thus completely blocking the entrance to the dining room.

What makes me angriest is that I hadn't run a backup since I added all that material to the new book, so those pages are gone. Since I'm so freaking furious, I can't really concentrate enough to recall what I wrote, either.

Fortunately, I still had the board-up company's information, so getting the window covered was easy. Untangling the chandelier from the sticker bushes was less so, and my arms appear to have gone three rounds with a Mixmaster. Naturally, both processes inspired new neighborhood petitions. Oh, what's that you say, Lululemon, Citizen Cane, and Elbow Patches? You're bothered by the boarded window? Join the fucking club.

We cordoned off the bathroom with the open floor and booked a handyman, although he can't be here until late next week, as apparently everyone in the Cambs is doing renovations.

Mac and I reached an uneasy truce, because I desperately hate being mad at anyone, particularly the person who's most important to me in the whole world. Mac was unbelievably contrite and helped me piece together a rudimentary work space until my new furniture arrives. So instead of tapping away on my desktop with the thirty-inch UltraSharp monitor while reclining in a posture-fit, multiadjustable Aeron chair, I've been parked in an ass-flattening metal folding chair, squinting at an old laptop that's sitting on top of a door supported by moving boxes on either side. The only way I've consoled myself is that the whole setup feels vaguely Amish.

All of that being said, one would think Mac might hang up his tool belt, but no. Then while I was out today, Mac decided to try to replace another toilet. He said he wanted to surprise me.

When I came home to find a second toilet shattered on the floor of the opposite end of the library—this time powder blue— trust me, I was surprised.

The weather's warming up and the house is stuffy and full of the stench of failure, so I'm going around opening windows. This will give me something to do with my hands, considering they seem to want to wrap themselves around Mac's neck at the moment.

Mac is right on my heels. "I said I'm sorry. I really thought I had it right this time, but toilets are a lot heavier than you'd think, especially the older ones."

I can't even look at him, because I'm afraid I'll lose my temper. "Uh-huh."

He continues. "I mean, I did all kinds of research on the Internet, and I referenced a couple of plumbing manuals, and other than dropping it, I did everything right. I blame the floors. I suspect they can't handle a live load."

"Mmm," I intone through closed lips.

"Listen, you can't be mad at me. I was just trying to help, and theoretically, everything should have worked."

We're in the living room now and I'm trying to get the big window open, although it appears to be a bit stuck. "Here's the thing, Mac. Your problem is that you're too theoretical."

"How so?"

I throw my weight into opening the window and it only budges a few inches. Argh. "Meaning you've spent your whole career designing computer networks but—Jesus, what's up with this window?—but I bet you'd be hard-pressed to actually build one yourself. Same thing with the plumbing. You absolutely understand the theory behind putting in a new toilet— Argh. Come on!" I step back, inspect my progress, and then throw my shoulder into getting it lifted.

I continue. "You have a profound understanding of the macro level of everything—networks, plumbing, weaponry, et cetera. But on the micro level, you're lacking. I suspect you don't even know what it is you don't know. There was probably a small installation facet you missed—*Damn. It. Open. Please.*—and that one tiny microdetail is probably the difference between my happily reading *Us* magazine on the john and having the commodes rain down in my office."

I begin to slam my whole side into the window while hoisting it up. "Want some help?" he offers.

"I've got it, thank you. You're like those guys who—*stuck hard, argh*—are so convinced they know where they're going—*oof*—that they refuse to ask for directions and—" I give the window one more tremendous shove and I'm suddenly enveloped by a warm spring breeze.

The window is open.

And by "open," I mean "lying in the sticker bushes outside."

I've somehow managed to knock the entire window out of its frame and onto the ground.

"Oh, my God, Mac! Help me! Shit! What did I do? Mac, can you help me get this damn thing back in?"

Mac moseys over to inspect the damage. "Well . . . theoretically, I understand why the window fell out, but in practice, I may simply not know what I'm doing. You see, on a macro level I have an idea of where you went wrong, but on a micro level . . ."

When we try to reinstall the window, it basically shatters into a million little pieces.

You know what? I can't take this.

I'm calling Babcia.

Chapter Ten
MUCH ADO ABOUT DRAWER PULLS

"You've got six weeks."

"I need more like three months."

"You've got six weeks."

I'm on the phone with my literary agent, Natalie, and we're discussing my deadline for *Rumspringa-ding-ding*. I'm critically behind schedule because I sold the book before I actually wrote it.[99] The manuscript is due in two weeks, but Nat was able to push that due date back till the end of June. Normally it takes me six to eight months to complete a novel, and at this point in the process, I should be finished writing. This is when I'm usually scrubbing the manuscript for errors and word choice.

---

99 Sounds crazy, but that's how publishing works sometimes.

Unfortunately, I've been somewhat distracted for the past few months, and most of what I've written is . . . craptacular. According to my niece Claire, I'm way off on my content. She tells me teenage girls don't spend much of their free time discussing drawer pulls, and by "much," she means "any." But my God, have you *been* to a custom cabinetry showroom lately? Not only does every choice come in a minimum of nine different metal finishes, like polished nickel, polished chrome, satin nickel, satin chrome, oil-rubbed bronze, antique bronze, pewter, wrought iron, and stainless steel, but they're also available in tons of other material, like art glass and granite and porcelain.

And shapes? Can we talk about shapes for a minute? There are bail pulls and cup pulls and bar pulls and finger pulls and pendant pulls! How about knobs? Don't even get me started on knobs! What's your poison? A square knob? A T-knob? Maybe a nice oval knob?

And all of that's before you even come close to making a decision on the cabinet itself. Do you want them stained? Glazed? Painted? Would you like an arched cabinet? A raised-panel cabinet? Beveled? Unbeveled? Oak? Maple? Rubberwood? Laminate? Stock? Semicustom? Custom? Framed? Unframed? *Argh!*

I told Claire that high school is easy; interior design is hard. I argued that kids should start plotting out their dream kitchens now, so they know what they want by the time they turn thirty-five, ergo Miriam and Rebecca's fourteen-page countertop-finish manifesto.[100] Claire told me that my book was giving her "bore-

---

100 Miriam's a sucker for durable and decorative cement countertops, but Rebecca's more of a traditionalist in that she prefers granite with an onyx tile backsplash.

dom cancer," and that's when I knew I had to scrap everything and start fresh.

I put my head down on my desk/door and exhale heavily. "Okay, I'll do what I can."

Natalie's frustration is obvious. "Mia, what is going on? Blowing a deadline isn't like you. I don't have to tell you that if you don't get this book in soon, you're going to cut the whole prepublicity push short. Long-lead magazines won't receive review copies. You're essentially hobbling yourself if you don't get on this. . . ."

I inadvertently wince when Nat says "hobbling." All authors do. I mean, we've all read/seen Stephen King's *Misery*, and we all remember when Annie Wilkes hobbled Paul Sheldon to keep him prisoner. Freaking terrifying. Every time I log on to my Facebook fan page and see someone calling herself my "number one fan," I feel around my desk to make sure my gun's still there.[101]

". . . so I want you to put aside whatever you're going through and concentrate, because, P.S., you don't get paid until you're done."

I'm too wiped out to tell her that Mac and I spent the past three days hauling wheelbarrows full of debris down our tenth-of-a-mile curved driveway because the Dumpster people left it in the wrong place. Nat doesn't want to discuss the kitchen cabinet that fell out of the wall, taking out the dishwasher and damaging the oven; nor is she interested in my frenetic rush to prepare for Babcia's visit.

All Nat wants to hear is that I'm on it.

"I'm on it," I lie.

"Good. Now, while I've got you on the phone, I have some

---

101   Fortunately it was still in its case when the toilet hobbled my desk.

interesting news. I got a call from a scout at HBO. The guy's a producer and his kid made him read your books. Sounds like he's interested in pursuing an option."

A healthy option check would go a long way toward easing my mind right now. With all the mishaps, things are getting too tight for comfort. Mac's set the deductible on our homeowner's insurance so high that all the repair costs are coming directly out of pocket. In his defense, a lower monthly payment sounded smart; he couldn't have foreseen it raining toilets in my office. Prevented it? Yes. Foreseen it? No.

So, the out-of-pocket expenses, plus what we've budgeted for a full kitchen rehab, plus replacing all the bathroom fixtures, plus all the petition-based repairs we've made, have gone through a huge chunk of our cushion. I mean, we've already spent a mint just because of the mailbox.

That damn mailbox has become the bane of my existence. When we moved in, the mailbox was housed in a big, crumbling brick-and-mortar pillar. The masonry seemed too far gone to try to repair, so Mac and I spent days swinging sledgehammers to bring it down, learning the hard way that "looks crumbling" doesn't mean "is crumbling."

The whole time we slaved away out there, Lululemon and Elbow Patches kept walking by us really slowly. After a while, we stopped even trying to say hello.

I found the most beautiful mailbox on eBay. It's a tall, red iron box with separate slots for mail and newspapers. According to the auction listing, it's an antique from India. If you squint at it just right, you might think it's an overgrown fire hydrant. I love it and it's unique and I actually spent a good deal of money on it. I thought it would really personalize the front yard—I mean, who doesn't like objets d'art from exotic locales? This is the first piece of art I ever bought, and I assumed it would be a nice gesture to share with the rest of the neighborhood.

I assumed wrong.

So very wrong.

First came the petition, which we chose to ignore, as it was signed by three families with enormous bass fish–shaped mailboxes, one with what looks like a birdhouse with a mail slot, and four with varying degrees of crumbled masonry posts. The only difference between my mailbox and theirs was that mine was beautiful. (Also, I didn't plant the ornamental purple cabbage around mine because I thought it clashed with the red.)

After we ignored the petition, our neighbors took additional action and we started getting letters from the city telling us our mailbox didn't "meet code." There's a mailbox code up here? Really? And who has the kind of time to go out and inspect mailboxes, anyway?

After receiving multiple fines for violating city ordinances, we've since taken down our beautiful Indian mailbox, which was no easy feat due to our having sunk it in cement. From the get-go, we've invested two thousand dollars in materials and fines, countless man-hours' worth of labor, and now we have to go to the post office to collect our mail, since the letter carrier won't deliver to our house, as we have no box. *Argh.*

Anyway, in terms of finances, there's always credit and a second mortgage, but I don't want to go that route.

"Does this indicate a possible bidding war between Persiflage and HBO?" *Oh, please, oh, please, oh, please.*

"That's my hope, anyway. But I want you to get back to work and I'll worry about Hollywood. Deal?"

"Deal." My voice belies a confidence I do not feel.

"Mia, one more thing? I don't want to impede your creative process, and I understand that in sci-fi/fantasy there's the obvious need to suspend disbelief, but I'm really having a hard time buying that teenage zombies in love have so much to say about wallpaper. Get it together; get it done. Talk soon!"

Natalie sounds harsh, but she's my agent, not my bestie. Her job is to make sure I'm delivering contracted work, not only on time, but of a certain caliber. She's actually being a good friend by being tough on me, and I'm always the one who says fifteen percent of nothing is nothing.

I need her to kick me in the ass.

I need to get my head on straight and write this book.

I need to finish on time.

I need to get paid.

But first, I need to address this drawer-pull situation.

And find a new mailbox.

"I bet she'd be more comfortable at a hotel. Matter of fact, I'm sure of it."

I keep my eyes on the piece of floor where I'm removing carpet tacks, saying nothing.

"Yes, yes," Mac continues, gathering steam. "A hotel sounds great. Perfect, in fact. I read about a boutique hotel in *Meridian Road* magazine and it's in downtown AC. Stag's Leap Inn. Won the Brides' Choice Award in 2010."

"They must be really proud of themselves," I note mildly.

"The inn's part of the National Trust for Historic Preservation. Their dining room's listed in the Distinguished Restaurants of North America guide."

"Fancy," I acquiesce, giving a particularly rusty spike a good, hard yank with my pliers. It finally releases and I stagger backward with the force of its removal.

Mac paces behind me as I work. "The amenities are top-notch: high-thread-count sheets, a flat-panel television in both rooms for suites *and* in the bathroom, plus L'Occitane products, a gourmet minibar, and your daily choice of three newspapers."

"Neat."

As soon as I'm finished removing all the carpet tacks/nails/other protrusions, we can start smoothing out the hardwood. I've got a little belt sander for the edges and the detail work, while Mac's responsible for running the rented orbital sander across the floors in the rest of this bedroom. We've already torn up the carpet[102] and ripped out the padding. Judging from the stains on both, someone here had dogs, many, many large, incontinent dogs.

"Their fitness room is state-of-the-art, and they do five kinds of massage in the spa."

"I was unaware five kinds of massage existed." My bangs keep falling in my face and I keep brushing them aside. I'm overdue for a haircut, but I kind of don't want to spend the money.

"They do and they have them. Full beauty salon, too, plus a twenty-four-hour concierge service."

I swat at those annoying stray strands again. "Interesting. So, are they paying you a commission?"

---

102 Fictional Jake Ryan family, what were you thinking when you installed mauve shag?

Before we can begin to sand, I have to hang wet bedsheets over the doorways. According to eHow.com, floor sanding creates a massive amount of sawdust. Since this house is already reminiscent of the Dust Bowl, circa 1930, I'm anxious to keep additional emissions to a minimum. I've got the windows open and I've turned off the air-conditioning so the grit has no possible way of circulating through the house.

"Of course not," he protests. "I'm just saying the place sounds very luxurious. Every night there's a free wine-and-cheese reception from five to seven. Babcia loves free stuff."

"True enough."

Babcia does love free stuff, although "free" is somewhat subjective. Babcia interprets it to mean every sugar, Splenda, and Sweet'n Low packet she runs across, the sugar bowl, the entire contents of the breadbasket plus the butter and a means with which to spread it, salt and pepper shakers—particularly the crystal ones—candleholders, candles, bud vases including the buds, guest soap, shoehorns, bath mats, towels, wineglasses, ashtrays, ice buckets, throw rugs, throw pillows, trash cans, the thick terry slippers you find in better hotels, the thick terry robes you find in better hotels, and any piece of artwork not bolted to the wall.

If Babcia stayed somewhere with a wine-and-cheese reception, she'd line her enormous satchel with foil and walk away with an entire platter and as many bottles as she could shove in her waistband.[103]

Admonishing Babcia about her sticky fingers is useless. I guess

---

103 Remind me to tell you about the Great 2007 Residence Inn by Marriott Free Breakfast Bar Massacre sometime.

once you live through childhood poverty, no matter how much money you have, you never forget the old days.

"Well, what do you think?" Mac's all forced smiles and anticipation.

"I think I'm going to need a tetanus shot after this." I squeeze my index finger to drain my puncture wound before wiping it on the edge of my T-shirt. Mac was supposed to help me with this part, but he says his fingers "aren't grippy enough."

"No, what do you think about Babcia staying in a hotel instead of with us?"

When my hair's fixed, I reply, "What I think is you need to not be terrified by an old lady. What do you expect to happen? Granted, she's a bit of an acquired taste, but she can't hurt you. You're safe as kittens around her."

Mac crosses his arms and levels his gaze. "Sal Domenico."

Ooh, kind of forgot about him. Sal Domenico lives in Babcia's building in Miami, and he's got that mob-boss-type slicked-back hair and wears fat gold chains and, um . . . may or may not walk with a limp now. "I suggest you don't take her parking space."

"Mrs. Irving Zielinski."

"Made the critical error of trying to cheat at Makao.[104] They were playing for quarters; what did you expect? Mrs. Z. is lucky Babcia didn't go more biblical on her and *actually* remove her hand."

"Frank Barnes?"

"Fluke. And probably faulty brakes."

"Bobby Chesney?"

---

104 A Polish version of Crazy Eights.

"Not a fluke, but also not unwarranted. Bet he never institutes a special assessment without condo board approval again."

"Roger Esparza, Wanda Shapiro, Ethel Wicker, and Samuel L. Jackson?"

"Mistake, mistake, accident, and should have never remade *Shaft*."

"I'm saying she's a lot more dangerous than you give her credit for and—"

" 'Shut yo' mouth!' " I sing.

"I'm serious, Mia. Babcia is scary and—"

I set down my pliers. "And she's my grandmother and she practically raised me. She's not perfect—some may say she's a complicated (wo)man—but I'm not shuttling her off to some motel. Can you dig it?"

"Hotel! It's a hotel! Award-winning!"

Patiently I explain, "Honey, people have said that same kind of stuff about you to me. If I'd have listened to Ann Marie's friend when she went on about what a jerk you were, we'd never be here now. What you have to do is look past Babcia's"—*do not say "history of violence," do not say "history of violence"*—"um, *tough exterior* and see her sweet center and huge heart. She has so many of the good qualities I see in you. How come you refuse to look for them in her?"

"But—"

"Honey," I say gently, "there is no 'but.' Babcia's coming next month, and all I ask is that we have one room done when she gets here. I realize it sounds like a lot of detailed work, but once we're finished, it will be perfect."

To prepare for Babcia's visit we're completely rehabbing the master suite. Once the floors are sanded and stained (we're leaning toward pickled oak), we'll top them off with a couple of coats of polyurethane. Once we remove the wallpaper, Mac will install a wide border of crown molding on the ceiling, and we'll give all the windows and existing woodwork a fresh coat of white paint.

After the trim's cleaned up, we'll repaint the ceiling, install the ceiling fan, and coat the walls with Benjamin Moore's Haystack (#317), which the brochure describes as "a clean, pure yellow that reminds us of a sun-drenched day at the beach." The test sample we painted has the same opalescent, mellow golden glow as a glass of sauvignon blanc and will be amazing with the blue Persian rug I found at the Winnetka Church of Christ rummage sale last fall.

The plumber's coming at the end of the week to reinstall the toilet, and then we'll DIY a travertine tile floor, which entails doing a dry layout of all the tiles, applying thin-set mortar, setting, notching, and grouting. Mac claimed we could install electric warming cables, but after he blew all the circuits on the first floor trying to install a dimmer switch, I nixed the idea.

We bought a new vanity from the Restoration Hardware outlet store in Pleasant Prairie, and its Italian Carrara marble topper should tie in nicely with the shower's existing subway tile—or will once we power-wash the rust stains off the grout.

After all the construction's done, Mac will hang the new linen curtains and rods, and we'll put the brand-new Tempur-Pedic mattress down and make the bed with a pale blue toile duvet. As the final touch, I'll place fresh-cut flowers in a clay pitcher on my mixed-woods copper-lined dry-sink dresser.[105]

I feel like it's important we get this room tackled for a couple of reasons. From a psychological perspective, we really need to have one room that isn't either painfully dated or utterly deconstructed. If we can do that, we'll have a retreat where we can just relax and not have a million constant visual reminders about how much we have yet to do. We could use the confidence boost that'll come from having done it ourselves, too. Personally, I need to feel like we're heading toward a victory so I can put this damn house out of my head for a while and write my book.

And it might be nice to work as a team and not be mad at Mac.

Seems that Mac didn't pay attention when I explained why I was taping an enormous Mr. Yuck symbol over the air-conditioning controls.

Between the blowing fan and the air intake vents, the whole house looks like a sawdust-filled snow globe.

I am not happy.

Correction, I am industrial-strength not happy.

Here's a pro tip for the DIY crowd: Just because oil-based paint can go over latex-based paint does not mean the converse is true.

Seems like *someone* might have inquired about that at Home Depot before he grabbed a couple of buckets.

In completely unrelated news, if you need instructions on

---

105   Hard to picture, but trust me, it's FAB.

how to strip every last bit of paint off a bathroom wall before completely starting over, I'm your gal.

Apparently Mac didn't rent an orbital sander for seventy-five dollars.

Apparently Mac thought it would be more cost-effective to *buy* an orbital sander.

For five thousand dollars.

He says we have a thousand places we can use it. Yet all I can think about is where I'd like to stick it.

So far this project is not bringing us together like I'd hoped.

Chapter Eleven
THE BIG REVEAL

"To be perfectly candid, I had my doubts we'd make it. Big doubts. The last two weeks have been entirely miserable. I feel like everything that might have gone wrong did, from the splotchy floor stain to the grout that changed colors to the door that swelled up and trapped me inside after I painted it. Nightmare, total nightmare. What really gets me is, with all the tools Mac bought, we could have easily done the room professionally for that price. Twice. Three times. Maybe more.

"Mac's obsessed with having the right tools for the job. He says that's why the bathrooms went so sideways. He said he was trying to half-ass something that should have been whole-assed.[106] Hence the major cash outlay that's causing me so much distress."

---

106   His expression, not mine.

He doesn't respond, naturally, so I continue. "I hate that I've been getting mad at Mac, because he listens but I don't know that he hears me. For example, I've been going over our budget with him and he insists we're 'fine.' The problem is, his version of 'fine' is way different from mine. 'Fine' to me is six months of living expenses saved up, plus a rainy-day fund, plus a little something foldable in the safe in case the bubble goes up."

I pause, then nod. "Mac says the expression is actually 'in case the balloon goes up,' but that doesn't make any sense either. Neither balloons nor bubbles are inherently threatening. Anyway, Mac's much more fast and loose in terms of fiscal responsibility. He says I'm stressing out needlessly, particularly since we'll get plenty of cash once I finish my book. But I'm terrified of not having enough in the interim."

I take his silence as tacit encouragement. "Right, you're right. Mac's concept of money being completely different than mine doesn't make it wrong. I mean, he grew up solidly middle-class. His folks weren't wealthy, but they were definitely comfortable. He never had to watch his mom's face burn with shame in the grocery store as the cashier took away items to bring the total under twenty dollars. He never heard his folks screaming at each other all night long because they couldn't pay the electric bill. My parents still loved each other when they split up, but ultimately, their marriage failed because they couldn't come together on finances. Buying this house may be the first time I haven't been completely fiscally conservative, and even that was with my accountant's blessing."

I take a couple of big breaths to gather my thoughts before I continue. "Oh, no, please, I have no regrets about buying the place.

I mean, Mac's living his dream of doing renovations, and I don't have to tell you again how important it was to live in Jake Ryan's house. You don't mess with destiny. I know I'm being silly and self-indulgent. Forgive me; I've been inhaling a lot of paint fumes; I'm not quite myself."

I pause a minute to take in my surroundings. I still can't get over how gorgeous and serene it is here. "To me, I see that house like Jake saw Samantha. Sure, he had Caroline, who was perfection on the outside. Put her and Samantha side by side and there'd be no contest on who embodied more of the classical elements of beauty. Blond hair, blue eyes, killer body, blah, blah, blah. But ultimately, Caroline didn't respect Jake enough to prevent her friends from trashing the joint, whereas Sam was pure and good and kind enough to lend her panties to a geek. Jake saw that in her. Jake realized that he'd be a better man with Samantha in his life."

There's no sound save for a light breeze ruffling the leaves and the distant hum of a lawn mower. "I'm not saying the house is going to make me a better person. But I'm really happy we didn't pick a Caroline of a house, all perfect and move-in ready. Maybe getting a Samantha kind of house takes a little more effort up front, but will end up being the better purchase in the long run. I'm going to learn something with the effort, you know? I feel like there's a real value in viewing this house not as a teardown, but as a place that will absolutely come to life with enough nurturing and love. Or it's like the kids in *The Breakfast Club*. Once they got past misleading exteriors and discovered one another's true selves, everything changed."

Even though it's almost June, the stone bench beneath me is ice-cold. I shift a bit, relocating to the sunny spot. "Mac? He's at home right now. He wanted to finish off the room himself. He—this is actually very cute—he wanted me to have the experience of a 'big reveal,' like they always do with the homeowners on TV, so he sent me away this morning. I spent quite a bit of time in Starbucks and I knocked out two chapters! Felt so good to have the words flow. I wrote the sweetest thing about how Rebecca tried to bite off Mose's ear and he stopped her with a first kiss—and . . . You know what? Details don't matter, because the scene just works and that's a huge relief.

"What's he doing? Oh, he's moving furniture back in and replacing outlet covers and hanging curtains and stuff. Actually, he said to be home by three o'clock, so I'm taking off now." I get up and start to walk away. "Oh, my gosh, you're right; I almost forgot! These are for you, sir. They're pretty in pink this week, pun intended." I grab the big bunch of peonies from their spot on the edge of the bench and set them down in front of him.

"It's 'really human of you to listen to all my bullshit.' Ha, I know, I know: Don't quote you to you. But in all sincerity, you understand me. You always understood me. So thank you. I'll see you next week."

Mac's in the kitchen arranging champagne in a bucket when I get home. I ease myself over the downed cabinet and wedge past the boxes of our salvaged dinnerware to get to him.

"Ooh, festive!" I exclaim.

"They always have booze at the end of *Holmes on Homes*, so I wanted to make the big reveal official." Mac hands me a plastic tumbler of Veuve. We stopped using real plates and glasses when the cabinet fell and the dishwasher was crushed. The kitchen's our

next project, and I'm cautiously optimistic we can do it ourselves.[107] We have yet to decide on cabinets and pulls, but that's
neither here nor there, and I'm not letting it mar this celebration.

Mac glances up from pouring. "How was he today?"

I respond, "Quiet," and Mac laughs.

"I'd be concerned if he weren't."

I recently let Mac in on the secret of my weekly pilgrimage,
because it felt weird keeping something from him.

Ever since we moved to the Cambs, I've . . . Okay, this might
sound a little strange. . . . I've been bringing flowers to John
Hughes's grave. At first I just did the floral equivalent of a dine-
and-dash. I'd practically run to his resting spot, dump my bouquet,
murmur a quick word, and sprint back to my car. Any further dal-
liance felt disrespectful.

It's common knowledge that Hughes was an extraordinarily
private man. Were he alive, I'd never go up to him on the street or
interrupt his dinner or say or do anything that might make him
uncomfortable. He left Hollywood to return to Illinois, coming
back for a quiet, more anonymous life. Even if I'd been presented
a chance to introduce myself, I'd likely have not felt worthy
enough to take it.

I've been to Jim Morrison's grave at the Père-Lachaise Cemetery in Paris, and the site was total chaos, covered in every bit of
detritus you can imagine—flowers, candles, graffiti, liquor bottles—
empty and full, plus ladies' panties and . . . a used condom.[108]
Crowds of people lined up so they could make "metal hands"

---

107 Very cautiously. Oh, so cautiously.

108 You should have seen the look on Ann Marie's face when she spotted that.

while posing for pictures with his headstone, and we had to wait awhile to even get close. The whole scene felt less like a place of quiet reflection and solitude, and more like a concert tailgate party, with kids singing and playing guitars, smoking pot, and having drinks.

I realize fans were simply trying to pay tribute to the life of the Lizard King and the iconic music he created. From everything I've ever read, Morrison probably would have loved that almost forty years later, the celebration rages on in his honor. But does that mean he'd have been okay with strangers spray-painting his lyrics on his grave? To me, the mess felt blatantly disrespectful. If fans want to keep his memory alive, wouldn't they be better served by making sure that each new generation hears his songs and reads his poetry?

Since I was there in the nineties, I understand guards have been employed to patrol the area. Given Morrison's tumultuous history with authority figures, I wonder how he'd have felt about that.

John Hughes's resting place is the polar opposite. Anyone who's cared enough about Hughes's work to seek him out has had self-restraint not to leave a permanent reminder of his or her presence. The plot is small and unremarkable, tucked under the evergreens in a particularly quiet corner of the cemetery, away from the showy mausoleums and ornately carved headstones closer to the water. You'd never find it unless you knew where to look. No guides shuffle carts of tourists past, and no one's selling maps to get there. There's something profound and sacred about his final resting spot, and I find myself lingering longer and longer now.

I started talking to him on my third visit. The minute I finally allowed myself to say something more than, "Thank you," the words started spilling out. I couldn't help it. I told him all about how he inspired me, and how, if I could provide teenagers with an iota of the kind of solace he gave Jess and me growing up, I'd consider myself a success.

I talked about how I wouldn't have a career without him. Then I apologized if I sounded like I was sucking up, but I truly felt like he had just as much cultural influence as Jim Morrison did, and how I was really glad none of Hughes's fans left him Mardi Gras beads or cheesy stuffed animals.

Anyway, perhaps it's a product of my overactive imagination, but I swear I feel his spirit when I'm there, because I'm always buoyed and inspired after I leave. I bet it's not coincidental that I do my best writing after a visit.

Or maybe it's just that I'm so prone to keeping everything bottled up that I feel better once I let it all out.

When I saw *Sixteen Candles* for the first time, I wasn't even a teenager yet. I wonder how I'd have felt knowing that movie would have such an influence on my life and career almost thirty years later?

"Mia?"

I snap back to attention. "Oh, sorry. Zoned out for a second."

Mac gives me a glass and takes my hand to help me over the rubble. "Are you ready to see your Fabulous! New! Master! Suite!" he says in his best HGTV-host imitation.

"Yay! Yes!" The big reveal's always my favorite part.

You know why I love HGTV? It's not just that I get a peek into other people's lives. It's that everyone's always thrilled with the end result, whether they're redecorating an unfortunate room, selling a house, or cleaning up another contractor's mess. I live for a happy ending, and HGTV is perpetually upbeat and optimistic. The shows are all about problem solving, not drama creating.

I used to be a huge *Trading Spaces* fan in the early days, and I was always so upset when the homeowners weren't happy. Sometimes their disappointment was justified—like the time Doug painted a newly refinished hardwood floor white,[109] or Hildi stapled something like ten thousand silk flowers to a bathroom wall. Seriously, can you imagine what a disaster that must have been to live with, let alone try to remove? The staples probably began to oxidize after the first shower, and I'm loath to picture how much dust and moisture those flowers trapped.

What infuriated me was when the homeowners would throw a fit over perfectly lovely rooms. I hated how, even though their friends and the designers and carpenters spent two days slaving away in their house, they couldn't get past how they "hate brown!" or "that's not where we keep the coffee table!" Sometimes they'd get all pissed off about the show's using lower-priced materials, even though the whole point of *Trading Spaces* was to demonstrate how to make improvements on a budget. Mac always knew what I was watching when he'd hear me shout stuff like, "If you want Brazilian cherry and not MDF,[110] pay for it yourself!"

Anyway, it's reveal time here, and I am, in fact, ready to see my Fabulous! New! Master! Suite! "Did you want me to wear a blindfold?" I ask Mac.

"No, and if I did, I'd make sure we were up the stairs first."

109 After the past two weeks of sanding and staining purgatory, trust me when I say I'd make sure something very bad happened to him.

110 Multiple density fiberboard.

Oh. Good point. The dogs dart in and out between us, and we have to step over Mac's cache of paint and stain cans and around the wall o' tools to get to the doorway on the second floor. "Ready?"

"Ready!" I clamp my eyes shut while Mac swings open the door.

When I open I almost can't believe what I'm seeing. I mean, I've been here for every step of the process and I know the room intimately. Trust me: I've shed DNA in this space. That's the spot on the floor where the rusty nail punched right through my shoe and into my foot when I was sanding.[111] That's the wall where I lost most of my knuckle skin wrestling off cherub-covered wallpaper that had been affixed with what was clearly the kind of glue used to hold airplanes together. That's the closet door that claimed most of my pinkie nail, and over there's the window that could easily do double duty as a guillotine.

But now? I'm transported to a place that's got the same kind of glow and luminosity as the inside of a seashell. The pickled floors are a cool, clean contrast to the multihued cornflower blue rug with its bold golden flowers and milk glass green swirls. The bed looks all fresh and inviting and squashy with the down-filled duvet, and the canopy curtains around it are white and billowy. This room is nestled next to a leafy old maple, and the view makes me feel like I'm in a tree house for grown-ups.

Unbeknownst to me, Mac refinished my rummage sale antique dresser with the dry sink and he shined up the copper lining. There are scores of creamy white roses in reclaimed glass

---

111 Yes, a tetanus shot was in order.

jars all over the room and tons of our black-and-white wedding photos.

Instead of linen, Mac suggested we go with lighter drapes for the coming summer, and the fabric he chose is unstructured and ethereal. Mac strategically placed candles that smell like honeysuckle and orange blossom around the room, too. On the hope chest at the foot of the bed, he's placed a woven tray laden with my favorite cheeses, candied nuts, and succulent grapes.[112]

The bathroom is equally inviting, with sparkly tiles and paint that's all Zen and the same pearly blue as the horizon at sunset.

"What do you think?" he asks.

I'm so enamored that it takes me a moment to find the proper words. "Oh, honey—I'm blown away. We did it! I can't believe we did it. I'm not going to lie to you: It was touch-and-go there for a hot minute, but this? This is spectacular! This is magic! This could be in a magazine! Babcia's going to love staying in here, and then we're going to spend many long, happy years in here."

Mac is beaming. "This room is tangible proof that we *can* do it ourselves."

I throw myself around him and kiss him with all my might before flitting off to inspect each corner of the room. "I should have never doubted you. I'm so sorry I've been a pill. I should have listened to you and trusted your instincts. Forgive me?"

"Maybe, if you come back over here." Mac's sitting on the bed and motioning toward me, and I quickly comply.

"I'm all over it, Mr. MacNamara." We both lie back in each other's arms and I start to kiss his neck.

---

112 And an oyster containing two tickets to that thing I love.

"Aw, shit, there's one small flaw," Mac says, gazing up at a small paint imperfection in the ceiling.

"It can wait," I insist.

"No, it'll make me crazy. Lemme just get this right here. . . ." Mac stands on the bed and pokes at the small outcropping, which is like a bubble or a balloon.

Years from now when we retell this story—and we will be retelling this story—I'm sure our recollection will go the way of any fish tale. The amount of water dispersed will likely swell from buckets to barrels, and the velocity at which it gushes down on me is prone to be exaggerated, sped up from a languid pour to a rushing river. And the ants that are washed down within that stagnant, brackish liquid will magically morph from carpenter size to Australian bulldog variety, maybe even with pincers and large enough to cast a shadow.

But right here, right now, and before my hands can inevitably grow farther and farther apart as I demonstrate that legendary fish's length, I can tell you one thing: I hop out of every ant-covered, sopping-wet piece of clothing faster than ORNESTEGA could imagine.

"Hi, this is Mia MacNamara, and I got your number off of Angie's List. . . . I understand you have twenty-four-hour service? . . . Super . . . Yeah, we need you right now. . . . Uh-huh . . . Bring a lot of poison. Buckets. Barrels. Whatever you've got. The address is 1407 . . ."

"Hey, it's Mia. Guess what, smarty-pants? You were wrong. We *don't* have Formosan subterranean termites. We have *Eastern* subterranean termites. Drywood, too. Oh, and at least three million carpenter ants. We have to fumigate. Call me back on my cell. And if you could keep the gloating to a minimum, I'd appreciate it."

"Hi, I'm hoping to book a couple of reservations. The first one is a standard room, right now for two people. You're dog-friendly, yes? . . . Cats, too? . . . Great . . . Uh-huh, two nights under 'Mia MacNamara' . . . Right, thanks . . . The second one is for June fourth through June seventh. . . . All you have left is the presidential suite? How much is that? . . . Ouch! . . . No, I was unaware that was Abington Cambs College graduation weekend. . . . Of course I realize prices reflect demand. . . . No problem . . . The name on that reservation is Josefa Grabowski. . . . Um, I'll be using my AmEx for both. The number is 3750 . . ."

"Hello, sir. Lovely day out here; hope you're enjoying it. Have a seat on the bench? Don't mind if I do. Went with the white peonies today, because I thought you might want to mix it up a bit after getting so many shades of pink ones. Anyway, do I have a week to share with you. Remember how I said neither balloons nor bubbles were inherently threatening? Yeah? I stand corrected."

Chapter Twelve
THE GOLABKI CLUB

"Thanks for coming, and we look forward to seeing your estimate!" I close the door behind the contractor, gingerly trying to keep the knob from falling out again.

Mac and I have spent the past few days interviewing general contractors, because the extent of the termite damage is far too much for us to take on by ourselves. Apparently those ravenous little bastards have been going at all the wood in our house so long and hard that we have to install new subflooring in some areas. We also have to replace floor joists and reinforce support beams.

FYI? I don't actually look forward to seeing the estimates for these repairs, despite Mac's rejoicing in his vindication when he found out weakened floors were the reason he kept dropping toilets into my office.

Yes. Because having to take out a second mortgage because of structural damage is totally cause for celebration.

The good news is, we're really enthusiastic about everyone we've interviewed, and we've narrowed the field down to three contractors who are the most top-notch. Not only do these three all have the highest ratings from the Better Business Bureau and are Best of Angie's List, but each one just slayed us with how they answered the interview questions.

We found an amazing resource on the Internet that advised us to lob a few "question grenades" during our fact-finding process, like whether their business was involved with any charity work. I was so impressed to learn how all of Bob's Builders employees get two paid weeks off each year to work for Habitat for Humanity. When I checked professional references for Larry Lambert Homes, I had to laugh when one of his suppliers was all, "Wait. Lambert's got an opening in his schedule? Tell him I need a sunroom!" And I loved how organized Miranda—owner of Do It Herself, Inc.—was, especially when I snuck out to take a peek in her truck.[113] Plus, she doesn't use any subcontractors and she's a huge proponent of going green. When she expressed her passion for sustainable building materials, I could suddenly envision a kitchen filled with bamboo flooring and agrifiber-based cabinets.

I tell Mac, "We'll have a tough decision on our hands. All of them seem completely competent, they each have impeccable references, and when I think of people I wouldn't mind having in my house for the next month, I'd be hard-pressed to find fault with any of them." Bob was just salt of the earth,

---

113 The guide told me to.

Larry was hilarious, and Miranda was a globe-trotting Peace Corps volunteer before she started her company and she seems like she's got tales to tell.

Mac agrees. "Our decision will ultimately come down to price. All things being equal, we're going to go with the lowest-cost provider."[114]

I collect our dirty Starbucks cups and napkins, tossing all the refuse in the trash before I catch myself. Oh, shit, if Miranda works here, I'll have to be a lot better about remembering to recycle.

I wipe off the perpetually gritty table and tell Mac, "Honey, we've got about twenty minutes to get ready to go to the airport, so if you've got to use the bathroom, I suggest you go now."

"Hey," Mac says from the doorway of the kitchen. "In a completely unrelated question—do we happen to have any straight-razor blades? Also, how long would you estimate it takes a person to"—he makes air quotes—"'bleed out'? Can this be accomplished in twenty minutes or less? I ask for no particular reason."

"I don't like car," Babcia says with a sneer when she sees Mac's Mercedes at the arrivals curb.

"Because it's German?" Babcia's not a huge fan of the Germans, having developed those feelings when she lived in Warsaw during WWII. Her opinion of all things Axis-power related explains why she also despises the Japanese, Italians, Hungarians, and Romanians. Of course, I'm hard-pressed to explain what she has against anyone who's from England, Canada, Mexico, China and Hong Kong, France, Vietnam, North and South Korea, or Switzerland. She has a

---

114 Oh, yeah, baby. Now you're talking my language.

particular affinity for the Swedes, though. I suspect that has more to do with the $2.99 meatball platter at IKEA and less with any socio-political aspect.

Babcia continues to scowl as she inspects the car from hood to trunk. "Is too fast-making."

As I settle her in the backseat, I say, "I promise Mac will drive home slowly."

I can see Mac blanch. I suspect he was planning to pilot this thing like the Batmobile on the way back, just to lessen their time together in such an enclosed space.

"How was your flight?" Mac gamely ventures.

"No talk while drive," she replies icily.

He gives me a desperate look while I offer a small shrug in return. "Babcia, does that mean no one talks or just Mac can't talk?"

"Warehouse."

"Warehouse? I'm not sure I follow you, Babcia." A little Babcia 101 for you? The question you ask often has little to no bearing on the question she'll answer.

"Warehouse."

"Do you want to go to Costco?" I probably don't even need to mention how Babcia feels about their liberal free-sample policies.

Or how she's since been banned from all Miami-Dade County locations after the whole Foreman Grill unpleasantness.

"WAREHOUSE."

"I think she's asking where the house is. We're about half an hour from here, depending on traffic, Babcia," Mac interjects helpfully, only to be met with a steely glare and a bony finger pointed in his direction. Realizing the error of his attempt to interpret, he slinks down so low in his seat I wonder if he can even see over the dashboard.

Then Babcia reaches around the seat in front of her and takes her bony finger and pokes me in the stomach so hard I think she hits my spine. "Why fat, *moja zabko*? Is baby?"

You know, it's possible this visit wasn't my best idea.

"I need you now!"

His desperation is palpable.

"Mac, let me finish getting the coffee together. You can spend thirty seconds alone with her." I roll my eyes and leisurely pour the carton of half-and-half into a white ceramic cow-shaped creamer. "Last I saw, she and Daisy were hanging out together on the couch in the living room, thick as thieves. How could that possibly be problematic?"

"Oh? Oh, really?" he questions me, his arms wrapped around himself in a very protective, albeit somewhat feminine position. "Then you're not at all concerned about her squeezing Daisy's hindquarters and muttering things like 'tender' and 'make delicious.'"

"Not even a little bit," I reply. That I put pep in my step filling the coffee cups and getting back to the living room is entirely coincidental.

I run a white dish towel over the coffee table before I set down the tray. With a couple of swipes, it turns completely gray. Even though we're not actively tearing anything down right now, the grit and dust remain. I look forward to this eventually not being the case. Today I started coughing, and from what I hacked up, you'd assume I was a coal miner.

While Mac attempts to make himself invisible on the opposite side of the couch, Babcia eyes me as I sit down. "You make movie."

I serve Babcia her coffee and hand her the cream, having pre-sweetened her coffee.[115] "I don't have a definitive answer yet. Maybe? A couple of places are interested in buying my stories, but my level of involvement may vary with each. If HBO— Wait. Do you know what HBO is?"

She nods with great conviction. "Tony Soprano."

"Right. If HBO wants it, then basically I've sold them the idea and they take my book and they hire someone else to write a pilot—first episode—based on it. If Persiflage—it's a film studio—wants it, then they'll have me rework the script I already wrote."

"What problem? You already write."

"Yes, but it doesn't quite work like you'd think it would. I'll know a little more today, because I've got a conference call with Persiflage." What I don't tell her is that this potential sale would more than pay for the repairs and renovations. We got our estimates back and they're all a little terrifying. As of now, our home-equity line of credit will just barely cover everything we need to do.

Babcia straightens in her seat and gets very serious. "You tell no turtle."

"Got it. No Teenage Mutant Ninja Turtles in my movie." When I first started writing, I explained to Babcia that I wrote stories for kids and that she wouldn't like them. As of now, she's not read any of my books. I hope to keep it that way, as I don't relish the thought of having to explain, "Why no zipper?" "Why no car?" "Why eat peoples?"

---

115 I learned a long time ago it's best just to eliminate any potential temptations.

"Mac, will you be around today at three o'clock? I'd like for someone to keep Babcia company while I'm on the phone," I request.

"Wow, you know I'd love to, but I can't. Meeting with the attorney this afternoon, remember?"

Mac's managed to schedule everything he's been procrastinating doing since we moved up here. In the past twenty-four hours, he's had breakfast with our accountant, he's gotten a cavity filled, he met with the guy from the security company about upgrading our alarm system, and after he sees the attorney this afternoon, he's playing a late round of golf[116] with our insurance agent in order to get a better idea about the differences between term and whole-life coverage.

In other words, yes, he *is* that desperate to get away from Babcia.

"Okay, honey, but if I'm going to be tied up, maybe you can take Babcia back to her hotel? I don't want her to be bored."

Mac turns about fifteen shades of purple, but before he can manufacture another excuse, Babcia says, "No. I stay. I cook." Then she gives Daisy a proprietary pat on the head.

So, yeah, I'll bring the dogs upstairs with me when I have my conference call.

"Very interested," I tell Natalie. "Superinterested. Persiflage sounds like this is a done deal if I want it to be. The conversation could not have gone better."

"Then why aren't you more excited?" she presses. "Are you worried about the workload? You said the book was coming along. Obviously you wouldn't start on any television project until you finished the work in progress."

---

116 A sport he normally calls "an excuse for morons to wear ugly pants."

I wrap the curly phone cord around a finger and gaze up at the ceiling. Oh, great. Water spot. I'll add that to the list. "No, it's not the writing—that, I love. I'm just . . . Well, it sounds like Persiflage is really hands-on. They'd want me in LA while I rewrote the script, and then they talked about me staying on while they did the casting and stuff."

"We'd negotiate to get you paid for each step of the process, no worries."

"Right, of course. That's not it. Truth is, I kind of hate the idea of being away from home for so long. I'd miss Mac and all the pets and my friends. I don't really have a life I can just step out of and run off to Los Angeles, you know?"

While we were on the phone, the more gung ho the producers got, the more reticent I became. I guess they're so used to people who'd sell their firstborn to get a screenplay sold that my hesitancy intrigued them. They kept putting me on hold to hash out details, and each time they came back on the line, they were more and more fired up.

"Mia, do you want to play in the big leagues or not?"

That is the million-dollar question. I desperately want to witness my characters coming to life on-screen. Seeing actors turn the characters I love so much into three-dimensional beings has been my goal since the day I started my first manuscript. I've lost myself in fantasy after fantasy of how the set would come across on-screen. Would the film be dark and foreboding in a nod to the culture of zombies within it? Or would producers opt to make the movie more of a rom-com, emphasizing the lighthearted moments, turning Amos and Miriam's love candy-colored and upbeat? The opportunity to have creative minds poring over my work, bringing every detail of the story to a mass audience, is something I'd do almost anything to experience.

For the most part.

What scares me is that I want no part of the celebrity that might come along with having my movie made. I don't want to end up *being* the story. I mean, I enjoy having the kind of job where people are familiar with my work, but the last thing I want is stringers for *TMZ* and Radar Online following me around trying to get candids of me buying coffee or shopping for toilet paper. I can't handle that kind of scrutiny.

I guess I always go back to John Hughes's example. He didn't drop out of sight because he wasn't producing work anymore. The reason Hughes went all J. D. Salinger is because he didn't like how the "Hollywood machine" used up his friends and colleagues. He hated the person the business was turning him into, so he brought his family back home to Illinois. Maybe I'm being silly to be so hesitant to travel down a path so fraught with potential hazards.

I mean, look at what Hollywood did to Vienna. She spent her first twenty years in luxury but obscurity. Vienna used to have real potential, maybe not as a terribly nice person, but definitely as a scholar. The tabloids never mention that she went to Brown University. She might have needed her parents' name to get into that college, but if she lasted three years, that's because she made the effort. It wasn't until she turned twenty-one and came into her trust fund that she hired herself a publicist, dropped out of school, and started chasing fame.

She probably never meant to become a caricature of herself, yet here she is. She chased fame and she caught it. And now fame/ Hollywood/the media has ruined her potential for being a person of value. I hate that, and I fear how even a tiny portion of drinking my own Kool-Aid could change me as a person.

And yet getting involved in the business by selling my rights would solve all our financial troubles, so I can't just dismiss it. On the one hand I'm flattered by their interest, and on the other, I'm terrified and I haven't a clue as to how to proceed.

Before I can give Nat an answer, I hear a commotion outside. I'm up in what was originally supposed to be my writing room before I annexed the library, and it affords an unencumbered view of the driveway. When I look out the window, I see what horror films would classify as "angry villagers," only instead of waving pitchforks and torches, they're shaking . . . ornamental cabbages?

"Listen, something's up here. Lemme call you back." I bang down the phone before Nat can get another word out. I'm not sure what's going on in my driveway, but as the casserole ship sailed long ago, it's definitely not the welcome wagon.

As I dash down the stairs, I'm stopped in my tracks by the smell of something delicious. I have to give Babcia extra props for volunteering to create a meal in our messed-up kitchen. She seems to have had no issues working around a downed cabinet and a bunch of rubble. I'm glad to note the oven's functional, even if the door is all bashed up.

The air is thick with the scent of simmering garlic and sautéed beef and pork and onions. My mouth begins to water. One whiff of Babcia's cooking and I'm instantly transported back to my childhood. Babcia must be in a good mood,[117] because she's making my favorite dish, golabki.

---

117 Even though it's almost impossible to tell.

I'm almost at the front door when I put the pieces of this particular puzzle together.

Golabki.

Babcia's cooking golabki.

We had a couple of pounds of ground beef and pork in the fridge from when I forbade Mac to make chili last time. Even though I'm not a huge cook, I always keep an ample stock of fresh onions in the house, and I'd be kicked out of my father's Italian side of the family if I didn't have an endless supply of garlic on hand. I had all the necessary pantry staples for golabki, too, like rice and beef stock.

But I did not have cabbage.

And I'm not walking distance from the grocery store.

Oh, sweet Jesus.

With great trepidation, I open the front door, whereupon Elbow Patches lunges at me with half a head of ornamental cabbage. "You did this! I know you did this! The trail of dirt leads directly from my planter beds to your front door! You wiped out half a block of our cabbage!" A host of angry neighbors stands behind him, all nodding grimly.

"I'm so, so sorry," I plead. "You see, I have an elderly, infirm relative here and she wanted to do some cooking and I think she just got confused. I understand how mad you all are and I can't apologize enough."

"You have to replace them," says a woman one row back.

"Yes, yes, of course. How do you want me to do this—shall I write you all a check or do you want me to—" Before I can figure out how to properly make amends to a dozen households, the screaming begins.

Lululemon's updated her look for summer and today she's sporting a colorful tennis skirt and racer-back tank. But we have no time for a sartorial discussion, as I'm pretty sure a blood vessel is about to pop in her forehead.

"*That woman flashed my children!*" I turn to see her gesturing at Babcia, who's materialized behind my right shoulder.

I'm pretty sure I don't want to hear what comes next.

And I'm pretty sure I have no choice.

"We were on our beach and we looked up and suddenly there she was! Naked! That crazy woman was naked on our beach!" Lululemon shrieks.

"Babcia, tell me this isn't true," I demand. She offers nothing but a shrug in return.

I take a couple of slow, steady breaths to compensate for having forgotten to breathe for the last minute.

One of the (many) things I didn't pay attention to when we bought this house was our odd plat of survey. Whereas it looks like we have full beach access in back, our property is actually shaped like a very big saucepan with a tiny handle, meaning we have only about twenty square feet of beach rights in that handle. And our part's a rocky outcropping. We can still get in the water (if we climb jagged rocks), but essentially any sand at the back of my house belongs to Lululemon.

"Can you at least give your version of events?" I beg.

"Is hot; I swim."

This is not the explanation Lululemon was looking for. "She was *naked!*"

"You weren't naked; tell me you weren't naked." *Oh, please, oh, please, oh, please.*

Babcia shrugs again. "Is hot; I swim. What? You want I swim clothing?" She flaps the ruffle of her collar at me. "Marc Jacobs don't like get wet."

Just when I think the situation can't get more awkward, Citizen Cane moves from the back of the group to the front and begins to bark, "Hey! I know her! She stole my cane! That's the woman who ran off with my cane in the restaurant at the Stag's Leap last night!"

I stand corrected; this situation *can indeed* be more awkward.

The temperature of the mob begins to shift from "angry" to something more akin to "lynch."

"She's eighty years old! I'm sure she thought she was grabbing her own cane. Please," I implore, "we can work this out. Babcia, you grabbed his cane by accident, right?"

"I want my cane! Look at me!" Citizen Cane waves a large Chicago Bears logo umbrella at me. "I have to use this to walk!" I remember the specifics of his cane now and I think I understand the problem.

"To *nie Polski!*[118] Eagle not belong you!" Sure, of course. Because, in Babcia's world, no one can possess anything with an eagle on it except for a Polish person. This is due to her great affinity for the Polish coat of arms. The eagle on the half dollar makes her crazy, and we don't even allow her to go to the mall with the American Eagle store anymore.[119]

Then, before I realize what's happening, Babcia sprints out the

118 "Not Polish!"

119 And by "we" I mean the management of the Shops at Sunset Place.

door and comes face-to-face with Citizen Cane, whereupon they stare each other down like Gamera versus Godzilla.

"What about my cabbage?" someone in the crowd shouts, causing others gathered to echo the same sentiments. This is followed by Lululemon demanding Babcia be charged as a sex predator.

The New Madrid fault line stretches through six states in the central part of America, including Indiana, Tennessee, Kentucky, Missouri, Arkansas, and Illinois. I learned about it in third-grade science class. Our teacher told us how it had the capacity to produce a quake up to a 7.7 magnitude. Growing up, I was terrified of a potential earthquake, and I lived in a constant state of worry that the earth would begin to violently shake and roll and fissures would open up and swallow me whole.

I'd sure like a fissure right about now.

Fortunately, I'm able to keep the situation from devolving further by writing some checks,[120] and eventually the crowd disperses.

As the last person exits the driveway, Babcia turns to me and gives me a triumphant smile.

"Golabki time."

For the record?

I'm pretty sure I'm out of the running for the dessert course at the next neighborhood progressive dinner.

---

120 Oh, so many checks.

Chapter Thirteen
CAREER OPPORTUNITIES

"After all that, did Babcia leave without incident?" Ann Marie asks during our weekly call. Because she's so busy, we actually have a standing appointment to catch up every Tuesday from noon to one thirty p.m. Her secretary blocks the time off on her calendar and brings down a world of hurt on anyone who tries to disturb us.[121]

I sigh. "Um, sort of. On Sunday, when I was upstairs writing and she was supposedly napping, she cornered Mac and told him she wanted to clean our house. Mac was so thrilled that she'd not only actually spoken to him directly but also seemed to be taking responsibility for her actions that he was all, 'Yes, of course, Babcia,

---

121 I never knew there was a younger, even scarier version of Ann Marie until I met her assistant.

anything you say.' So she and some random crew of Polish ladies—mind you, I have no idea who they were or where they came from—they got this place spotless. When they finished, Mac was all, 'Thank you!' and then Babcia goes, 'Four hundred dollars. Plus tip. Big tip. Babcia don't like cheap.'"

"He never saw it coming, did he?"

I laugh despite the six-hundred-dollar hit on our bank account. "We've been married how long, ten years? And the poor guy has yet to figure out how Babcia operates. This is what happens when he doesn't communicate with me. Had he just run the cleaning idea past me, I'd have stopped them both. I mean, did he forget that Christmas when we stayed with her and she tried to charge him for using hot water?"[122]

"I can't help but adore her. Someday when I'm old, I'm going to stop being so nice to people and be more like Babcia," Ann Marie replies wistfully.

I kind of hope I'm not alive to see that.

She continues. "So, construction, how's that going? Please tell me you've finally started making decisions about that house with your head and not your heart."

I'm very pleased to tell her, "We did a ton of research on how to select a contractor, and we conducted a number of interviews."

"Why, Grasshopper, there may be hope for you yet. When does work begin?"

"That's still TBD."

"Oh, did they all run away screaming when they saw the

---

122   I didn't let him pay her, of course, although I suspect she may be the reason his three-hundred-dollar Allen Edmonds loafers went missing on that trip. Poor guy had to head to Christmas dinner in a sport coat and a pair of running shoes.

place, too?" We're on speakerphone, which means I can hear her tapping a box of Marlboro Reds, followed by the tearing of cellophane. Then I note the familiar clink of a crystal ashtray being placed on her desk, the whoosh of a lighter, and a deep intake of breath. I've heard it all a million times before.

Ann Marie's secret shame is that she hasn't been able to conquer her addiction to smoking. She's done the patch, the gum, Chantix, acupuncture, hypnosis, aromatherapy, psychotherapy, support groups, herbal cigarettes, an ill-advised weekend in a sweat lodge, and cold turkey/sheer willpower. Every time she fails, it's . . . not pretty.

You know how families stage interventions to force their loved ones to stop a destructive behavior like drugs or alcohol? Ann Marie's husband gathered all her friends, family, and associates to beg her to please start smoking again because her attempts at quitting were ruining the lives of everyone around her.

She's gotten her habit down to the point that she'll smoke only at work. Her office is located in a municipal building—not only does everyone in the building turn the other way when she blatantly violates the city's no-smoking statute, but her boss even had a special fan and vent system installed for her. In college we used to call her "the Bear," which was short for "Don't taunt the bear."

"No, smarty-pants, they didn't. None of our top choices were available, and I'm so disappointed. The one guy would have kept us in stitches, and there was a female contractor who was just so cool and interesting. The third guy was all Zen and socially responsible and I loved knowing that my hiring him would directly benefit Habitat for Humanity."

While we chat, I'm lying on the couch in the library, staring up at the gaping holes in the ceiling. Because we have such extensive termite damage, the handyman we contacted after the fact couldn't repair the openings and we have to wait for our contractor. On the one hand, I'm a fan of how much more light this room gets, but on the other, I'm not so thrilled by the source. Given the choice, I'd rather have a dark library and two additional functioning bathrooms.

I go on: "Plus, I really looked forward to having coffee with them before they started work for the day. I'd try to make them happy to come to the job site with theme breakfasts and stuff. Monday could be Munchkin Doughnut Day, followed by Turkey Bacon Tuesday and Waffle Wednesday. I can't think of anything for Thursday yet, but we'd have Fresh Fruit Friday and, if they wanted overtime, Sausage, Egg, and Cheese (Biscuit) Saturday."

"That's not the worst idea you ever had." When she says it like that, I'm not sure I want to ask her what my worst idea ever was, because I suspect I don't want to hear the answer.

"Um, thank you? Anyway, the guide actually stressed hiring someone you'd want to have over for dinner. Doing quality work is only one aspect. When you're going to have a person managing a team in your house for what could be months, you have to make sure your personalities mesh or the experience is going to be awful for everyone."

Ann Marie is noncommittal on her end of the phone. "I see. Go on."

"I guess it's understandable that these contractors are all busy, because they interviewed so well. The guide said you don't want a contractor who actually *needs* the work. But that's kind of weird to me. Like, why are they even going out to talk to potential new clients if they won't have time to take you on?"

"Ours is not to ask why," Ann Marie replies. See? Do you see how much calmer and more serene she is while she's smoking? One of her tricks is to deny herself cigarettes when she's going to court because it makes her extra aggressive.[123]

"What really sucks is that none of the B-teams we interviewed can take our job, either. I guess with summer coming on, everyone's really ratcheting up the home repairs."

I can hear Ann Marie exhale sharply on the other end of the line. "None of them? How many second choices did you have?"

"We did seven interviews in all, three we loved and four we really liked. All of them came highly recommended."

"Uh-huh, and did they all seem interested in the job when you first approached them?" She's trying to get at something, but I'm not too concerned. She's *always* trying to get at something. She sees conspiracy theories everywhere. When her kids were younger and she'd watch children's programming with them, she'd always go on and on about the *Sesame Street* industrial complex.[124]

"Well, yeah, or else they wouldn't have met with us. As of now, to fix everything in this place, it's a six-figure job. We had to take out a second mortgage to pay for it all."

When I say the cost out loud, I get a stomach cramp. I knew everything would be expensive and that the home's price reflected the need for updates, but there's still something about seeing all

---

123 One of my tricks is to always have a pack of her brand in my purse whenever we're together. Her husband keeps a spare carton in the freezer for the same reason.

124 Oh, honey—sometimes "B" is for "Bitch Be Crazy."

those zeroes on a piece of paper that makes me more than a little queasy. Do you know how much melodramatic zombie longing I'll have to write to compensate for that kind of money? For six figures, I may even have to let Mose and Ishmael get to second base with their crushes.[125] Argh.

"To recap, you've met with seven contractors and you already have your financing secured. This is a big-ticket job and it's the kind of project that will keep crews working all summer. Am I right so far?"

"You are." Ann Marie's always been a recapper. Back in college, we'd lie in our bunk beds at night and she'd be all, "So after he kissed you at the formal, you went outside and barfed blackberry schnapps into the fountain? And then you lost your shoe when? On the bus or before you fell down the stairs?"[126]

I can hear Ann Marie push smoke out of her nose, something she does only when she's ruminating. "Mmm-hmm, so what you're telling me is that in a depressed economy and in a market where new housing starts are down by an average of seventy-three percent since their peak in January 2006, all the decent contractors in your area are too busy to take hundreds of thousands of dollars from you."

Now I'm confused. "I guess so?"

"Mia, I'd like you to do me a favor. Call every available contractor in your area, interview them immediately, right this minute, and if you find someone decent, sign a contract on the spot. Can you do that for me?"

---

125 But not Jebediah. Never Jebediah.

126 I miss college.

"But the guide says—"

"Do you trust me?"

I don't even have to mull this over. "With my life. But Mac will—"

"*Thank me.* Mac will thank me. Call them all. Now. We'll cut our call short so you can get started. Off you go."

Wow. That was even bossier than usual.

I bet she's been smoking light cigarettes again.

"How many other jobs does your company have going right now?" Mac asks the gentleman sitting across from us at the kitchen table.

The man scratches his head while he thinks, a task made far more challenging due to his blond dreadlocks. He shifts his eyes upward and starts counting off on his grubby fingers. "Um . . . I guess that would be . . . none at the moment. Hey, you got any more coffee?" He shakes his cup at me. "Sugar, too. I like them little cubes." I cross to the counter to retrieve the sugar bowl and he ignores the small silver tongs, choosing instead to plunge in bare-handed. I do my best to conceal my shudder.

Mac is undeterred. "When you're on a job, what kind of hours do you put in on a typical day?"

The man yawns and stretches in such a way that he exposes the bulk of his hirsute belly. "I like to get in when I get in and work until I don't want to work anymore."

"Can you clarify? Are you more likely to start early or stay late?" Mac questions.

"I'm more likely to start late and finish early. I like to be done for the day around, *ahem*, four twenty." Then he waggles his bushy, unkempt eyebrows at us, causing some random bit of crud to fall off his face. I try hard not to retch.

I tacitly ignore the implication of drug usage and then I hit him with a couple of my own questions. "Who'll be on-site managing the project every day?"

"I try to be on-site every day. But some days . . . eh, you know how it is. If I'm not here, I send in Nugget. If Nugget can't make it, I send in Cheeba. If Cheeba can't make it, then it musta been some party the night before." Then he laughs so hard his dreads shake.

Mac and I aren't quite as amused. "Okay, then. How many people work for you?"

"Lemme see," he says, having just discovered that his coffee spoon works well for all those hard-to-reach itches. "I got Stash and Loadie on full-time, Cheeba and Nugget when they're not following Phish, and Lucy and Shaggy when needed. So that's"—he pauses to add on his fingers again—"nine. I got nine."

"No," I reply, "that's seven. Including yourself, that's seven."

"Whoa."

Whoa, indeed.

In terms of hiring people with whom I might like to dine, this man ranks somewhere on my list between Mussolini and Hitler. And it's not because of anything as superficial as his silly coiffure. Actually, during my freshman year of college I had a crush on a guy who was all into grunge and had the white-guy dreadlocks. But then he spent the summer working at a fishery in Alaska and he had to shave them off because of the bugs. He seemed way less cute after that.

Anyway, my issue is that this guy has not only blown every question we've asked him, but then he used the bathroom without flushing *or* washing *or* closing the door, and on top of a plethora of other blatant personal hygiene problems, he was an hour and seventeen minutes late for our meeting. Say what you will about Mussolini, but at least the trains ran on time.

"Okay, yes," I say, pushing off from the table, "I think that about does it. We look forward to receiving your bid, Chronic." Mac and I make a beeline to the door while Chronic ambles along behind us. When he tries to shake my hand, I cough and tuck mine into my armpits, saying, "Ooh, sorry. Cold and flu season, you know how it is."

"Yeah, man, that's cool," he agrees.

And then he hugs me instead.

Mac finds this hilarious until Chronic hugs him, too.

"Do you belong to any trade associations?"

"Come again?"

"Trade associations, you know, like NARI or NAHB?"

"Knob? What's that?"

"National Association of Home Builders."

"Never heard of 'em. Must be new."

"They've been around since 1942 and have a hundred and seventy-five thousand members. Their members are responsible for building eighty percent of all new homes. They work closely with Congress to promote a probuilder agenda. Does any of this sound familiar?"

"Not ringing any bells."

"Do you use subs?"

"Do I sub what?"

"Subs. Subcontractors. What's your policy on subcontractors?"

"I don't know what those are."

"What kind of liability insurance do you carry?"

"For what?"

"Are you bonded?"

"Listen, lady, what people do in the privacy of their own bedrooms is none of your business."

"Do you have any references?"

"My mom thinks I'd do a great job. Does that count?"

"Is this your first job ever?"

"Yes. Is that a problem?"

"And finally, I like to be paid in cash. Cash up front. See, cash makes it easier to, y'know, grease the skids and the like."

"Are there many skids to be greased?" I ask, trying desperately to sound enthusiastic. When I told my dad how much trouble we were having finding a contractor, he made some calls and got ahold of his cousin Big Joey, who referred us to his "associate" Lucky. In the past half hour, I've heard all about how Lucky and Co. keep their pinkie-ring-clad fingers in many businesses . . . waste management, vending machines, concession trucks, cell phones, and, of course, building construction.

"Lotta skids, kid, whole lotta skids. So my associates and me, we find cash makes everything nice and easy. Cash makes workers less, y'know, *likely to have an accident* on the job."

"Yes, of course," I agree.

There's no way I'm going to hire this cut-rate John Gotti, but if I'm not polite, it will get back to my dad's cousin, and then my father and then I'll never hear the end of it at Thanksgiving. "It's good to hear you have standards," I add.

"Plus, we got a service that if the neighbors get too, y'know, *inquisitive* about the permits, we can take care of that."

"That's just covered in awesome sauce," I say.

Although honestly, after the latest petition,[127] I'm a tiny bit tempted to learn more, but I fight that urge. I glance at my watch to see how much more time I've got to kill with this guy before I can make it seem like I've given him my full consideration.

Then he moves in all conspiratorially. "Hey, your cousin tells me you make books. Funny, we got something in common. I make book, too. What's your taste of the vig?"

When the bell rings, the dogs come dashing to the door with me to meet the next candidate. I open the door to a gentleman who, from the looks of him, is neither stoner, nor greenhorn, nor small-time mobster. I swear, if this guy can swing a hammer in the general direction of a nail, he's hired.

"Hi," I say, grabbing hold of the dogs' collars. "Please give me a minute. I've got to put these guys out back and then we can chat."

He bends down to the dogs' level. "Hey, is that a pit bull?"

"Yes, her name is Daisy. Isn't she beautiful? Say hello, Daisy!" She doesn't speak but instead chooses to wag her whole body in response while Duckie paws and licks at the air beside her.

The contractor leans against the doorway. "You ever fight her?"

"I'm sorry?"

"Dogfights—you ever put her in the ring and see what she can do?"

---

127 Which essentially calls for us to not exist.

"Are you serious?"

"Between us, you can make a lot of money fighting dogs. If you want, I've got a place—"

I don't hear the rest because I've slammed the door.

"Oh, my God, I can't believe I'm here! I can't believe I'm sitting at your table! Is this where you write? Is this where you come up with your stories?"

So, the good news is that I have fans who aren't thirteen-year-old girls. Did not know that. Apparently I'm beloved not only by young ladies who've yet to graduate from training bras, but also by at least one forty-six-year-old male builder.

He gushes on: "I see so much of myself in Mose and Amos. They're both hardworking and dedicated and they're drawn to women who want to eat them."

Mac kicks me under the table. I ignore him.

My fan/possible contractor/probable eventual restraining-order recipient continues. "I mean, not literally. No, that'd be weird and gross. Spiritually. All the women I date are spiritual vampires."

"Listen, Nick, we don't really use the v-word around here," Mac tells him, making air quotes when he says "v-word."

The contractor turns ashen. "OH, NO, I'M SO SORRY! PLEASE DON'T BE MAD AT ME! I'D DIE!"

"No, Nick, he's kidding." I shoot Mac an angry look. "Tell him that was a joke."

"Sorry, man."

The contractor gives me the kind of adoring gaze that's supersweet coming from a tween, but something entirely different from an adult. "Seriously, can I, like, touch your beautiful brain? Not in a weird way—I just want to see if your energy transports into me."

"Is it okay if we don't?" I always try to be as kind as possible to my fans; they're the reason I have a career. But come on, creepy is creepy. When his face falls at my response, I add, "I just got my hair done."

"Yeah, yeah, of course. That was really inappropriate of me. I'm sorry."

Mac tries to break his reverie by asking, "What else do you need to know to bid out this project?"

"What do I need?" He rests his chin in his palms and stares into the distance. "Um, I guess what I really need is to find out if Amish and zombie teenagers in love ever find a way to live between their two worlds. I need to know if it does indeed get better. I need confirmation that their love will conquer anything."

Nick looks down at his wide, capable hands. I wonder whether, when he reads descriptions of how small and delicate Miriam's tiny zombie fingers look resting in Amos's broad, wide palm, he pictures his own calluses and scarred knuckles.

I wonder whether, when I talk about the pain and melodrama associated with coming of age, he sees his own teen years, and if he can find peace with the decisions he made long ago. And I'm curious whether somehow these stories help him make sense of his own life. Knowing that my words have an impact on an entirely unintended audience really touches me and I can't help but smile.

Nick is apparently emboldened by my encouraging grin. "Also, I need to find out if Amos and Miriam ever get it on, and if so, will you please be describing their union in graphic detail with anatomically correct terms?"

As it stands, I can live in a squalid house or I can hire someone completely repugnant to fix it.

Talk about your Sophie's choice.

Chapter Fourteen
EAT, PRAY, SHOVE

"Hi, Chronic. It's Mia MacNamara! . . . Yes, the lady with the sugar cubes . . . You're welcome. I'm glad you liked them. . . . The grocery store, I guess . . . Yes, probably any grocer will have them. . . . I can't really say; I've never checked for them at the 7-Eleven. Anyway, I'm calling because we'd like to hire you to do our renovations. . . . Oh, no, really? . . . Well, I guess that's great for you guys. . . . Shoot. Okay, if anything changes and the band breaks up again, please let us know."

"Hi, this is Mia MacNamara; may I speak with Lucky? . . . No, I didn't realize . . . Do you know how long he'll be gone? . . . Yeah, our renovations probably can't wait eight years. . . . No, not even with good behavior . . . I agree, racketeering *is* a bitch. Thanks, anyway."

★   ★   ★

"Hi, this is Mia MacNamara. . . . Right, right, the nosy woman with all the questions. Listen, I'm calling to find out about your availability. . . . You're kidding. Booked solid? All summer? . . . Okay, then good luck with your new business, and please let us know if your schedule opens up."

"I don't know, Mac. I don't understand why, either."

Between the two of us, Mac and I have called every general contractor/builder/carpenter/handyman/plumber/electrician in a hundred-mile radius, and we can't even get anyone to give us an estimate, let alone commit to taking on our project. I wonder whether the folks who write newscasts and newspapers have talked to builders in our area, because it sounds like the housing boom is back.

"What are we going to do? I can't keep living like this," I say, surveying the wreckage of my kitchen, which is adjacent to the dining room with the crumbled wall, across from the library with all the ceiling holes, across from the living room with the aggressively ugly monkey wallpaper. Plumbing issues have crippled two more bathrooms and we're down to one functioning toilet and shower. We've yet to get the smell of rotting carpenter ants out of the master, the mustiness emanating from the covered hot tub is almost unbearable, and there's something alive and well in the wall of my writing room.

"We have no choice," Mac says in a determined tone.

"You realize I'll go to jail if the dogfighter steps into this house," I remind him. People who are cruel to animals bring out my inner Swayze. I'll show him exactly how *not nice* I can be, and

I'll probably still be more humane than those barbarians are with sweet, innocent doggies.

"That's not who I meant."

That's when I feel my heart drop into my stomach.

"Mac, noooo! Nick was way too creepy! I seriously don't want to be alone in the house all day with my number one fan!" I plead.

"I have plenty more vacation time," Mac reasons. "I can take it now so you won't be alone with him initially."

"I can't." I curl into myself just imagining having that weirdo in my house.

Mac is firm. "You can."

"I won't."

Mac stares me down. "You won't what? Imagine how nice it might be to have the capacity to wash dishes? Use a toilet other than in the basement? Breathe in air that's not full of drywall dust? Walk across a floor without shoes or with the confidence that it won't give way at any time?"

I cross my arms in front of me and rock slightly back and forth in my chair. I don't know what to do. Do I agree to have someone in my home who makes me unbearably uncomfortable, or do I suck it up and keep trying to find someone—anyone— else?

I need a sign.

As I rock forward, the leg of my chair punches through the hardwood and I topple out of my seat and onto the floor.

Okay, universe, I hear you loud and clear.

With great resignation, I say, "Fine. Call the pervert." I'm too immobilized by the general feeling of ickiness[128] to bother sitting upright. The dogs rush over to lie beside me.

"Good dog," I whisper into the rough of Duckie's neck while I glower at Mac. "You'd never make me hang out with a perv-o-potamus."

Mac whips out his cell phone and retrieves Nick's number. He dials quickly and walks into the dining room as the call goes through. "Nick, John MacNamara here. How are you? . . . Good, glad to hear it. Hey, Mia and I wanted to see if you're still available to spearhead our project. . . . What's that? . . . You're joking. . . . You're serious? Are you sure? . . . Everyone? . . . Is there any way to— . . . Shit . . . Well, yes, this is obviously going to affect her work. . . . Yes, we have been encountering— . . . Fucking hell . . . Nope, wasn't aware of that, either . . ."

I sit up, trying to hear more of the conversation, but Mac's since paced into the living room. I get up to follow and the dogs trail along behind me.

". . . and that's what it would take? . . . There's no other way? . . . You're sure? I don't want her to have to— . . . No, you don't need to swear on your love of *It's Raining Mennonites*. . . . Okay. Let me run it up the flagpole and I'll get back to you."

Mac walks over to where I'm standing in the doorway. "So, how badly do you want the house fixed?"

"On a scale of one to a hundred? At least ninety-eight."[129]

"Are you willing to make a sacrifice?"

128 And fear of being hobbled.

129 I don't want to be greedy.

"Like what? Going down two and a half flights of stairs in the night to go to the bathroom? Washing dishes in the bathtub? Already been there, thanks."

"No, I mean a different kind of sacrifice. One that could temporarily compromise your principles."

"I don't follow you."

"How much are you willing to give in order to get this ball rolling?"

Mac looks as cagey as he did the time he tried to keep the oven fire a secret.[130] "You're talking in circles. Out with it."

Mac puts his hand on my shoulder. "So, remember when *TMZ* said Vienna was out for revenge?"

"Yeah, what of it? That was, like, two months and one cover of *People* with the headline *Eat, Pray, Shove* ago."

"Then I guess revenge is a dish best served cold. She got her revenge; we just weren't aware of it. You know how no one will work on our house? There's a reason for that. Mia, we've been blackballed."

Blackballed? Like a sorority pledge who made out with someone else's date, then barfed in a fountain, lost her shoe, wiped out six active members while she tumbled down the stairs, and *didn't* have Ann Marie pleading her case? "What does that mean?"

"Vienna's family issued a moratorium on any contractor who works with us or on this property. No one can take the job."

"Oh, come on," I protest. "They can't legally do that."

"No," he agrees, "but they're huge real estate developers—the biggest in the country, actually. They can't legally stop their subs

---

130 As if I wasn't going to notice all the smoke and extinguisher foam and firemen.

from doing work with us, but they can make sure they don't get any more family business. At least, that's what Nick was told."

I clench my fists and rub my eyes with them. "Aw, shit, this is what Ann Marie was worried about when we talked last week. *That's* why she wanted me to lock someone in with a contract. Goddamn it."

"You knew about this?" Mac's eyes fly open in surprise.

I wave him off. "I thought this was just another one of Ann Marie's wacky conspiracy theories, like how she thought we had termites and how our home inspector was senile."

Mac's lips narrow into a tight white line. "We *did* have termites, and according to Nick, Mr. Sandhurst has just been admitted to the Alzheimer's wing of the Abington Cambs Assisted Living Center."

I slump down the doorway into a heap on the floor. "Oh, my God, now what do we do?"

He sits down next to me. "There's a solution, but you may not like it."

"Whatever it is, I'll like it more than this." I reach out beside me and grab one of the thousands of handfuls of dust, debris, and broken nails that are free-range all over our floors.

"Nick knows a guy who can fix our house. His name is Vladimir, and he's not exactly on the up-and-up, but he's skilled. I guess he does a lot of work out of town, and he's so under the radar that Vienna's family probably doesn't even know about him. Nick said he'd give us his contact information."

I perk up immediately. "Great! Call him! Let's go!"

"Yeah, there's one thing," Mac says with some hesitation. "We've got to do something for Nick in exchange for his sticking his neck out."

"What does he want? I'll get him anything—signed first editions, other authors' books, an introduction to my agent. Whatever." I glance around at the squalor of our living conditions. "I am willing to do anything."

Mac's face twists with a wry grin. "Well, then, in exchange for Vlad's info, your task is to write Nick a sex scene featuring Amos and Miriam."

Damn you, Vienna.

Damn you.

I thought about finding some erotic fan fiction and trying to pass it off to Nick, but ultimately I couldn't put my name on something I didn't write, even if it was under duress.

I decided the most expedient route was to pay homage to the fridge scene from *9½ Weeks*, only I changed the setting from the kitchen floor to the ground in the milking barn. Instead of strawberries and whipped cream, Amos feeds Miriam friendship bread and dumplings and the very tip of his thumb. And then . . . other stuff happens under the watchful eyes of a barn full of Holsteins and two goats.

I feel dirty and disgusting after I'm done writing.

Then again, that might just be the end result of having our only shower break.

"You got big fucking mess on your hands."

"Thank you for noticing," Mac dryly replies.

"No, I'm serious. This is big fucking mess."

We've just conducted the whole-house tour with Vladimir,

our new contractor. He's agreed to take the job, and I couldn't be more relieved.

Mac seems to have his doubts, though. First, Mac noticed Vlad's 3AKA3 MO CCCP[131] Komandirskie watch. Then, when Vlad nudged the downed cabinet with his toe, Mac whispered that his boots were also Soviet army issue. When Mac tried to find out where exactly Vlad is from, it sounded like "Somewhere-istan." I assume whatever country he's from no longer exists, in which case I feel like we shouldn't bug him about it. Maybe he's sensitive.

Mac has an inherent distrust of all things Soviet, which he claims comes from his army background, but I'm willing to bet originated when Ivan Drago killed poor Apollo Creed in *Rocky IV*. Personally, I don't care about his watch or his boots, and if this guy wants to totter around in Carrie Bradshaw's Manolos, I'm fine as long as he makes my house more livable.

"Did you bring a contract with you or do we need to wait for you to draw one up?" Mac asks. Nick explained that Vlad won't do contracts, but Mac tries anyway.

"No contracts, too much paper trail. I like to stay . . . how you say . . . undetected. Not on grid. Quiet. Is better," Vlad tells us.

"That doesn't sound ominous at all," Mac replies, giving me a plaintive look. I shrug at him in silent response. This isn't exactly my first choice either, but what else are we supposed to do?

Vlad nods. "I got enemies. Long time back. Is bad situation."

"I hear that," I agree.

---

131 Translation: By the order of the Ministry of Defense.

Vlad suddenly becomes very alert, swiveling his head back and forth over his shoulders. "What do you hear?"

"No, I mean I feel you." Vlad's still confused and concerned. "I *understand* you." Vlad visibly relaxes and I continue. "I get the whole enemies thing. That's why no one will work with us." I briefly recap our issues with Vienna just to make sure he's cognizant of the whole situation. I don't want him ripping everything up and then deciding midstream he's too afraid of the Hyatts to continue. As of now, everything's an enormous mess, but a lot of the rooms are still functional with actual walls and floors. Once renovations begin, there's no going back or stopping halfway.

"You got money to pay?" Vlad questions.

"Of course," I reply. "I can give you a deposit right now if you'd like."

Vlad coolly appraises me. "Then we got no problem. We got big fucking mess, but we got no problem. Tomorrow we come, begin tear everything down. Is good?"

"Is good." Oh, crap. I've already started to mimic his speech. That used to happen to me all the time when I got sick as a kid. I'd be home alone for a couple of days with Babcia, and by the time I was well enough to go back to school, I'd adopted her cadence, telling my teachers, "Yes, have excuse in bag. Very sick. Better now."

"Okay, tomorrow," he says, before marching out the door.

As it shuts behind him, Mac says, "I have a bad feeling about this. I get a real ex-KGB vibe from him."

"Please don't start getting squirrelly on me now," I beg. "Do you realize what I had to go through to even get his contact information?" Every time I remember what I wrote about Miriam and Amos . . . and the udders . . . and the milking stool, I die a little inside. "We agreed we were going to do this. We have no other options."

"We still have the one," Mac argues.

Mac volunteered to quit his day job and work on renovating our house full-time. He's already drafted preliminary plans about how he'd need to upgrade his garage workshop in order to accommodate the project.

If Mac were interviewing for a job, I'd tell him to bring up the meticulous-planning aspect of his personality if asked about his greatest strengths and weaknesses. If Mac's properly prepared, he can blow through a task in a heartbeat, like when he mounted a shelf for me in college. The installation took ten minutes, zip, zip, zip, done. Buying the tool belt, gathering all the right screws, selecting the most appropriate hammer, and finding the studs and a lever and the right brackets took two weeks, and I was at the point where I was fine with my books living on the floor. Sometimes I need more execution and less planning, you know? Our infrequent fights almost always boil down to me getting on him to move faster, or him reacting to feeling rushed.

What's ironic is that as much as he plans and readies his tools, he's terrible at following instructions, because he secretly believes that he can figure out a better way; ergo, blue stew for dinner.

In order to do our renovations himself, Mac said he'd get his buddies to help him on the weekends.

Yeah, *that* was a selling point, let me tell you. I'm not sure which of those prospects strikes the most terror in my heart. He's friends with Luke, whom you may have seen on the news last year when he set his garage on fire trying to deep-fry a turducken on

Thanksgiving. Then there's Charlie, who knocked out a Wrigleyville gas main when he attempted to dig out an inground pool with a stolen forklift one night after a Cubs game. How about Phil, who ended up in a body cast after adding a nitrous booster to his riding lawn mower?

Or perhaps he'll bypass all of the aforementioned and he'll hit up his fraternity brother Bobby, who seemed normal enough until we set him up with Kara. Remember how cool and romantic it was when an eighteen-year-old Lloyd Dobler stood outside Diane Court's window with the boom box raised over his head? The scene is decidedly less romantic when a thirty-five-year-old does it, especially after having gone on only one uninspired date, where he spent the entire time crying[132] about his ex. Did I mention he pulled the boom-box stunt in the lobby of Kara's office at the paper? Every year since then, she's received a Peter Gabriel CD at her company's gift exchange.

I am resolute. "Not an option, honey."

"I don't like it." Mac pouts.

"The way I see it, our luck is about to change. Everything that could go wrong has. Things are about to get better. Trust me," I assure him.

Had Agent Jack Bauer not knocked a hammer through one of the holes in the ceiling right as I said this, I might even believe myself.

---

132 Literally.

Chapter Fifteen
NOBODY EXPECTS THE KYRGYZSTAN INQUISITION

"Hi, Mia speaking."

"I've been outed!"

"I'm sorry?"

"I've been outed!" Kara wails. "My parents know about the column!"

I sink heavily onto the floor, as all the furniture is under dust-covers. "Sweetie, are you sure?"

Kara's frantic on the other end of the line, and I can hear her bangles jangling in the background. "Yes! No. Or I'm not sure, at least a hundred percent. My sister called and said my parents were in a lather about something after talking to my cousin Parvati's mother. Parvati's family has been all over her about breaking off her engagement and I think she may have thrown me under the bus to deflect."

"Parv's not engaged anymore?"

"No, she caught her fiancé cheating with some chick from work, so she dumped him."

"That poor kid." I don't know Parvati very well, but I like her because she's so much like Kara—all hugs and kind words and frenetic energy. "Would Parv do that? She doesn't seem like the type to squeal on you."

"Not intentionally, no. But if she was under scrutiny, she may have cracked. Like when I got busted smoking in high school and I blurted, 'At least I wasn't drinking, like Parvati does!' Mia, you can't comprehend what it's like having my mom or her sister grill you—it's like waterboarding, only instead of water, they use guilt. The government should have my mother question terror suspects. We'd have bin Laden before she finished her tea."

"Okay, that may be, but I still don't follow how you know you've been outed."

Kara's breaths are quick and ragged. "While I'm on the phone with my sister, I get a voice mail from my mother telling me in no uncertain terms that I *am* coming to dinner up there Friday night, and that we *will* be having a talk. Honest to God, I want to puke right now, I'm so nervous."

From the clicking in the background, I can tell she's pacing. I do my best to calm her. "Kara, the simple fact is, you haven't done anything wrong. Your column helps people. People have problems. They come to you for a solution. You're providing a public service."

Her voice is small. "I guess. . . ."

"Think of all the success stories you've told me—like that woman who was afraid to let her boyfriend see her stretch marks, or the guy who was too shy to make the first move with his platonic roommate, or the kid who didn't know how to end her friendship with a mean girl. Happy endings, all of them! Yeah, sometimes you write about sex, but big deal; you do it in a clinical way. Your mom stares at lady parts all day. You think she doesn't field some of the exact same questions you get?"

Kara warms a tiny bit. "Maybe. Go on."

"Honey, you're writing for newspapers—hundreds of them— not *Penthouse* Forum! You do nothing salacious. You never started a column, 'I never thought it would happen to me, but . . .' If anything, your parents should be proud. Now, tell me what you're going to do when you talk to them."

Kara launches back into panic mode. "What am I going to do? I'm going to do exactly what Parvati did! Deflect, deflect, deflect! She told me she once kissed a girl at a party; I'm probably going to lead with that and follow up with the time she walked out of Macy's without paying for a bra. Totally accidental, but I'll leave that part out."

I try to speak in a slow, calm voice to make sure she's actually listening and not just plotting how to screw over her cousin. "K, that's a temporary solution and you know it. You've got to come clean, because the longer you drag this out, the worse it's going to be when you tell them. And you'll feel so much better when you do," I try to reassure her. "Let me ask you this—if someone in the same situation wrote to you, what would you tell them?"

"I'd tell them they were thirty-four years old and that it was time to man up. I'd tell them the only way to get their parents' respect would be to demand it as an adult, as an equal."

"That sounds like excellent advice. Why don't you follow it?"

"Because I'm chickenshit."

"Kara, you're not—"

She bursts in, "Wait. I've got it! I've got the perfect solution! I'm going to bring you with me to dinner, because she won't yell at me if you're with me. My parents won't make a scene if you're there. Yes, that's it! Tell me you'll come! You have to come! Meet me at their house on Friday night, six p.m., please!"

"Of course. I'll be there if you need me. But I swear you'll feel better if you face—"

"Mia, I am currently hiding in a closet thirty miles away from my parents in Abington Cambs. Clearly I am not ready to face anything. Now please distract me. Since you won't tell me any dirty stories because you're boring—"

"Hey," I protest. "That's not fair. I'm not boring; I'm private."

She snorts. "You weren't private in college—at least, not according to Ann Marie."

I frown and this time my forehead actually furrows, since I haven't wanted to waste money on Botox lately. "Ann Marie has a big mouth."

"Ha, I'll say. She told me about one time that you and her and four Sigma Chis—"

"Excuse me," I interrupt. "Do you want me to come to dinner or not?"

"Fine. But you really are Amish now." She laughs.

I nod. "You wouldn't be the first person to say so."

"How's the rehab going?"

I glance at my surroundings and sigh. "I'm not sure how to describe it," I say. "I guess it's going well? Vlad told me living here would feel worse before it felt better. We're definitely in the 'worse' part right now. Everything has been ripped out, and I mean everything. Last week they demoed the kitchen and they took it all away—the nasty old cabinets, the Formica counters, the twenty-year-old appliances. All we have left is our wine fridge and a toaster oven, and we brought those with us." Unless Mac brings home carryout, I've been subsisting on grilled cheese toasties and wine coolers.

I can't describe how depressing it feels to be here. When everything was ugly, that was one thing, but at least I could mentally redecorate, swapping out Formica for granite and a banged-up enamel sectional sink for something deep and wide of the farmhouse variety.

I hated the window treatments in the dining room, but when I looked at them, I was briefly reminded of the end of *Sixteen Candles* and remembered why we wanted this place. Plus I enjoyed painting over the living room's chintz wallpaper in my head, but now that the walls are down to studs in here, I'm having trouble picturing anything.

Vlad suggested we move out while they work, but where are we supposed to go? All our money's tied up in this project. We can't afford a rental, because we had to pay for almost everything up front, since Vlad doesn't have lines of credit anywhere. I suppose we could move into the tiny apartment over the detached garage, but no one's touched it since the sixties. I went up there once to scope it out and practically threw myself out the window when I tangled with a bat.[133]

I lean against one of the few standing lath-and-plaster walls.

---

133 Why do they always fly directly at your hair? Why?

"The basement's a wreck because most of our stuff is in storage down there. The upstairs here isn't so bad, except every single bath fixture has been ripped out."

"Toilets and everything?"

"Yep. We've got a Porta Potti stationed outside of the back door, and oh, boy, are the neighbors excited about that! Like this was intentional, as clearly my dream has always been to poop outdoors. Yesterday I was using the hose to wash my hands afterward and Lululemon came over to bitch about something. The thing is, she kind of snuck up on me, so when I spun around, I blasted her with the hose." Pow. Right in the kisser. It was both awesome and awful.

Kara giggles, which is a good sign she's starting to unclench. "Classic! What'd she do?"

"What does everyone do around me? Swore revenge and stomped off." I have to admit to laughing while she stormed away trailing water, but I'm not looking forward to how she might retaliate.

"Wait. Where are you showering?"

"At the gym. That's kind of a pain, but I figure it's all temporary. Vlad said he's going to start on a bathroom today, now that he's shored up the floor underneath it. Speaking of Vlad, I wonder where he is? It's almost ten a.m., and they're always here by now."

"I'm sure they're just at the lumberyard or something. Now, how's the book going?"

I try to shake off the vague feeling of uneasiness stemming from the crew's absence. I shouldn't worry, because so far, everything's run smoothly on the project. Plus, I feel comfortable around Vlad, because his no-nonsense approach reminds me of my grandmother. He doesn't believe in idle chitchat, and he works with dogged, albeit brusque, efficiency. He's been plowing through this place like a machine, and his one nod to being human and not, like, a robot or something is the occasional brief, curt cell phone call. Would I want to have him over for dinner? Not really. But I'll be able to prepare dinner only because of his efforts, so I'm okay with that.

Vlad's team has done excellent work so far, too. I expected them to be a little more . . . I don't know, fast and loose. Ribald and raucous or something. I mean, you always hear stories about construction workers ogling ladies and joking around over their lunch pails, but that's not the case here. These guys move with the steady, focused purpose of men in battle. They don't even listen to the radio while they work. Once we had a shower repaired in a rental house, and the guys our landlord hired did nothing but horse around and listen to daytime talk shows on their mini TV.

Naturally, Mac is suspicious of all the crew, because they seem to hail from the former Soviet republic of Somewhere-istan. Again, I suspect this is less because of the work they're doing and more because of *Red Dawn*. Mac came home from work early one day last week and I swore I heard him shouting, "Wolverines!" in the driveway, but he says he didn't. But who else could it have been? Citizen Cane? Elbow Patches? Doubtful.

Mac should lighten up, because the crew has done nothing but prove to have an innate understanding of all that needs to happen here. I'm wowed by their efficiency, and Vlad's already placed orders for every single item we're going to need, from tiles to appliances to fixtures to pipe fittings. He even made it easy to decide what drawer pulls I wanted. He brought over ten different styles and colors and told me to choose among them. Done and done!

So I should be all happy and relaxed, but still . . . why aren't they here?

"Mia? You listening?"

"Sorry. I was distracted for a second. You were saying?"

"I asked how the writing is coming."

"Better. I'm working in what was Jake Ryan's bedroom, because it's the farthest away from the noise. I'm not in love with a lot of what I've written, but at least I'm closing in on getting done. I've got about six chapters to go."

"Then you get paid?"

"Pfft, I wish it were that easy. Then I turn in the manuscript, my editor requests rewrites, I turn those in, *then* I get paid. If I get this done next week when it's due, I'm looking at at least six to eight weeks before I see any money. That's about when Vlad and Co. anticipate being finished with the house."

"Cool. Bet you can't wait. Anyway, it's after ten, so I should probably come out of the closet and get to work."

"You going to be okay?" I ask.

"As long as you come with me on Friday, I'm golden. Thank you for talking me down."

"Bye, Kara."

"Go write! Be brilliant! See you in a few!"

I'm glad I was able to calm Kara, but as I head up the stairs to my office, I can't help but feel a twinge of something stress related.

Where are they already?

Twelve o'clock and they're not here. Not panicking.

★　　★　　★

I come downstairs for an apple juice at one thirty. I kind of hoped the guys had simply been working quietly and I just didn't know they were here. My eyes immediately dart to the bucket of Monday Munchkins I set out this morning.

They're completely untouched.

Trying really hard not to panic.

At two, I call Vlad and get his voice mail.

At three, I text him, and keep doing so at ten-minute intervals throughout the afternoon.

At five p.m., I receive a text back from Vlad.

It contains one word:

Revolution

With my heart in my throat, I drag the television out from under its tarp and turn it on, flipping to the first news channel I can find. After Anderson Cooper finishes his think piece on Miley Cyrus, he mentions a violent flare-up in Kyrgyzstan between Uzbek and Kyrgyz forces. While he speaks, they smash-cut to footage of opposing armies.

I can't help but notice how half of the soldiers are clad in outfits *exactly like my builders wear*.

My builders.

Who should be installing my toilet but instead are likely on the other side of the world engaging in civil war.

With all my money.

I briefly wonder if the cash for my six-headed steam shower is helping fund this revolution.

Yeah. I can probably panic now.

Chapter Sixteen
DON'T TAZE ME, BRO

I scan the Web page in front of me to make sure I've ordered everything we need.

Your Amazon.com Shopping Cart Items—To Buy Now

Bathroom Remodeling for Dummies
The Complete Idiot's Guide to Electrical Repair
Home Improvement for Dummies
Kitchen Remodeling for Dummies
Landscaping for Dummies
Painting Do-It-Yourself for Dummies
Plumbing Do-It-Yourself for Dummies

Before I press "Proceed to Checkout," I add one more item.

Wilderness Survival for Dummies

There. That ought to cover it.

"Hello, sir, hope you're enjoying the weather today. How am I? Better than I was on Monday. I guess the bright spot in our contractor's absconding with our whole renovation budget is that it wasn't intentional. Nobody expects the Kyrgyzstan Inquisition, right?" I laugh bitterly.

I lean back and let the sunlight hit my face. "No, I don't really know what I meant by that either; it just sounded funny. Ironically I was unaware Kyrgyzstan even existed last week, and now it's pretty much all I talk about. Want to know about the city of Bishkek or Lake Issyk-Kul? I'm well versed. Did you know their national sport is horse riding, and no one in the EU will allow planes registered in Kyrgyzstan to fly in their airspace because of security concerns? Because I do. Shall I go on? I'm kind of an expert now.

"Anyway, boring, I know. Point? At first I thought this was all an elaborate ruse by Vienna to completely screw us, but I gave her far more credit than she was due. She's more low-grade thug than criminal mastermind. Turns out Vlad isn't a thief so much as he is a mercenary with terrible timing."

I glance down at the flowers I'm holding. I cut wild roses from the backyard today because peonies don't come cheap. "On Wednesday, the supplies he said he ordered began to arrive. So far we've received the spa tub for the master, a whole bunch of toilets,[134] Sheetrock and cement backer board, boxes and boxes of

---

134   All of them white and matching!

various tiles, and I just got a call that our countertops will be delivered next week. Granted, Vlad still has all the money earmarked for labor, so it's not exactly like we're ahead of the game, but it could be worse."

I smile and nod. "You're right; I've got to stop saying that. Every time I say it could get worse, it gets worse. Speaking of, Mac's started his leave of absence—unpaid, of course. At least he'll still have his job once we get these projects knocked out. But I'm not looking forward to the process. When I get home, we're bringing the tub upstairs; then he and his friend Luke are working on plumbing. I'm a little afraid."

I pick a damaged petal off one of the roses, and, not knowing what else to do with it, I stuff it in my pocket. This is not the kind of place where I want to litter. "I got a one-week extension on my book. Yep, that's it; that's all Nat could arrange after the first one. I've got to kick ass this week, because I'm out of second chances. And that's what's going on. I should probably scoot but I didn't want to leave you hanging."

I place the roses on the ground.

"See you next week, sir. And thank you for listening."

Many things can put the strength of your marriage to the test.

Infidelity.

Alcoholism.

Family conflict.

Children.

Illness.

Dishonesty.

Financial issues.

Yet I'm convinced nothing puts more strain on marital com-munication than trying to haul a whirlpool tub up a flight of stairs, which we're currently in the process of doing. I'm at the front of the tub, attempting to navigate, while Mac and his idiot friend Luke hoist up the rear. To say it's not going well would be like saying the *Hindenburg* ran into a bit of turbulence.

The problem isn't the tub's weight, per se. At the most this thing weighs a hundred pounds. Spa tubs really get heavy only once they're filled with water (and bodies), and if Vlad hadn't re-inforced the floor upstairs before he ran off to start an uprising,[135] this would have been a nonissue because we couldn't have used it.

The problem is the size of the tub. We couldn't fit it in the front door, so we had to go all the way around the back and try to get it in through the sliding glass doors. After much sweating and swearing, we couldn't fit it in that way either, and both Mac and Luke started to make elaborate plans to pull the windows out of their casings in an effort to establish a wide enough entry when it occurred to me that maybe we should just take the damn thing out of the box.

Did I mention both Mac and Luke are engineers by trade? Granted, Mac designed telecom networks before he got promoted to management, but Luke's a full-on civil engineer. He's respon-sible for designing bridges and buildings and roads, which means he's supposed to have a basic working knowledge of geometry. When they were debating Operation Window, I should have left them both to their devices, but no, I wanted to *help*, so that's what I did.

---

135 Or down an uprising—I'm not actually sure which side is paying him.

We began to maneuver our way through the sliding glass doors, me in front and Luke and Mac in the back. Our kitten Agent Jack Bauer—who at nine months old is almost twenty pounds—waited until we were all positioned halfway through the door before making a break for it through our legs and into the woods behind the house.

When I attempted to chase after him, Mac screamed at me not to drop the tub, and I was stuck. I'm sure the cat will be fine, as he's escaped a couple of times before and there's very little traffic on this street. My concern is for any woodland creature that crosses his path. Agent Jack Bauer is precisely as deadly as his namesake, only our Jack Bauer is more likely to kill chipmunks, not terrorists. Actually, all of our kittens are ass kickers, hence their names: General Patton,[136] Charles Bronson,[137] and Sun Tzu.[138]

So, through the house we went, and now we're at the turn in the stairwell and we're thoroughly and profoundly stuck.

"Guys, we need to angle it up and to the left to get it over the newel," I instruct.

"No, I think we have to wedge it more this way," Luke disagrees, turning and shoving the lip of the tub until it's firmly lodged between two wide wood balusters.

"Wrong!" Mac chimes in. "We've got to go even more to the right." And then Mac bashes the corner into the riser.

"You guys, please! I've got the better vantage point. Up and to the left!" I plead.

---

136 Whom I call Paddy.

137 Whom I call Brawny.

138 Whom I call Sunny.

"How about if I try this?" Mac asks, shoving his section of the tub into the stringer, which leaves an enormous gash and makes me wince. The stairs, up until five minutes ago, were the one undamaged portion of this whole house.

"Or what about this?" Luke throws his weight into the side of the tub and hits something, causing it to splinter.

"That didn't sound right," Mac says, and Luke agrees.

The fiberglass begins to get slippery. "I'm starting to lose my hold on this thing. Can you just do what I ask and go up and to the left?"

"That's why you need to wear gloves for this kind of project. See here, Mac? I've got the rubber dots on these and they grip like crazy. It's like the tub would stick to my hands even if I let go."

"Please do not let go!" I call from my perch on the landing.

"I go more for the high-tech gloves," Mac says. He rests his shoulder against the tub and shows Luke his hands. "For me, I'm all about the gel inserts. They aren't quite as grippy as what you've got, but I find they go a long way in shock absorption. Hey, when we're done, I should show you my new shooting gloves. The Palm Swell protects all the nerves in the center of your hand so you don't get so tired when you're on the range. Fatigue is the number one cause of misfired—"

"I'm about to drop the tub!" I shout, as the fiberglass slips out of my non-rubber-tipped, non-gel-coated, non-shock-absorbed hands. My end flips forward while the portion the boys are carrying wedges tightly in the stairwell.

The tub is lodged almost completely upright. I can't see around it, but from the sounds of it, the guys are fine.

"Hey, what happened?" Mac asks.

"I guess I couldn't hold on to a hundred-pound tub myself," I acidly reply.

"You should probably get some gloves," Luke adds helpfully.

Argh.

I grab the tub on either side and shake it in hopes of dislodging it. No such luck. "You guys, try it from your end!"

I hear huffing and shoving, and if I position myself right, I can see the guys through the tub's drain hole. Luke's hurling himself into the tub while Mac tries to lift.

"Yeah, it's stuck, all right," Luke confirms.

"Well, unstick it, please; I've got plans later." In a little while I'm supposed to meet Kara at her parents' house for her big outing. Poor thing was so nervous that she made herself sick and had to take the day off work. I've been trying to talk her off the ledge all day.

Mac takes charge. "Let me see what I can do. Luke, what we need here are tools. Let's go."

"Wait. Don't go. Maybe we—" But by then it's too late. They head directly out the front door toward Mac's workbench in the detached garage, leaving me alone at the top of the stairs with my thoughts.

I have two thoughts right now. One, that I should have never offered to emcee the goat rodeo that is carrying a tub up the stairs, and two, that I deeply, desperately, urgently need to pee.

I wait for at least twenty minutes before they return, crossing my legs the entire time. We don't have any functional bathrooms yet and we're still going in the Porta Potti. As soon as we got the tub upstairs, the guys were going to work on the toilet. I suggested they do the toilet first, what with my deep and abiding love of using the restroom indoors, but they insisted it would be easier to get the tub out of the way.

Yeah. Easy.

"What the hell, you guys?" I ask when they finally return.

"Oh, sorry," Mac replies. "Luke wanted to see my new impact driver, so we were looking at that."

"Can we please get me out of here? I'm about to wet my pants!"

"Then use the bathroom," Luke suggests.

"I would, but you guys haven't installed it yet! Hurry, please; I'm dying!"

"Whatever you do, don't think of waterfalls or swimming or anything," Luke instructs.

"That was very helpful, thank you," I seethe.

"Hey," Mac says, "we can probably fit a coffee can or something over the top of the tub and you can go in that."

"What are you talking about?" Luke argues. "When's the last time you saw anyone buy a can of coffee? What are you, eighty years old? Gonna use your S&H Green Stamps to buy something nice before you listen to your Pat Boone album? Coffee can, ha! She could probably go in a Starbucks bag, but I'm not sure they're watertight. Oh, hey, have you tried those VIA packets? Not bad. I keep them in my desk at work—"

Through clenched teeth, I say, "A can isn't going to fit. Can we please stop talking about coffee now and start moving the tub?"

"Okay," says Mac, finally taking charge. "Here's how we're going to do this. Mia, you're going to stand at the top and push, and Luke and I are going to come underneath and pull."

We try this for a few minutes and manage only to jam the tub in more. Then the guys lift the bottom as I pull up and back. We make a tiny bit of progress, but it's a hollow victory, due to how much this gouges the balusters. We're just starting to get somewhere when Luke stops us. "Listen, guys, I'm having a low-blood-sugar crash. I think I had too many VIAs today. They're just so easy to make! You just rip 'em open and add hot water! Bam, that's it! Anyway, I can't do this until I eat. Do you have something with protein in it?"

"We're not doing a lot of cooking here, but we may have some hot dogs in the back of the minifridge," Mac tells him. "You can heat it up in the microwave in the corner." The microwave Vlad ordered has arrived, and not a moment too soon. I was getting really tired of eating my SpaghettiOs hobo-style.

Luke starts to trot off, but then stops himself. "Wait. Where are my manners—Mia, would you like a hot dog?"

I would like to scream, I would like to cry, and I would like to hit something or someone. Yet in this moment, I'm probably best off following the path of least resistance. "Sure."

Luke's back in a minute.[139] "Here ya go, Mia!" I don't understand how he's going to give the hot dog to me until I see the end of it poking out of the drain.[140]

For lack of a better idea, I eat my hot dog. It's not bad.

The protein seems to refresh Luke, who comes up with the idea of removing the banister and spindles. Ultimately this will

---

139 Remember when it used to take, like, ten minutes to cook a hot dog? Those were dark days, my friend.

140 I wonder if this is how the Larry Craig scandal started?

cause more work on the back end, but will likely save hundreds in repair costs. "Let's do it."

I could wait in any of the bedrooms or up in the loft, but I feel like if I'm not within earshot managing this process, the boys will get distracted. I have to pee so badly my entire body is humming. I'd hoped the salt and nitrates in the hot dog would somehow make me want to go less, but now I'm about to bust *and* I'm thirsty.

"How's it coming?" I ask.

"Almost there!" Mac assures me.

"Can I be doing anything?"

"Well . . ." Luke considers. "You might want to, um, you know . . ." But before he can articulate "Hold on to your end," he pulls the final balustrade, and the tub releases, sails down the length of stairs, banks off the wall, and careens into the foyer, where the force of a hundred pounds of sweat-slicked fiberglass flies across the tiles and knocks the front door wide-open.

I'm off like a shot behind it, making a mad dash to the Porta Potti. As I sprint out the door and over the tub, I slam directly into two Abington Cambs police officers.

"Where's the fire, ma'am?" says the taller, older one.

"I'm sorry. I was just trapped and—" And that's when it occurs to me that I have two Abington Cambs police officers in my driveway. "Wait. I'm sorry. Can I help you officers with something?"

The younger, shorter one addresses me. "Ma'am, does a Mr. Bauer live here?"

"Come again?"

The older one takes over. "Mr. Bauer, does he or does he not reside at this residence?"

I am beyond confused. "Agent Jack Bauer?"

"Yes, ma'am, Mr. Bauer."

"You know Mr. Bauer is a cat, right? Not a person?" Then I'm suddenly consumed with dread. "Is he okay?"

"So you confirm he does live here?" demands Officer Younger.

"Yes. Do you have him? Has anything happened to him?" I worry that not only might Agent Jack Bauer be hurt, but that someone could have had an accident avoiding him. We live up on a bluff and the roads back here are winding. One wrong turn and someone could find himself down a ravine or in the lake.[141]

The younger one flips open a notepad before he continues. "We've had a complaint about your cat. He was seen at eighteen hundred hours urinating on a neighborhood lawn."

"He got out a couple of hours ago and I was tied up and couldn't chase after him. But how would you know that? Wait. Someone called you guys? Because a cat peed outside? Are you kidding me? Is this a joke?"

"Vandalism is no joking matter, ma'am," says the older cop.

And that's when I snap.

Or go all Swayze.[142]

I can't stop what comes out of me next. "Do I seriously pay thousands of dollars in property taxes so you two can harass me about my cat getting outside? Is that where my money is going? I'm sorry; is it illegal for creatures to relieve themselves in this

---

141 Big lake.

142 Your choice.

town? Are you going to buy all the squirrels tiny little diapers? Gonna give the chipmunks catheters? Hey, wait. A bird crapped on my windshield! Better call nine-one-one! I think that's a hate crime! I'm not kidding; this is singularly the dumbest god-damned—"

"Language, ma'am," says Officer Older.

Rage bubbles up inside me. "Forgive me. What I meant to say is that this is singularly the dumbest *gosh-darned* thing I've ever heard. You tell Lululemon and Citizen Cane and Elbow Patches or anyone else in this neighborhood who has you two rent-a-cops in their pocket that I will not be harassed any longer! I live here! I'm not leaving! But you? You are wasting my time, you're wasting taxpayers' time, and I'm about to commit my own hate crime if you don't get out of my way so I can use the bathroom."

I stare them down so hard that Officer Younger finally says, "We'll get Mr. Bauer for you." Then he goes to the backseat and plucks one seriously confused kitten out of it before handing him to me.

"What, no shackles?" I demand.

As they begin to back away, the older one says, "One more thing, ma'am?"

"What?!"

"You really can't keep your bathtub on the front porch."

After Mac and Luke convince the police not to Taser me, they all turn into fast friends over a conversation about their sidearms. The cops impart some wisdom on how to properly seat a toilet on a wax seal, and only then do we finally get something accomplished. Now, like Agent Jack Bauer, I shall whiz indoors exclusively.

Right before I go to bed, I finally think to check my messages. I have an increasingly panicked string of texts from Kara beginning at five fifty p.m., ending with the final one that says simply:

where were u?

Shit.

Chapter Seventeen
SPANISH TILE

"It's a jungle out there."

"You got that right," Mac agrees from behind his *American Rifleman*'s annual "It's the End of the World as We Know It" edition.

I come up to him at the table and bend his magazine down. "No, it's a jungle out *there*." I point out the window. "You promised me you were going to take care of the yard."

He sips his coffee before returning to his reading. "I will, as soon as I finish fixing the light."

Instead of letting any of the fight grenades in these statements explode and have the shrapnel ruin yet another day, I simply walk away. I'm tired of being angry. Yet I'm not sure which frustrates me more—the yard or the goddamned light.

A couple of weeks ago we had to discontinue the landscaping service because we can't afford to keep paying ninety dollars a week for a little mowing and some light weed whacking. A lot of our property is woods, so our place doesn't require nearly as much upkeep as one might think.[143] We have some flowering perennials out front, and I've done a fine job[144] of keeping them up myself. When I get blocked in my writing, it's nice to go outside and take my frustrations out on the weeds.

Given my current level of frustration, those beds are impeccable.

However, we do have lawn on the side and in the back of the house, and it's almost up to Daisy's shoulders now. The grass doesn't look like single blades anymore so much as short stalks of wheat and corn. One more good rainstorm and the yard might swallow her whole. As is, I can barely get her out there. I've been quietly resenting the yard for a while now, especially since the novelty wore off for the dogs. Sometimes I think they'd be happier back in the city, because the smells there were so much more interesting.

Mac's been promising to run the mower, but it rained most of last week and he didn't get the chance. Then he was supposed to do it a couple of days ago, but that's when the light on the garage blew out. I asked him to change it because the fixture is below the peak of the roof between the two garage doors and he's better on a ladder than I am. I'm not afraid of heights so much as I am particularly susceptible to gravity.

---

143 And there's certainly no reason in the world to have gardeners *on staff*. You know what? Three months later and that still pisses me off.

144 At least well enough to keep our neighbors from complaining.

Mac agreed to change the light before tackling the yard, and I estimated this project would take, what? Eight minutes start to finish if he actually put the ladder away and six if he didn't.

But no.

Nothing is that simple in this goddamned house.

"The four-packs of floodlight bulbs are in the hall closet," I told him.

"I'm not using a regular bulb out there," he replied. "I'm installing an EcoSmart LED light. I figure if I'm going to all that trouble of replacing it, I want a bulb that's long-lasting. I've got to go to Home Depot to pick one up."

"Can't you just save yourself a trip and stick in a regular bulb and take that time to cut the lawn?" I asked, mentally adding at least an hour and a half to the task, since he'd involved the Depot.[145]

"Being able to see the garage is a priority. I'll be back in a few minutes," he said.

Two hours later, Mac arrived home and was, ostensibly, ready to tackle the task at hand. However, I had to wait another fifteen minutes while he "strapped on his bags," because God knows you can't change a lightbulb without donning thirty pounds of tool belt. There's got to be a joke about how many do-it-yourselfers it takes to change a lightbulb, but my sense of humor was such that I probably wouldn't have appreciated it had I heard it.

When he was finally ready to climb the ladder, I positioned myself at the bottom, primed to hand him stuff as needed. While

---

145 Ladies, if your man can get in and out of that godforsaken place in less than an hour, please give him a medal or a lap dance or a pie or something. That kind of time management needs to be rewarded.

he removed the glass around the lantern and unscrewed the old bulb, I inspected the new one. That thing didn't look like the regular kind of bulb you'd see popping up in thought bubbles over cartoon characters' heads when they got bright ideas about how to best roadrunners and wascally wabbits. Instead the bulb had a flat glass surface in the middle that was surrounded by what appeared to be white plastic gills or spokes. Odd.

"What's so special about this?" I asked.

"This bulb is extra bright and environmentally friendly, and it's guaranteed to last five years. According to the manufacturer, it should save us two hundred dollars over its life span. That's why it costs a little more," Mac told me.

My ears instantly pricked up. "How much more?"

"A lot more," he admitted.

I did not care for the sound of that. "How much?"

Mac appeared to be very interested in the fixture when he answered me. "Forty-five dollars."

I practically crushed the bulb with my bare hands when I heard that. "Are you shitting me? Forty-five dollars? For a frigging lightbulb? Are you high or do you just hate money? I could buy groceries for the week with forty-five bucks! For two of these bulbs, I could pay for a week of landscaping! Forty-five dollars is insane!"

Mac steadied himself against the garage. "Can you stop shaking the ladder, please? We need it, it will last, end of story. My dad always says buy cheap, buy twice. This may not sound like a great idea now, but when we have five full years of a clear, cost-effective lighting solution, you'll thank me."

I snorted. "Yeah, talk to me in five years about that."

"Hand it up, please; I'm ready for it." I did and then he screwed the Hope diamond of lightbulbs into the socket. "Okay, now go into the garage and flip the switch."

What I thought was, *Oh, I'll flip something, all right.*

What I said was, "Got it."

I entered the garage, located the yellowed switch plate, and flipped the first switch on the right. "Done."

I walked back out as Mac called to me, "Mia! Flip the switch!"

"I did."

"Clearly you didn't, because the light's still off. You must have hit the wrong switch."

"No, I did the one on the far right. You probably just have a bum bulb."

With a tad more condescension than I'd deem appropriate, Mac said, "Mia, Home Depot doesn't sell defective forty-five-dollar bulbs. Now please get back in there and flip all the switches."

So I did . . . and nothing happened.

Mac didn't believe me, so he got down from the ladder and kept trying all the switches himself. "I don't get it," he said, and then he snapped his fingers. "Oh, wait. I figured it out. This fixture has got to be thirty years old. I'm sure that's the problem. I'm going back to the Depot to buy a nice new wall-mount outdoor lantern. I'll be back soon."

"What about the lawn?" I asked, trailing behind him.

"I'll do it as soon as I'm done with this," he promised, and I mentally braced myself for the inevitable arrival of the "You Need to Either Mow or Buy a Goat" petition.

Another hour and a half went by before Mac finally returned with a new lantern. "What do you think?" he asked, proudly displaying the two-hundred-and-thirty-dollar Beaumont fruitwood fixture.

"I think you should try a regular bulb before you go to all the effort of installing a new lantern. My way costs four dollars. Your way costs, so far, two hundred and seventy-five bucks. Not including labor."

"I'm not having this discussion with you," he fumed, stalking off toward the garage. So I went back to my office to work.[146] From my vantage point, I observed him burning all the available daylight in trying to get his fancy new light/lantern combination to work.

Yesterday he spent his morning installing a new switch that cost only four dollars but took three hours. After this bit of fecklessness, he replaced the whole junction box with zero success, and today he plans on rewiring the whole garage.

You know what? I'm just going to mow the lawn myself.

I change into old sneakers, cutoff sweatpants, and an ancient sorority T-shirt, stick in my earbuds, and select my sounds-of-the-nineties playlist as I plod down to the garage. I glower at the lantern and it's all I can do not to throw a couple of landscaping rocks at it.

We inherited a lawn mower with the house, and like everything else here, it's completely antiquated. Mac cleaned the blade and filled it with gas and he says it works, but considering it looks like a prop from the movie *Road Warrior*, I'm a bit skeptical. I wheel it down the driveway and let myself into the gated part of the yard.

---

146 And Google "how much do goats cost?"

I bend across the rusty motor and give the toggle dealie a tentative yank. I don't want to pull too hard, because I feel like the rope will break. Nothing happens, so I pull harder. The engine sputters to life and then dies, so I probably have no choice but to tug harder. I yank the toggle with all my might and the mower roars to life. And I do mean roar. Even with my iPod up full blast, I can't make out a single word Alanis Morissette is singing, so I turn it off. I don't need to hear her to understand exactly how ironic this whole situation is. I do leave the earbuds in to protect my hearing.

Cutting the grass isn't as hard as I anticipated, because this mower surprisingly has one of the self-propelling features. I thought I'd have to push this aging bucket of bolts like Sisyphus and his boulder, but really it's more a matter of steering. What's frustrating is that the grass is so long that I have to empty the bag every five minutes.

Also, apparently since we no longer have landscapers, we no longer have people who are paid to pick up dog crap. I retrieve what I can see, but due to the height of the grass, most of those treasures are hidden. Every time I run over poop, the pile explodes into tiny shards that spray me in the legs. I figure the tetanus shot I had last month will protect me from any doody-borne pathogens, so I keep going.

By the time I complete this chore, I've filled six brown paper landscaping bags, and now I have to haul them all the way up to the curb for pickup.

I'd ask for Mac's help, but he's taken off for the Depot *again*. I'd simply leave the bags for him, but since I want this done now,[147]

---

147 As opposed to never.

I'm stuck humping everything a tenth of a mile down the drive. The gravel grates so hard against the bottom when I drag them that a couple of the bags burst and then I have to rake up all the clippings and shards o' crap before it occurs to me to use the wheelbarrow.

By the time I finish the job, I stink and I'm itchy and I'm coated with sweat and grass clippings and dog poop, plus I'm pretty much dyed green from the knees down. I put everything away in the garage and find myself entertaining very unhappy thoughts every time I glance at the dead light fixture.

Then, like Wile E. Coyote or Elmer Fudd, I get a lightbulb of an idea.

I dash back to the house, grab a cheap floodlight bulb, and hoof it back to the garage. I gingerly set the ladder against the garage and, with much trepidation, begin to climb. I've nestled the bulb in my cleavage for safekeeping. Once I'm at the top, I unscrew the fixture, take out the new bulb, and screw in the one from my shirt.

I scurry back down the ladder and hit the switch and . . . in the words of Clark W. Griswold . . . *Hallelujah!*

Initially I'm thrilled the lamp finally works, but then I add up the expense and opportunity costs we racked up because Mac wouldn't listen to me and I begin to seethe.

I'm still standing in front of the garage when Mac pulls up. "Hey, I fixed it! It's working! I guess the wires righted themselves somehow."

I pull the forty-five-dollar bulb out of my shirt and silently point to it.

"So the bulb was the problem from the get-go? Huh. Well,

hand it over. I'm going to take it back to Home Depot and give them a piece of my mind," Mac huffs.

Then I take the pricey bulb and fling it against the closed garage door with all of my time-wasted, fecal-matter-splattered might. Because of its odd construction, I don't get the same satisfaction of shattering, say, a fluorescent bulb, but it fractures enough to truly be good and broken.

"There," I say. "Saved you a trip."

Okay, Mia, focus. You can do this.

I look down at my hands hovering over my keyboard and I will them to move.

Nothing.

No response.

My fingers are as immobile as a couple of teamsters on a coffee break.

I wonder if writer's block used to feel more devastating back when people wrote on typewriters. A blinking cursor on an empty Word document is bad enough, but then I imagine how much worse it would be to have a whole empty sheet of paper in front of me, with a ream of pristine pages sitting undisturbed in a box on my desk, taunting me with the sheer volume of incomplete work. I bet there'd be something satisfying about a wire trash can full of balled-up pages, though. At least then I'd have a visual measure of having tried. Right now all I have is a blank screen.

I'm desperate to get this damn novel finished. I'm so close, but I can't pull it all together because my ending feels forced and false. I want to wrap this manuscript up in a big, happy bow but I'm not feeling it.

Part of it stems from the whole Amos-and-Miriam thing. I can barely (figuratively) look them in the eye. Even though their sex scene wasn't for public consumption, I feel ashamed that I sold out their innocence for the dream of granite countertops and indoor flush toilets and cabinets actually attached to the walls.

And now I don't even have any of those things, and I'm too embarrassed to carry on their story line.

I so want to be done with this, yet I lack the inspiration to get there.

Maybe the problem is that I tend to draw for inspiration on my relationship with Mac, and right now, that's not terribly inspiring. The strain of living in this shell of a house is starting to show. We're both stressed-out and anxious, and he blames me for talking him into this place, and I blame him for not having the DIY competence he's always claimed. We're at a stalemate. A subfloor-covered, bare-walled-having stalemate.

I don't even know where he is right now. He stormed off earlier after I may or may not have gotten a bit shrieky about our credit card statement. But he spent *eight thousand dollars* this month at Home Depot in readying his workshop for our renovations, and all we have to show for it is one flushing toilet. We don't even have a functional shower yet. Last night we struggled so long and hard to install a kitchen cabinet that when we finally gave up, I was covered with sweat and filth. It was too late to hit the gym, so I took my towel and a little plastic caddy full of shampoo and soap down to the lake to bathe.

There's something particularly shameful about being a thirty-something adult with no choice but to wash my own ass outdoors.

My point is, if I'd known we had eight thousand dollars to

throw around, I'd have spent that on a rental house with a fully functional bathroom.

Anyway, it's probably best he's not here. I'm in no mood for conversation. I just need to concentrate and maybe, just maybe, I'll get through this.

Tock, tock, tock, tock, tock, tock, tock!

What is that noise? I look up from my manuscript and glance over at the dogs. Is Duckie scratching or something? Nope, he and Daisy are both out cold on their doggy beds. Weird.

Tock, tock, tock, tock, tock, tock, tock!

Okay, that's annoying.

Tock, tock, tock, tock, tock, tock, tock!

And it needs to stop.

Tock, tock, tock, tock, tock, tock, tock!

No, really, what is that?

Tock, tock, tock, tock, tock, tock, tock!

Is someone at the door?

Tock, tock, tock, tock, tock, tock, tock!

A very annoying someone?

Tock, tock, tock, tock, tock, tock, tock!

Why don't they ring the bell?

Tock, tock, tock, tock, tock, tock, tock!

I get up from my desk and pound down the stairs. God help them if they're Jehovah's Witnesses. Although given my current mood, I might not even be nice to cookie-peddling Girl Scouts.

Tock, tock, tock, tock, tock, tock, tock!

Tock, tock, tock, tock, tock, tock, tock!

Tock, tock, tock, tock, tock, tock, tock!

"I'm coming, goddamn it!" I shout.

When I haul the front door open, I don't see anyone on or near my porch or retreating up the winding driveway. *Argh*.

I head to the kitchen to grab a banana. Not long after I get back up the stairs, I hear it again.

Tock, tock, tock, tock, tock, tock, tock!

This time I peer out the window. I don't spot anything at first, but then I hear the *tock-tock-tock*ing and I catch a flash of red coming from the tree across from me. I look closer and see the downy, light gray feathery belly of a woodpecker.

Well, this is just what I need.

Tock, tock, tock, tock, tock, tock, tock!

I whip open the window and try to shoo the bird. He pauses briefly to give me what I swear is a haughty look and then continues on his merry way.

Tock, tock, tock, tock, tock, tock, tock!

I spin around and grab the first item I can find—a half-full paper Starbucks cup. Without even thinking, I chuck it directly at the bird and then I instantly feel bad. I don't want to hurt him—I just want him to go away.

The good news is, I don't have Vienna's prowess when it comes to pitching and I miss him by a mile.

The bad news is, I do not, however, miss the UPS man, who's here to deliver a load of drawer pulls.

After I help towel all the Cinnamon Dolce latte off his uniform and write what seems like an unnaturally large check for dry cleaning,[148] I return to my desk.

---

148 Although I'm in no position to argue.

Tock, tock, tock, tock, tock, tock, tock!

I holler at the bird some more, hoping that I'll scare him off. No such luck. Then I throw my banana peel at him—not to hit him, but to let him know that he's treading on my turf and he needs to "tock" it the hell off.

Can birds be smug? Because this little asshole looks mighty smug as he continues to bore into my tree.

Tock, tock, tock, tock, tock, tock, tock!

Clearly I need to alter my approach. I'm getting upset, and that's not doing anything for my writer's block. I need to find a way to unwind and just ignore the bird. I always find that a nice, hot bath soothes me, but that's not really an option, now, is it?

Maybe I need a drink. Yes. That's the ticket—a drink! A quick cocktail will calm me down and maybe open up my chi or something. I don't really even know what my chi is, but it's best to—

Tock, tock, tock, tock, tock, tock, tock!

—err on the side of caution.

Tock, tock, tock, tock, tock, tock, tock!

I grit my teeth and square my shoulders. I am not about to be bested by one pound of beak and feathers.

So I'm just going to have one quick drink and that should solve everything.

Fruuuuiiiittty deeelish vodka 'n' Hawaiiiiiian Punch!

Om nom nom!

I wake up late afternoon and hear the *tock-tock-tock* again. I'm about to start shouting when I realize it's just the pounding of my head. In retrospect, I should have realized that vodka has a higher alcohol content than, say, Baileys Irish Cream. Let's file that under "lessons learned," shall we?

I poke around the house but Mac's not here. Looks like he might have stopped in for lunch, judging from the empty McDonald's cup, but he's not around now. Whatever. I'm still mad at him, especially as I could have used his help with the woodpecker today.

When I glance out the front door, I see a pile of objects ranging from books to CDs to notepads to blank-faced Amish dolls to Barbies. Pretty much everything I could have thrown in the woodpecker's direction, I did. Somehow this must have all made a great deal of sense in my drunken stupor.

And this? Right here? Is why I never drink Stoli.

I go outside and begin to pick the objects up one by one, but I get dizzy every time I bend over. I come back inside and grab the shovel we'd used to scoop up piles of lath and plaster and decide I'm just going to dump everything in a bucket and deal with putting it away later.

Tock, tock, tock, tock, tock, tock, tock!

Oh, goddamn it, he's back.

"Stop it! I hate you! You're making me crazy! Go away!" I bellow, shaking my shovel at the sky.

Tock, tock, tock, tock, tock, tock, tock!

With my shovel in one hand, I try to scale the tree with the other, thinking that maybe I can scare the bird away with a combination of yelling and shovel shaking. But I quickly learn that I do not, in fact, have the dexterity or upper-body strength of a monkey, and I slide down the tree and into the dirt, slamming the bejesus out of my tailbone. The string of profanity that escapes my lips surprises even me.

I'm just gathering up my shovel—loudly—when behind me I hear, "For the love of all that is holy, would you please shut up?"

I spin around and come face-to-bicycle-shorts with Lululemon. I guess we're cross-training today.

She continues her tirade while I attempt to stand up. "Do you hate children? Is that your problem? Did you move here with the sole purpose of disturbing and traumatizing my babies? Is that your endgame? Do you realize they still ask me about the crazy old naked lady on the beach? They won't even set foot on the sand anymore! I have to take them to the pool to swim!"

I say nothing, instead opting to simply stare at her through my haze of alcohol and throbbing butt pain.

She moves in closer to me. "Well, say something, you moron."

I begin to inch back toward my house, and that's when it happens and I prove that clichés do, in fact, have a basis in reality. My heel connects with the banana peel I'd tossed hours earlier and, in overcorrecting my balance, I lurch forward toward Lululemon with my shovel. The scoop connects with where the tops of her sneakers would have been if she hadn't hopped right before I hit the dirt.

From my spot splayed on the ground I see her beating a hasty retreat down the drive. *"You attacked me! You're going to pay for this. I mean it!"*

For the record?

The drunk tank in the Abington Cambs police headquarters is more luxurious than most Holiday Inns, with its fluffy duvet covers, soft sheets, cheerily painted walls, and nice, hot showers. Better yet, the officers allow me a pad of paper and a pen and I'm finally able to get some writing done in peace.[149]

Mac was cleared to pick me up first thing this morning, but I asked him to wait until noon, because I want to take another shower and they're serving fried chicken for lunch.

Because the officers couldn't prove I'd committed any real crime, the charges were dropped and I'm back in my office typing up my notes from yesterday.

Mac is none too pleased with me, but I don't care. If he'd actually been here yesterday instead of pouting at the movie theater, this whole incident could have been avoided. He's at the gym right now and that's fine. I didn't join him because I already bathed today. In jail.

I figured the best way to resolve the whole Miriam/Amos plotline was to—okay, this is cheap and sensational and not at all how I normally do things—trap them in a well together. By the time the next book rolls around, I'll know what to do with them, but for now, they're out of sight and off my plate. Hopefully fans will actually enjoy having a bit of a cliff-hanger.

I've got to plow through the final chapter and then I'm officially done, at least with the book. *Then* I have an entire house to rebuild on a nonexistent budget and . . . Okay, if I start thinking about it I'll get all stressy and won't be able to concentrate.

All righty, let's do this. I'm immersing myself in this book. I'm not in this enormous, drafty construction site that I hate with

---

149 Had I known you *could* write in jail, I'd have taken care of Vienna long ago and then none of this would have ever happened.

every fiber of my being. Instead, I'm strolling the verdant green hills of Nappanee, Indiana.

Is it hilly there? I should probably check.

Scratch that; I'm strolling the verdant green *fields* of Nappanee, Indiana. I'm engaging all my senses now so I can experience the scene. The air is warm but not sticky, and I feel the sunlight on my face over the brim of my bonnet. I smell the rich, damp earth and I lightly trail my fingers across the scratchy wooden posts of the cattle fence as I walk by. Later, after I've done my chores, I'll feast on hot baked biscuits topped with honey and freshly churned butter. In the distance I hear the wind ruffling the trees and the gentle trickle of the creek. The bell on our old milking cow Bessie tinkles and—

Tock, tock, tock, tock, tock, tock, tock!

Son of a bitch.

Ignore it. You're so close, Mia. Just put in the earplugs Mac bought you. You can do it.

Tock, tock, tock, tock, tock, tock, tock!

Ahem, green fields, trickling stream, nice cow—

Tock, tock, tock, tock, tock, tock, tock!

You know what? I need to think more like the Amish. I've got to get inside their heads. How would they deal with this? WWMD?[150]

And then it comes to me. My plain-talking, straight-shooting characters wouldn't mess around with the symptoms—they'd directly address the cause.

I head down to Mac's workshop and grab some protective

---

150 What Would Mose Do?

goggles and his good shootin' gloves. And then I pick up the chain saw and march back to the house.

That tree is going down.

"All rise."

We rise.

"You may be seated."

We sit. Then I rise again when my attorney pokes me, because everyone's supposed to sit but me.

The judge begins to speak. "This is Mia MacNamara, case number 0360144237. Good afternoon, Ms. MacNamara. I understand you want to plead guilty to the charge of an unlawful discharge of a firearm, code 13-3107."

"Yes, Your Honor."

The judge glances up from his files to take his first look at me. He peers long and hard over his half-glasses.

"Ms. MacNamara, what is this all about?"

"Your Honor, have you ever seen *Sixteen Candles*?"

"Ms. MacNamara, I ask the questions around here."

"Sorry. It's just that it's superrelevant. Anyway, long story short, we bought this house that was featured in that movie almost three decades ago and we made a stupid, emotional decision, and because of a birthday cake and a song and John Hughes we bought a money pit that we thought we could fix up ourselves and we couldn't, and then a contractor ran off to fight a war in some former part of the Soviet Union and he took all our cash and I don't have a shower or a kitchen and I got covered in ants and now the only way we'll have enough funds to finish the house and start living like human beings again and not like bears or something is for me to turn in my manuscript, which I couldn't do because a stupid woodpecker wouldn't shut up already, so I threw shoes at it and shook a shovel at it and then cut its tree down and after all that I kind of lost my mind a little bit and I shot at it and I'm sorry but I almost don't even want to go home because my husband is mad at me and because I want to take another shower and because they're serving spaghetti for lunch at the jail today."

I gasp for air because all that came out in one big breath. "So, yes," I continue, "I'm guilty. I'm sorry, but I'm guilty. Whatever my punishment is, I'll take it, but please know there were extenuating circumstances that led to my discharging the firearm."

The entire courthouse is quiet after my soliloquy, and the judge takes a long time before he says anything. He takes off his half-glasses and rubs his eyes.

"Ms. MacNamara, what do you know about Spanish tile?"

I shrug. "Virtually nothing, Your Honor."

"My wife loves Spanish tile. In fact, she loves it so much she decided to have our kitchen redone in it. The whole job was supposed to take a week. 'One week, that's it,' she promised. We'd have the contractors do the renovations while we were on vacation. We'd be out, they'd go in, and we'd come back to a brand-new kitchen. Piece of cake." He swings around in his big chair to face his bailiff. "Remember that, Marcus? When I told you it would take a week?"

"Mmm-hmmm," Marcus the bailiff replies.

"And what did you say to me?"

"I said, 'Take however long they told you it'd take, double it, and then double it again.' "

"So four weeks," the judge says. "I did your math and I estimated the job would, at worst, take four weeks."

The bailiff simply chuckles in response.

"But the project didn't take four weeks. After the contractors ordered mismatched tiles and put in the wrong-size cabinets, my wife decided she didn't like her initial choices because they weren't 'Spanish enough,' whatever that means. So she had the contractors order different items. Then she liked what she picked, so we waited for them to be installed. You remember that, Marcus?"

"Mmm-hmmm."

"This whole time, I don't have a kitchen. I've got men in and out of my house every day, except for the days when they flat-out don't show up. No call, no e-mail, no texts, they just flat-out don't come. When I'd protest, they'd apologize and then not show up the next day. Seemed like they were intent on teaching me who really was boss."

Marcus is nodding the whole time. "I remember those days."

"Then, just as I thought we'd seen the light at the end of the tunnel, they broke a water main and flooded my basement. My finished basement. Ms. MacNamara, do you have any idea how long they were in my house?"

"Two months?" I guess.

"Try six. Six months. I lost my kitchen and my basement TV room for the better part of six months. I had to watch the World Series on the little TV my wife keeps in her sewing room. That was the year the White Sox were in the series. Instead of seeing the action on a sixty-inch plasma, I saw it all unfold on twelve inches of screen. Every pitch, every catch, every strikeout. Twelve inches."

"I'm really sorry," I tell him, for lack of anything else to say.

"I don't believe you're dangerous, Ms. MacNamara. I don't

believe this is something you'll do again. I'm willing to take your extenuating circumstances and let you off with a warning, this one time. But if I see you in here again, I will not be so understanding. Do I make myself clear, Ms. MacNamara?"

"Crystal clear, Your Honor, and thank you so much." Relief washes over me.

"One more thing, Ms. MacNamara. There is the matter of the tree."

"I'm sorry?"

"You chopped down a tree that was more than four inches in circumference. I understand the circumstances surrounding your actions, but the city of Abington Cambs strictly enforces this ordinance, so there is a fine involved."

Then the judge addresses the rest of the court. "The defendant, Mia MacNamara, is free on her own recognizance but will make restitution to the town of Abington Cambs in the amount of fifteen hundred dollars. Case dismissed."

He bangs his gavel and I'm free to go.

As soon as I figure out where to get fifteen hundred dollars.

But I did finish my book while in jail.

So there's that.

Chapter Eighteen
ALONE, HOME

"For what it's worth, Kara's not returning my calls, either," Tracey tells me.

It's been a week since I accidentally missed Kara's come-to-Jesus meeting with her parents. In between my stays at the Abington Cambs jail, I've frantically tried to get hold of her so I can tell her how sorry I am. I even maxed out my credit card to send her an extravagant wine-and-flowers-and-chocolate care package, but I haven't heard a peep back.

"I was going to go down to her place a few days ago and stake her out, but, you know, prison. I feel sick that she had to face her parents alone."

"Mia, it wasn't like you were trying to avoid her. This kind of thing happens." She quickly amends that statement. "Wait, no. This kind of thing happens to you, I mean. No one else gets trapped by bathtubs. Anyway, Kara finally standing up to her folks may be exactly what she needed. I bet you inadvertently did her a favor."

"If so, I sure wish I'd hear that from her," I reply. "I'll just add Kara to the list of things about which I'm panicking."

"But you finished your book. Why are you stressed?"

"Apparently you forget I live in a barn."

"Actually I kind of did. Are you ever sorry you decided to—cough*notlistentome*cough—I mean live up there and not just face ORNESTEGA and his band of idiots?"

"Lately? Every minute of every day," I mournfully reply. "Things are not great. Our nerves are shot and we're both overreacting to everything. Like last night, when we tried to mount a cabinet? I thought we were going to spontaneously burst into divorce."

We're both unbelievably sick of carryout, delivery, and hot dogs, so we decided we'd try to tackle the kitchen. First, Mac tried to do the cabinet bases himself, but the floor's so uneven that he ran out of shims trying to get them level. So he decided we should change courses and try to work on hanging the cabinets again.

When we attempted this last week, the whole incident ended in tears because Mac didn't know we weren't supposed to hang them with the doors on, and they were so heavy I kept dropping them. Realizing his mistake, he thought we could do it this time, particularly if we used a ladder to help balance the load.

To mount a cabinet on the wall, a strong person needs to stand underneath while someone with good dexterity anchors the cabinet to the wall.

As it turns out, I am neither.

First, we put me underneath the cabinet, with part of the weight being supported by a ladder, but mostly by me holding it up like Atlas tried to hold up the world, while Mac dicked around with anchors and drill bits. By the time he'd finally load up his drill, my arms would get wobbly and I'd have to set the cabinet down.

Since he didn't learn last time exactly how much I can bench-press, he decided it would be smart to bolt some of the cabinets together, so I wasn't just trying to hold up one—in some cases I was trying to do two or three.

Once we realized I didn't have the endurance to hold cabinets up for the twenty minutes it would take to get them anchored, we swapped jobs and I had to work the power tools. Mac got all squawky that I was "countersinking!" or "not countersinking!" and ruining the anchor holes and stuff.

In the end, we got a couple of cabinets up, but it turns out Mac measured wrong and now we have to rip them back down and start again. The whole ordeal was a nightmare, and I feel like I'm at my breaking point.

"Do you need to vent?"

"Yes and no. Remember how I've always had a policy of not saying anything about Mac that I wouldn't first say to Mac?" This is one of my rules for a happy marriage. I believe every time you bring someone else into a confidence that you don't share with your spouse, it forms a wedge between you and your beloved. Problems should either be addressed directly or, as sometimes is the case with me, shoved down into a little ball where they're hopefully forgotten.

"Of course."

"I'm having trouble keeping it all in and tamping it down. We're angry all the time now. I feel like if we could just get this damn house straightened out, we could get back on track. I know that'll happen eventually—the skirmishes in Kyrgyzstan can't go on forever—but I worry that in the interim, we're going to let our anger build up so much that we'll say stuff we can't unsay. Because we both want to avoid this, we're avoiding each other."

"If you change your mind and decide you want to talk, I want to listen."

"Thanks, honey. So what about you? How'd the date go last night?"

Tracey giggles like a tween. "I hate to jinx it by gloating, but we had an amazing time. He took me to a show at the Goodman and afterward we had the most delectable dinner at Nightwood. For the first course, we split hand-cut pasta with veal meatballs. Then I had weather-vane scallops in a tomato broth and he got a braised pork belly that—"

I moan, "Stop, you're killing me! You know what I ate today? Peanut butter and lemon curd on an English muffin. Untoasted. Yesterday I had a tortilla filled with ham and mustard, a can of chicken broth, a drive-through cheeseburger, and a mushy apple. I'm considering robbing a 7-Eleven just so I can go back to jail and get a hot meal."

"When will your kitchen be up and running?"

"As it stands now? A quarter past never, because the cabinets are just impossible and they need to go up before we move on to anything else. We're at a stopping point and we've barely even started."

"Why don't you buy or rent those support things that hold up the cabinets while you drill?"

Hold the phone—what? "What are you talking about?"

"Here, let me Google it; I think I just saw them use something like this on *This Old House* last week. Ah, here we go, I'm looking at the T-JAK all-purpose support tool. Says here 'the lightweight, multipurpose T-JAK tool is designed to ease the installation of kitchen cabinets, drywall ceilings, door and window headers,' et cetera. Lemme see if I can find a price . . . Okay, yes. They start at seventy-nine fifty."

I slump down in disappointment. "Oh, well, no wonder Mac didn't buy one. We can't afford seven thousand nine hundred and fifty dollars."

"No, Mia, it's just seventy-nine dollars."

"Tracey, I'm going to need to call you back." I hastily put down the phone and rush out to Mac's workshop.

"Mac! Mac!" I race to the garage with the dogs right on my heels. Mac's at his worktable, studying plans. "Honey! Our problems are solved! All we need is a T-JAK! It's some kind of support that'll hold up the ceiling when we drywall it and that way I won't get all crippled trying to install the cabinets either! It's a miracle! It's, well, it's probably some kind of tube and platform and—"

"I know what a T-JAK is."

That stops me dead in my tracks. "You do?"

"Of course I do."

"Then why don't we have one?"

He shrugs. "Because I heard pros don't use them. They're for amateurs."

I think about the debacle we had a couple of days ago, when

we ruined a whole sheet of drywall trying to install it on the ceiling, and reflect on how much my shoulders hurt from trying to hoist cabinets and the resulting tension, and I can't stop what comes out of my mouth next. *"What the fuck do you think we are?"*

The stack of bills in front of me is the same height as my mug of tea. I have them sorted into stacks of "late," "very late," and "they're probably going to send some guys." Every time I look at them, I hyperventilate. Now that I've finished my book, the money's going to come, but I won't see a check until I finish my revisions, and then another good six weeks. These bills need to be paid now. Each time the phone rings I'm shot through with anxiety and I hate it. I've gone my entire adult life making careful financial decisions specifically to never have to deal with a situation like this.

I've been running spreadsheets of our household expenses and I'm trying to cut every last bit of fat. While I pore over my paperwork, Mac strolls by eating an apple. There's something about his cavalier attitude that makes a tiny part of me fantasize about stuffing the apple in his mouth and roasting him over a spit.

"Mac, can you come here for a minute?"

"What's up?" He leans over my shoulder to see my array of paperwork.

"I've found an area where we can economize."

Mac attempts to not roll his eyes. "Mia, this is all going to be fine in a month. I don't know why you're torturing yourself right now."

"Why am I 'torturing myself'? This is why." I begin to slap envelopes down in front of him. "ComEd, North Shore Gas, AT&T, Comcast, Abington Cambs Department of Water Management,

Abington Cambs Bank and Trust, Chubb, Geico, MasterCard, MasterCard, MasterCard, Visa, American Express, Discover Card, U.S. Department of Education, and . . . Macy's? Why do we have a Macy's bill?"

Mac shrugs and takes a loud, wet bite. "I needed some new shorts."

Argh.

Calm down, I tell myself. *You love this man, and this situation is only temporary. Stop thinking of places you can insert that apple.* Through gritted teeth and a bitten tongue, I tell him, "I found a way to save a couple of hundred dollars this month."

"Cool. What are we doing, switching to cheaper toilet paper?"

"Yes," I hiss. "We're going to stop wiping our asses on bonds and start using Charmin."

He takes a step back and coolly appraises me. "Sarcasm doesn't suit you, Mia."

I stiffen. "Noted. Anyway, what we need to do is cancel our gym membership. We're month-to-month anyway, so we're not going to lose a huge membership fee. Plus, we're getting quite a workout here." All the physical exertion of rebuilding this place coupled with stress has had a marked reflection on my waistline. I've easily dropped fifteen pounds.[151]

Mac takes another noisy bite. "No can do. Where would we shower?"

"Here's a novel idea," I suggest. "Why don't you quit screwing around in your workshop and wandering the aisles of Home

---

151 The good news is, I can fit into my high school jeans again. The bad news is, they're acid washed.

Depot and actually install one of the new showers? Or hook up the tub; I'm really not picky at this point."

He says nothing, opting instead to chew his apple slowly. I continue. "I just saw one of those save-the-children things on TV. You know, where some organization visits underprivileged families in Appalachia and brings the kids candy bars and crayons and stuff? The announcer was all, 'This family only has cold running water in their bathroom,' and I got jealous over their ability to take a chilly shower! Mac, we live in what was—and hopefully someday will again be—a mansion, yet I envy people who receive charity. What's wrong with this picture?"

He finishes his apple with a slurp and attempts a three-point shot into the garbage with the core. Only he hits the can in such a way that the whole wastebasket tips over. "Fine. I'll do it tomorrow, or as soon as I get the west wall of the workshop organized." Then he stalks off, most likely to do something inane and useless, like sort screws by length and diameter.

I'll admit that the few projects we've completed successfully happened because Mac could immediately locate packets of molly bolts in his huge workshop. When he needed to whittle down a door edge, I was grudgingly impressed by how he'd labeled all his various wood planes by function, e.g., for smoothing, polishing, routing, etc. So perhaps there's some merit in being orderly, yet a tidy workshop does little to negate the fact that *I can't bathe in my home.*

I call the gym and cancel my membership immediately, and it's only once I hang up that I realize my mistake. I haven't showered yet today. If I call back and leave my membership open until tomorrow, I'll be charged for another whole month. As I see it,

I've got three choices: I can go without, I can hop in the lake, or I can get arrested.

My stomach growls, causing me to longingly recall the oatmeal chocolate-chip cookies I had in the holding cell. Yet as understanding as the judge was, I really can't risk another appearance at the Abington Cambs lockup. I'm all sweaty and dirty from yanking weeds, so I guess it's time to hit the lake.

I grab my shower bucket and towel, and because I just do not care at this point, I take the trail through the woods and to the sand instead of climbing down our rocky promontory.

I haven't even gotten in up to my waist when I realize I'm not alone. In my peripheral vision, I notice a familiar apple-cheeked toddler wandering into the light surf. I'm shocked to see that the kid isn't all done up in zinc oxide and floaties and a sun hat, because I get a real protective vibe from that family.

I crane my neck to see Lululemon, and brace myself for her ire at being on her beach, but she's nowhere in sight.

Hold on a second—is that kid down here *by himself*? He can't be more than two years old!

I haul ass *Baywatch*-style to the shore and scoop up the toddler right before he goes under a gentle wave. He seems to be having a fine adventure, whereas I'm pretty sure I've headed into atrial fibrillation.

My heart banging away in my chest, I climb the wide teakwood stairs up the bluff to Lululemon's impeccably maintained backyard and pass through the open gate. Even though I'm on a mission, I can't help but appreciate the surroundings. She's got dozens of small garden areas sectioned off with stacked pavers, and they're all filled with the most glorious assortment of prairie grasses and yellow and purple native flowers. She's got larkspur and lobelia and silky aster blended with meadow blazing star and wild senna. The grasses come in a host of varying shades of green, yellow, and magenta. Some are stout with broad leaves, and some are so tall and willowy they're practically my height. I love all the varieties of coneflowers, with their delicate petals sprouting out of the spiny center disk. They contrast beautifully with hoary vervain and wild leek, some with blooms so heavy and dewy they're practically doubled over.[152] This garden is nothing short of magical.

The pool house is the size of the ranch I grew up in on Spring Street, with a peaked roof, shake siding, and window boxes, and her pool's surrounded by bluestone and dotted with artfully staged rocks meant to look like natural formations, complete with waterfalls.

Lululemon's perched on the edge of a basil-green-and-white-striped double lounge chair, talking into her cell phone while Calliope plays with a doll at her feet. Lululemon's face runs the gamut from rage to shock to pure fear as she puts the pieces together and she drops her phone and runs to us.

"Missing something?" I ask, holding the child out to her.

"Gregor! Oh, my God, what happened? Where did you— How did you— Is he—" She's red faced and sputtering and crying and, for the first moment since we met, seems almost human.

"He was on the beach about to get in the water. He was having the time of his life,[153] so I don't think he's going to be scarred by the memory or anything."

---

152 FTR, Stephenie, that's how *I'd* describe a meadow.

153 And wasn't scared of being on the sand *at all*.

Lululemon shakes her head in disbelief. "I don't understand. I just sat down for a second to take a call and . . . I didn't even know he was gone. I didn't know." She sinks heavily into the lawn chair and buries her face into Gregor's chest. "I didn't know."

I stand there awkwardly in my bathing suit and I'm not really sure what to do next, as I've never been around her when she's not shouting at me. Do I just leave? Do I reassure her? This is all new territory for me. I begin to back away and she stops me.

"How can I possibly repay you? You saved Gregor's life. My family is in your debt."

I look her up and down, and for a second my mind races to all the things I could request. I get the feeling I'm in the position to name my own price, considering the garden alone on this place is easily worth six figures. Oh, and I bet the ladies in this neighborhood would have a field day if they heard about this little incident. I could probably even get pool-house-shower access if I play my cards right.

And then I instantly feel guilty for even imagining capitalizing on this incident. Doing right by someone else isn't about getting paid back.

"Two things," I say. "First, I want to be left alone. Let me be very clear about that. If you don't approve of the construction noise or the flowers I've planted or my mailbox, I want you to keep it to yourself. According to all sixteen of the petitions I've received, you, Mrs. A. J. Bain, are the neighborhood president; ergo, you're in charge. I imagine you have the power to call off the dogs. Everyone around here follows your lead; am I right?"

Numbly, she nods.

"And number two?" She braces herself for what I'm about to

say next, knowing she's in no position to negotiate. "I want to know your first name."

Her expression's colored with caution and suspicion. "That's it?"

"Yep."

"Nothing else?"

"Nope."

She exhales heavily, never once letting up her death grip on her son. "My name is Amanda."

"Then it's nice to meet you. I'm Mia." We regard each other long and hard. I have sincere doubts that we'll ever be friends, but I bet maybe, just maybe, if I needed some sugar she'd lend it to me.

"I can never thank you enough."

"No need." Things are going to be different from here on out. And you know what? I'm fine with that.

I begin to make my way back to the gate and then I remember something. "One more thing, though? I have to go wash my hair in the lake now and I'd appreciate not getting a petition about it. See you later."

It's amazing what a little passive aggression can accomplish.

I ease back into the tub as the water pours down on my feet. This is far and away the finest bath I've ever taken. Perhaps Mac believed I meant business yesterday after I impaled his apple core on the satellite antenna of his car with a note attached that read, *You're next*, so he had a whole parade of friends up here today to install this tub. I hate that I had to be so childish to get his attention, yet I can't argue with the results.

The jets aren't hooked up yet, and this bathroom's still pretty torn up, but the idea of getting clean in my own home is such a novelty that I don't even care.

Mac, Luke, and Charlie headed out to celebrate their "massive victory" (their words, not mine—mine were more along the lines of "bare minimum"), so it's just me, a mug of tea, and Cecily von Ziegesar's newest book.[154]

I take turns alternating the taps with my toes. First the water's too hot, so I have to cool it down, and then it's too cold, so vice versa. The taps feel a little loose, but I imagine they'll tighten up with use. When I hit the cold water, I hear an annoying little whistle, but it's not nearly as bothersome as, say, washing my hair in the lake or bathing with a bunch of Japanese industrialists, so I ignore it.

I slide down into the water and let my hair fan out around me. This? I could get used to this. I sit up and take a sip of chamomile and then dry the tips of my fingers on a towel so I can turn the page.

Oh, Chuck Bass, you are my favorite bad boy.

My mind drifts to the author—I wonder if she'd ever compromise *her* principles to write a gritty sex scene in exchange for drywall and fresh paint? My guess is no.

I just ran the hot and I've practically poached myself, so I opt to cool things down. With my right foot, I reach the whistling tap and nudge it just a tiny bit to the right. A slow stream pours out and the whistling grows louder.

As I lean in to get a closer look, the faucet makes a clanking sound and then—*wham!* The tap launches itself off the wall and

---

154　Methinks Blair Waldorf would make an excellent zombie.

pegs me directly in the chest and is immediately followed by a fire hose–worthy stream of water that's coming out so fast and hard that I'm pinned to the back of the tub.

I drop my book in the water and begin to shriek. I spend about ten seconds immobile from shock before I finally scramble forward to reach the tap. I try to block the water, but when I do, it shoots directly upward, drenching all the fresh new drywall hung on the ceiling. *Shit!*

I attempt to rise, but the water's coming out so hard and fast that I keep losing my footing and falling backward into the tub. Tidal waves of bathwater spill out over the newly grouted floor and are most likely seeping into the subflooring as I struggle and scream. I fish around in the water for the tap and attempt to screw it back over the gushing water, but the pressure's so high I can't get it connected.

I finally get the bright idea to stanch the flow with a towel, and I'm able to crawl, freezing and furious, out of the bath.

From what I ascertain, in their haste to celebrate their victory in assembling the tub, one of Mac's dim-witted cohorts forgot to tighten the tap with a wrench, and the buildup of water pressure caused it to fly off and, essentially, waterboard me.

I have to gather up every towel in the house to sop up all the water on the floor. I slip in puddles twice, soaking my shorts all the way down to my underwear, so I yank off my bottoms and continue my mopping in the buff from the waist down. Every time I saturate a towel, I toss it in the tub, which now appears to be overflowing with terry cloth.

I'm all bent over getting up the last of the water when I hear a noise behind me.

Fortunately it's just Mac and not a couple of Japanese investors. He's somewhat unsteady after a night out, and he seems more than a little puzzled about my state of undress.

"Hey, where are your pants?" He squints as he takes in the scene. "And what'd ya do to the ceiling?"

I say nothing, choosing instead to pitch my waterlogged copy of *Don't You Forget About Me* at him. I miss him by a mile and I'm perversely disappointed by this.

I bet Blair Waldorf never had to put up with this shit from Chuck Bass.

Chapter Nineteen
YOU KNOW, LIKE A RAT

What fresh hell is this?

Judging from the commotion coming from downstairs, I'm guessing it's a bunch of monkeys clanging metal pipes with wrenches.

Because it's absolutely impossible to concentrate on my last few book revisions with all this racket, I go downstairs to grab a Diet Coke and find out the source of the noise. When I reach the kitchen, I stumble across Charlie, who is, ironically, underneath the cabinet, clanging a metal pipe with a monkey wrench.

"Should I even ask?" I inquire, glancing down at Charlie, who appears to be doing nothing but playing a jaunty tune on the kitchen plumbing.

Mac shakes his head. "It's probably best if you don't."

I nod and return to my office. I fool around with my manuscript a little more, doing my best to scrub any and all Restoration Hardware references from everyone's conversations. Then I glance down at my watch and realize I'm almost late for my call with Ann Marie. I dial quickly and she answers on the first ring.

"How are you holding up?" she asks by way of greeting.

"I've been better," I admit.

"Are things coming together at all?"

What seems like a simple yes-or-no question really isn't. "Somewhat? Sort of but not really? More items arrive every day, so that's a bonus. Our new fridge came yesterday. I was so excited to be able to stock up on cold food that I even bought stuff without using coupons!"

Ann Marie snickers. "Living the dream, eh?"

"Ha. Hardly."

"Are you satisfied with the progress you've made on the house? Would you classify your living conditions more as 'tar-paper shack' or have you upgraded to 'post-Katrina New Orleans' yet?"

I make a mental inventory of everything we've accomplished so far. Seems like every time we take a step forward, we take a step back. Like when we got the drywall up on the ceiling in the dining room finally? That felt like a victory. But then when Mac went up into the eaves to mount the chandelier, he slipped on a slat and his legs came crashing through the drywall and we had to start over.

"I'd say post-Katrina. We don't need FEMA anymore, although you can see it from here. Actually, after I threw the book at Mac—"

Ann Marie sounds sympathetic, but she may just be breathless from taking in a lungful of smoke. "Big fight?"

"No, not a euphemism—I mean after I pitched the new *Gossip Girl* at him—Mac shifted into gear. He's not wasting nearly as much time preparing to work. Now he's actually performing tasks with mixed results. Take yesterday, for example, when we plugged in the new fridge. Every time I touched it, I felt a weird, low-level vibration run through me."

"Like a shock?"

"Yeah, but not painful, per se. But real, and I definitely felt it. So after the initial few shocks, I made Mac touch the fridge and he said he didn't feel anything. Then I said I did and he said I was crazy and we ended up having a stupid argument over it. But I knew something wasn't right, because refrigerators are not supposed to send pulses of electricity through your body. Although I bet you could sell fridges with a built-in electrical shock to dieters all over the country. Talk about your negative reinforcement!" I hear scratching in the background. "Hey, are you writing that down?"

"Mia, I have no idea of what you speak."

Right. Swear to God, if some kind of dieter's shock fridge comes on the market in the next few years, I'll know who's profiting from it.

"Anyway, clearly something is wrong with the damn thing, so I go upstairs and start Googling different iterations of getting shocked while touching a household appliance. Turns out I was right! When Mac rewired the outlet, there was some sort of ground-fault reversal and I was, in fact, getting shocked."

"Let me guess," Ann Marie interjects. "Mac didn't feel it because he was wearing rubber-soled shoes and you were barefoot?"

After all my run-ins with rusty nails, you'd think I'd have the common sense to wear shoes over my socks in this place. You'd think that, anyway.

"Bingo. What infuriates me isn't that he wired the outlet wrong—relatively speaking, that's small potatoes. What pisses me off is that he refused to believe me."

"Frustrating, I agree." When we talk, I get the feeling Ann Marie's responses take the exact amount of time it takes her to exhale.

"Then, after that little debacle, he goes to rewire another junction box. Now that he's savvy enough not to cause a ground fault, that's a step forward, right?"

"I'd say so, yes."

"And here's where the step back comes in. He had to cut a hole in the drywall. Oh, by the way, when we hung drywall last time, Mac learned the hard way that you're supposed to cut it with a utility knife and not a saber saw. You would not believe the flying debris a couple of quick swipes with a power saw can produce. Anyway, so he slices open a big hole and then he wanders off. When he comes back, he finishes his wiring project and then he patches the hole."

"Was the fire department involved at any point in this little scenario?" Ann Marie asks.

"No."

"Then you have to give him credit for his progress. The learning curve just got a little less steep."

I laugh but it comes out more like a snort. "No, it's more like, 'Congratulations on becoming king of the dipshits.' And you know what? I hate talking about him like this, but I've already expressed all these opinions to him and he doesn't seem to be taking the hint."

"Everyone can agree he's a decent man, Mia, but no one ever said he can't be dense about some matters."

"Exactly. But the wiring is not my point; he's got that down finally, and God bless him for it. He's not making the same mistake over and over—he keeps making new ones, because he refuses to accept the fact that he's not automatically good at stuff he's never tried before. He won't touch any of the repairs-for-dummies books, preferring to figure it out himself. I guess because he was instantly good at being in the army and later at his job, he's convinced that he's somehow inherently skilled in all things, like home repair and cooking. He can't seem to grasp that having the right tools and a positive outlook is only part of the equation."

I've been leaving HGTV on nonstop because I'm hoping he picks up some tips by osmosis. So far no luck.

"Anyway, I'm in the kitchen unloading all kinds of yogurt and cheese and lunch meat into the new fridge, and I hear Agent Jack Bauer meow. I check and don't see him anywhere, so I just assume he's in one of the empty cardboard appliance boxes. Later, I feed the kittens dinner and he's nowhere to be seen, but I can hear him."

"Is he fine? Don't tell me any more of this story unless you can confirm he's fine." I forget sometimes that Ann Marie has a soft spot for cats. In related news, Ann Marie prosecuted a guy who now holds the state's longest sentence ever given for animal cruelty.

"Agent Bauer is in fine shape, no worries. But I went all over the kitchen looking for him and it's like he was a ghost, all sounds and no sight. Then I heard the tiniest little thud in the wall and I put the pieces together."

"No."

"*Yes*. Mac sealed the cat in the goddamned wall."

"What did you do?"

I can't stop clenching my fists as I relate this story. "We had to cut a cat-shaped hole out of the wall just like you see on cartoons! Fortunately, Agent Bauer was completely undaunted and we're learning that drywall's pretty simple to fix once it's hung. A little joint compound, a little sanding, dry overnight, and voilà! Good as new."

"For what it's worth, I'm sure Mac meant no ill will."

"Of course he didn't! He felt awful, and he spent the whole night hugging Agent Bauer and giving him extra treats. But that level of carelessness just—" But before I can finish my sentence, the phone goes dead. I tap the switch hook a couple of times but nothing happens. Damn it.

We've had a few connectivity problems—of course we have— and I've become an expert on how to fix them. I get up from my desk and trek down to the network area in the panic room. What I have to do is recycle the router, which is a fancy way of saying unplug and then replug it.

Once I reach the networking area, this whole task shouldn't take more than a minute. I get to the panic room and heave open the heavy metal door. I quietly fume that while this room helped sell Mac on this house, he hasn't done much with it except to stow the most basic of disaster supplies and some of his second-tier tools. Should the unthinkable happen, we're good for two days, tops.

While I wait for the router to complete a cycle, Charlie pops into the room. "Mac sent me down for a different wrench." I have to suppress a giggle—Mac treats his tools like his children, and I'm sure Charlie's banging the pipes hurt him as much as it annoyed me. Mac's sending Charlie down here for the old stuff tells me everything I need to know about Charlie's plumbing prowess and the status of the sink installation.

"The toolbox is over there," I say, pointing to the corner nearest the door.

"Got it!" Charlie grabs something off the top of the box and then trots out the door, shutting it behind him.

I get to a thirty count and then turn the router back on. I wait as each little green light lights up, and when I have a row of them, I know our Internet connection[155] has been restored.

Before I go back up, I poke around the few supplies Mac has stashed. We've got a couple of army MREs,[156] a three-day supply of bottled water, a few first-aid products, and an Army Ranger survival guide. Apparently in the case of home invasion or nuclear holocaust, Mac might like to get in a bit of light reading.

I walk over to the door and open it.

Rather, I try to pull it open, but it's really heavy. I put both hands on the knob and give it a good yank.

Nothing happens.

I jimmy the handle and then, using both hands, I pull on it while bracing myself against the doorjamb with one of my feet. The handle gives way, but unfortunately not in the manner I'd

---

155 And IP phone line.

156 Meals ready to eat.

hoped. It takes me a couple of seconds to process that the knob has come off in my hand. *Uh-oh.*

If nothing else, living in this house has made me resourceful. Instead of panicking, I root around in Mac's tool bag and come up with an old pair of pliers. I use them to manipulate the pin of the door handle, simultaneously pulling and bracing again.

This time the pin comes off in my hand.

So I resort to my second option.

Yelling.

I shout with all my might and bang on the inside of the door with the pliers.

What I quickly find out is that bombproof rooms are also soundproof rooms.

I whip out my cell phone and attempt to call Mac, but I'm not getting a signal. Awesome.

I start going over every inch of this room, because surely there's some sort of two-way communication device in here. I mean, no one would put this much effort into a room and then . . . And then I remember where I am. I am in the middle of the House Where Shit Goes Horribly Awry, and there is no fail-safe in this room.

If I were to disconnect the Internet, Mac would know to come down here, but he's not at his computer right now and probably won't be for a while. The best that I can hope for is that he comes looking for me sooner rather than later.

For lack of anything else to do, I settle on a metal cot covered in a scratchy army blanket and begin to read the survival guide.

According to the manual, I should remain calm. Noted. I don't think remaining calm while I'm in here is my problem. I imagine needing to remain calm will come into play *after* I'm out of here.

As I peruse the chapter on planning and survival packs, I make a note that Mac's kit contains neither a snare nor a solar blanket nor water purification tablets. Also, Mac hasn't stored pudding cups down here. The guide doesn't say specifically that we need them, but I feel this is a serious omission.

I wish I'd run across the chapter on contact dermatitis before now. That bit of knowledge might have gone a long way in educating me in why one should wear long pants to mow the lawn. In related news, poison oak leaves actually look an awful lot like regular oak leaves and should be retrieved while wearing gloves or with a rake.

Ask me how I learned this.

The guide provides excellent advice in regard to starting a fire. Good thing I'm not cold down here, because there seems to be a dearth of flint, convex lenses, spongy threads of dead puffball, or birch shavings.

I'm greatly enjoying the "dangerous lizard" chapter. I can't imagine I'll ever need to put this learning to use, but if I ever get a lizard question in Trivial Pursuit, I'll be all over it.

Oh, Mexican beaded lizard,[157] I've got my eye on you.

*   *   *

---

157 *Heloderma horridum.* Come on, is that not the best Latin name you've ever heard?

A few hours into my captivity, I find myself sizing up the electrical panel. Possibly it's because I'm so rife with new survival skills, or perhaps because I'm too much of a dumb ass to have thought of it sooner, but I've just discerned my means of egress.

I pocket a flashlight from Mac's supplies and walk over to the electrical panel. I open the metal box and systematically begin to flip every switch. The last tab I flip bathes the room in darkness, but I'm confident it won't be for long. I switch on my flashlight and return to the cot.

Less than two minutes later, Mac opens the door with his own flashlight in hand and he's greeted by my bellowing, "*Do not shut the door!*" Mac prides himself on his inability to be spooked, yet odds are good my ethereally lit presence causes him to shart himself.

"What were you doing in here?" he demands.

I reach the junction box first and turn all the switches back. "Boning up on my survival skills."

After I fully explain the whats and the hows of my imprisonment, that son of a bitch has the audacity to laugh.

"Yes, yuk it up. This is hilarious," I snap.

Mac wipes his eyes and tries to stop smiling. "Listen, I'm sorry, but it's funny. You should call the Guinness book people, because you have to have set some kind of record for 'number of times trapped' by now." He then goes on to list every time and place I've been stuck in the past five years and he starts to snicker again.

I say nothing in response, instead just crossing my arms and tapping my foot, waiting for him to finish.

"Are you done yet?"

"Yes. No! The tub! I forgot about the tub. Now I'm done."

"Good."

I turn to leave, and Mac, who's staying behind to fix the door, calls after me, "Where are you going now?"

"I have to call Ann Marie back and I want to eat some pudding. But first, I need to punch Charlie in the head."

"I got the call. I got the call and I haven't any idea how to proceed. What do I do? Where do I go from here?"

I'm not on my usual cement bench today. Instead, I'm up and pacing back and forth, because I've got too much nervous energy coursing though me. "I mean, I'm thrilled and I'm excited, because this is everything I've worked for, but at the same time I'm scared, because now what? I mean, this is a life changer. This is big-time. Hollywood, baby!"

Although we're in late summer and the sun is high and bright, I feel chilled and I wrap my arms around myself. "I'm afraid; I guess that's what it is. I'm afraid if I leave, then whatever's unsaid, whatever isn't working between Mac and me, is going to fester and decay and we'll never be able to get back to where we were once upon a time.

"Funny, I always thought that if we were ever going to break up, there'd be some huge incident, clear and unarguable. We'd suffer the marital equivalent of thermonuclear war, and *bang!* Mutually assured destruction. There'd be no question as to whether we should proceed in life together. But this? This isn't one mass detonation; it's a million tiny explosions, but we're at the same crossroads.

"I don't know what to do. Persiflage Films wants me to hop on a plane tonight, right now, in fact, and be ready to start taking meetings tomorrow. But there's so much to be said, so much to resolve. . . . Do I just go and hope we can work it out over the phone? Honestly, that seems like running away, and I already do that far too much. Or, like lately, I completely lose my shit and start yelling and throwing small, breakable objects. We've always been so good about talking things out, but now I'm so frustrated that I can't seem to stop going from completely passive to overly aggressive. I've lost the ability to find middle ground."

I collapse onto the bench, suddenly exhausted by all the adrenaline dumped in my body after I found out that Persiflage actually agreed to meet my asking price for my books' rights. My agents are currently hammering out the last few specifics on gross and net points and production credits and such, but the bottom line is, I'm about to be wealthy.

The big catch is that the film company wants me to be an active participant in the process from start to finish. They're buying not only my words, but also my "artistic vision."[158] They need me in LA as soon as possible and for an undetermined amount of time.

"Mac wasn't home when I got the call, and I couldn't reach him by cell, so he doesn't even know. Last thing he said was that he was going to the plumbing specialty store, so I imagine he'll be off the radar for a while. I talked to Ann Marie, who doesn't want me to do anything without her reading my contract—go figure— and to my family. Jessica and Claire are beside themselves, especially as Claire's going to be the coolest girl in eighth grade when the film comes out. My mom was totally psyched, and Babcia, well . . . Babcia is Babcia."

---

158 Their words, not mine. And yes, I had to choke back a laugh when they said that, too.

No matter what the situation, Babcia's reaction is totally unpredictable, and I find that charming. "Babcia's exact words were, 'Life not movie. Good guy lose, everybody die, love not cocoa all.' I had no idea what that was supposed to mean, but Jessica said Babcia signed up for a Netflix membership and she's been watching a bunch of Kevin Spacey movies lately. Apparently she thinks he looks like her dead husband. Anyway, Jessica suspects this is some bastardization of a quote from *Swimming with Sharks*. Oh, boy, I can't wait until she starts grilling me about who Keyser Söze is."

The truth is, I've been avoiding Babcia a little bit ever since Vlad ran off. The rest of my family knows about our current housing predicament, but we didn't want to tell Babcia because we don't want her to worry.[159]

I glance down at my watch and see that I've been away from home for a while now. "Time to go. I'll see you next week. Or maybe not? I guess that's still to be decided. Tell you what, if you could send me some kind of sign, I'd appreciate it. Bye for now."

When I get back home, Mac's car is in the driveway, but I don't see a sign of him downstairs. The dogs seem to be gone, too. I wonder if they're outside. I search the backyard and around all the boxes in the basement. For good measure, I even peek my head in the panic room, but it's just as I left it last week, save for the addition of a case of pudding cups.

He's not upstairs, either. Weird. Maybe everyone's out for a walk?

I'm still not sure what I'm going to do about leaving for LA,

---

159 Or have something bad happen to Vlad's family. With Babcia, you kind of never know.

but just in case, I should probably toss in a load of laundry. Our new washer and dryer arrived not long ago, and every time I'm able to wash a sheet or towel in my house, as opposed to the Laundromat two towns over,[160] I want to hug someone.

There's a small maid's quarters off the laundry room, and when I pass it, I hear swearing. I wonder what he's doing in here. This part of the house was one of the numerous additions, and it's so awkwardly located that there's no reason ever to come in here. Plus it's built over a crawl space instead of a basement, so it's perpetually hotter than the rest of the house.

"Mac?"

"Miiiiiaaaaaa!"

"Where are you?" I poke my head into the attached bath, and that's when I find the dogs. They're both staring into a hole in the floor and wagging their tails. I gaze down into it and, under a maze of new copper pipes, see Mac. "What the . . . ?"

"Miiiiiiaaaaaa!"

I can't even begin to figure out what's happening here. Mac appears to be—judging from his level of agitation—unharmed. But trapped. Clearly trapped. He's down under the subflooring in the crawl space, and there're a whole bunch of pipes blocking the hole in the floor between where he's sitting and the bathroom above it.

"Is there an explanation for all of this?" I ask. The dogs flop down on either side of me, still peering into the hole.

"Yes, but can I have a bottle of water first? I'm dying of thirst."

"Um . . . okay." I scurry to the kitchen, grab a bottle from the

---

160　Like Abington Cambs would ever allow a Laundromat to sully their town green!

fridge, and trot back to the bathroom. "Do you want me to just . . . throw it down there?"

"Yes, please." He unscrews the cap and downs the whole thing in a single swig.

"Is it safe for me to come closer? Did you fall in? Do I need to call the police?" Actually, I wouldn't mind giving Officers Older and Younger a buzz. Might be nice for them to see it's not me doing the stupid stuff around here for once.

"Yes, it's safe, and no, I didn't fall in. I cut the floorboards back to the joists, so anything you stand on is supported."

"Good to know." I sit down at the lip of the hole and dangle my legs in. "So . . . how was your day? Were the dogs well behaved? Did they finally want to play outside? Oh, and did anything interesting happen?"

His voice gets a wee bit accusatory. "*You* wanted a working shower."

"Mmm," I agree. "I did want a shower. But what I got is a husband doing the world's largest termite impersonation. Tell me, are you drywood or Formosan subterranean?"

"Not funny, Mia."

"That's where you're wrong, honey. This is *so* funny." There's a certain amount of poetic justice here. I've been trapped in bathrooms a dozen times, but I've never actually been stuck *under* one.

"Anyway, this shower was the quickest fix, because we're not replacing tile or a tub surround or anything in the walls. All I needed to do was patch a couple of leaky pipes with new sections. I started doing the repair on the bathroom floor and I felt like I was working upside down. I thought if I climbed into the crawl space I'd have an easier time accessing all the pipes. And I did. Everything soldered together perfectly. Check out my work—it's professional-grade."

"Do most professionals wind up piping themselves in?" I query.

"I see you've discovered the one small flaw in my plan."

"Why don't you just disconnect the pipes and pull yourself out? Isn't that the most logical solution?"

"Because it will ultimately be easier and faster to patch the floor than it will be to redo the pipes. What I need you to do is grab the cordless handheld saw and pass it down to me. That way I can cut myself out without damaging the joists."

I find the saw and Mac manages to extricate himself as quickly as promised.

As we patch up the subflooring, we seem to have developed a tentative truce. This is the first time in a long time we've had a conversation without snapping at each other.

And that's when it occurs to me that the floor was a sign.

We need the money to bring in an outside professional to get this house done if we're to have any hope of a future together. I imagine we'd have to pay a premium to put up a whole crew of folks from an area outside of Vienna's family's reach, but as much as we love each other, we can't continue to live like this. If our formerly rock-solid relationship is already on shaky ground after three months, I can't bear to think of where we might be in three more. I hate to leave, but I think that's the only chance we've got to stay together.

Los Angeles, here I come.

Chapter Twenty
MOSE(Y) GOES TO HOLLYWOOD

"Just so you know, I'm comfortable with nudity. Very comfortable. In fact, I prefer it. I'm, like, naked all the time in my apartment. My roommates, too!"

I sneak little glances at everyone sitting at the table with me. As no one else seems on the verge of collapsing in nervous laughter, I guess they've all heard auditioning actresses say this stuff before.

I'm sitting in a casting session. I've been in LA for about two weeks and we're just starting to test people for principal roles. Since I've been here, we (meaning a big team of people who seem to know what they're doing, and me, who does not) have done a lot of the legwork that happens before a film goes into production.

Before I even signed on, financing was secured[161] and now key personnel have been hired, casting directors have been engaged, scouts are checking out potential locations, etc.

To be honest, I still don't really understand the process. I tried to do research before I came out here but, surprisingly, Google didn't have a lot of answers when I typed in, *I sold my book to a movie studio for a whole bunch of money; now what?*

My agents are thrilled this film wasn't only green-lighted but also fast-tracked, which is fancy movie talk for "going a bit too quickly for my liking." Two and a half weeks ago I was staring into a hole in the bathroom floor, and now I'm in meetings with a bunch of suits estimating opening-weekend box-office sales. It's surreal.

On the one hand, the more swiftly this process moves, the sooner I can go home to my husband and pets and albatross of a house. On the other, I fear we're rushing and getting sloppy. Can't we all have a minute to get our bearings?

Also, and more important, I thought my job out here would be, you know, *writing*. I penned the initial screenplay for *Buggies Are the New Black* years ago between books, because I was told that everyone in Hollywood is lazy and that no one would want to convert my writing from a novel to a screenplay.

Actually, I enjoyed the challenge, because it was fun to dabble in such a different medium. At first I was all, *How different could it be? Words are words*, but that's not the case. When you adapt a book, all you have to work with is dialogue. You can't really set the scene other than a line noting where the scene takes place. Plus, you're

---

161 Apparently this is a big deal.

not supposed to provide too much background in scene headings or include many parentheticals,[162] because that's for a director to interpret.

I was worried that someone would get hold of my story and change it too drastically, so I wrote the screenplay myself to avoid all of that. Yet here I am in a casting session while some writer I never met gives my screenplay a "polish." I'm told he's going to be listed as one of the cowriters in the credits. Somehow this feels wrong.

But in terms of wrong, nothing's been more wrong than the parade of bimbos who have tottered through here today. Seriously, can we talk about Miriam for a second? She's supposed to be a quiet, reserved, gentle Amish girl who inadvertently gets turned into a zombie. (Although, really, does anyone go zombie *advertently*?) But Miriam's propensity for goodness is such that she keeps all her undead flesh eating to a minimum, and that's how she earns Amos's trust and love.

Yes, I know her story sounds a tad *Twilight*-y.

Yes, more than a little.

I know.

I know.

I'll thank you all to quit pointing it out, and did you ever consider that MAYBE I HAD THE DAMN IDEA FIRST AND THAT ASSHAT STEPHENIE—

Ahem. Moving on.

Anyway, when I picture my Miriam, I envision someone slight and darkly lovely, with luminous skin the color of fresh milk and

---

162 When you give instruction on how an actor's supposed to say a line, e.g., "dryly."

enormous, soulful, haunted eyes—kind of like a young Winona Ryder before all the bat-shittery.

Miriam might appear weak and unassuming, but she's got a well of hidden strength. She should dwell in that netherworld somewhere between childhood and adulthood, maybe sixteen or seventeen years old. I'm looking for an actress who possesses a certain innocence, someone who can portray the kind of child/woman who knows of disappointment and adult problems but hasn't yet been jaded by the world. Every time she curls her delicate lip or raises her eyebrow, I want her to be able to telegraph the emotion she's expressing all the way to the back row of the theater.

When I explained this to the casting coordinator, he was all, "Oh, yeah, like Kristen Stewart?"

NO, NOT LIKE KRISTEN STEWART.

But I'd take K-Stew in a second over these ridiculously implanted *Rock of Love* girl wannabes.

Ladies?

For the record?

The Amish don't have hair extensions, and *that* I know for a fact.

The woman auditioning now claims to be twenty-two, but she's as close to twenty-two as I am. In what I imagine is her nod to the Amish, she's plaited her blond hair (with pink highlights) into two braids and tied her completely unbuttoned shirt under where her bra would hit, were she wearing one. She's clad in shorty-short cutoff jeans, and the charm hanging out of her belly-button piercing is a cowboy boot. If she were auditioning for the porn version of *The Beverly Hillbillies*, yeah, I could see her being appropriate, but otherwise? *Blech.*

"That was great, Amberleigh, just great, thanks! Hope to see you back again," says Seth. He's running the show here and was brought in by the studio executives to head up my film. I keep trying to defer to him, because he's the one with all the experience, but *damn*.

As soon as she steps out of the room, I whip around to face him. "You were joking, right?"

He's the very picture of innocence. "Whatever do you mean?"

"I mean she was thirty years old and probably spends her weekends in the grotto at Hef's pool."

Seth seems genuinely puzzled. "You didn't think she had a certain farm-fresh innocence about her?"

"She's as fresh as Bea Arthur[163] and innocent as Paris Hilton."

"Hey, that's an idea! We ought to talk to Paris about playing Rebecca! What a twist, huh?"

Words escape me, so I simply shake my head in mute frustration.

When the next actress enters, I get an overwhelming feeling of déjà vu. She seems so familiar. I lean in and whisper, "Hey, what's she been in? How do I know her?"

"That's America's sweetheart."

"Who?"

Seth's whole face lights up at the mention of her name. "That's *Lolly*. Everyone knows *Lolly*."

I've been trying to sound cheery and upbeat and not utterly and completely frustrated at everything that comes out of this man's mouth. If I didn't know better, I'd swear he was screwing

---

163 RIP.

this up on purpose. One of my author friends got to sit in during the casting session for her movie, and she said every actress was more perfect than the next, and all of them were better than she could have ever imagined. But here, unless I imagine Miriam as someone who'd make out with Flavor Flav in a bathtub, that's not the case.

"Everyone except for me, Seth. I'm drawing a blank. Help me out?"

"Mia, she's been on the cover of every tabloid for two months."

"Forgive me; I haven't really been to the grocery store for a while."

Or, I have been. I just haven't had the cash to throw around on four-dollar celebrity rags.

"Lolly was the bachelorette who got dumped at the altar! How did you miss it? She was all over the news."

"Whoa," I say, a little louder than I mean to. Lolly stops and the cameraman has to tell her to keep going. "Now I remember. She was the superslutty one who had sex with all the guys on their fantasy dates."

"Yes, that's her." Seth nods enthusiastically. "We were really lucky to get her in here. She's a hot commodity now."

"And . . . and you find the woman who's famous for banging a whole bunch of unemployed dudes on national television to be the most appropriate choice to play a seventeen-year-old Amish virgin?"

"Absolutely!"

Oh, my God, I can't believe this joker is in charge of this whole goddamned production; ergo, my fate.

Think of your house, think of your house, think of your house, I mentally repeat before I say something career killing out of anger. I pose the next question as gently as I possibly can, even though it kills me to do so.

"Um, Seth, I'm curious—have you read the script yet?"

With complete sincerity he says to me, "No. But I plan to real soon."

Now, tell me that's not a sign.

"Ready to kill self-slash-others yet?"

"Tracey, you have no idea." I'm talking to Tracey on the phone from the living room of my fancy suite at the Four Seasons in Beverly Hills.

The studio's spared no expense in making me comfortable in my home away from home. A few months ago, I'd have been in my glory in here. But now? The suite feels way too luxurious. I have two bathrooms in here! Two! For one person! There's no possible way I could use both the massive soaking tub and the powder room shower at the same time. This room is double the size of our old place on Spring Street, and it feels more than a little excessive. If putting me up here is the reason that movie tickets cost fifteen dollars a pop, then I'm really sorry, America.

When I step out on one of my three[164] balconies, I have un-encumbered views of the city and the mountains. I could have probably gotten by with one balcony—or none—considering how gorgeous the pool area is, with all the massive teak loungers and tented private cabanas.

I have a sitting area and a dining area *and* a separate bedroom

---

164 Three!

with a canopy bed. With solid walls and finished floors and ceilings that don't gush carpenter ants! The studio doesn't realize it, but they could have put me up in a motel on the off-ramp and I'd have been satisfied.[165]

Yet despite my million-dollar surroundings, I'm not happy.

I miss my stupid, chaotic, taking-baths-in-the-lake life desperately. I miss my husband. I miss my dogs. I miss my friends. I miss having nemeses who are at least forthcoming enough to try to firebomb my house or have me arrested or blackballed, rather than this passive-aggressive trying-to-ruin-my-movie shit that's going on out here.

I gaze out the window and I fail to be charmed by the scenery. I sip my tea and tell Tracey, "Did I mention Seth's determined to destroy this film?"

"You keep saying that. But if he's in charge, why would he deliberately sabotage it?"

"The craft table scuttlebutt is, he didn't want to work on this project. I guess he got passed over for some Tom Cruise film and now he's taking his frustration out on me."

Tracey's not yet certain of what I'm convinced is fact. "Are you sure he's not just incompetent? Hollywood's rife with nepotism. Is it possible he's someone's kid or cousin?"

I stir honey and lemon into my tea while I consider this possibility. "No one could be this incompetent. Sabotage is the only explanation for the decisions he's made."

"Like what?"

"Well, for one, he wants to film at the beach."

---

165 Nat's been very clear that I should not actually verbalize this sentiment.

"Come again?"

"*The beach*. He claims audiences love an ocean view. Granted, I'm not as well versed as I should be in Amish culture, but for Christ's sake, I'm pretty sure none of them live in Malibu!"

"It's very difficult to maneuver a buggy through the canyons. So many sharp turns," Tracey adds.

"Yeah, that part is not actually a problem, because Seth let this cowriter kid totally mangle my script. Apparently General Motors is willing to pony up big bucks for product placement, so guess what they're driving? Think horsepower, not horses. Might I remind you this film is called *Buggies Are the New Black*? GM's rep wants to set up a cross-promotional Web site—CallMeIshmaelsRide. com—and it'll feature the cars from the movie."

"You're shitting me."

"I wish. I always say that the Amish bit is a device and I don't really need it to tell the story of what it's like to be a teenager, right? Well, Seth took that thought one step further by trying to completely eliminate all Amish parts of the movie. He wanted to make it more 'hip and modern,' like that 1996 version of *Romeo and Juliet*."

"No offense, Mia, but that movie version worked because Shakespeare wrote the original."

"None taken." I pluck a grape from my daily fruit plate and chew it angrily. "Ooh, and guess who he tried to cast as Mose? No, wait. Don't answer—you'll never guess, because it's too ridiculous. He wanted the guy from the Old Spice commercials!"

" 'I'm on a horse'?"

"Yep. The man your man could smell like. And I love that guy and I bought Mac a bunch of Old Spice products because of him, but once we got him in to read he was all, 'Um, you want me to play an eighteen-year-old white boy?' He was a total class act, but it was mortifying!"

"Mia, that really sucks. How does Mac feel about everything?"

Oh, *Mac.*

What am I going to do with him?

He's yet to visit, even though the studio will fly him out at their expense. He keeps making lame excuses, like about not being able to leave the dogs. I slump back into the chaise. "On the one hand, he's been really supportive when I bitch about how things are going out here, full of advice on how to not be so passive about everything. But then when I ask him about the house, he suddenly gets distant and distracted and has to hang up. I thought it was a onetime thing, but it's been happening each time we talk. So I don't know what that means. I wonder if he's even trying at this point, or if he's just waiting for the money to roll in. I get the vibe that he doesn't even care whether or not he's made any progress on the house, and I find that really distressing. At the moment, I feel like I'm the only one who cares about the foundation of our house *or* our marriage."

Tracey's as perplexed as I am. "That seems so out of character. Not his personality. He'd go down in a hail of bullets, not a blaze of apathy."

"Right? I can't even fathom why he's just given up. Maybe I was just too awful at the end, there. I did turn into a shrew."

"With good reason, Mia. Don't forget I was there the day it rained toilets."

"I guess. If Kara would ever get back to me, I'd make her put on her advice columnist hat and tell me what to do next."

"Have you talked at all? I saw her once in the past six weeks, and we literally bumped into each other on Michigan Avenue. She seems happy but we didn't get a chance to chat—she was running to a meeting. She keeps e-mailing saying we should get together, but she's been booked all the dates I suggest."

"We've exchanged a couple of texts, but we haven't had a conversation since I missed her outing. She's not one to hold a grudge usually, but I must have really let her down. Seems to be a trend lately."

"Yes, Mia. Self-pity. That's exactly what the doctor ordered. Much as I'd love to wallow with you, I've got to bolt in a few minutes. I'm meeting my new man for dinner."

Tracey's been seeing this new guy for a couple of months now. She's been particularly cagey about details and says everything will make sense once we meet him.

"Is he coming to get you now?" I ask. "And is he driving fifteen miles an hour the whole way with his blinker on and seat belt hanging out the door?"

"You're going to eat those words, Mia."

"I look forward to it. I'll see you . . . Shit, I don't know when. But hopefully soon."

"Take care, kiddo."

"Bye, Trace. Big love."

I have some time to kill before this afternoon's casting meeting, so I decide to check out my Facebook fan page. My tweens are completely losing their minds over the book becoming a movie. Their wall comments are full of excellent suggestions for whom they want to see on-screen. For female leads, they're all about Miley Cyrus, Dakota Fanning, and Selena Gomez, and for the male leads, they'd like to see Zac Efron and at least one Jonas brother. They're all dying for Justin Bieber, too, but honestly, he's so pretty I'd lean toward slapping a wig on him and casting him as Rebecca.

Funny, not one of them envisions a thirtysomething ex–porn actress for any of these roles. Except for Nick, of course. He's hoping we'll consider Traci Lords.

I tab over to read my Facebook messages and I run across a couple of familiar names in the in-box. Looks like I've gotten notes from both Amberleigh and Lolly. Of course, they're both dead wrong for the parts, but I do appreciate anyone who sends a thank-you note. Manners still count, you know?

I open Amberleigh's first.

Hiya Miya,

Small pet peeve here, if I may? My name is three letters and I get a wee bit stabby when people spell it wrong.

I dunno if you rememumber me but I ~~and aoud ott~~ tried out for Marion.

Oh, honey, I won't forget you *or* your jeans shorts.

You should cast me becuz I LOVE your books!

Plus ten points for the bimbo.

Vampries turn me on and I would totally have a three-way with Edward and Jacob.

And . . . thanks for coming out. Delete.

Then I begin to read Lolly's letter.

> *Mia,*
>
> *Thank you for the opportunity to audition. I'm currently awaiting a callback.*

What's the expression I'm looking for?

Ah, yes, over my dead body.

> *Your books are superfun and I know I'd be a great Mary Ann.*

Unfortunately we're not casting any Mary Anns.

> *If you cast me in your movie, I am willing to do the following to you:*

I scan the list and . . . Yikes. She really wants this part.

A lot.

I'm not sure number sixteen is even legal.

I feel dirty even knowing some of this stuff exists.

Um, wow.

I always heard rumors that the casting couch existed. Guess I never realized one day I might be running the couch.

I think that's enough fan mail for the day.

I'm going to get ready for this afternoon's casting session now. By taking a *Silkwood* shower.

★　　★　　★

I'm almost late for the meeting because I couldn't stop scrubbing. Most of the team is assembled and we're here to discuss final callbacks for principal roles. I pretty much hate everyone Seth likes, and what sucks is that I don't have right of first refusal. Per my contract, I'm allowed input on the decisions, but I don't get final say. As EP, Seth is the one with all the power. I guess the trade-off is that I get a really big check.

I settle into my seat at the conference table and grab a bottle of Fiji water. I'm probably not even going to drink it; I just like to take them, since they're free. I've got quite the collection of them back in my hotel room just in case the Four Seasons runs out of water and I need to wash my hair or something.[166]

Seth opens the meeting with a bombshell. "Good news, everyone! We've found our Marion!"

"Miriam," I correct in a tone that I mean to sound firm but instead comes across as passive-aggressive. There's a low rumble of whispered conversations and collective surprise at the table. Sounds like none of us were part of this decision.

"Right, right! Miriam, I meant to say." He flashes me a shiny white, fully veneered, completely insincere smile. "We needed someone new and fresh, but she had to be the kind of person who would get audiences talking—I mean, really talking! So I figured, why not go for broke? Why not reach for the stars? Why not bring on the biggest It Girl out there?"

The room instantly begins to buzz. Who is it? Who'd he get? Who possesses such star power that he didn't even have her read

---

166 Am scarred from our old bathroom situation.

for us? Big, huge names are bandied about the room as Seth goes
to retrieve our Miriam.

My mind races with possibilities—is it Taylor Swift? She could
be amazing in the role. My tweens would love her, and adults
would appreciate her charm and authenticity. What about Amanda
Seyfried? She's a triple threat, and her eyes are so expressive. She's
not what I envisioned as Miriam's physical type, but the truth is,
she'd be perfect with all her blue-eyed innocence. Blake Lively
would bring grace and a timeless elegance to the role, and Emma
Stone could be great in that she'd bring such comedic timing.
Ooh, what about Carey Mulligan? How spectacular would it be
to have an Oscar nominee speaking my words on the big screen?

The air is electric with anticipation as the door swings open.
Seth's wearing a triumphant smile as he heads to the end of the
table. "Ladies and gentlemen, may I present . . . Miriam!"

"My name isn't Miriam, you douche."

It takes me a second to realize that this is not, in fact, a nightmare, and that the woman standing in front of us clad in a leopard-
print catsuit and ermine wrap is indeed Vienna Hyatt.

"I'm, like, totally an actress now."

And I'm, like, totally done here.

Chapter Twenty-one
PLANES, AUTOMOBILES, NO TRAINS

"So I ran away. I went back to my hotel room and packed up all my stuff, even all my silly hoarded bottles of water, and I caught the red-eye home. Except I didn't go home, because I can't face being there, either."

After Seth's big announcement, I simply stood up from the table, grabbed my Fiji water, and left the studio. I could not willingly participate in the destruction of my own work.

"And you know what really gets me? Vienna didn't recognize me. Neither my name nor my face rang a bell. The bitch pretty much set the destruction of my home, my career, and my marriage in motion, and she didn't have the courtesy to remember who I was.

"I was out there only three weeks, and I absolutely see why

you had to get out of that town. The things regular people are willing to do to become famous and crap that powerful people pull to stay that way . . . it makes me sick, the whole business. How did I want this for so long?"

The sun is the perfect shade of pink-gold in the sky. Movie people call this the magic hour, and they spend scads of money to film at this time of day. So I guess I learned something valuable, albeit esoteric, while I was in LA.

"The one bright spot is that Kara was there for me immediately when I called her. She admitted she was initially avoiding me after her outing, but then she got involved in other stuff and lost track of everything, so we're totally cool now. Maybe even stronger than before, having weathered our first friend fight. She lent me her new car to drive up here this afternoon. Funny story, after she had it out with her parents, she realized her problem is that she needed to grow up. She figured the easiest way to start would be to buy a new car so she didn't have to rely on her parents when her old one broke down.

"The car salesman was cute and Indian, they hit it off immediately, and they've spent every second together since they met. Kara's all mad at herself because she says she's become one of those girls who forgets her friends when she gets a boyfriend. But I think we're all giving her a pass on that. Plus, her family loves the guy—he's working at CarMax only while he gets his PhD—and everyone's happy. Folks love a happy ending."

I bite at a cuticle and stare off in the direction of the lake. "I'm glad it worked out for her. As for me? Everything's a shit show right now. I keep letting studio calls go to voice mail, same with my agents, and the one person I want to talk to isn't picking up.

"I need to go home, but I don't want to. I'm terrified to see the place, because I haven't a clue what to expect. I'm so scared that if I get there and Mac hasn't made any effort in getting things together that it's the symbolic end of us. I feel like that stupid house is a metaphor for our entire marriage right now. I'm desperate to find out where we stand, but I'm afraid to get a definitive answer. What's that line that Allison Reynolds says in *The Breakfast Club*? You want to but you can't and then you do and you wish you hadn't? That's how I feel about going home.

"Why is life so hard to navigate now? It wasn't always so hard. I got through my teenage years without a lot of problems, in many ways because of your guidance. You taught an entire generation how to deal with every problem we faced—insecurity and first love and bullies and mean girls and pressure. Personally, you helped me figure out how to forge bonds across socioeconomic classes and how to navigate cliques by showing me that, deep down, we were all going through the same stuff. You gave me the confidence to go forth and be my best self.

"But I'm all grown-up now and you're gone, and I don't think I know how to be an adult without your guidance. You didn't leave a trail of bread crumbs for us to follow. The greatest tragedy is that we lost you before you had a chance to teach my generation what to do next."

I stare at the unmarked headstone for a long time. As the light changes, I'm aware that it's time to do something, but what? I'm not sure.

I get off the bench and kneel in the grass. "Sir, if you're out there, if there's any part of you that still exists—and there has to be, because you left a little piece of yourself with an entire generation—please give me a little nudge. Point me in the right direction. I'm begging you for a sign, one small clue as to how to take the first step in the rest of my life. Please. Something."

But nothing happens.

I wait for it and I wait for it, but nothing happens.

I am truly on my own.

And that breaks my heart.

So I stay where I am, on my knees in the dying light of late afternoon. I need to get up and do something, go somewhere, but I just feel paralyzed.

I stay there for what feels like hours, bent over with my face in my hands, trying to figure out where to go once I finally muster the strength to stand.

". . . go home."

And then I almost jump right out of my skin.

I stare down at the headstone. Did . . . did John Hughes just say something to me? Is that possible?

"Ma'am, I'm sorry to disturb you, but we're closing the gates shortly. Visiting hours are over and it's time to go home."

That's when I realize I'm being addressed by a groundskeeper standing at the edge of the grass, and not a voice from the great beyond.

But damn it, a sign's a sign.

Thank you, sir.

You've still got my back.

I live only a couple of miles from the cemetery, but the ride home takes forever. When I finally reach my street, Lululemon—I mean, *Amanda*—is out for a jog, propelling two happy toddlers in the stroller in front of her. When she sees me, I get the briefest flash of a smile and a barely perceptible wave, yet that greeting smacks of what Admiral Dewey must have felt when he returned to New York from the Pacific.

When I slowly pull down my driveway, I look for anything that might give me a clue as to what's been happening inside.

The first thing I notice is that the Dumpster is gone and that someone must have power-washed the area underneath it, because my drive is clean and clear for the first time since Mac ripped down the first sheet of drywall.

The next thing I notice is the windows, as in, we have actual windows in each and every frame and not just half a dozen strategically placed boards. Plus, my perennials seem healthy and strong, and someone even removed the stump from the tree I executed.

All of these are positive omens, but I'm not really going to have a grasp on where things stand until I see Mac.

The front door opens and I run to throw myself into Mac's arms when I realize that Mac is suddenly taller.

And burlier.

And blonder.

And dressed kind of like the construction guy from the Village People.

What the . . . ?

"Hey, there, ya must be Mia. Heard ya may be comin' home today. We'd hoped to be finished, but you're a little early and we're still cleanin' up."

Wait. I know that voice. It's all confident and businesslike and vaguely Canadian.

"The name's Mike Holmes. Glad to meet ya." He holds out a meaty palm and gives my hand a firm shake.

I'm speechless.

"Speechless, eh? Let's give ya a little tour and show ya what we've done." Numbly I walk in the front door, and I'm in such a state of shock that for a moment I don't even realize my dogs are jumping on me.

I snap out of it. "Hi, guys, Mummy's home. Yes! That's right! Mummy is home!" I let them romp and bark and kiss me for a couple of minutes, because that's happening whether I want them to or not.

Greeting the dogs has given me time to collect my thoughts. "So, you're here. How are you here? And where's Mac? And are there cameras—is this for a show? I'm sorry; I'm a little lost."

"Nope, not filmin', just helping ya out, doin' the right thing. I gotta tell ya, this place was a mess when we got here. I can't believe ya were livin' like that. We almost thought ya were pullin' a prank when we got your husband's call."

"Mac called you?"

"Oh, he's been callin' the production office for a while, couple of months at least. We had your house on the list for potential sites to scout, but we're not filmin' the new season yet."

As Mike talks, I start to look around my house. In the foyer, the hideous black and white tiles have been replaced with wide-plank dark walnut floors, and they go as far as I can see. When I inspect the walls, I don't see lath and plaster or drywall;[167] instead I see smooth, even walls painted a light yellowish green. The ceil-

---

167 Or nothing.

ing not only exists, but it's a really clean white, and it's bordered by four inches of glossy crown molding.

I don't understand. "Then . . . how are you here?"

"Funny story. I was on vacation in Miami with the family, and your grandmother tracked us down. She"—he pauses and flinches just the tiniest bit—"convinced us to come up here."

That doesn't make sense. "How'd she even know? No one in my family wanted to tell her, because we didn't want her to freak out. She's old and kind of delicate."

Mike shrugs. "I guess Mac called her and asked for her help. Turns out it's a real small world, because her company cleans the condo where we were staying, and let's just say she can be very, very persuasive. Also, I'm not so sure about the delicate part." Then he kind of bites his lip and looks off in the distance for a second. "Anyway, are ya ready to see your new kitchen?"

We pass the library, and I can't help but notice that all my gorgeous paneling has been repaired and restored, and also that the enormous gilded cross Babcia gave us as a housewarming gift is now mounted over the fireplace.

You know what? I can live with that.

Mike shows me all the features of my brand-new kitchen, with the warming drawer and extra refrigerated drawer in the island. The cabinets are a painted cream finish with antiquing in the crevices, with oil-rubbed bronze fixtures and pulls. The counters are a sand-colored granite with cambered edges. Although I'm both shocked and awed, I'm not surprised by how well it all coordinates, because they used all the stuff Vlad and I picked out. The guy might have been a mercenary and possibly a thief, but he was definitely an aesthete.

"All of the appliances work?" I ask tentatively. "I can have hot or cold food whenever I want?"

"Of course it works! Our job is to make it right around here!" Mike booms.

The rest of the house is equally overwhelming, and I ooh and ahh over every closable door and flushable toilet. Holmes and company even put in a fail-safe opening in the panic room, and they got rid of the Jacuzzi.[168]

"Is Mac coming home soon?" I ask. All of what I'm seeing is amazing, but what's really making me happy is the effort Mac made to make it all right. And he called Babcia! That's what blows me away more than anything. The only possible interpretation of all this is that even though we hit a rough patch, his love for me didn't waver.

"Should be here shortly. Said he had to pick up your grandmother from the hotel, and then he said something about a birthday cake and someone named Jake Ryan? It was all supposed to be part of your homecoming celebration, but like I said, you're a little early. Hope that's still okay."

Mac wanted me to finally have my Thompson Twins "If You Were Here" moment in the new house?

Yeah, I'd say that's more than okay.

"You put Kevin Spacey in movie. He good boy."

We're in the living room and I'm curled up in Mac's arms and covered in dogs and cats. I'd be hard-pressed to determine which creatures in this house missed me the most.

---

168 Apparently it wasn't hard to remove once it was cut in half.

Babcia's sitting across from us on the oversize chaise. She looks like a little kid, because her feet don't touch the ground. Yet she still manages to be eighty pounds of imperious.

"Babcia, I don't have that kind of decision-making power. Plus, I ran away. I'm not even sure I'm allowed to go back."

She says nothing in response, instead choosing to fix her gaze on Mac. "Babcia need drink." Mac sprints to the kitchen to fix Babcia's cocktail.

I'll never quite know the price he paid to get Babcia here and involved, but whatever it is, I'll do my best to make it up to him for the rest of our lives.

Our reunion was brief but meaningful.

I think Mac's exact words were, "Are we cool now?"

And yes, we are indeed cool.

"But you can't go all distant on me again," I told him. "I didn't know what to think, so I thought the worst."

"I didn't want to distract you or ruin the surprise," he replied. "I wanted to prove to you I could do it."

I raised a Botox-free eyebrow at him.

"Or, technically, that Mike Holmes could do it."

"But not knowing what was going on distracted me."

"I really am sorry, Mia."

"Me, too, Mac." He pulled me to him and we stood there for a long time, just remembering what it was like to be together.

"Promise me one thing, though?" I asked when we finally broke apart.

"What's that?"

"That you'll never buy a forty-five-dollar lightbulb again."

He said he wouldn't . . . but I may lock down his workshop just to be sure.

The doorbell rings and I hop up to answer it. It's a little late, but Kara and Tracey are dying to see what's been done to the place, and I need to give Kara back her car.

Kara arrives first with a gorgeous Indian guy in tow. "This is Leo!"

We exchange pleasantries, and at no point does Leo stop gazing adoringly at Kara. He's smitten, and it's adorable and everything I could wish for my friend.

Mac serves everyone a cocktail and hands me a Scotch and soda. I take a tentative sip. Not bad. I'll probably sneak some ginger ale into it when Mac's not looking, but hey, at least it's not pink.

Progress, yes?

We're barely past introductions when the bell rings again. It's Tracey and her date. "Hey, girl!" I give her a big hug, and only after we unclench do I notice the man by her side.

Although calling him a man may be pushing it.

"Um, who's this?" I ask gamely.

"This is my date, Trevor."

Kara and I exchange extraordinarily meaningful glances.

"Hi, Trevor, welcome! Come on in! Let's show you around!"

While Trevor and Tracey get cocktails in the kitchen, Kara and I put our heads together. "Shouldn't you card him before you serve him liquor?"

"What is he, fifteen?" I ask in a low tone.

"I wonder if she had to cut his meat at dinner?" she whispers back.

"You think his mommy lets him be out so late on a school night?"

It's almost like Tracey has bionic hearing—or just knows us really well—and she shouts from the kitchen, "He's twenty-four, you assholes."

I'm not sure what the biggest shock of all today has been—that my house is in order, that my grandmother is here, or that Tracey's gone straight to Cougar Town, but I swear it feels like my birthday.[169]

Once we're all gathered in the living room, the discussion turns back to my movie again.

"The bottom line is, I'm not running the show. And even if I were, I don't want to be out there anymore. I've had enough LA to last me the rest of my life," I tell everyone.

"Legally, what are your options?" Tracey asks.

"The rights are sold. Legally I've got bubkes. Trust me, I had my entertainment attorney and Ann Marie tear that contract apart, and it's ironclad. I mean, the studio heads wanted me out there for my artistic vision,[170] but they're not at all obligated to accept my input."

"Did you just want to die when the producer paraded Vienna into the room?" Kara queries.

"Die, kill, something," I reply.

"Won't a subpar film dilute your whole brand?" Trevor asks.

Kara mouths, *He's adorable*, and pantomimes pinching his cheek behind Tracey's back. I answer, "Yes, and that's a major concern. But what else can I do?"

---

169 And no one fucking forgot it.

170 Yep, still funny.

"I can go out and straighten them out," Mac postures.

"Much as I'd like you to punch that shitweasel in the neck, that's not the answer," I say before I kiss him on the cheek.

Babcia mumbles something from the depths of her chair.

"What's that, Babcia?" I ask.

"Fight. You movie, you write, you fight. You go back, go over head. Talk to person write you check. Fight."

"It's not that simple, Babcia."

She pulls herself up to her full (almost) five feet. "Wrong. Is simple. You fight. You go plane tomorrow. Fight. Win. Kevin Spacey say greatest trick ever pull, devil world not exist. You make movie. Yes."

I glance around the room and everyone seems to be behind Babcia, even if they are a little confused by her mangled *Usual Suspects* quote.

"Is it crazy? Do I go back?" I ask the group.

"What, you need sign? I give sign. Sign say go. Be not stupid girl. Be smart girl. Go."

"I don't know. . . ."

Babcia looks over both of her shoulders and leans forward to say something sotto voce, which somehow makes her all the more menacing. "Is deal—you get on plane? Babcia find Vlad. Then he pay."

She's no Mafia don, and yet I'm pretty sure she just made me an offer I can't refuse. Mac blanches in sympathy for whatever bad, bad thing is about to befall Vlad.

"I'll do it."

"Good. But first, get Babcia drink."

Chapter Twenty-two
JUST VISITING

"Take me to Persiflage Films, please."

This time around, I'm not arriving at the studio in a chauffeur-driven Town Car.

This time I'm in a regular cab I caught at LAX. I didn't even pack anything more than an extra pair of underwear and a toothbrush, because I'm not planning on staying. I'm finished in this town.

Whether that's literal or figurative, I'm not yet sure.

The cab drops me off in front of Persiflage, and I'm able to get on the lot because I still have my pass. But instead of heading to the offices, where—at least according to my old itinerary—I'm supposed to be meeting with costume designers,[171] I make my way to the office of the studio's twin presidents, Will and Phil Bernstein.

---

171 No doubt to pick out Miriam's bikini.

I'm not at all sure what my plan is, having chosen to remain in denial the entire flight out here.[172] But I'm here, and now I'm basically ready to throw up from anxiety.

Although my game plan is hazy, my mission is clear. I need to wrest control of this movie out of the hands of that overly veneered jackass. I don't have to (or want to) be in charge, but I'll never forgive myself if I don't at least plead my case.

When I arrive on the executive floor, I stop at the Bernstein brothers' second assistant's desk. The girl behind it looks friendly and seems like she might, just maybe, not call security on me before I finish making my plea for five minutes of a Bernstein's time.

The second assistant is cute and fresh-scrubbed Midwestern, not all plastic, like every other woman I've seen out here. I think she's sporting her real hair color, and the only makeup she wears comes in the form of the tube of cherry ChapStick on her desk. She's speaking into her headset while I approach, which gives me a couple of seconds to determine what I want to say.

And that's when I see it—my lifeline, my ticket in, my *sign*.

When she disconnects, I point to her desk and say, "You're reading my book."

Instead of getting the typical blasé oh-yeah-well-Brad-Pitt-and-I-share-a-pool-boy response, the girl actually squeals and leaps out of her seat. "Oh, my God, are you Mia MacNamara? I love you! My little sister turned me on to your books and I can't stop reading them! I'm so excited to meet you! Hello! I'm Jasmine!"

"Hold on," I say. "You're excited to meet *me*? Don't you get, like, A-list movie stars in here every five minutes?"

---

172 Babcia paid for first class on my solemn word that I would create a role for Kevin Spacey.

"Oh, yeah," she says. "You just missed Will Smith. Although he's actually really cool, because he acknowledges us out here. But most of them are just empty suits. Actors, they just say the lines. I'm more impressed with people who write the stuff that makes them sound good. That might seem weird, but I just graduated from USC's School of Cinematic Arts, and I did a ton of writing, so that's what I'm into. Trust me, I'm an anomaly around here. Everyone else is a total star fucker." Jasmine claps her hand over her mouth. "Didn't mean to swear. Sorry! Terrible habit. So, anyway, did you have an appointment? I don't remember seeing you on the schedule. I'd have noticed."

I give Jasmine the condensed version of my situation, and I tell her that if there's any way I could get five minutes of a twin's time without getting her fired, that she could potentially save my film from, if not obscurity, then at least a solid panning on Pajiba. com.

"They cast Vienna Hyatt? As Miriam? Is that a fucking joke?" She slaps her hand over her mouth again. "Shit, I've got to stop swearing at work. Goddamn it, I did it again!" She pulls up the twins' schedules and tells me, "I can get you ten minutes with Phil in about an hour."

"And that won't get you in trouble?" I already love this kid, and I don't want to jeopardize her job.

"Oh, please." She waves me off. "If anything goes wrong, I'll blame it on Brittany, the first assistant. She's a Bernstein niece, and she's a total space cadet. She screws stuff up every day and everyone lets her coast. She just scheduled Jennifer Aniston and Angelina Jolie in back-to-back meetings with the twins. I mean, are you kidding me? Who does that? But she's Teflon and everything slides off her.

She'll probably run this place someday. Trust me, Mia, I'm all over this."

Jasmine puts me in the schedule and directs me to the waiting room down the hall after setting me up with a latte and a stack of magazines.

An hour later, she comes to get me, and just as I get ready to walk into Phil Bernstein's office, she whispers to me, "Do it for Miriam."

And then I prepare myself for the fight of my—no, our—lives.

I don't want to say I went Swayze all over the Bernstein brother.

But I went Swayze all over the Bernstein brother.

In my ten minutes, I managed to not only convince him to dump Vienna, but also to assign a totally new producer and start the whole casting process from scratch. He even promised to call in a favor from Kevin Spacey to do a cameo as Amos's father.

I'd like to say my powers of persuasion were top-notch and that I unleashed a little bit of my inner Ann Marie.[173]

But the truth is, Mr. Bernstein's daughters are huge fans, and they stopped talking to their dad the minute they found out Vienna had been cast.

You know what? A victory's a victory, even if it comes from a forfeit.

The best part is, I get to do my own rewrites, and I don't have to be on-site for the whole process. Mr. Bernstein is pulling a couple of producers who worked on the *Harry Potter* and *Twilight* films to head up *Buggies*, and I'm confident they'll make it great.

---

173 You don't spend four years living with someone without learning a few of her tricks.

Did I mention I got Vienna fired?

Yeah, that's worth noting twice.

I finally feel like my baby's in good hands. And now I can go home to begin the rest of my life.

Mac and I are picking up the last of the garbage from our house-warming party. Tonight was even more fun than our wedding reception, and *that* went on all night and well into brunch the next day.

Everyone was here—all of our friends, my whole family, and even Ann Marie was able to make it out, although she's presently passed out in my writing room. We offered her a regular guest room, but she said she wanted to sleep on the couch in "Jake Ryan's bedroom." I'm telling you, even though he was fictional, and despite the movie having come out twenty-seven years ago, you can't negate the influence his character had on an entire generation of ladies.

At one point in the night, we all went outside and poured out a little bit of our drinks in John Hughes's honor, and then we came in to dance to the *Pretty in Pink* sound track. I could not imagine having a better time. Lulu—no, *Amanda* even stopped by, and she and Ann Marie became instant besties.

I fear what this depraved pairing might bring forth.

I'm just locking the front door when I see an odd flash of light outside. "Mac?" I call. "Come check this out."

Mac flips off the porch light and we both peer into the darkness. In the distance we see a car idling at the end of our driveway.

"Mac, is that a . . . Bentley?"

Mac cranes his neck to get a better view. "How about that? It is. Did you invite any latecomers who drive a Bentley?"

I wave him off. "Pfft, I don't know anyone who drives a Bentley. What, is Puffy going to show up at our housewarming? Kanye? A Kardashian? Be real. The only time I've ever even seen a Bentley is when Vienna used to—"

"Speak of the devil." Mac and I have been heading quietly down the driveway in the shadows and now have a much better vantage point of what's happening at the end of our drive.

"Is that her?"

"You don't recognize the hair extensions?"

I'm not entirely surprised that Vienna's showed up here. To say she was pissed about getting fired would be an understatement. Apparently she'd already gotten "Miriam" tattooed across the small of her back when she got the news. We've been expecting some kind of revenge but weren't sure of the form it would take until now.

Vienna's standing outside of her car with a Dom Pérignon bottle, and it would appear that she's created a Molotov cocktail of her own. We quietly observe her sticking a strip of cloth in the bottle, and we step back into the brush line while she lights it. Then, with all her might, she hurls it in the direction of our house.

The problem is, we've got this big old black mailbox at the end of our driveway. Remember how our mailbox caused so much consternation in the neighborhood when we put up the beautiful red iron one? After we'd installed it, we shone an uplight on it so people could see it in the dark and they wouldn't accidentally hit it with their cars on our winding street.

But everyone threw such a fit over our tacky[174] mailbox that in a fit of goodwill, we took it down and replaced it with the old,

---

174 Their words, not ours.

boring, big black box. Then we unplugged the light because it was causing everyone so much aesthetic distress.

Vienna's standing ten feet away from the mailbox, but because of its color and the late hour, it's practically invisible. When she tosses her Molotov cocktail, she's not, in fact, throwing it into all the dry brush surrounding the front of our house. Instead, what happens is that the bottle shatters when it hits the mailbox, and because she's standing so close to it, she becomes covered in its flammable contents, which ignite when her lit cigarette falls out of her agape mouth.

And that's when we're all taught a little chemistry lesson, although it's Vienna who really learns that polystyrene hair extensions work as an ad hoc wick, and her entire head goes up in flames.

Before Mac can jog back to the house to grab a hose, Vienna's flunky immediately douses her with Diet Snapple and whacks her flaming do with the new Marc Jacobs hobo bag while Vienna sheds every inch of her flaming clothing. Then they both hop into her car and scream off into the night.

"Mac," I say, "I'm pretty sure we haven't heard the last of Vienna."

"I suspect you're right," he agrees.

Then I lean back into his arms. "Do you care?"

"Right now? Not a bit."

"Want to know what's funny?" I ask.

"Hmm?"

"If ORNESTEGA taught us anything, it was to wear a full set of drawers before trying to set someone's house on fire. Also? I bet Vienna would kill for a pair of Spider-Man underpants right about now."

Chapter Twenty-three
HAPPILY EVER AFTER

Now that our house is done and our neighbors' hatred has morphed from active to dormant, I'm ready to enjoy every amenity this community has to offer.

Huh.

Somehow I thought there'd be more amenities.

Is it possible that twenty-plus years of John Hughes movies built unrealistic expectations?

Epilogue

"Hello, sir, it's been a while, hasn't it? Six months, to be exact. I know, I know; I meant to come, but I guess we've just been a little preoccupied. Mac's been back at work for a while, and he got a big promotion, and the commute's been making him crazy. Me? I've been busy working on a new book that I kind of love. It's a departure in that I'm giving the Amish a little vacation for now and I'm writing more of what I know. This one takes place in a regular suburban high school."

I fiddle with the package in my hand and shift from foot to foot to warm up. There's a ton of snow on my usual bench, so I don't sit down. "I guess the big news is . . . we bought a house back in the city. Turns out once our place was finished we realized how bored we are in Abington Cambs. Seriously, they roll the streets up at eight p.m. around here, and I've got zip in common with the Ladies Who Lunch or the Ladies Who Life Time (Fitness). This would be an amazing place to raise kids, but it's just not for us.

"No, we're not selling the place. My family plans to expand the business to the Midwest and they need a base of operations, so Babcia and Jessica and her family are going to stay in my house. So I'll be around. Not as much, but I'll stop by from time to time.

"Anyway, I brought you a little something different today. I hope you like it. And because I can't say it enough, thanks for everything, sir."

Then I place a copy of my new manuscript on the ground before I walk away.

I'm calling it *Sixteen Zombies*.

Acknowledgments

Before I get to the thanking part, I have to apologize to the owners of the house featured in *Sixteen Candles*. This home (the outside, at least—haven't been peeking in anyone's windows) (yet) is
nothing short of spectacular, and I'm sure the neighbors are lovely.
Should this book cause people to drive by the place, then I'm
supersorry, but my guess is, if you bought Jake Ryan's house, you
probably expect a few rubberneckers, yes?

Anyway, a million thanks go out to my readers, who make
everything possible! I hope you enjoyed reading my first foray into
fiction as much as I did writing it.

To everyone at NAL, I couldn't be more grateful, particularly
to my editor, Danielle Perez, who totally got it when I pitched this
idea . . . a month before an entirely different book was due. Thank
you for trusting my instincts. Much gratitude also goes to Kara
Welsh, Claire Zion, Craig Burke, Melissa Broder, sales and market-
ing, and especially the art department for creating my favorite

cover ever. And, of course, thanks to Kate Garrick of DeFiore and Co., who's been with me from day one. (Seriously, six books? How'd we get here?)

Big love to my own personal Breakfast Club—Stacey Ballis, Gina Barge, and Tracey Stone—and my Algonquin Round Table—Caprice Crane, Karyn Bosnak, Sarah Grace McCandless, Jolene Siana, and Amy Lamare—who inspired the teenage-Amish-zombies-in-love bit. And to my Indian Wells Six-Feet-I'm-Pacing-It-Off Beach Buddies—Angie, Poppy, Blackbird, and Wendy—same time next year?

Of course, nothing's possible without Fletch. I'm sorry for all the times I confused you with Mac and got mad when you'd attempt a home repair. (But seriously, never buy one of those stupid lightbulbs again.) For the record, Fletch is actually quite handy, and yes, I'm willing to put that in print.

The best part of writing this book was studying up on John Hughes and revisiting all his work. In particular, I found books by Susannah Gora, Jaime Clark and Ally Sheedy, and Thomas A. Christie to be not only full of insight but also fascinating. Also of note is the film *Don't You Forget About Me.* These writers and film-makers confirmed what I already suspected—that Hughes was truly a genius and his work will continue to influence generations to come. Thank you for not forgetting about him.

About the Author

Jen Lancaster is the *New York Times* bestselling author of six books. She has appeared on *Today*, *The Joy Behar Show*, and NPR's *All Things Considered*, and she is a regular columnist for Tribune Media Services. She resides in the suburbs of Chicago with her husband and their ever-expanding menagerie of ill-behaved pets.

Jen Lancaster

If You Were Here

A CONVERSATION WITH
JEN LANCASTER

Q. Readers know you as a memoir author, so why did you choose to write a novel?

A. Of all the questions I've been asked about *If You Were Here*, I've heard this one the most. I decided to write a novel for a couple of reasons—first, I like to believe that I learn something about myself every time I write a memoir. In *Bitter*, my takeaway was that I'd never be happy until I lived my life on my terms. *Bright Lights* was a lesson on accepting reality, *Such a Pretty Fat* on making better decisions, *Pretty in Plaid* on learning from the past, and *My Fair Lazy* about being open to change and improvement.

The upside to all this hard-won self-awareness is that our lives are, by design, as free from conflict as possible. I'm never writing another *Bitter* because (please, God) Fletch and I have made the kinds of decisions to prevent having to relive those days.

The downside is that conflict makes for a funny read. Because I mine my own life for material, I find that when I'm in a ridiculous situation, I tend to stick around to see what happens instead of just removing myself like any sane person would do.

I realized that if I wrote a novel, I could include tons of conflict and awkward situations, yet I wouldn't actually have to experience any of them myself. Plus, I could branch out as a writer, which was really important to me.

Now, I'd originally planned to pen a memoir about moving to the suburbs. Yet, as we started the buying process, we realized we'd spent so much time and effort researching best home-buying practices that we weren't going to screw it up. (A first! Thank you, HGTV!) Try as I might, there's nothing inherently funny about things going exactly as planned.

Although we debated purchasing a fixer-upper for the sake of a story, we actually listened to experts and friends who told us that idea was terrible and that we'd either get divorced or shoot each other with a nail gun. Frankly, neither of these eventualities appealed to us, so ultimately we bought a place (within our budget, which was key) that needed no work except for some wallpaper removal.

Instead, I decided to create an alternate universe in which "Jen" and "Fletch" would be played by Mia and Mac and the first couple of chapters borrow heavily from our real lives, save for the Paris Hilton doppelgänger. But the more I wrote, the more I realized Mac and Mia had their own quirks and nuances and motivations that were very different from ours. I've always heard fiction writers saying stuff like "the characters told me what they wanted," but I kind of thought they were full of shit until I did it myself. My bad.

Despite intentional similarities in the beginning (like the neighborhood in which we wanted to buy and our deep and abiding love for John Hughes), the minute those characters made a poor investment, our stories diverged.

In my first outline, Mia and Mac's reasons for buying their house were very different. Mia and Mac were motivated by pride, having been scarred by poor childhoods. Also, the story was going to be darker. (I planned to call this book Apocalypse House: A Journey into the Heart of Darkness of Home Renovation.)

In the time between selling the proposal and actually writing the book, the housing market crashed and the economy took a dump. I realized that Mac and Mia wouldn't be sympathetic if they were throwing money around while real people struggled to keep their own homes. I needed more of an emotional core for what I was writing, but I wasn't sure what that might be. Also, the world suddenly seemed dark enough and I didn't want to add to it.

While we were looking for a home, Cameron's house from *Ferris Bueller's Day Off* hit the market. Everything about the place was wrong for us, starting with an asking price that would pretty much guarantee we'd both need to find a second job and unload a kidney. The inside was totally eighties, and I don't mean that in a delightfully kitschy, girls-who-listen-to-Duran-Duran way. Plus, the home was built on a ravine. If we lived there, the dogs would tumble down the hill like so many classic Ferrari convertibles. Yet such is my connection to John Hughes, I knew that if I set foot in that place, I'd find a way to make it happen; so we never allowed ourselves to see it.

We'd already moved into our house when I began to write this book in earnest. One day I was stuck because I wasn't sure how to move the story forward. Whenever I have writer's block, the best thing for me is to get up from my desk and do something distracting. I moved to the town where John Hughes lived preceding his passing, and I'd been planning to pay my respects at the cemetery; the day I was blocked seemed like as good a time as any to visit.

Before I left the house, I stopped to cut three perfect pink roses—one for each of my favorite Molly Ringwald movies—to leave at his grave. I'm not sure what I was expecting when I got to the cemetery. I guess I thought that with the impact he made on so many of my generation, I'd have to stand in line to pay my respects, à la Jim Morrison. Instead, I found a place of undisturbed serenity.

While I was there, I thanked him for writing the characters and making the kinds of movies that have stayed with me for more than a quarter of a century. I mean, what teen didn't wish for Ferris's quiet confidence? Whose heart didn't break for the different yet no less detrimental types of abuse suffered by Brian Johnson and John Bender? Who didn't cheer for what was really Duckie's revenge when Keith chose Watts over Miss Amanda Jones? And who among us wouldn't give her panties to a geek, should such circumstances arise?

As I stood there in the quiet green meadow, I realized that I loved what he had created so much that with a touch less self-control, I'd have made the emotional decision to purchase Cameron's house and we'd likely have found ourselves in a world of trouble.

On my way back from the cemetery, I decided to swing by the location that had been Jake Ryan's house since it was only a few miles down the lakeshore. I'd planned on taking an ad hoc John Hughes Memorial Tour soon, so I already had the address with me.

When I pulled up to that familiar iconic Tudor, I lost my breath because it was so magnificent. I wondered how John Hughes reacted when he saw the place for the first time—maybe he felt the same way?

Make no mistake, in real life this house is the polar opposite of a fixer-upper. Few in this country could manage the six-figure property taxes on it, let alone the mortgage. But as I gawped at it from the street, taking in the garage that held a fictitious Mr. Ryan's Rolls, the driveway once paved with beer cans, and the forked tree from which the Donger dropped, I was positive that even the most casual Hughes fan would have lost her sense of reason upon seeing it.

And that's when I realized I'd found Mia's motivation.

Not long after that, I was listening to the sound track from *Sixteen Candles* for inspiration. The songs Hughes selected were as poignant then as they are now, and as the opening instrumental to the Thompson Twins' "If You Were Here" came up, I was hit with the same rush of joy and anticipation that Samantha Baker must have felt while waiting for her cake and her kiss.

A title was born.

So that's the *Behind the Music* on *If You Were Here*.

Please stay tuned because Mia and Mac AND Jen and Fletch will be back, coming soon to a bookstore near you.

I love hearing feedback from readers, yet my schedule doesn't always permit me to reply to each query. Accordingly, I've compiled a list of the most frequently asked questions I've received.

Q. What events in If You Were Here *are based on your real life?*

A. Since this book was published, I've learned that without additional information, people tend to fill in the blanks. Many readers have assumed that this is really our story, so I'm pleased to have the chance to set the record straight.

A minimum of 90 percent of the events in this book is completely fabricated, particularly all the dramatic ones. I've never carried a bathtub, mowed a lawn larger than a postage stamp, or discharged a firearm. I've not removed one square of tile nor have ex-KGB contractors ever run off with a penny of my money. Although we had run-ins with gang members, no one ever tried to set us on fire. (But we did decide to make the move to the burbs when I read that someone sacrificed two goats in an alley near us. HOW MESSED UP IS THAT??)

In terms of truth, most of what's real came from our initial house hunt. I absolutely saw (and fell in love with) a pink-and-green-toile-wallpapered room with block letters spelling out "Sophia," and I did pass on viewing a home after I realized it had been owned by a convicted sex offender. I did move to a nicer town, but unless I pull a Mr. T and level all the trees in my yard, I anticipate we'll live here without incident.

Q. But the characters felt so familiar—how real were they?

A. I drew from my life a little more liberally here and many of the characters are an amalgamation of my friends, albeit an exaggeration. Babcia definitely shared some of my grandmother's more pragmatic traits, yet my Noni wasn't terrifying. Much. The villains, however, are pure fiction. To date, we've not only never had an issue with a suburban neighbor—we've never even met any of them. Yeah, it might have been nice to receive a welcome basket, but I'd prefer to buy my own wine and cheese than be hassled about my landscaping.

Q. How do Mia and Mac differ from you and Fletch?

A. Mia holds her tongue in order to be polite and often internalizes her problems. As evidenced by my memoirs, clearly that's never been an issue with me.

Clearly.

In terms of being a couple, Fletch and I faced a number of problems along the way, but the reason we work is because we approach issues as a team, rather than as two individuals with opposing wants and needs.

Fletch is a lot less serious than Mac, and he isn't nearly so quick to escalate. What's funny is that it wasn't until after I finished *IYWH* that Fletch began to mirror some of Mac's traits. (Do not get me started on the $3,000 dresser refinishing project.) However, we're both communicators, so the issue was more of a charming annoyance than anything else.

Mia and I share the ability to learn from our mistakes, though. I've always disliked when some authors write the same story again and again, all "Oh, no! We maxed out our credit cards again!" For my memoirs, I like to say that in each one I find an entirely new way to screw up my life. You'll see this with Mia in the next book, too. She'll be getting a handle on her mousiness and the problems that ensue stem from her switching from the passive to the aggressive.

Q. Are you going to write a teenage-Amish-zombies-in-love book?

A. Thought about it, but likely won't. That's too far outside my comfort zone to sustain for more than a couple of pages. Besides, the best part about it would have been making up the book titles, and I already spilled all my clever ideas.

Q. *Which do you prefer writing, novels or memoirs?*

A. Writing a novel allowed me to flex different creative muscles. When you've written as many memoirs (and supplemental blogs, tweets, and Facebook posts) as I have, there's a lot less of what Chuck Palahniuk calls "unpacking." I don't have to set the scene for what my husband's like or how my dogs behave—there's automatic shorthand to understanding. Fiction is a different ball game and requires much more unpacking.

Ultimately, my goal is to switch back and forth between genres so I'm perpetually refreshed for whatever my next project is. For a first effort, I loved the idea of blurring fact and fiction, but going forward, fantasy and reality are going to inhabit their own worlds.

And with that, I thank you for reading whichever genre you prefer!

QUESTIONS FOR DISCUSSION

1. How would you compare Mia's relationship with her family to that with her friends and with Mac? Why are these relationships so different?

2. *If You Were Here* is clearly an homage to filmmaker John Hughes. What other tributes or nods to pop culture can you find?

3. Why do you feel Mia connects so much with the teenage generation yet is so opposed to the notion of having her own children?

4. How do Mia and Mac's adventures in home renovation compare to your own? Are you more or less likely to try to "do it yourself" after reading their story?

5. Mia tends to keep her anger under wraps until she reaches a breaking point. How might events have changed if she were quick to escalate? For memoir fans, how would Jen have handled each wrench in the works?

6. In what ways are Mac and Mia different? In what ways are they similar? With whom do you sympathize more? How would this tale unfold if told from Mac's perspective?

7. Which character do you relate to the most?

8. How do the concepts of money and materialism contribute to Mac and Mia's downfall?

9. The suburbanites featured in this story are almost wholly cold and unwelcoming. Do you believe this is a function of moving to an upscale neighborhood, or is this due to Mac and Mia's refusal to try to fit in?

10. Putting yourself in Mia's shoes, how would you have handled her friend breakup with Kara?

11. Mia was inspired to make an emotional decision based on her love of John Hughes movies. In your own life, who inspires you to step outside of your comfort zone?

12. If you were making *If You Were Here* into a movie, who would you choose for the lead roles? If you were making a movie of your own life, who would you cast?

13. Fast-forward to the future: Where do you see Mia and Mac in ten years? How about Vienna and ORNESTEGA?

Please read on for a sneak preview
of Jen Lancaster's hilarious new memoir,

GENERATION X

Coming in May from New American Library.

When Douglas Coupland wrote *Generation X*, he was writing about me.

I mean figuratively, not literally.

I read *Generation X* in my second[1] senior year of college, in the time in which I briefly traded my loafers for Birkenstocks, khakis for flannel, and Wham! for Nirvana. As a poster child for all things considered "slacker,"[2] I clearly recall nodding my head and saying, "Yeah, man. You *get* it."

Until I stumbled across *Bridget Jones's Diary* six years later, I'd never identified more with a novel. Coupland gave voice to the ennui that every twentysomething felt at the time, back in the day when we were long on promise and short on opportunity. He understood us because he was one of us—trapped between the

---

1 Of six total.

2 Including cynicism, apathy, and un-cute plaid shirts.

perpetual collective optimism of those he labeled "Global Teens"[3] and their Baby Boomer parents, our generation defined ourselves by . . . nothing.

Technically, that's not true. Our generation defined ourselves by our perpetual fear of a Soviet invasion, playing Cold War mixtapes on our Walkmans. *Oh, Sting,* we'd lament, *we also hope the Russians love their children, too.* If iPods had been around back then, we'd have had entire thermonuclear war playlists, filled with songs like "99 Luftballons," "Wind of Change," and "Toy Soldier."

Before John Hughes made them household names, we had Matthew Broderick and Ally Sheedy in *WarGames* trying to persuade a Soviet supercomputer via dial-up modem that the only way to win a nuclear war is not to play.

We had *Red Dawn* and a pre–*Dirty Dancing* Jennifer Grey carrying not a watermelon, but an AK-47.

We had "Wolverines"!

Then, just like that, the Cold War ended and we lost the one thing that made our generation unique.

Those of us born between 1965 and 1980 had none of the benefits of the generations that came before or after us. We know nothing of the kinder, simpler America from the Camelot days, nor were we born with an innate understanding of how to operate Microsoft Windows.

Today, we're a beeper generation in a smartphone world.

Complicating matters is that neither the generation that came before us nor the one that's come after has demonstrated any real desire to act like adults themselves. Financial-planning advertise-

---

3 Later characterized as Generation Y or the Millennials.

ments show Baby Boomers running away from corporate life to pursue dreams that, in this economy, are downright ridiculous. This is *not*, in fact, the time to quit your job with your 401(k) and health insurance to go build custom boats. I know Dennis Hopper told everyone it was okay, but he's dead now.[4]

On top of that, we've got folks in their late twenties to early thirties so wrapped up in quasipolitical Facebook friend requests and Spotify and FarmVille that Soviet troops could *actually* roll down Main Street and they'd never even notice. Or care.

Of course this doesn't pertain to every member of Generation Y,[5] but it's not that far-fetched either. Um, hey, Counselor, can you stop streaming *Gilmore Girls* on Netflix long enough to present your case to the jury? KTHXBAI.

Watching this generation operate makes me very glad that people my age understand that tools like technology and social media are a means to an end and not the end itself.

My generation didn't play soccer, so we know that at the end of the game, not everyone gets a trophy. Yet here we are, trapped in middle management between two massive cases of generational arrested development.

And what we've determined from watching everyone else is that deciding to grow up has been our ultimate act of rebellion.

So that's what those of us in Generation X have done to define ourselves. We've become the only adults in a world full of children.

I mean, if I could finally grow up, anyone can.

---

4 And he had the kind of cash and cachet only Hollywood could create.

5 Or Baby Boomer, for that matter. Or you, no matter what your generation, as you've shown remarkably good sense in having picked this book.

Maybe I've moved to the dark side, but it's clean and nice and we never run out of toilet paper. And honestly, getting here wasn't that hard. All I had to do was make the conscious decision to grow up.

Whether you're a Boomer, a Millennial, or still-reluctant Xer who's not yet read the memo because you don't understand how to download attachments on your phone, *Jeneration X* is your invitation to join me because it's never too late.

I know it sounds hard, but fear not: I've done the legwork for you! Each chapter in this book illustrates a painful lesson I learned about becoming more of an adult, so I hope you'll find this guide useful.

Although this book will help you navigate the treacherous waters of many aspects of reluctant adulthood, if I leave you with no piece of wisdom but this, please understand that at a certain age your body can no longer efficiently process all the artificial colors in a dinner-sized serving of Froot Loops, regardless of how delicious they may be.[6]

And you won't realize this until it's already too late.

Far, far too late.

Unless you have a particular affinity for crying on the toilet, you may just want to trust me on this one.

Best,

Jen Lancaster

---

6 Particularly with a dash of half-and-half.